AFTERSHOCK

A Novel

Richard, hope you
enjoy...
Jim McFarlin

JAMES D. MCFARLIN

PREFACE

Although AFTERSHOCK is a work of fiction, many of the circumstances in the book are real. As this updated edition goes to press America sits on the precipice of a war the likes of which it has never before experienced.

Cyberwarfare is a game changer which levels the playing field between the military powers possessed by major nations such as the United States and less militarized smaller nations, extremist terrorist groups and others who would attack America. The weapons of cyberwarfare strike silently and without warning, respect no national borders, require no missiles or complex delivery vehicles and leave little if any trace of the aggressor's identity.

In this new theater of war the power grids, security markets, electronic communications networks, and all aspects of the critical infrastructures which enable our modern way of life are at risk.

Former Secretary of Defense Leon Panetta and Homeland Security Secretary Janet

Napolitano have both warned of the serious dangers cyberattacks pose to American national security. U.S. intelligence agencies, including the CIA and FBI, now classify cyberterrorism as the number one threat facing the United States.

Despite of this high level of awareness, America currently possesses no effective defenses against cyberattacks. This may seem strange for the most advanced technological nation on the globe to be in such a position, but is in fact true.

Why? In addition to their sophisticated underlying technology, cyber defense systems are a function of both human factors and politics. Human factors run the range from attitudes of disbelief in the board room to lax cybersecurity practices and malicious employees such as Edward Snowden who misappropriate and publish U.S. national security plans for the world to see. Politics drive both the deployment of offensive cyber weapons as well as intelligence operations. Politics were recently onstage as demonstrated by the crippling of some National Security Agency electronic surveillance capabilities which are expressly designed to detect and prevent terrorist attacks against the United States.

The full extent of the challenges and dangers from this new world of cyberspace will unfold as time and future events present them. By taking you behind the scenes to the U.S. political and military maneuvering which follow crippling attacks against America's power grids, AFTERSHOCK pulls back the curtain to increase your awareness of this looming threat to America's national security and to our way of life.

James D. McFarlin
Rancho Mirage, California
March 1, 2014

PROLOGUE

The early morning rays of the winter sun have yet to seep through the dense winter fog as the first attacks strike San Francisco.

Power is the first to go, stilling electrical equipment and draping the city in a carpet of darkness. Electric Muni buses stall in the streets. Lacking control signals with which to operate, Southern Pacific trains sit motionless on their tracks. The Bank of America tower, Transamerica Pyramid and other skyscrapers hang over the city like shadowed spires, towering monuments from an age past.

Attempts to use cell phones yield only the wailing cadence of circuits-busy signals. Land line, cable and Internet transmissions have vanished as though they never existed, reducing television and computer screens to blank, darkened slates of glass. Only battery-powered computing and communications devices cling on to their electronic lives, their bright screens sparking initial relief, even child-like joy, of cherished familiar devices still responding to command. It is a relief to be quickly snatched away by the reality of a world where Internet connections seemingly do not exist.

Anxious residents cluster in small groups on the streets outside their homes, hands stuffed in jacket pockets for warmth. As to whether they had experienced an earthquake – they thought not. Nor were there claims of having heard explosions. Many clutch laptops, iPads and smartphones, anxiously searching for answers. But answers were not to come.

In the moments when talk falls into a lull, the awareness of the absence of sound envelops them like a cloak. No buses. No clanging of cable cars. No swishing sounds of tires on wet pavement. Only silence. Increasingly, conversations turn from nervous banter to speculation, private whispers of possibilities, but to no result except to feed a spreading dread of things imagined but not known, growing fears felt but not spoken.

When a fragmented e-mail, Tweet or Facebook posting flashes, flickering on a screen, cries of excitement rise with the sound of a crow's shriek, only to turn to moans of disappointment following the inevitable loss of signal. Following rumors of the closure of area airports, scores of residents anxiously toss personal belongings into their vehicles and rush to leave the city, only to find bridges and major arteries out of San Francisco blocked by squads of armed National Guardsmen.

The growing anxiety is fueled by the increasingly frequent sounds of military helicopters clawing their way over the city like massive birds of prey, the frequent sightings of filled National Guard vehicles streaming through the streets, and the growing wail of emergency sirens, seemingly from every direction. Something big, something bad, is happening in San Francisco, perhaps all across the United States.

As residents of San Francisco recoil from the shock of the morning's attacks, 3,000 miles away in the nation's capital an aftershock of infinitely greater magnitude threatens to trigger massive worldwide repercussions in the days to come.

CHAPTER 1

Homeland Security Secretary Dustin Clayton felt the anxious tension filling the air the moment he entered the rear of the White House press room. The air was warm, stuffy and stale, every seat filled with representatives from the media. Additional correspondents, a few men Clayton recognized from Defense, members of Congress and several senators crowded two-deep along the walls.

Silenced closed-circuit displays of downtown San Francisco played across the screens. Images of the Golden Gate Bridge showed its towering fog-enshrouded spans eerily empty of traffic except for military vehicles. In the financial district, a stream of emergency vehicles with lights flashing raced past darkened traffic signals. A bright red banner streaming across the base of each screen proclaimed "ACCESS TO SAN FRANCISCO CLOSED BY HOMELAND SECURITY."

President William Anston, shoulders back and face drawn with worry, stood stiffly behind the lectern at the head of the press room, his press secretary behind him. The president preferred to speak to the press without the phalanx of senior cabinet and military officers with whom many presidents had typically surrounded themselves.

Clayton caught the eye of Admiral Ace Rutledge, Chairman of the Joint Chiefs of Staff, and eased through the parting crowd in the chairman's direction. Rutledge's ramrod—straight military pose and crisp tailored Navy blues always reminded Clayton of his own thirty-six years in uniform. He had missed the military dress many days since his retirement a year earlier and the way the uniforms fit his conditioned physique. His transition to dark suits, white shirts and patterned ties had been an adjustment that he was just getting used to. He edged through the crowd until he was next to the admiral.

"Where are we?" Clayton said.

Without taking his eyes from the president, the admiral answered, "Q & A."

Clayton studied Rutledge. "And…?"

Rutledge lowered his voice, speaking out of the corner of his mouth. "This briefing is a self-inflicted disaster in the making, if you ask me."

Clayton tightened his jaw as he considered the remark. He regretted having missed the president's prepared remarks, but the morning's events had left him little choice.

President Anston called on a broad-shouldered reporter toward the front of the room. The reporter stood with his question. Clayton recognized the thick black hair tied in a pony tail as belonging to Sal Sonsini, technology reporter for the *New York Times.*

"I'm a bit confused, Mr. President," the reporter said in a fast-paced, clipped tone. "While the terrorist group calling itself New Tomorrow has publicly claimed responsibility for this morning's attacks and has blatantly distributed a message over the Internet, you have stated that we *still* don't know who the attackers are? Are we experiencing yet another failure in our intelligence agencies, or is there something you aren't telling us?"

Clayton noted that Anston didn't project a visible reaction to the question. The president took a sip of water, nodded, and then replied in a level tone, "The terrorists didn't walk into the White House, hand us a business card and leave that message," Mr. Sonsini, if that's what you mean." Scattered laughter rippled across the room. "You, Mr. Sonsini, perhaps more than the rest of us, are aware of the difficulty faced tracking the origin of disguised, or as you techies call them, "false flag" messages, on the Internet. As soon as our intelligence agencies have something substantial to report, you will hear from us."

The reporter remained standing. "One follow-up question, Mr. President. Are you planning military action anywhere in the world as a result of today's attacks?"

The president nodded. "I will say to all of you – and to the terrorists who have perpetuated this atrocious and unprovoked act on the American people – that all options, including military action, are on the table."

A chorus of voices rose in unison from media representatives wanting to be next.

Rutledge leaned closer to Clayton, "The President is not looking good here."

Anston pointed to the slender raised hand of an attractive blond female journalist.

The journalist rose. "Marsha McCollum, Washington Post. My question is in regard to the Safeguard missile defense," she said.

Clayton reached to his inside jacket pocket. He removed and quietly unfolded a sheet of paper handed to him on the way in by the president's chief of staff, who commented to him, "This was just released on the Internet."

Clayton pressed close to the wall, keeping the page close to his face. The words "Terrorist e-mail message" were handwritten across the top of the sheet. He ran his hand through his wavy silver hair as he scanned the message and then read it more carefully a second time:

President Anston,
Our disruptions in San Francisco are just our opening hand. Imagine your air traffic

control systems going down? Or transmissions of financial data between your Federal Reserve and member banks somehow being scrambled? If you do not announce the immediate cancellation of America's Safeguard missile-defense system during your upcoming State of the Union address, you will find out.

–New Tomorrow.

Clayton frowned. The president's address was five days from now. Not much time at all to deal with a crisis of this magnitude. He had witnessed several game-changing points in warfare in his 38-year career. The proliferation of nuclear weapons was one. The global spread of extremist terrorism that led to and followed 9/11 was the other. This, he thought, may be the third.

The blond reporter's voice drifted into Clayton's consciousness: "What is your response, Mr. President, to the terrorist's demand that we cease all work on the Safeguard missile defense system?"

Anston's face tightened. "We have never negotiated with terrorists, and I don't intend to start now."

The reporter remained standing. "Does that mean, sir, that you are willing to risk American lives to retain Safeguard?"

The room fell silent.

President Anston shifted uneasily and then replied, "I believe I've just answered that question." He pointed to a raised hand in the front row. "Yes?"

The journalist stood. "Mr. President," he began, glancing at some notes, "securities markets to be closed to trading, rendering investor's assets illiquid . . . massive anticipated withdrawals of funds from U.S. banks by foreign institutions . . . the dollar plunging in overseas markets . . . possible wholesale liquidation of U.S. treasuries by international banks and sovereign funds . . . a financial system reeling toward collapse. Sir, what steps are you taking to ensure to the American people the stability of our financial system?"

Anston shook his head. "The closing of securities exchanges is viewed by my economic advisors as a prudent step to head off panic trading, surprise 'flash crashes' like Wall Street saw in 2010, and will serve to protect and preserve the investments owned by American citizens. In addition, the Federal Reserve is meeting at this moment with Treasury officials and executives of all leading financial institutions. It is too early to be specific but I can assure you every possible measure available to us will be taken to ensure the soundness and strength of our monetary and financial system. When those details are available you will hear them from me directly."

"Might that agenda include a bank holiday?" the journalist asked.

A perplexed look flashed across the president's face for a moment. "Let me say that. . ." The president's press secretary stepped to the lectern and whispered something into Anston's ear. Anston glanced back to the journalist. ". . . I will get back to you on that."

A senior CNN correspondent rose. "Mr. President, Twitter and Facebook feeds from residents who have fled San Francisco report massive traffic jams and a major influx of military vehicles and drones overhead. YouTube posts confirm these reports. Can you tell us if additional attacks on the city are anticipated?"

Clayton stirred. The question struck to the heart of the problem lurking in everyone's mind. But he noted that word of the naval ships speeding toward San Francisco to clear the offshore waters and provide emergency communications had not yet spread.

Anston took a sip of water. "Again, we are taking whatever measures necessary to protect our citizens."

"But the military attack drones?" the correspondent asked, pursuing the point. "Some might consider such action overkill – unless there is something you are not telling us, Mr. President."

Rutledge tilted his head toward Clayton and said, "This situation calls for all-out military response, not a fleet of flying toys."

"I've said all that I can say at this time," Anston said. He held up both hands. "I'm afraid my presence is required elsewhere, so we will have one final question. . ." He pointed to a thin bearded man in a dark suit sitting in front of Clayton.

"Bloomberg, Mr. President," the journalist said. "Citizens in San Francisco and the bay area are huddled together for warmth, desperately trying to contact loved ones, and worried about food supplies. Across the country, Americans are scared. Will the Orion Project guarantee defense against further cyber attacks?"

Clayton felt Rutledge studying him. His management team had assured him the cyber defense capabilities of the Orion Project would provide an effective deterrent against additional attacks. What he was not certain of was the timing of the availability of that defense. So he was also concerned about what might happen if the blackouts continued several days longer. What would be the effect on hospitals and those in emergency situations?

"How we will defeat them is something the terrorists will have to find out on their own, and not in this press conference," Anston answered. "I will say to you that the Orion Project will play a major role in that defeat."

Clayton expected Anston to conclude at that point, but the president stayed at the lectern, straightened his tie, and scanned the audience.

"I have an announcement before you all leave," Anston said. "Based on the recommendation of the Joint Chiefs of Staff I have issued an order grounding all flights and closing U.S. airports effective immediately. In addition, our military has been brought to DEFCON 3 status."

An explosion of voices filled the room like a thunderclap. The last time the United States had reached DEFCON 3 was during the September 11, 2001 attacks. Dozens of hands shot in the air, seeking the chance to ask a question.

Clayton shot a glance at Rutledge, who was already looking at him. A thin smile covered the admiral's face. "And what now, Mr. Homeland Secretary?"

Clayton returned the stare for a moment, attempting to gauge the intent of Rutledge's remark before returning his attention to the president.

Anston raised his hand above his head to silence the crowd. "Details of these announcements will be available on the press section of the White House website within fifteen minutes. Thank you all very much." Anston turned and exited down the hallway to his rear.

Clayton observed the journalists as they dispersed, attempting to gauge reactions to the press conference. Many stayed in their seats, heads down, working their keyboards to get their stories transmitted. Others shared comments with colleagues as they passed by him toward the exit. From the segments of conversation Clayton picked up, he sensed uneasiness, concern, even anger. Many made comments about leaving with many more unanswered questions than those answered. He worried that if the media's concerns and speculation flared out of hand, public fears and outrage would become more and more difficult to control.

He couldn't really blame the public. Since 9/11, America's intelligence services had effectively disrupted the communications, travel, and money that fueled terrorism in all its forms around the world. Citizens had become comfortable with their security. Earlier that day, as a result of attacks no one in the government could explain, and from an enemy the nation's military and intelligence agencies could not identify, faith in that comfort had been shattered.

Clayton turned toward Rutledge, but the admiral was gone.

CHAPTER 2

As many times as he had visited the Oval Office, Clayton never failed to sense its history and power. But from the unbelieving atmosphere permeating the press briefing, he had the ominous feeling that the power of the office was being threatened by more than terrorists.

Admiral Rutledge was already seated, speaking in quiet tones to Stuart Ibbs, the Director of National Intelligence. Clayton nodded to the two men. Ibbs had been called abrasive and foul-mouthed, but was also considered brilliant and a dedicated public servant. It would be interesting to hear Ibbs' perspective on the attacks, Clayton thought.

President Anston was on the telephone, his back to Clayton. Behind Anston the flags of the four services flanked the tall windows overlooking the south lawn. A layer of snow from the previous night's snowfall dusted the grass like a thin coat of white paint.

Clayton nodded to the others but remained standing, waiting for the president. A moment later, Anston finished his call and came around the desk, motioning Clayton to sit. "Please take a seat, Dusty."

Clayton eased into a chair and waited, trying to gauge the president's frame of mind after the press conference. He did not have long to wait.

The president asked, "You were all there. How do you think the press conference went?" He stared at Admiral Rutledge as he asked the question.

Rutledge shook his head and spoke slowly. "We are in trouble on three sides: the terrorists pushing from the front, the media ramping up the rhetoric and enflaming emotions, and the public pushing for answers and action from the back. In my mind, Mr. President, we need to counter with aggressive, decisive action. Now."

"Stuart?" the president asked, switching his stare to the National Intelligence Director. Stuart Ibbs stared at his hands for a moment before looking at the president and answering, "We are not just at war with the terrorists, Mr. President, but also with public opinion. I concur with the admiral that the press was not wholly satisfied, which means public perception will follow within the hour. I agree we must take forceful and purposeful steps at once."

Clayton ran a series of scenarios through his mind, attempting to decode what the Director of National Intelligence had said. He had shuddered when Ibbs had been named DNI a year earlier. Although qualified for senior responsibility by virtue of a lifetime of government service and senior posts at Defense and State, Ibbs was an avowed hawk who did not provide the president with a balanced view of intelligence matters. In fact, Ibbs had for years given the clear signals that he had been waiting for another opportunity like 9/11 as a reason to use America's military force to finish dealing with terrorists once and for all. Perhaps in the latest terrorist attacks he had found his opportunity.

Clayton noticed the president was staring at him.

"You with us, Dusty?" Anston asked. His face held a questioning expression.

"Yes, of course, Mr. President," Clayton answered, pulling his thoughts to the present. "I have similar reactions to the press conference, but see a different agenda for response. With many regions of the world waiting like tinderboxes for a spark to ignite them to explosive conflict, I believe reasoned response, even at the potential expense of public opinion, is preferable to inflammable actions."

The president settled into a stuffed chair across from the three men, tented his fingers and stared over them at the group. "So there we have it. Okay — let's get started."

Ibbs glanced around the room, a puzzled look on his lean face. "Is Defense going to be represented, Mr. President?"

"For the time being, Defense Secretary Witt and the vice-president are remaining at the Asian nuclear arms summit," Anston replied.

"Because of the sensitivity of what we will be discussing today," the president continued, "I'm limiting our meeting to this group, plus Secretary of State Karlin."

Clayton turned his head and watched as a painting on the side wall slid noiselessly upward into a hidden panel, revealing a large wall-mounted video monitor. The image of Secretary Karlin's matronly face, surrounded by her full mane of silver-white hair, filled the screen.

"Mr. President. Gentlemen. Sorry to miss out on the testosterone rush filling the Oval Office," Secretary Karlin said. "We're running around like squirrels during harvest time here at State."

Clayton shook his head and smiled. Karlin would never lose remnants of her Texas upbringing, no matter how long she was in Washington. He was pleased with her inclusion in the meeting; her grounded, common-sense style would bring balance to a discussion he knew would center on aggressive counter-attack strategies.

"Let's start with you, Stuart," Anston said, locking his attention on the DNI. "Where are we on intelligence?"

"Still no trace on the message the terrorists sent to you," the Director of National Intelligence answered. "It came in over the secure White House priority communications network. Must have bounced off half a dozen satellites and been routed through a maze of servers around the world. Bottom line, the message is untraceable."

Anston kept his attention on Ibbs for a moment, as if about to press further, but then asked Joan Karlin, "What's your take on this New Tomorrow group? Think it's North Korea?"

"In my book, Mr. President," Karlin replied, "those charlatans couldn't scrape together enough technical talent in the entire God-forsaken wasteland they call a country to do this."

"China?" Anston asked her. "They've fought the defense system every step of the way."

"President Cheung and his blow-hard warriors would give up Opium and half their Wal-Mart business to stop our missile shield," Karlin responded. "But during the Asian nuclear summit? That would be a peculiar form of Zen-based Oriental thinking that exceeds even my Texas-sized comprehension."

"Peculiar, yes," Anston answered. "Machiavellian, no."

Ibbs cleared his throat. "No nation on earth would take this kind of chance, Mr. President, particularly the Chinese. They want to restrain us, not provoke us. I believe the attacks were planned, and perhaps even executed, by the new leadership in Al Qaeda."

Anston nodded. "As yet another part of their retribution for our killing Bin Laden?"

"And the others," Ibbs answered.

"And how does this New Tomorrow group fit into your view?" the president continued.

"Most likely a front or one of the semi-autonomous Al Qaeda cells," Ibbs said.

The president leaned forward in his chair. "And you have proof?"

"Concrete proof, no," Ibbs said, "but we do know Al Qaeda has been planning attacks on the U.S. and that they have recruited hundreds of highly skilled technical resources."

Anston shifted his attention to Admiral Rutledge. "What do you think?"

"I would place my money on al-Qaeda or Iran," Rutledge replied. Both have motives, and Iran is still smarting over their belief that we started all of this cyberterrorism with Israel and that Stuxnet attack in 2010."

Clayton nodded his head. It was a poorly kept secret that the United States played a major role with Israel in developing the so-called Stuxnet computer worm attack that disabled portions of Iran's nuclear reactor at Bushehr in September of 2010.

"But I will have to defer to Secretary Clayton," Rutledge said, directing a sharp stare at Clayton. "My impression is he has an organization whose job is to identify and stop terrorist actions such as these."

Clayton knew Rutledge would take every opportunity to minimize the value of the Orion

Project. But now was not the time to do battle. "I've realigned our priorities at the Orion Project, focusing every available resource on these attacks. But have we identified the terrorists? No. Can we stop them at this moment? No."

"You mean to tell me," Rutledge asked, his attention on Clayton, "that the massive technological resources your organization has been given can't track down a ragtag band of techie geeks holed up in some basement in Afghanistan?"

"We aren't dealing with drive-by hackers here, Ace," Clayton said, choosing his words carefully. "These were sophisticated attacks that entered highly secure systems and shut them down. We're dealing with people who have experienced technical resources, extensive funding, and as we see from their Safeguard demand, a cause."

Rutledge shook his head. "Sad."

"What's your point?" Anston asked Rutledge.

"My point, Mr. President, is that we can't place hopes for the safety of our country on Secretary Clayton's mythical cyber defense programs that don't defend."

Clayton worked to keep his voice level. "And your solution, Admiral?"

"Clearly, we have only one course of action," Rutledge answered. "Those responsible for these attacks will understand one thing and one thing only. The use of force."

"Now there's some original thinking, Admiral," Karlin interjected. "Seems we just heard we don't have a clue who these fellows are. Did I miss something?"

Ibbs pulled a brilliant red binder from his attaché and set it on his lap. He patted its cover. "I think what Admiral Rutledge is saying is that we have a response crafted and ready for just this situation. Perhaps it's time we used it."

Karlin's face twisted into disapproval. "You're speaking of Operation Hydra?"

Rutledge glanced at Ibbs, and then took the response. "Precisely what we're saying. Operation Hydra will finish the job we started with the killing of Bin Laden and crush these terrorist networks once and for all."

A sudden chill streamed across Clayton's back. No circumstances, even those they now faced, justified unleashing the horror of Operation Hydra. The super-secret operation would mean the immediate, in many cases indiscriminate, worldwide elimination of thousands of possible terrorists and suspected terrorist supporters. With Hydra there would be no questions, no proof of guilt, and no prisoners. Just a swath of death that would surely take the lives of many civilians. Clayton studied Anston, trying to gauge the president's reaction.

Anston gave Rutledge a stern look. "Admiral, we've got a situation that demands cool heads and global massacre isn't on the top of my list." He scanned the three faces in the room. "Am I making myself clear?"

After a moment, Stuart Ibbs shifted in his chair. "If I may offer this: September 11 was the result of our weak responses to barbaric acts of terrorism throughout the 1990's. Following 9/11 we got bogged down in tribal and religious warfare instead of relentlessly pursuing the terrorists who attacked us. If we don't react forcibly, and swiftly, Mr. President, every terrorist organization on this earth will think the United States of America is fair game."

Ibbs paused, staring directly at the president, then added, "At that point we will have lost any measure of control over the safety of our citizens. Our country will become a war zone. So if I can be so bold, Mr. President, now is not the time for a weak or hesitant response from the United States of America."

Clayton shifted his attention to Rutledge. As Ibbs spoke, the admiral's eyes glowed with increasing brightness. Two inches lower on his face, the tip of his tongue licked his lips like he was preparing for a savory feast. Clayton knew the look. Many flag rank officers dreamt of the opportunity to show their contemporaries, their country, yes, the world, their true selves, what they were *really capable of.* Even in a long career, it is rare when such chances present themselves, and sometimes the opportunity to make one's mark in history must first be created. Then, when the timing is right, they seized it with a vengeance. Clayton felt a slight chill down his spine as he studied America's senior military officer more closely. Was four-star Admiral Richard Rutledge, Chief of Staff and leader of the massively devastating power possessed by the military forces of the United States of America, at that point?

Anston's voice broke Clayton out of his thoughts. "Joan, you've been in contact with our allies. What's their reaction to the attacks?"

"Pucker-level fear," she responded, "and failure to understand why the United States, with all of our gee-whiz computer power, can't fend off these attackers."

Anston frowned. "Fear? Worried they're next?"

"No, Mr. President. Fear. . ." She stared at Rutledge and Ibbs ". . . of some idiotic response from the United States of America. They're aghast, for example, by our launching of killer drones over the heads of our own citizens in San Francisco."

"Looking for signs of terrorism, nothing more," Ibbs said, rolling his eyes. "So you want us to just sit back and let them use bombs to topple the Bank of America building into the financial district?"

Karlin shook her head in a sign of disgust. "Please note I have voiced my disapproval."

"So noted," Anston said. He scanned the group. "Options everyone?"

Clayton had remained silent, watching the interchange, but his mind whirled, considering the implications of what he had just heard. "In my opinion, Mr. President, a military response, particularly something as harsh as Operation Hydra, will only further solidify world opinion against the

United States, massacre thousands of innocent people, and will not address the problem."

"Fine," Anston said. "Your recommendation?"

"Give me seventy-two hours for the Orion Project to ID the terrorists and complete a defense against further attacks."

Admiral Rutledge leaned toward Clayton, the muscles in his neck standing out like taut ropes. "Jesus, our country's under siege, and you're suggesting we take a three-day holiday and bet the farm on your over-promised, hocus-pocus cyber defense system? Have you lost your—"

"Cut it, Admiral," Anston said. "We've just had dress rehearsal for a national disaster. I don't need to referee a free-for-all between you two."

Anston let his words hang in the air before turning his attention to Intelligence Chief Ibbs. "Stuart?"

"Seventy-two hours is a gift to the terrorists that we'll pay dearly for," Ibbs said, tapping his knuckles on the red notebook. "I propose we move decisively. Now. Before further attacks throw the country into chaos."

Anston stared at Ibbs, looking as though he were about to explode.

Joan Karlin spoke, breaking the quiet. "I vote with Dusty, Mr. President. Let's keep the waters calm out there, work our intelligence channels, and buy time for his folks to make progress."

Anston glanced at Clayton, tapping his fingers on the arm of his chair. When he spoke, his voice was calm again, but his tone strong and unyielding. "We're going to take the seventy-two hours. Joan, I want you to apply the pressure on our allies to put their intelligence services to work on our behalf. I want every known and suspected cyber terrorist on this earth rooted out, interrogated, his equipment confiscated, incarcerated if needed, and threatened within an inch of his life. I want to know who's doing this to us. Second," he continued, "give them fair warning that the United States is not going to stand down on this and may make aggressive military moves to show our might."

Karlin returned an approving nod. "Guess I'd better get my kickin' boots on, Mr. President. If you gentlemen will excuse me?" The silver-haired image faded from the screen.

"As for intelligence," Anston continued, focusing on the National Director of Intelligence, "I want a full contingent of CIA, FBI and military intelligence teams in the field tracking down all suspected cyber hackers, crackers, terrorists and thieves, and that means every available agent. No action, no mission, anywhere in the world has higher priority." He hesitated, his words hanging in the air. "Any issue on this?"

"We're already deploying our full available force of agents, Mr. President," Ibbs replied.

Anston leaned toward Ibbs and said, "Find some more goddamn agents. Drag them out of retirement. Pull them off their cushy desk assignments. Use an executive order to draft them from their lucrative private sector jobs. I don't give a damn what you do, but get them. You have twenty-four hours. Now get going."

"Ace," Anston said, turning to Admiral Rutledge, "I want our naval forces in the Middle East moved to a position for a potential attack that scares the you-know-what out of Iran. I will also be sending a communication to President Ahmadinejad through the Swiss embassy making clear our intentions to move militarily if we find his country is behind these attacks."

"Mr. President?" Ron Comber, Anston's chief of staff, stood in the doorway to the anteroom outside the Oval Office. "Senate leader Cannell and Speaker Robinson are here to see you."

Anston waved in acknowledgement. "Three minutes."

"Are you still planning the Houston trip, sir?" Comber asked.

"I'm going," the president replied.

Clayton remembered that Anston was addressing the conference of Republican governors that evening in Houston. The president had to continue his duties; to do anything less would send further panic across the country.

Anston pushed out of his chair and walked to the tall windows looking out on the winter day. "That unfriendly contingent waiting outside wants progress on the terrorists or they're going to be after my head." The president paused, then added, "I expect you gentlemen to see to it such an exercise is not necessary."

Rutledge cleared his throat. "Mr. President, I will execute your orders, but once again, I strongly believe we should not waste the next seventy-two hours. We must begin immediate preparations for Operation Hydra."

Anston whirled away from the window and pointed his glasses at Rutledge. "Listen carefully to me. Your father's shining military record came as the result of intelligent warfare, not a quick trigger. You might remember that if you get an itchy finger contemplating World War III."

"And, Dusty," the president said, focusing his attention on Clayton, "I didn't pull the former head of the Joint Chiefs from retirement to head Homeland Security because we grew up two hundred miles apart in northern Oklahoma. I expect you to do whatever you have to do to find a way to repel these damn terrorist attacks. If you can't deliver, you leave me with few options, and I believe you just heard one of them."

CHAPTER 3

Kirsten Lockhart pushed her way from the crowded elevator on the third level of the Pentagon's E-Ring and scanned the stark, gray-walled corridor. Waves of military officers, aides and civilians, speaking in rapid, cryptic phrases, their faces tight with anticipation and purpose, shouldered past her as she edged her way into the flow. She could feel, even smell the tension that crackled through the hallway.

These were men and women who had spent their lives since 9/11 preparing, rehearsing, and re-rehearsing intricate plans to prevent, and in the event of necessity, respond to terrorist attacks against the United States.

Hours earlier, shattering the still of San Francisco's winter darkness, those strikes had come.

Kirsten took a moment to adjust to the stark fluorescent illumination, bright in its reflection from the shiny walls and polished floors. She scanned a bank of video displays facing the elevators as she moved with the throng. She had seen visuals of the situation in San Francisco taken from military helicopters and satellite cameras in a security briefing thirty minutes earlier; she watched, searching for anything new.

An off-screen announcer was saying, "The suspected terrorist attacks early this Sunday morning that left citizens of San Francisco without heat, power, and communications have pushed the city into a state of restlessness and growing panic. Homeland Security Secretary Dustin Clayton has deployed National Guard units to seal off access to the city, emphasizing that residents should remain calm and at home until further notice. Public transportation and all Bay Area airports remain closed until further notice. Secretary Clayton gave no clear answer when asked why he believed the Orion Project, Homeland Security's massive counter-cyberterrorism effort, had not prevented or given warning of the attacks."

Kirsten thought back to her security briefing showing videos and satellite images not carried on the news, images of citizens packing up their families and rushing to leave the city before the next shoe dropped. She shook her head. No, the

Orion Project had not been ready. Now the operative question was *when would it be ready?*

She shifted her attention to an adjacent screen where Maria Bartiromo of CNBC was saying ". . . pre-market indices in Asian market stock futures is indicating a massive selloff of U.S. equities of epic proportions as our markets open tomorrow. For Americans who saw the value of their investments evaporate in the 2008 economic crisis, this will be yet another financial blow, particularly for the retired, who rely on their investments for income . . . ."

Kirsten thought back to the cyberterrorism attack simulations she had participated in and the devastating potential of what could lay ahead: loss of heat, power and communications nationwide, hoarding and scarcity of food, looting of stores and homes, overwhelmed police, fire and medical resources, followed by widespread panic, plunging securities markets, runs on the banks . . . . Possible end games included potential financial collapse, chaos in Washington, and massive U.S. military engagement across the globe on a manhunt to identify, locate and kill the perpetuators.

Unless the attacks were stopped.

Kirsten swore under her breath and mouthed a silent vow. *It should never have come to this.* Brushing her hair from her face, she got her bearings and joined the moving crowd, edging toward the Chief of Staff's office, where she had been instructed to meet Secretary Clayton. The question in her mind was *why* he wanted to see her. She would soon find out.

She moved through the corridor, aware of the glances in her direction. She had grown accustomed to the looks, appreciated them, when the time was right. Although only five-foot-six, she dressed well and possessed a fit, lithe figure men admired. Many had shared that the way she moved, with the smoothness of a cat or leopard, created an allure they found hard to resist. She pushed such distractions out of her head. Secretary Clayton was her immediate concern, not some lonely naval commander or defense department aide.

The crowd moved quickly and in unison, like fish swimming downstream. The atmosphere of calm control and sense of purpose that she had felt on prior visits to the Pentagon still prevailed. Only the intensity had changed. Much like going from a three to a seven on the Richter scale.

She strained to see over the moving sea of tall shoulders surrounding her and saw Clayton, engaged in close conversation with a small group of senior military officers. On the wall beyond them, a satellite video image displayed a swath of darkness stretching from the Monterey Peninsula through Silicon Valley and San Francisco and extending eastward into the Sacramento Delta river region. She knew the closure of San Francisco was Homeland Security taking no chances on the cyber attacks being followed up by physical attacks in the form of dirty bombs or chemical weapons. But protecting an area the size shown on the display…? She shook her head. Protection would be a massive effort, and most likely impossible.

She approached and waited. Over the mixed jumble of voices in the corridor, she could make out pieces of an exchange between Clayton and a tall, erect Navy admiral. "The military is not your affair anymore, Mr. Secretary," the admiral was saying. 'I will do what I am charged to do."

Clayton appeared as though he was going to respond to the officer's remark when he glanced in Kirsten's direction. "I'll catch up with you and we'll talk further on this," he said to the group. The officers nodded and dispersed.

Clayton took a step forward and offered his hand. "I understand we plucked you from a flight in Atlanta."

"Yes, sir, on my way to a technology conference," Kirsten said.

"You've been through your security briefing?"

"On the Air Force plane you sent to get me."

"I've just come from the White House. Things are in disarray, and I need your impressions on the attacks."

Kirsten carefully framed her response. "This was a highly sophisticated attack, months in the making. In my opinion, it required a team of top rate software engineers whose objective was to get one or more worms inside our power grid." She paused before adding, "As you may remember, unlike a virus, which is created to attack computer code, worms are designed to actually take over and control computer systems. This attack was absolutely worm-driven."

Clayton nodded. "Who could do this?"

"A well-funded private entity which has reason to do us harm. Or a state sponsored project with a political or military motive."

"You have an opinion?"

"China or Iran top my list, as both possess advanced cyber warfare development programs – and a past history of using them."

Clayton raised an eyebrow. "That Anonymous group?"

"Possible. Their cyber assaults against corporate targets such as Visa, MasterCard and eBay did some damage. And we do have some indications of their interest in more destructive attacks. But I question their having a motive."

"And if they did have a motive, it would be...?"

She let out a long breath. "I'm guessing. Power, prestige. Not to mention money."

"You haven't mentioned al-Qaeda."

"Since bin Laden's death we know there has been a surge in Al Qaeda's cyber warfare interests, but they don't possess the know-how. Not on the sophisticated level of today's attacks."

"So to summarize, we aren't sure who is advanced enough to pull off attacks like we saw this morning."

"Well, sir, one of them just jumped two years ahead of us."

Somewhere down the hall an alarm suddenly blared and Kirsten quickly stepped aside to avoid three military policemen pushing through the crowd.

Clayton nodded. "What else?"

"An effort as significant as these attacks will definitely have an end game. I suspect we'll hear something from the attackers soon, in less than twenty-four hours."

"Excellent insight, Kirsten." Clayton tilted his head toward the elevators. "I'm late for a briefing. Let's talk as we walk."

At six-foot-two, Clayton moved through the crowd with ease, acknowledging greetings and nodding to those he knew. Kirsten still marveled at how well Clayton had kept himself in shape, in spite of the demands placed on him by his grueling schedule. He had maintained his rugged good looks, much like an older George Clooney, she had always thought. Few men under the pressure he must feel on a daily basis would do so well. She hurried to keep up with his long strides, waiting for him to speak.

"I'll get to the point," he said, shooting her a sideways glance. "I hope you appreciate that these latest strikes have changed our priorities on the Orion Project."

Kirsten frowned, wondering where the conversation was heading, but remained silent.

"You know I agree your advanced cyber defense research program holds extraordinary potential as an alternative to the efforts underway in the Orion Project."

"Thank you, sir," she said, feeling a warning chill shoot up her spine.

"What I also need you to know," he continued, "is that I need every available resource focused on the more immediate terrorist threats. That means focusing on the Orion Project."

"Meaning exactly what, sir?"

Clayton stopped and faced her. "I've put in the order transferring your staff – for now – to support the Orion Project. I wanted to tell you personally, of course."

Kirsten felt like she had been slammed in the chest with a baseball bat. *No. Something was dreadfully wrong here.* Her hands shot to her hips as she felt the shock well up inside of her, flushing her cheeks with heat. "Excuse my candor, sir. You know I'm on the verge of some cutting edge breakthroughs in cyber defense. Derailing my effort now would be a serious mistake."

Clayton started toward the elevators again. "These breakthroughs of yours. Are they operational?"

"No, but…"

"In beta testing?"

"Scheduled to start this—"

He waved her to silence. "I understand your disappointment. For now, I need your staff working with the Orion Project. We'll take up the question of your cyber defense system once this crisis is past."

Kirsten's temples ached, compounding her headache. This couldn't be happening. "So my people will be reporting to Zachary?" she asked.

"That's correct. For now."

"And Zachary, he had nothing to do with –" Kirsten stopped before she caused herself harm with Clayton. She had long known that Zachary Ishmel, the head of the Orion Project, had resented her and would never rest until she was out of his turf. So this was his scheme to take advantage of the crisis to strip her of responsibility, hoping she would pack her bags and take the next flight back to Silicon Valley. Slick.

"This is my decision and mine alone, Kirsten."

She let out a breath to calm her anger. "And my security and access privileges?"

"Of course you will maintain full privileges and security clearances. You'll need them. I want you to focus on identifying the terrorists – who they are and where they are."

"We may never find out who they are, or where they are. And if we do, it doesn't matter."

"I'm missing your logic."

Kirsten shrugged. "They could be anywhere on the globe. And quite frankly, *where* they are doesn't matter. It's the nature of their attacks that matter. That's why the only defense is one that actually stops their attacks. That is what my project offers."

"And that is exactly what the Orion Project is close to delivering," he said, his tone a bit harder.

Sure, she thought. "Pardon me for being out of line, sir. But what if this thinking is all wrong and the Orion Project cyber defense can't be brought on line? What is the backup plan?"

Clayton shot her a penetrating stare. "I've made my decision, Kirsten."

Kirsten shook her head and looked away. Her attention was focused nowhere in particular. She was vaguely aware of the figures moving past, moving in slow motion, as her thoughts raced forward in light speed. Dustin Clayton, the only man who could have convinced her to drop her Silicon Valley career to come serve her country in Washington. Dustin Clayton, one of the few men she knew she could trust. Where was the trust in this? Her thoughts came back to the present just as she formulated an alternate appeal.

They reached the elevators and she turned toward Clayton. "Suggestion, sir?"

"Yes?"

"Since the Orion Project needs additional resources, why not go outside and get the best professionals we can find? I will even offer to locate them for you."

"Give me a name."

"Terry Sailor, for one. He is arguably one of the brightest Internet software engineers in the country. I understand he's living outside of Tucson."

Clayton frowned. "The outspoken security guru who was run out of government service for making strident claims to the media about our technology vulnerabilities? No, Sailor is a loose cannon, and that I don't need."

"With all due respect, perhaps if the politicians had listened to him, we might not be in the fix we're in today."

Clayton shot her a sharp glance but did not reply.

Kirsten instantly knew she had overstepped her boundaries, but at this point didn't care. "There are others; I know many of them."

The elevator arrived and Clayton edged closer to Kirsten, his tone softer. "I asked you to come to the Orion Project to bring the entrepreneurial vigor of Silicon Valley to a lumbering bureaucracy that needed a fresh spirit." He reached out and squeezed her shoulder. "You have your father's relentless drive and intensity. Use those talents to benefit your country. I have an assignment for you. I want you to focus on finding these terrorists. Will you do that?"

Kirsten looked down for a moment, trying to calm herself and then stared at Clayton, silent.

Clayton stepped inside the elevator, his eyes still on her. "I'm counting on you, Kirsten. Find those goddamn terrorists – then we'll talk about your project."

The polished elevator doors closed with a quiet hiss, reflecting the image of a news commentator on the large video screen on the wall behind her: "Following the rapid spread of power and communications outages eastward from San Francisco, a White House spokeswoman confirmed that President William Anston has issued an order closing all securities and bond exchanges effective tomorrow. On Wall Street, financial experts were sharply divided on whether the closings would stave off or increase the chances of financial panic, perhaps spiral the country into another crushing recession."

Kirsten could feel her eyes harden. But she would take the war to the terrorists, whoever they were, wherever they were.

But first she would find out what was going on inside the Orion Project.

CHAPTER 4

Following a quick stop at her office to pick up a surprise package for Zachary Ishmel, Kirsten strode past row after row of computer workstations in the Orion Project cyber center, past the dozens of teams of computer scientists and communications technicians bent over their workstations, speaking in small groups or studying the massive wall screens depicting every facet of operations in the cyber center. The massive room hummed and crackled with a special tension and energy that morning, much like it might be inside an active beehive.

The center always held that distinct smell that resulted from hundreds of miles of wires, connectors, cables, and thousands of electronic parts, tied together into a massively powerful computing machine that was collectively hundreds of thousands of times more powerful than the sum of its parts.

She shook her head as she contemplated, as she always did when visiting the center; she was inside an incredibly complex hybrid man/cyber machine, joined to battle other teams of technicians with their cyber machines somewhere across the globe.

This morning the other teams had fired the first shot, made the first real strike in what would certainly become known as America's first full-scale cyber warfare battle. And at the moment, America's team was losing.

She slowed her stride as she heard the announcement overhead: "Launch aborted! Repeat. Launch aborted!" She had heard similar announcements in recent days as system tests of Orion 5, the latest release of the Orion Project's counter-cyberterrorism software, had also failed. She wondered how such announcements affected those pouring every ounce of their soul into progress, only to hear announcement after announcement of failure. She pushed her thoughts of the implications of such failures aside. At the moment she had to focus on Zachary Ishmel.

On the way from the Pentagon, Kirsten had considered how she would approach Ishmel in a way that would get her what she wanted. She had long ago tired of the competition between them, where Ishmel was Director in charge of the Orion

Project, developing cyber defense systems. She had been added to the mix by Secretary Clayton as Director of Advanced Research to go past the incremental, to leapfrog cyber defense technology to new heights. Unfortunately, Ishmel had not been able to push past his feelings that she was the privileged one, sanctioned by Clayton. If she succeeded, it would mean he had failed. And Ishmel showed his disdain; there had been scant cordial interactions between them over the past eight months, few professional courtesies. Although both occupied the same building and their staffs worked adjacent to one another, she worked in her realm; he in his, like separate cocoons.

But she felt that today was the day when *she* should be feeling these sentiments of anger, of jealousy. After all, it was *her* people who were being transferred to Ishmel, *her* project that was being put on hold. Further, she was certain that Ishmel had sold Clayton on the organizational change, like the bill of goods it was. But instead, she was coming to Zachary Ishmel in a happy mood. Happy because he was going to gladly give her something she wanted. A bit of trickery was all it would take. And trick him she was going to do. Right in front of his own staff.

She saw Ishmel ahead, in his control center at the front of the cyber center, observing a cluster of computer workstations with a small group of other men. He stood erect and formal, dressed in his usual style - black three piece pinstriped suit with bright white cotton starched shirt and perfectly knotted, muted tie. Black shoes shined to a mirror gloss. She wondered, as she had many times before, why did he always look like he was on his way to see the President? She had sometimes wanted to scream to him to lighten up a bit, throw on some chinos and an open collar shirt, mix with the crew. But she had seen that for what it was, a worthless cause, and ended up submerging her impulses.

She approached him with a reserved, friendly smile, but not so friendly as to seem phony. She was, after all, the victim, the loser in his mind, in his game of power and deceit. He stopped his conversation and looked at her blankly, as if deciding on an appropriate greeting. Two of the men behind him carried expressions of deep worry on their faces, like those who were working to free trapped coal miners mine before they asphyxiated. The third man, who she knew only as Mario, stared at her with the look of an important man being interrupted. Mario also wore a tailored, tight-fitting suit that covered his stocky, muscular frame much as she could imagine how the notorious gangster Al Capone might have looked years earlier. Mario was Ishmel's go-to guy, an enforcer, the one who made things happen that needed to happen around the Orion Project. Kirsten had never heard or seen Mario's last name and did not care if she ever did.

Ishmel took a step toward her and said in his thick guttural accent, "What is it, Kirsten? We're busy here."

Kirsten discarded her thoughts about what she was interrupting. She would complete her mission and leave, quickly. She stepped forward and said to Ishmel, "Congratulations on the additions to your team."

Ishmel hesitated and cleared his throat. "You mean—"

"My people," she said, cutting him short. "Best cyber security experts in the business."

Ishmel gave a smile but his eyes were dark. "Of course. Excellent staff. I'll take good care of them."

She found this an ironic statement. In staff meetings Ishmel had gone out of his way more than once to berate her, one time referring to her as a "gun-slinging loose cannon from Silicon Valley" and likening her project as "some free-for-all love fest where she threw the taxpayer's money at tattooed, ring-nosed programmers whose only credentials were that they had chased the last social network computer fad."

Kirsten looked around the cyber center and then gave Ishmel a wide-eyed look like a girl scout on a field trip. "I heard the abort announcements as I came in. How are things on Orion 6?" She did not expect any information from Ishmel but could not pass up putting in the jab.

Ishmel's eyes darkened. "I really don't have time to talk."

"Sure." Kirsten shook her head. "But I do want to say it's too bad about the timing on these terrorist attacks. Not the best timing for you."

Ishmel suddenly held a puzzled look. "What do you mean?"

"You know . . . the cyber security czar position at the White House you're gunning for." In Kirsten's thinking, if he had spent half as much time on the Orion Project as he did lobbying for the White House position, the Orion defense against the terrorists would already be operational. "But I understand congratulations are in order – word is you are down to the finals in the confirmation process."

He pulled back his shoulders to the point where his lapels pulled away from his shirt collar. "Just trying to be of service to my country."

Sure you are. "I know how you feel."

"Beg your pardon?"

"Well, you know, giving up my hand-picked team of cyber security experts to give the Orion Project a better chance at success. Good feeling, that service. Hits me right in the gut."

Ishmel looked at her without speaking, so Kirsten continued. "Not a good time for trouble, that's all I'm saying. Things could go wrong here."

Mario suddenly broke from the group and whispered something in Ishmel's ear in a gravelly voice. It struck Kirsten at that moment that she could not recall ever seeing a smile on Mario's stern, bulldog-like face, and today was no exception. She could not make out what was being said but saw Ishmel's jaw tighten. *Oops. Not good news,* she thought.

Ishmel turned his attention back to her. "I must go."

"I'm certain you do," Kirsten said, and then added, on a whim, "anything I can help with?"

Ishmel stiffened. "I dare say not. Now if you will excuse—"

"Oh, you might want this—" she reached in her pocket and retrieved the present she had picked up for Ishmel in her office and dangled it in front of him like a sister taunting her younger brother with a special piece of candy. "This flash drive contains the access keys to my project's software modules. The modules are protected with three layers of Zorb/Heissman encryption. Can't be too careful these days, you know," she said, winking in Mario's direction.

He reached for the drive and cradled it in his palm as if he were Cortez holding an artifact of Montezuma's gold. "I doubt that we will need access to your systems—"

She waved him to silence. "The software is not 100% complete, as you know, but there are some zippy software routines in there you might find fascinating. You never know when you might need a bit of help. Am I right?"

Ishmel smiled but his dark eyes turned cold. "I am honored."

I'm certain you are not, Kirsten thought, then said, "Oh, just a bit of housekeeping – the access codes automatically reset every sixty minutes, which means you have. . . ." she glanced at her watch ". . . .thirty-seven minutes to download. Just be sure to download on your primary command console. That way you will always have access, even when the codes reset."

Ishmel nodded and handed the flash drive to Mario, who in turn tossed it to one of the others and pointed to the command console. "Anything else?" Ishmel asked.

"Just wanted to say you did a nice sales job on Secretary Clayton, getting him to transfer my staff. I hope he doesn't have to regret his decision."

Ishmel shot her a hard stare.

"Well," Kirsten said, giving a cheerful wave. "Gotta go. Oh, and good luck with that White House thing."

As she hurried up the aisle toward the exit Kirsten allowed herself a thin smile. Ishmel would soon find he had 'read-only' access to her group's software, meaning he could take nothing, change nothing. That should tighten his starchy collar. And within minutes, without Ishmel's knowledge, a hidden module on the USB drive would be directing his command console to transmit his private network security access codes to her Android mobile device. The Orion Project's secrets would soon be her secrets. She was now on to the next step in her plan.

Her smile widened. All in all, a satisfying conclusion to what had been an otherwise unforgettably miserable morning.

Sweet!

CHAPTER 5

Kirsten frowned as her attention lingered on the information filling the computer screen. The euphoria she had felt an hour earlier from obtaining Ishmel's computer access codes had evaporated like an early morning mist on a sunny day. Her scanning of Ishmel's internal files had discovered no evidence – or even hints – of trouble in the Orion Project cyber defense system. To the contrary, all software modules were reported to be on schedule and system integration of all key components was where she would expect it to be. All of this was contrary to rumors of delays she had heard, and the abort announcement she had heard when visiting Ishmel in the cyber center.

She tapped her fingers on the desk in a rhythmic cadence like a military drummer. She had reached a dead end. Still, something about the information nagged at her but she could not place the feeling. Her thoughts drifted to Ishmel. He by now had discovered that the gift of her system she had presented to him was inaccessible. Her software would beckon him with the allure of a mermaid, but was locked and beyond his grasp. He was probably wishing at this moment that Clayton had cancelled her Orion Project security access. But it was too late for that. *Neat job* she said to herself.

Kirsten put aside her feelings about Ishmel and focused on the Orion Project. The strange feeling that was troubling her about Ishmel's data suddenly became clear: the Orion Project "On Schedule" progress reporting was all too perfect, too neat. And for good reason. Clayton's staff would have access to Ishmel's progress information. Things *had* to look perfect, on schedule, as planned. How was this possible? She shook her head, wondering why the revelation had taken her so long. In intelligence jargon, the data had been cleansed. With no further sources of information, she had reached a dead end.

She lay her head back and stared at the ceiling, thinking. It was one thing, Ishmel getting to her. But it was quite another with Clayton drinking Ishmel's Kool-Aid, shifting her promising work aside, doubling down on Ishmel's promises.

She had not left the success, power and excitement of Silicon Valley to come here and see the United States betrayed from within.

She got up, pushed her chair away and moved past a bookcase containing technical journals and mementos of days past and stopped in front of the credenza behind her desk. Project proposals, system design specs, executive presentations, and implementation plans for her advanced counterterrorism system lay in neatly labeled folders across the top of the surface. Plans that would never see completion. *Damn Ishmel.* In one swift motion, she swept the folders off the credenza, scattering their contents across the floor.

She stared at the littered mess she had created. Nothing in her accelerated track to a PhD at Stanford or years of success in the insane, intense world of computer technology had prepared her for the anger and pangs of emptiness that gripped her.

"Two years in D.C. to chase goofy hackers? For what?" her friends had asked her eight months earlier, laughing over beers that night at Bucks restaurant in Woodside where many of the deals in Silicon Valley were born. "You're going to gridlock city, where innovation is a foreign word. Get real, Kirsten. By the time you return, we'll be three product generations ahead, well into our vesting for the next round of options."

Her friends' words echoed through her head. She had come east for Clayton, of course. A call out of the blue from a family friend, offering her the opportunity to give something back to her country. The offer felt somehow good to her and after some consideration she had accepted the request. But for this?

Perhaps her friends had been right. Had she been so ill-equipped for an environment where any sense of purpose other than advancement of personal agendas was checked at the door that she was blinded to Ishmel's maneuvering? Perhaps government service was no place for her.

She blinked to clear her eyes and stared at the bookcase against the wall. Neat rows of technical journals and reference books were mixed in with pictures and mementos of days past. Happier days, mostly.

She slowly scanned the items on the bookcase: the PR photo of the brash Silicon Valley real estate developer who had spent sixteen months rarely present as her husband, a picture kept as a reminder to be wary of trusting false promises of love; a silicon-framed photograph of her division's startup team in their polo shirts, hoisting beers at the first product shipment; the Wall Street Journal announcement of the IPO; the *Inc.* magazine cover article with her picture on the cover with the caption "Wonder Woman: The Ice Queen of the Cyber Security World"; the hand-signed congratulatory notes from the crew at CNBC following her appearances.

She laughed a small, private laugh. She had not been that tough, but the image had built, like those gunslinger legends from the Wild West.

Yes, there had been success – tremendous success many had said – with all the trappings of power, money, and celebrity status.

How quickly those eight years had whirled by. And how quickly eight months could change everything. She had known the transition to government culture would present challenges. Silicon Valley, with its obsession with Internet time, shrimp and Chardonnay receptions, grueling work regimen, frenetic entrepreneurs stretching for the brass IPO ring, and fire-red Ferraris piloted by thirty-something venture capitalists now seemed as though it existed on a different planet than the nation's Capital.

The talk had begun shortly after her arrival at the Orion Project — she was here because of a family relationship with Clayton. Her business success was due to the luck of timing. She was a lightweight glamour queen not suited to the massive software complexities of the Orion Project.

Had she been right in dismissing the innuendos as merely chatter caused by envy? Or was there something more to the talk than she would admit? Was she a "loose cannon" as Ishmel had impolitely put it more than once? Yes, she had butted heads with the best of them in Silicon Valley, taken chances, lots of them, but not recklessly so.

There had been hurdles and setbacks, of course, but she had prided herself in her ability to see the promise on the other side of the mountain, to build the loyalty that enabled her to lead her team places even they doubted they could reach. In the end, she had always delivered.

She pulled the *Inc.* magazine from the stack and examined the cover picture, her short-cropped copper hair framing the attractive face, gleaming emerald eyes projecting the intense confidence of a young woman driven by purpose. Once the company had gone public and the stock soared, the recruiter's calls had coursed into her life like a flood. Now those days seemed like a misty memory. The phone calls dwindled several months after her move east, and then had stopped.

Eight months. For what? Perhaps it was time to fold the tent and go home?

Images returned of Clayton delivering the bad news. Of Ishmel strutting in front of his team, their whispered, secretive discussions. Something more than political maneuvering and crisis reaction to the San Francisco attacks was going on in the Orion Project. But what?

The picture of the startup team came back into focus, chins up and eyes defiant as if daring defeat to take a shot. Long hitters all. Not a quitter in the lot, especially not Kirsten Lockhart, rising superstar vice president of software development.

No, she was not a quitter. She would stay, if for no other reason than to give Ishmel his due. But before that, she would find out what deeper problems were troubling the Orion Project and determine what could be done to stop the terrorists.

But who would risk Ishmel's ire – perhaps even an entire professional future – to help her? A face emerged from her swirling thoughts, someone on Ishmel's staff who might have the guts to take her behind the veil of misinformation that Ishmel had constructed.

She reached for her phone and tapped an extension, kicking at the scattered papers on the floor as she listened to the buzzing of the phone at the other end. "I would like to see you," she said when her party answered. "Now."

CHAPTER 6

Kirsten skipped rapidly up one flight of stairs and pushed into the busy hallway. Karl Breskin was waiting outside his office. He waved in a way to attract her attention, but she could not have missed his large frame and full head of wavy dark hair in the crowd. She noticed as she reached him that Karl's perpetual smile had been replaced by creases of worry.

He placed a large hand on her shoulder. "You and your project took the hit for the San Francisco attacks. I'm sorry to hear that." He had a deep voice, almost hoarse, his words measured and deliberate.

"There's a bit more to it," she said, keeping her tone neutral so as not to reflect her inner turmoil.

"Ishmel?" he asked, raising his eyebrows in question.

Kirsten nodded. She searched his eyes for clues to his sentiment, trying to decode how she should approach him. She and Karl had built a good working relationship over the past eight months, the only such rapport she enjoyed with any of Ishmel's managers. Her visit was going to put that rapport to the test, and she hoped she wasn't placing Karl in a career-endangering position by asking his help. One of Breskin's responsibilities as director of operations was to monitor software development progress in the Orion Project. If anyone could provide the insight she sought, it would be him.

"I need to talk to you," she said, glancing around. "In private."

"Of course." He turned down the corridor and motioned her to follow.

"What do you think about the attacks?" he asked as they wove their way through the crowd.

"I think we got caught with our pants down," she replied.

"How so?"

"You know the answer. We should have been ready. Orion software versions 3 and 4 were flawed in design and had critical failures. And so here we sit, the country undefended, waiting for a version that is actually operational."

Breskin paused a beat before replying. "I'm told it's an extremely complex set of software. Nothing like it has ever been done before."

Kirsten put aside his comment and asked, "What's your take?"

He glanced away. "You know my role in the Orion Project is internal operations, to keep the trains running on schedule, so to speak."

Kirsten searched his face. "And are the trains running on schedule?"

Breskin stopped them at a private elevator and pressed the call button. As he turned toward her, he raised a finger to his lips. "We'll talk when we get downstairs."

Kirsten followed him into the elevator and watched as he inserted a pass card into a slot. As the doors slid silently closed, a surveillance camera overhead winked on.

They both stared straight ahead as they rode in silence. The car stopped at Sub Level 4, deep below the operations of the Orion Project. Breskin was out and heading down the hall before the doors were completely open.

Kirsten followed. She had not been this deep in the Orion Project before, and found the empty, silent corridor a stark contrast to the bright, bustling activity above. They moved swiftly along the narrow hallway around two turns before Breskin stopped in front of a large steel door labeled POWER SYSTEMS.

"Know where you are?" Breskin glanced at Kirsten as he pressed a button that opened a panel to the right of the door, revealing a biometric reader and a microphone.

Kirsten remembered mention of the Orion Project's power systems in her site briefings, but only recalled that access to the area was severely limited. She shrugged. "Backup power for the cyber center?"

"That's the cover story. This room is a whole lot more than that." He tilted his head toward the reader. "Want to give it a try?"

Kirsten stared at him. "But I—"

"You're cleared for entry."

"Really?"

"Really. Secretary Clayton saw to that. He told Ishmel he wanted you to be familiar with all critical functions in the Orion Project. Clayton evidently has complete trust in you."

Kirsten put her thoughts of Clayton's trust aside for the moment, instead fighting a flash of simmering anger with Ishmel. Ishmel had never shown this facility to her, never even mentioned its existence.

"Go ahead," Breskin said.

Kirsten pressed her index finger on the reader and stated her name into the small microphone and waited for identity verification to be completed. A moment later the locking mechanism clicked twice and the door swung open.

Kirsten followed him inside and surveyed the room as the door closed behind them with the solid click of metal on metal. Row upon row of tall steel-clad boxes adorned with panels of blinking colored lights mixed in with racks containing servers cast shadows from the overhead lights across the floor like monuments in the noonday sun. Kirsten let out a long breath. The room appeared to extend the length of half a football field, perhaps more. Except for the faint hum of the equipment, the room was silent, and as far as she could tell, empty of other people. Two floor-mounted swivel chairs sat in front of large curved control console housing banks of computer screens. Smaller versions of the display screens matching those in the Cyber Center were mounted on the wall above the console. She instantly recognized the center screen, which displayed cyber threats across the U.S.

He motioned Kirsten to a chair and dropped in the other, then swiveled to face her. "Welcome to Colossus."

"Which is . . ?" Kirsten wondered what this massive computer center was all about but waited for him to continue.

"The fastest computer ever created. Faster than the Cray XT5 Jaguar, faster even than China's new Tianhe-1A, which is – excuse me – one hell of a machine. Colossus is a different design completely, consisting of an array of optical computer processors, making up one of the few optical computers in existence. It contains processing power thousands of times more powerful than the fastest silicon-chip computers anywhere."

"Optical processors?" Kirsten said. "I thought their commercial capabilities were five or more years away."

Breskin gave her a tight smile. "Exactly what we want the rest of the world to think."

Kirsten scanned the room again. "Where is everyone?"

Breskin shook his head. "Colossus is fully automated. We only have people here for software updates and in case of emergencies."

"You're going to tell me what this facility is for?"

"Cyber attack simulations, primarily. We have continuous feeds on cyber attack activity around the globe from the NSA, CIA, FBI and all U.S. and allies' intelligence agencies. Colossus also monitors networks around the globe and analyzes intelligence information and all known cyber-related events, running complex simulations, looking for patterns. Potential threats to the United States or our allies are identified and prioritized flash notifications issued for defensive action.

Kirsten got it. "And the results are fed upstairs?"

"And to Homeland Security's cyber defense center."

Kirsten asked the obvious question tugging at her mind. "You're telling me we saw the San Francisco attacks coming?"

"Yes, but with so little notice all that could be done was to begin preparations for military deployment to secure the city."

Kirsten scanned the screens, reflecting on what she had just heard. "So . . . if Orion 5 had been ready we could have prevented the attacks from happening."

He paused for a moment, as if framing his response. "That's the theory, yes."

"And in practice?"

"Don't know. We have never had a live situation to test against a fully operational Orion defense."

Kirsten was edging closer to the information she came for. "And how close are we to having a 'fully operational Orion defense?'"

Breskin looked away. "I'm not comfortable going that direction."

Kirsten decided to ease up and come back at him later. "Okay. So what else do we have here?"

"This is our emergency operations center, containing mirror-image files of all Orion Project software systems, displays of cyber attack activity across the U.S., fuel cells strong enough to power this facility for months – and an emergency escape mechanism that I hope we never have to use."

Kirsten's mind flooded with questions, but she let Karl continue.

"Our fiber optic communications network down here is independent from the rest of the Orion Project. All of Washington D.C., could be bombed and this center would continue to operate Orion Project cyber defense systems, totally unattended." He paused, his eyes scanning the equipment, before returning his attention to Kirsten.

Kirsten felt an eerie feeling come over her as though she had been injected with an intoxicating drug while Breskin's words echoed in her head: *All of Washington D.C. could be bombed and his facility would continue to operate its cyber defense systems, totally unattended.* It was as though the developed human race could be extinguished and the computers would continue their fighting. Until when? For what purpose?

"And you mentioned an escape mechanism," she said. "To where?"

Karl tipped his head to a single blue door on the wall beyond the console. "Non-stop elevator to the surface, opens inside of a double-locked fake electric transformer box to hide its purpose. The box contains weapons, smartphones, emergency rations, gas mask, even a motorcycle."

Kirsten's eyes were riveted on the blue door as she considered the "last man standing" scenario sweeping through her mind. When her thoughts returned to the present she noticed Breskin staring at her. "Sorry," she said. "I just was thinking—"

"I know what you're feeling. It's spooky. I've been exactly where you are."

"Do the feelings ever get better?"

"Perhaps." His eyes studied her for several moments, and then he leaned toward her, hands clasped in his lap. "You've come to see me for a reason, Kirsten. What's on your mind?"

Kirsten studied the serious face across from her. "I first thought today's organizational change was more of the political maneuvering we see around here, but there's much more going on, isn't there?"

Breskin's bushy gray eyebrows knitted together in a frown. "Your people were needed elsewhere."

"Why?"

"That's a sensitive question. If Ishmel knew I was discussing this with you, I would pay dearly."

"Today's critical Orion 6 test aborted. Ishmel's staff is panicked. I was there. For God's sake, Karl, if there's any reason the Orion Project isn't going to be able to counter the terrorist attacks, something needs to be done."

Breskin averted his eyes.

Kirsten leaned toward him and pressed forward. "Karl, the networks that the entire U.S. technology infrastructure – military, financial, power and communications grids, everything – are at risk. You know that. The Orion Project is the only potential defense the country has to stop further attacks, and we are running out of time. If there are problems, perhaps I can help. But I need to know exactly where Orion 5 and 6 stand."

He studied the computer screens, and then turned his face to her. "What I'm about to say can never come back to me."

"You have my word."

He blew out a long breath. "Several days ago, we experienced an increase in Orion software failures. The problems started as we were completing final system tests and preparing for distribution to critical computer networks nationwide."

"Go on," she said.

"Ishmel was having fits. Time was running out and he desperately needed to pinpoint the source of the failures. As the level of software failures increased, Ishmel came up with the idea of sidelining your project, to provide additional resources to locate the problems in Orion 5. Last night's attacks brought everything to a head, and in a desperate move, Ishmel convinced Secretary Clayton that the transfer of your staff would ensure completion of Orion 5. You know the rest."

Kirsten let out a long whistle. "Ishmel is hanging out there big time."

"You might say that."

"Ishmel's ploy was also a convenient way to get me pushed aside," Kirsten added.

He nodded. "And to keep you from poking around and discovering things Ishmel doesn't want to get to Clayton."

"Such as what?"

"Such as any information on the nature of the delays. Ishmel hopes to keep it quiet and fix the problem on his own."

"Doesn't want to lose face," Kirsten said.

"You got it."

Kirsten felt disgust rise up inside of her. *Well, that's keeping your priorities straight.*

Breskin glanced at his watch and stood. "I really must get back."

Kirsten realized her throat had gone dry. The Orion 5 software provided a powerful defense against cyber terrorist attacks, but the next generation product, Orion 6, was a thousand times more powerful.

"If we're going to stop the terrorists, Karl, we need Orion 5. Now." Kirsten waited.

He locked his eyes on hers. "God help me if Ishmel hears I said this, but someone needs to know that progress on the Orion Project has come to a halt."

CHAPTER 7

Brett Logan studied the worn four-story building through the rain-streaked side window of the staff car. "What the hell is this?" he said quietly under his breath. The windowless structure in the industrial area of Bethesda was unmarked except for an aging large blue and white sign running up the corner that read "Millennium Transport" in block letters. The dark glass double entry doors showed no light from within.

The driver glanced at Brett in the rear view mirror. "We have a problem?"

"You certain this is the place?"

"Absolutely certain."

Logan shook his head. Two hours earlier he had been absorbed in analyzing intelligence data on North Korea's latest surface to air missile sites. Urgent orders had pulled him from his work, directing him to report for a surveillance assignment. But at a transport firm?

"Very well," Logan said, and angled his broad shoulders through the door. He watched the staff car pull away and disappear around the corner, not noticing the sharp darts of icy rain against his face, wondering what Millennium Transport held for him. He shot one more look at the aging sign, and then strode across the wet sidewalk and entered the building.

Logan assessed the reception area as the doors slid closed behind him. The room at first appeared ordinary, with an arrangement of muted-blue upholstered chairs and magazines stacked neatly on low tables. Background music relieved the sense of total silence. The two unsmiling guards dressed in black ninja uniforms behind a thick glass partition, their attention locked on him, however, created an atmosphere quite different than the traditional waiting room. These were not garden-variety rent-a-cops sleepwalking through their shift, but two highly trained, armed professionals.

Logan glanced above the two security men. A trio of video cameras swept the room. To their left a double metal door filled half of the wall. His senses screamed at him that Millennium Transport was not what it appeared to be. But what was it?

The guard nearest to him rose, a man not yet out of his thirties, still fit and filling his uniform. His face was neutral but guarded, his eyes a serious, cold gray.

"Help you, sir?"

Logan met the man's stare as he closed the distance to the partition in three long steps. He retrieved his CIA identification from his inside jacket pocket and slid it through the opening in the bulletproof glass.

"Agent Logan," he said in an even tone.

Without removing his attention from Logan, the guard handed the ID to the second security officer who scanned it through a reader attached to a flat computer screen.

"Reason for your visit?" the guard asked.

Logan told him all that he had been told. "Meeting."

The guard's eyebrows shot up a notch as he scanned the computer screen. "Seems Mr. Washington, the director of security, will be greeting you personally," he said to Logan.

Logan thought that over and then said, "Is that the good news or the bad news?"

"In your case, the latter," the guard replied. He pointed to the steel doors at the end of the room which had begun to swing open. "An elevator at the end of the corridor will be waiting for you."

Logan stared at the guard, his hand held extended. "My identification?"

The guard stared back, unblinking. "You will have it before you leave."

Logan started to protest, but knew he had no choice. He stepped through the massive doors and hesitated as they hissed closed with a solid click behind him, taking a moment to get his bearings. He stood in a windowless steel tube forty to fifty feet long devoid of décor or furnishings. A pair of unmarked elevator doors filled the far wall like twin monuments. His glance at the ceiling confirmed what he had expected to see, security cameras and small apertures next to the fire sprinkler heads, probably for tear gas. *No easy way into this place, or out.*

He wondered again what Millennium Transport really was and why he was here. And what was going on with the security director – the Washington fellow? He really was not in the frame of mind for more CIA chicanery. His last field assignment had been one too many. All he wanted was a quiet desk and his intelligence information, distanced from the horrors of war, where he could suppress the memories of death that still haunted him. In two more years he would walk away with an adequate pension and start a new life, restoring that small winery his parents had left him. But for now, he had to dispense with the mystery of Millennium Transport, which he had every intention of doing in short order.

As he approached the end of the corridor two ramrod straight armed marines appeared through a sliding door to his right, their attention focused on him. Brett waved and threw off a friendly smile. *Anyone who isn't supposed to get this far and hasn't been gassed, will be shot on sight.*

The senior marine, perhaps a kid of 25, tilted his head ever so slightly toward the elevators without speaking. The left door slid silently open as Brett approached. He entered, turned, and waved at the young men as if they had all just finished having a beer together.

He smiled as the door slid closed. *These kids today need to loosen up.* The interior of the elevator was unlike any he had seen before. The polished metal cab was topped with a softly illuminated ceiling and held no buttons, controls, floor indicator lights or emergency phone. A brief glance at the ceiling confirmed the presence of security cameras and – yes – more tear gas. *Three times dead.*

The descent of the elevator was so subtle it took Logan a moment to realize he was moving. He was going underground. He started counting to himself and had reached twenty-eight when he felt the tiniest sensation of the car stopping. Assuming fifteen feet per level and two seconds travel time per floor he had dropped ten levels. Approximately one hundred fifty feet below street level. *Where was he?*

He was taken out of his thoughts as the door opened. A tall, muscled black man in a well-tailored dark suit, hands hanging loosely at his side, glowered at him, blocking his exit into a hallway that appeared to be identical to that from which he had just come. This must be the mysterious Walt Washington, head of security, he thought.

Brett examined the other man as he waited for him to speak. Washington – if it were indeed Washington – held himself with the grace of an athlete, balancing his weight on the front of his feet as if ready for an assault. His large brown eyes swept over Brett in one swift motion, never dropping their hardness.

The man's quick about-face and swift movement down the hall was all the invitation Logan needed to follow. After a few turns down an empty hall, the man entered an office and held the door open for Logan to enter.

"We won't be long – you may stand," the man said, then eased into a leather desk chair and stared at Logan.

With little need to play Washington's little power game, Logan looked elsewhere, taking in the office.

In addition to a telephone and computer monitor and keyboard, the credenza behind Washington held two framed photographs and a Navy SEAL plaque. In one picture, two smiling school-age girls were dressed in their Sunday best, hair done up in brightly colored beads. In the other, a decorated navy chief Walt Washington in dress whites was shaking hands with President Anston. A handwritten note and the president's large, flowing signature filled the lower right corner of the photograph.

Except for an outbox containing neatly stacked documents and a prominent name plate

displaying the Orion Project seal and the words
"DIRECTOR OF SECURITY", the surface of
Washington's desk was as bare and polished as
the smooth, shaved surface of the black Navy
SEAL's head. Logan's ID lay in the center of
the desk. Logan started to let his mind wan-
der as to how his identification card made it to
Washington's office before he did, but let it drop.
He just wanted to get this exercise over with, have
his meeting, and return to Langley.

Washington finally spoke, his tone measured
and gravelly, like a smoker's voice: "I know who
you are and you know who I am so let's dispense
with the introductions. Why are you here?"

"As I told your security officers, I have a
meeting," Logan answered, feeling a surge of
frustration.

"With whom?"

"Don't know."

"To discuss what?"

"I don't know that either."

"'Don't know. Don't know.'" Washington said
in a mocking, sarcastic tone. "Jesus – where do we
get you people?"

Logan put aside Washington's question and
parried with one of his own. "Don't care much
for those of us in intelligence, do you?"

Washington placed his massive hands on the
desk and leaned toward Logan. "Listen to me,
Agent Logan. I run a tight, secure government
facility. I want things neat and clean. I don't care
for messes. Neither do I care for blue-suited,

flag-waving self-styled Langley hotshots who roll in here in the name of national security, interfere with my mission, and create a great…big…mess."

"Thank you for that job description,'" Logan answered, glancing at his watch. "Now may I get processed in and on to my meeting?"

Washington stood and thrust the ID card just far enough forward that Logan had to lean across the desk to retrieve it. "Processing is two doors down on the right."

Logan slid the card into his jacket pocket. "I didn't expect to see this until leaving."

"Trust me, Logan. You will be leaving immediately following your meeting. I will see to it personally."

My pleasure, Logan said to himself.

After proceeding through digital fingerprinting, a retina scan, and a security discussion, Logan expected his meeting room - Room 7 it said on the door to be crammed with cubicles occupied by busy fellow agents. But the space he stepped into when the door slid open puzzled him.

The windowless room was shaped like a blunt bullet with straight, bare smooth walls curved to a rounded point at the far end. The only furnishings were a highly polished half-circle conference table with six black leather chairs facing away from him toward the nose of the room. Brett studied the table, his attention on a computer screen set into the polished wood surface.

He glanced at the door. If he activated the screen before his host arrived, perhaps some of the mystery of Millennium Transport would be revealed. Brett's thoughts drifted to the pert young blond who had conducted his security processing and the way her hand had held his a moment longer than necessary. "The biometric transmitter I've inserted under the skin in your wrist will provide limited computer access and permit entry to those areas where you are authorized," she had said, "and to keep you honest our internal positioning system will track and record everywhere you go, everything you do."

"Everything?" he had parried, with an innocent look.

It always started that way. Some attributed it to his engaging, crooked Harrison Ford grin, or perhaps his blue eyes set off by the light brown hair and strong athletic jaw that some said gave his forty-one years and six foot tall frame a youthful magnetism. Not that any of his endearing qualities had led him beyond a series of relationships, six to eight months was the norm, before his restlessness, or hers, moved him on.

He glanced at the door, then back to the screen. Millennium Transport, or whatever it truly was, was gaining a hold on his imagination. *What the hell.* He skimmed his wrist over the computer screen, which turned a bright blue. "Welcome to the Orion Project, Agent Logan," a pleasant female voice intoned.

So that's where he was – the Orion Project. He knew of the Orion Project and that it would be involved in countering last night's cyber attacks against San Francisco. Not his specialty. So why would he be called?

"For a view of the activity on the floor of the Orion Project cyber center," the female voice continued, "touch the View icon."

Logan tapped his index finger on the View symbol. Lights in the room dimmed. The bullet-nosed wall split at its center and the two sections silently slid apart, revealing a curved expanse of floor-to-ceiling windows. He took a step toward the glass. The room below him was shaped like a large amphitheater the size and shape of a major league baseball field. Dozens of rows of computer workstations, their screens flashing, squatted on a field of computer desks that stretched from wall to wall. Several hundred people, perhaps more, he estimated, were in motion about the room, hunched over terminals, or talking in small groups. Two massive digital displays dominated the wall furthest from him.

The voice continued: "The Orion Project cyber center below you, home to America's war against cyberterrorism, was built in the shell of a former nuclear blast shelter. The operation is bomb-hardened and sealed through multi-layered security from outside threats."

Logan turned his attention from the voice. The Orion Project had nothing to do with him. He was suddenly gripped with the desire to be out of Room 7 and out of the Orion Project. He glanced at his watch. *Where was his briefing officer?*

"You can listen to the sounds of activity from the floor," the voice continued. "If I can provide additional information, please touch the Information icon."

A hum of activity from the center replaced the woman's voice. Brett focused on what sounded like an announcement: "Entering final countdown," a crisp male voice intoned.

Not understanding which final countdown was being entered, Logan touched the Information icon and waited.

The woman's image appeared. "There are three levels of defense against cyber attacks: anticipation, defense, and attack. In the first level, the Orion Project aggregates feeds from U.S. and foreign intelligence agencies on cyber attack activity around the globe and runs highly sophisticated simulation models to predict and prioritize where and when in the United States attacks might occur."

Nice job predicting the San Francisco attacks, Logan said to himself.

"The second level is defense," the woman continued. "The primary mission of the Orion Project is to build defenses to intercept and stop attacks against United States computer networks when they do occur."

Logan scanned the computer center below, thinking about the massive deployment of resources being dedicated to cyber defenses. And for what result? So far, as much as he could tell, the Orion Project was zero for two on the attacks. "What about level three – attacking?" he asked.

"Sorry, sir, you are not cleared for that information."

Logan could have guessed as much. He let his eyes wander over the information icons until he came to one titled "STAFF". He suddenly wondered who else from the Agency might be at the Orion Project. He quickly skimmed through the Staff section, then stopped and smiled at the sight of a familiar name and made a mental note of the individual's location.

Behind him, the door to Room 7 hissed open. He swiveled, expecting a routine case officer, assignment in hand. The face he saw stopped his breath. Nate Sherwin, a twenty-seven year veteran of the agency, stood at the door, empty hands loosely at his side, observing Brett in the manner of a prey assessing his quarry. As deputy chief of staff to the CIA director, Sherwin handled the delicate assignments, most never spoken of except in whispers in private places.

"Surprised to see me, Logan?"

CHAPTER 8

Logan stared at Nate Sherwin through narrowed eyes, making no effort to mask his disgust. The CIA deputy chief of staff's clean-shaven, perpetually tanned head seemed even larger in proportion to his average frame than Brett had remembered, but Sherwin's erect posture and air of supreme confidence had not changed. In his single prior experience with Sherwin, Logan had found the man ruthless in pursuit of his objective, regardless of the cost, human or otherwise. Logan had no desire to repeat the experience.

Sherwin unbuttoned his tailored suit jacket and came around the table next to Logan. He placed his hands behind him and spoke to the windows that overlooked the cyber center. "What a sorry goddamn mess."

Now more than ever, Logan was more confused than ever about his being at the Orion Project. He kept his eyes on Sherwin but remained silent.

"Dustin Clayton's misconceived, misguided, massively expensive field of dreams," Sherwin added. "The Orion Project, site of the Homeland Security Department's war on cyberterrorism." Sherwin pointed a long manicured finger at the window. "Look at them down there. Overpaid computer nerds scurrying like rats in a maze between their satellite-tethered electronic screens, like the medieval sorcerers who deceived the emperors into believing their alchemy would cure the ills of the day. And for what?"

"I seem to be missing your point," Logan said.

"If you haven't noticed, San Francisco is a disaster area. Hospitals are jammed with freezing, ill, frightened citizens. Fires are breaking out across the city from people attempting to stay warm. Public transportation and BART trains are inoperable. The 911 phone systems are out. People wander the streets, unable to leave the city or call their families on the jammed cellular circuits, searching for an open restaurant, an operational television, or any source of information."

Logan was tiring of the tirade. "Which has exactly what to do with me?"

"I have an assignment for you."

"I'm on assignment."

Sherwin turned and pushed his face close to Logan's.

"Now you have another."

"Not in this place I don't. I was clearly briefed by the security director that my welcome in this facility ends with this meeting."

Sherwin laughed a wheezing laugh while shaking his head. "Security Director Washington is throwing his weight around, finessing you." His face took on a dark cast. "Just like you were finessed into that trap in Tehran, Logan. Except that your misjudgment there cost us three good men."

Logan started toward Sherwin, fists clinched, but stopped himself halfway through the first step. He would find a way to deal with Sherwin in due time.

"That's it, Logan," Sherwin said, his eyes glittering with excitement. "Hit me. Add that to your list of failures and see where it gets you. No wonder you're running out your days to retirement in a basement cubicle analyzing satellite photos of North Korean missile sites instead of doing something worthwhile."

Logan stared back, not caring if his eyes reflected the distaste he held for Sherwin. "I'm not your man for this assignment."

"This is a routine surveillance job." Sherwin gave a sardonic smile. "You know, something even you can handle."

The crisp voice from below interrupted them: "Twenty seconds to application launch."

Logan bristled at Sherwin's sarcasm, but held his tongue. If he said what he was thinking, Sherwin would be looking for someone else for the assignment, and Brett would find himself at the end of twenty years in Army intelligence and then the CIA, his career abruptly ended without benefits or pension. Sherwin had the power and the malice to make that happen. He wondered why Sherwin was handling a routine surveillance assignment, if the Orion Project assignment truly was routine. With Sherwin, he knew truth lay hidden behind a veil of purposely constructed misdirection.

"Ten seconds," the voice continued.

Logan kept his eyes locked on Sherwin. "This is a technology operation. You know I'm not a computer guy."

Sherwin waved him to silence. "For what you're going to do, it doesn't matter." He pulled a USB flash drive from his jacket pocket and extended it to Logan between two fingers.

"Application launch!" the voice from the speaker announced.

Logan noted the tension in the crisp voice and turned his attention to the room below. Movement in the cyber center had ceased. The technicians sat motionless in their chairs. All eyes seemed to be intent on their computer terminals or on the large wall mounted screens.

Sherwin shoved the flash drive forward, almost touching Logan's stomach. He glanced toward the computer screen imbedded in the table. "Insert this in the terminal."

The large screens in the cyber center below erupted in a blaze of lights. To the crisp voice was now added a shrill tone: "Launch aborted! Repeat. Launch aborted!"

Sherwin looked below and snorted. "What a joke. I rest my case."

Logan did not accept the drive. He wanted out. Now. "You need someone else."

"You're on thin ground, Logan. You understand that? You don't decide what assignments you take or don't take. I'm the arbiter of your future. So don't push me."

"Tell me, Sherwin. What is it you have for breakfast that makes you such an asshole?"

Sherwin's face reddened. "Take the goddamn drive."

Logan slowly grasped the flash drive and slipped it into a slot adjacent to the computer screen.

"Now we're talking." Sherwin tilted his head toward the glass. "The waiting for this misguided counter—cyberterrorism effort to produce results is over. San Francisco was only the terrorist's first stop. We're going to find them, whoever they are, wherever they are, and dispose of them. And you, Logan, like it or not, are part of the plan."

The flash drive blinked red several times and the computer screen came to life.

"Say hello to your new partner," Sherwin said, tilting his head back with an air of supremacy. "Computer savant Peter Olson will more than compensate for your sorry lack of technical skills."

The screen filled with the fair-skinned face of a stocky young man with military-cut blond hair and intense blue eyes. Logan couldn't help thinking that Olson looked more like a college athlete and about as far from a computer jockey as he could imagine.

The image dissolved and Logan scanned the short bio on Olson that filled the screen: Masters in computer science with honors from MIT. Former U.S. Army captain, seven years service, Ranger qualified but worked in counterterrorism. Three years with an Internet security software company. Two years with the Agency.

Logan rolled the information about Olson over in his mind. Why hadn't Olson been tapped for this assignment rather than him?

"I'm still missing what this has to do with me."

A smirk crossed Sherwin's face. "Mark it up to personal business. Your assignment is to locate and apprehend Sidney Hirschfield, a prime suspect in the terrorist actions."

One piece of the puzzle fell into place. "Hirschfield? The young Internet grand master from Stanford featured on *Sixty Minutes*?"

"One and the same."

The image of a lanky twenty-something youth with dark curly hair filled Logan's consciousness. He had met Hirschfield while on assignment in Silicon Valley a year earlier. Hirschfield operated at hyper-speed genius level, had problems with authority, and clearly demonstrated a wild streak, but a criminal?

"Certainly you have stronger suspects than a college student working on his latest degree."

"Listen and look at this." Sherwin touched the computer screen. The notation above the picture of Hirschfield read "Top of the most wanted list for cyber crimes against the U.S. government, fled the country, whereabouts unknown."

"Starting to get the picture?" Sherwin asked.

Logan tuned Sherwin out, concentrating on the image that filled the screen. Sidney Hirschfield, thin cheeks and fair skin framed by Buddy Holly-style black frame glasses stared back at him. Logan paged to the next screen and scanned the text: "Sidney Hirschfield, known as the Phantom. Wanted on charges of illegal entry, tampering, and theft of top secret information at Department of Defense, Los Alamos, NASA, and other secure computing sites.

"Age 26 years. Raised in the San Francisco bay area. Graduated Stanford with a doctorate with highest honors in computer science. Studied in Paris during his junior year. Dropped from view five months ago following unsuccessful arrest attempt. Current location unknown but believed to be out of the country. Parents uncooperative, even following seizure of assets, search of properties, and repeated interrogation. Communication taps are in effect but to date have been unproductive. Hirschfield Facebook, Twitter, and Instagram accounts in monitoring status and show no activity."

Logan hesitated at the mention of property seizure, then continued reading. "Interrogations with Stanford students and faculty established that Hirschfield had developed sophisticated, undetectable network entry tools using new technology developed while in his Ph.D. program."

Logan had read enough. He looked away from the screen toward Sherwin. "Did I miss the evidence linking Hirschfield with the terrorists?"

"Hirschfield is guilty of illegally removing confidential CIA information relating to, shall we say, U.S. plans for certain high-ranking officials in the Iranian government. If he makes this information public we will have a major embarrassment on our hands."

Logan considered the implications of what Sherwin had said. The worldwide hacker network that called itself Anonymous had proven itself vicious in spreading malicious information and in hacking into corporate and government networks. But they had not been labeled as terrorists, to Logan's knowledge. "Need I ask my question about the terrorist connection again?" Logan asked.

"It's confidential."

Logan shook his head. "I think I'm getting the picture. The CIA is about to be embarrassed for not maintaining control of its internal black ops plans, so you start grasping at straws, and I'm one of them."

"Let's be clear, Logan. Give me one chance and you'll be freezing your measly balls off counting Chinese satellites from the outer tip of the Aleutian chain. Don't think I wouldn't relish the opportunity."

Logan stared at Sherwin in silence. There was electricity in Sherwin's energy that bestowed him power, power only a foolish man would consider harmless. He knew Sherwin could easily make good on the threat, that his future would be determined by what happened over the next few minutes. He had no course except to play along.

"Go ahead," Logan said finally.

"It's simple," Sherwin said. "I need Hirschfield and you're perfectly suited to lead us to him."

"Because I've met him?"

"No, because you've been close to someone who is going to lead us to Hirschfield, and if we play our cards right, to the terrorists."

"'Been close to someone who is going to lead us to Hirschfield?'" Logan studied Sherwin, trying to unscramble the riddle. Was it his imagination, or was Sherwin savoring this interchange?

"Well, well." Sherwin pointed at the glass to the floor of the center below. "I believe I see your quarry at this very moment."

Logan's eyes followed Sherwin's gesture. He blinked once, then again, conscious of the increase in his heart rate. Rushing between rows of desks, an attractive woman with brilliant copper hair sped toward the front of the massive cyber center. *Kirsten Lockhart, here, in Washington?* He had given up trying to reach her after months of unreturned calls, e-mails, and messages left with her company. But now, she was here, one floor below.

"I guess I could say she's all yours," Sherwin said, watching Logan with a grin, "but we wouldn't want to get your hopes up, would we? After all, your last little romp with her was at the Westin hotel in Palo Alto – room 319 as I remember. Of course it cost you a chateaubriand dinner and two bottles of 2003 Markham cabernet. Too bad, a better man could have done the same with just one bottle, as I'm sure many have before and after you."

"Go fuck yourself, Sherwin," Logan said, spitting out the words. Suddenly he imagined grabbing Sherwin by the back of the neck and bashing his face again and again against the viewing windows until, nose broken, forehead slashed and lips bleeding; Sherwin's blood would run down the glass to the floor. But he knew baiting when he saw it and turned away.

"I love it when you get angry, Logan." Sherwin's eyes took on a dark cast. "Now all you have to work on is channeling those flaring energies toward your assignment."

Logan ignored Sherwin and focused on lowering the racing of his heart. The pieces had fallen into place. Kirsten had been friends with Hirschfield, perhaps even had stayed in contact when she left California. He fought back words that were too harsh to speak. Sherwin had placed him on a collision course against himself, and clearly was enjoying every second of the journey.

After a moment, Logan found his voice. "What makes you believe she'll contact Hirschfield?"

"Because she is as of today out of the loop in the Orion Project. But not totally out of the game. If she decides to go after the terrorists she will need help. Hirschfield can help her, even if he is a fugitive. Shall I quote from her psychological profile? How about this: 'Risk taker, lives on the edge. Only feels truly alive when she has it all on the line.'" Sherwin leaned close to Logan. "Is that the way she was, Logan? Must have been thrilling. Does she put it all on the line in bed also?"

Although simmering inside, Logan eased away and waited. He would not win this battle.

"Ah, yes, where were we?" Sherwin dropped the smile. "So that's why you're here, Logan. To flush out the quail. For starters, we've set up surveillance of her apartment and office communications systems. Agent Olson will brief you."

Logan struggled to push the image of Kirsten aside. "What am I supposed to do if I happen to find Hirschfield?"

"We're at war. Acts of terrorism involving American citizens are treason of the highest order and must be dealt with."

"Meaning?"

Sherwin paused, his look once again appraising Logan. "You're armed, aren't you?

Logan stared at Sherwin, chilled at what he was hearing. "You're out of your mind."

A wicked smirk crossed Sherwin's face. "The assignment too much for you, once again?" Then, in an instant, the smirk was gone. "Do your job on this one, Logan, or you're through."

Logan looked away. He was trapped, no matter what he did.

"As for the Lockhart woman," Sherwin continued, "she's close to Hirschfield and operates on her own agenda. There's no telling what she might do when confronted with his capture."

At that moment Logan knew he would pursue Hirschfield, if only to protect Kirsten from the possibility that someone else would be assigned the job, possibly resulting in unknown consequences.

Sherwin buttoned his jacket and pulled himself to his full height. "This mission is in motion. The terrorists have a timetable, and so do we. The director expects you to find Hirschfield. You have seventy-two hours."

Logan stared coldly at Sherwin and remained silent.

Sherwin retrieved the flash drive from the terminal and tossed it on the table. "All the information you need to know about the Orion Project and your assignment is there."

Logan grasped the drive, thoughts lingering on the crop of copper hair one level below.

Sherwin turned to go. "I expect to be kept abreast of your actions. Any questions?"

Logan ignored Sherwin and stared at the frenzied activity in the cyber center, struck by how the activity mirrored the current state of his life. After a moment, he shook his head.

"Good. So we understand each other."
Sherwin strode to the door and then faced
Logan. "One other thing, Major Logan," he said.
"You don't mind if I use your old rank do you?
The director says we don't want another failed
Tehran mission on our hands. Think hard about
that as you're making your decisions." Sherwin
turned and disappeared through the doorway as
it slid open and was gone.

The stinging remark hung in the air, refusing
to leave. Logan stared at his image in the glass, as
though through an act of will he could make the
painful memories disappear and return his pulse
to normal. *No, director. There will not be another
Tehran. Ever.*

CHAPTER 9

Logan made his way down the main aisle of the Orion Cyber Center and saw the familiar figure he was searching for. He had not seen Kansas Morningstar since they worked together on a delicate CIA assignment researching China's nuclear missile program eighteen months earlier. And there she was, twenty feet from him, engaged in deep conversation with a young dark-haired man. He paused and waited, not wanting to interrupt. Morningstar hadn't changed. Her jet black hair, showing a streak of gray, was tied as always behind her head in a short pony tail.

Logan marveled at Morningstar as she worked. She was fiercely proud that she had reached the highest position ever realized by a Native American in the CIA – one of only several in the organization – and she was determined to prove herself and go higher. He hoped this position was a step in that direction.

As though sensing his arrival, she looked his way, a flash of surprise covering her face. She broke into a deep smile. "Well, well, well! Look who drug himself out of the basement." She pulled away her microphone headset and threw Logan a broad smile as she extended both hands in greeting. "To what do I owe this honor?"

Logan returned the smile and took her firm grip, happy to be staring into a friendly face for the first time since entering the Orion Project.

Logan tilted his head to the mezzanine where he had been twenty minutes earlier. "Just got my orders from Nate Sherwin, so here I am."

"Sherwin?" Morningstar rolled her eyes. "Boy, the Orion Project stumbles and they bring out the wolves. Watch yourself, Brett."

"I'll do that." Logan glanced around the cavernous cyber center which surrounded them like a giant balloon. "I was surprised to see your name on the assignment roster. This isn't exactly a CIA project."

Morningstar swept a hand toward rows of computer terminals behind her staffed by a dozen or so intelligence analysts and to the immense digitized wall display of the United States. "I'm on loan, running the Orion Project's intrusion detection systems."

"Intrusion detection systems? Care to put that in English?" Logan asked.

Morningstar smiled. "IDS, for short. Look at them as technological burglar alarms, alerting us to possible attacks on key computer sites. So while the Orion Project's mission is to deter cyber attacks on the country's technology infrastructure, my group's mission is to detect those attacks, or attempted attacks, and attempt to trace them to a source."

Logan shoved his hands in his pockets and took in a moment to survey his surroundings. The Orion Project cyber center seemed far larger from floor level than when he had viewed it from above with Sherwin. He scanned the digitized U.S. display, past the analysts at their terminals who seemed so young they could have been from a high school science project, and looked at Morningstar.

"So you're watching for the next attack?" he asked.

"You got it. The terrorists have announced plans for a second strike, and our CIA leader Ibbs wants an ID, a location, anything that may give us even a country of origin for the attackers. He's in quite a state since this morning's attacks."

Logan glanced again at her staff. "Looks as though you're ready."

"Get real, Brett. Everything in this country, from finance, communications, transportation, and health, to military operations, is based on computer technology. The United States is one big fat cyber target. The volume of sophisticated viruses, denial of service attacks, classified information thefts by China, and malicious entries from Iran and eastern Europe, coupled with domestic attempts to loot or damage sensitive computer sites, is rampant. Less than one-tenth of one percent of everything we see is potentially a serious cyber terrorist attack, so we have to sort out the bad from the good."

She motioned to the blue wall screen. "Our U.S. display shows key computer sites and networks we're monitoring for cyber attacks. Plus, we have feeds from CERT at Carnegie-Mellon, the National Infrastructure Protection operation, the National Cybersecurity Center, and CYBERCOM, our military counterpart. Any major computer infrastructure site in the U.S. under attack is shown in blinking red. If the site is compromised, the lights go to solid red."

Logan nodded but kept silent. Morningstar had built a reputation in the Agency as a brilliant intelligence analyst. She could recognize patterns and draw conclusions while others were still trying to interpret the raw data. Developing patterns of recognition for cyber attacks seemed like the perfect assignment for her.

"What happened last night with your – ah - IDS systems that we don't know the identity of the San Francisco attackers?" he asked.

"This is a game of strike and respond, and the terrorists are always ahead. We try to anticipate attacks and take defensive action, but the truth is, intrusion detection systems are only responsive tools. Nothing we have is predictive of when the next attacks will occur."

Morningstar led Logan to a young Asian woman who faced a trio of computer terminals. "Agent Kim was the first to detect the San Francisco strike. We have a twenty-second window for tracing attacks, but by the time we were able to initiate any effort at a trace, the terrorists had done their damage and were gone."

"No clues?" Logan asked.

Morningstar shook her head. "Most intruders leave a signature, a unique *modus operandi*, which we either recognize or can research and match up, like you do fingerprints. The San Francisco attackers probably routed their attacks through a mirror maze of hundreds of computers they employed, without the computer owners' knowledge, to run the intrusion. The attackers left no traces."

Logan wondered about the probabilities of picking a true cyber terrorist strike out of a mass of thousands of attacks, identify and lock on to an incoming signal, and then trace it through a myriad of computer sites, all in less than twenty seconds. "Challenging assignment you drew here."

Morningstar shot a piercing look Logan's way. "If that's what you want to call a dead end."

"What's that?"

"This assignment is about as far from the CIA main line as you can get."

Suddenly Logan got it. He knew from past discussions with her that she had felt held back unfairly because of her heritage.

"You want a field assignment," he said, thinking how different his desires were from hers. She wanted to be on the front lines, to prove herself, again and again. He started to comment on how her stint at the Orion Project might actually gain her notice, but the stone look on Morningstar's face stopped him.

"Enough about my problems," she said after a moment, letting out a deep breath. "Is there any way I can be of help to you?"

Logan cocked a curious eyebrow and watched her carefully. "Ever hear of a Sidney Hirschfield?"

"Hirschfield, the Phantom? Who hasn't?" She gave Logan a curious look. "Why?"

"Professional interest." Logan motioned toward the wall screen. "Seen anything of him lately?"

"No, but that's not unusual. His signature is no signature at all. Silent entry, no trace. He's in and gone before anyone knows their systems have been compromised."

A bell went off in Logan's head. "Just like the San Francisco attacks?"

Behind Morningstar, a shrill sound began to rise in pitch. She jerked her head toward the U.S. display map.

"Possible incoming at Cheyenne Mountain," the young Asian agent Morningstar was speaking with earlier announced.

"Cheyenne Mountain is the Space Defense Command," Morningstar said in a clipped tone to

Logan. "This may be the terrorist's second attack we've been waiting for."

Logan squinted at the electronic mosaic of flashing lights, mind still on Sidney. The dossier on Hirschfield was typically one-sided, focusing on his actions and transgressions. But what was inside the kid? What was it that made him what he was? And what would those feelings drive him to do?

The lights on the blue display stopped blinking red. "All clear," agent Kim said.

"Keep the traces open, just in case they hit again," Morningstar replied, and then returned her attention to Logan. "Hirschfield. Is he a suspect in the attacks?"

"You tell me."

Morningstar blew out a long breath. "Listen, we have fewer than a dozen true internet geniuses on the planet, the guys with the intelligence and hard core skills that can take them wherever they want to go in cyberspace, whenever they choose. Hirschfield is one of them. Could he have pulled off the SF strike? Probably. But why?"

"Perhaps he has anger, a desire for retribution, something driving him. Have you heard anything?"

"I've heard he's got some serious problems stemming from being hounded by the Feds, driven from his country, and his family being harassed. Other than that, who knows what motivates a guy like that?"

The high-pitched whine rose again from behind Morningstar. Computer monitors flashed red. Workers adjusted their headsets, gluing their faces to a three-tiered array of computer screens. Logan could sense the atmosphere instantly change from one of professional attention to detail to intense focus on the sources of the alarm.

"Here we go," Morningstar said, pulling the microphone to her lips.

Logan glanced to the wall display. A cluster of lights flashed red in Colorado.

"It's Cheyenne," Agent Kim stated in a formal, elevated tone. "They're in."

CHAPTER 10

Kirsten closed the door to her office and stood motionless, thinking. Ishmel had engineered the transfer of her group because he desperately needed her people - and he wanted her out of the way. Having her removed was the icing on the cake.

The Orion Project was in trouble, and something had to be done. But what? By whom? With no staff, no official position, and no support from Clayton, what could she do?

She needed more information. Kirsten dropped into her chair, faced her computer, and clicked on the NEWS icon. She entered a search for recent Webcasts on the topic of terrorist methods. She selected a CNN.com interview from the search list, and the screen filled with the image of a young man in a LINUX FOREVER sweatshirt with curly red hair in front of a banner reading Computer Emergency Response Team. Behind him, a computer center lined with large wall-mounted screens was packed with a phalanx of young men and women, heads down over their computer workstations.

The reporter began, "I have with me Gerry Wozniak, a computer scientist with the Carnegie-Mellon Computer Emergency Response Team, or CERT, which is well known for its efforts in tracking and analyzing acts of cyber terrorism.

"First of all, Mr. Wozniak, given the substantial attention and funding the United States gives to preventing cyber terrorist attacks, how do you explain how last night's San Francisco attacks could have happened at all?"

"Actually, most of us here at CERT are on the other side of that question. We're amazed such attacks haven't happened sooner."

The reporter looked puzzled. "Why?"

"Couple of reasons. First, our country's infrastructure is totally dependent on computer technology and communications networks to operate. Eighty-five percent of the technology infrastructure in our country is operated by the private sector, but the government still has responsibility for the nation's defense. That's all fine, but there is a fundamental distrust between the private and public sectors. The two don't communicate effectively or work well together, and the government has chosen to play a weak role in defining and mandating standardized cyber defense methods. The result? Gaping holes in our cyber defenses. In the case of San Francisco, the terrorists found one of the holes, and we have seen the result."

"You mentioned two reasons," the reporter asked.

"Sure. Quite simply, the terrorists have a compelling advantage. They aren't restricted by national boundaries, politics, or physical location, and neither are they deterred by the barriers the Department of Homeland Security has erected to protect the United States from physical attack. They operate in a parallel universe, silently watching and waiting, with their own rules, picking their battles. Unseen, untraceable, and unknown."

"That's chilling news," the reporter said.

The young man shrugged. "We need to wake up to the fact that we're dealing with a quantum shift in warfare. Physical force is no longer the terrorist's default stock in trade."

"The terrorists have promised a second attack," the reporter continued. "Where do you think those strikes may hit?"

The young man pushed a hand through his curly hair. "I can't speculate on a physical location, but last night's attacks did tell us something about the characteristics of potential targets. The West Coast power grid was compromised by an attack initiated through the Internet. The on-line operations of the grid were not brought down. The computer systems that control the grid are operated on older mainframe computers. These mainframe systems are supposedly bullet-proof, firewall protected in our terms, from Internet access."

"So how did the terrorists get from the Internet to the protected insides of these mainframe systems?"

"We have theories and are working on that question around the clock. When we have the answer, we'll be able to identify other computer sites around the country that are vulnerable to similar attacks, and steps can be taken to protect them."

"Any clues on the identity of the attackers?" the reporter asked.

The young man from CERT shook his head. "We have a long list of possibilities, but to answer your question, no."

Kirsten clicked off her computer and sat in the silence. Even the so-called experts didn't have answers to what happened the evening before, only more questions. The terrorists had weak U.S. cyber defenses, surprise and time on their side. The United States had the Orion Project, which was fumbling the ball. Badly.

She needed support if she were to help the Orion Project. She ran quickly through her top associates in Silicon Valley, and discarded them, one by one. They would have their own mountain of projects, anyway. Then she remembered Terry Sailor, the consultant who had single-handedly driven through their first product launch. Her suggestion to Clayton to call on Sailor had fallen on deaf ears, but that did not stop her from taking action on her own.

She grasped her smartphone and selected her travel app, looking for airline schedules. Yes, she could be in Tucson tomorrow morning.

She searched her address book for Terry Sailor's cell number. She hit the CALL button and rushed for the door, gathering her attaché and overcoat as she went.

He answered on the first chime. "Kirsten, what a pleasant surprise."

She spoke without a greeting. "Terry, I need to see you."

CHAPTER 11

Logan watched as Kansas Morningstar's team responded to the latest attack. The quiet intentness that had greeted him on his arrival had been replaced by excited voices, the rapid movement of technicians between computer stations, and the shrill ping of alarms.

Morningstar's voice, which normally carried a warm, melodic tone, was sharp, rising over the noise from her intelligence team: *"Alert the FedCIRC team, and get me a lock on the incoming signals."*

"FedCIRC's on it," one of the agents replied.

"Have the Space Defense Command move to the alternate system, now," Morningstar ordered.

"Roger," another shot back.

"Give me a trace, somebody!" Morningstar paced behind the rows of terminals, looking over the shoulders of her staff and their computer screens. "Come on! Come on!"

Logan stepped aside, dodging a specialist speeding to a bank of computer terminals. His eyes fell on a page taped to one of the computer displays manned by a young specialist in front of him. The sign read WE OWN THE WEB in large block letters, underlined with a large lightning bolt. Given the events of the past twenty-four hours, he wondered how true that was.

Suddenly, the pulsing red lights in Colorado blinked to dark. The attack was over. "Anything at all?" Morningstar scanned the faces of her staff. "Anyone?"

The bustle of activity dropped as quickly as it had sprung to life. One by one, intelligence specialists pulled their attention away from their monitors and turned in Morningstar's direction.

Morningstar scanned the faces. "No reports?"

The area was silent.

"Okay," she said finally, clearly not trying to disguise the dissatisfaction covering her face. "Standard reset, everyone." She motioned to Agent Kim. "Close out with Cheyenne, then give me a debrief."

Morningstar motioned Logan to a chair and fell into one next to him. "Welcome to another day in paradise." Her tone was filled with the resignation that accompanies acceptance of a long journey.

"Did you learn anything?" Logan asked.

"Don't know yet. This is a continuous battle. They sniff us, looking for weaknesses, points of entry, around the clock, day after day, probing our defenses. Kind of like World War III on the installment plan."

"With all of this whiz-bang setup, I'd have bet you could trace the intruders down in their bedrooms."

Morningstar sighed. "I've got a top notch team, an unlimited budget, the latest equipment, but sometimes I think we'd do better with an Ouija board. One quick strike and they're gone into the ether. They could be operating from the Supreme Court building, for all we know."

Agent Kim approached Morningstar's chair, paging through screens on a hand held display unit. "Not much to go on. But the attack tools have patterns indicating they were sourced from eTerror."

Logan leaned closer to listen to the conversation. He remembered eTerror from security briefings: arms merchant to the global cyber terrorist community. The organization, referred to by some as the eBay of cyber terrorism, operated an internet-based business that matched terrorists with cyber attack tools. The tools were available for instant transmission to successful bidders via worldwide auction, twenty-four hours a day. In spite of massive efforts on the part of the U.S. and friendly intelligence agencies around the globe, no one had learned who ran eTerror or its location.

"Cheyenne did capture a portion of the attack script in its honey pot," Kim said. "We'll have it in a few moments."

Morningstar nodded her thanks, and Kim turned away.

"Honey pot?" Logan asked.

"It's an electronic trap we set to lure the attackers, a computer system visible and interesting to the prospective intruder, vulnerable to the point of allowing entry with some work, but armed with attack sensors and surveillance tools. We hope to have the intruder stay long enough to leave some clues, traces, M.O.'s, or anything. Then we have something to go on for identification. In this case, he may have figured out the trap."

Logan checked his watch. He had to move on to the subject of Kirsten. "I understand Sidney has a friend here in the Orion Project."

Morningstar's eyes narrowed. "Kirsten?"

"Yes."

"Is she why you're here?"

"Not really. What does she think about Hirschfield?"

"You're wasting your time with her. She and Sidney go back a ways and that's it. You know that."

"So she would think he's innocent?"

"I think you should ask her yourself," Morningstar said, her tone colder, as she started toward the front of the intelligence area.

"I plan to," Logan said, following.

Morningstar stopped and faced him. "You know she lost her position this morning?"

Logan hesitated. *Sherwin hadn't said anything about this.* "What happened?"

"She got off to a bad start here. She blew in to the Orion Project with Clayton's blessings, flush with success from a software security firm in Silicon Valley, practically as a celebrity. She pushed hard for new approaches to software development, accelerated schedules, that sort of thing. Ishmel and his old-guard crew resented her approach and believed her advanced research project was encroaching on their work. Behind her back they called her the 'valley girl,' a lightweight who made it out West because she was in the right place at the right time. Their view has always been that she had no place here."

"They have a point?"

Morningstar placed her hands on her hips and studied Logan. "Absolutely not. Ishmel's staff felt threatened by her energy, her creativity, her new ways of doing things."

"Okay, the deck's been reshuffled," Logan said. "What does she do now?"

A pitched alarm sounded behind them. Agent Kim motioned from her computer. "Our sensors are picking up something in Houston."

Morningstar moved to go, and then turned back, facing Logan. "I can't guess what she'll do next. But knowing her, doing nothing is not an option."

"Incoming. Starting countdown," Agent Kim called.

"Better let you go," Logan said.

Morningstar grasped his arm. "Listen to me. They won't rest until Kirsten's completely out of here, no matter what it takes. Watch out for her."

Logan returned Morningstar's burning stare. "Well, that's not exactly my assignment."

"Don't 'well' me, Brett Logan. I happen to know you owe her one."

The U.S. display erupted with red lights over Houston.

CHAPTER 12

Dustin Clayton rolled his shoulders and tried to ignore the tightness that arched across his back. He paced in front of the windows of his office overlooking the Orion Project cyber center, and then dropped into one of the upholstered armchairs circling the conference table in front of his desk.

He drummed his fingers on the polished surface, lines of concern creasing his forehead. What had happened to America's vast superiority on land, on the sea, in air, and space? Was this new dimension of warfare in cyberspace a place where the military no longer reigned and the country he had served all of his life was no longer safe?

Kansas Morningstar's image materialized on a large wall-mounted video display on the opposite wall. "I have an update, Mr. Secretary.

Clayton swiveled the chair and faced the screen. "What have you got?"

"Looks like a surgical attack on power and communications systems, Mr. Secretary," Morningstar replied.

"Like San Francisco?"

"We're comparing methods now. I'll have that answer within the hour."

"Make that thirty minutes. Now what about Space Defense Command?"

"The attackers were in and out of Cheyenne in a matter of seconds. The good news is that no apparent damage was done."

"Get any intel?" he asked, knowing that the theft of military strategies, war plans, cyber defense tools — all were at risk, no matter how strong the defenses.

"No, sir."

"Probes?" he asked.

"More than that."

Clayton stopped pacing. "Go on."

"This has happened before, but we didn't catch the pattern until now. They seem to be testing our defenses, our response capabilities, and then retreating."

"Testing for what?"

"Who knows. It makes sense that the attackers may tire pretty soon of putting out lights and disrupting telephone calls."

The dominant thought that coursed through Clayton's mind was that of an enemy putting together its attack plan. But for what? "What else do you have?"

The door to the office hissed open. Zachary Ishmel stood stiffly, arms at his side, and Clayton waved him toward the conference table.

Morningstar shook her head. "Sorry to be less than informative, Mr. Secretary, but that's all we know. The attackers seem to know our methods and response time for identifying and tracing their strikes, and they exit just before we have a bead on them."

"Sounds like an enemy who knows too much."

"My thought exactly, sir."

"Damn," Clayton said under his breath. He was tiring of the lack of intelligence on who the enemy was, where they were, and how they managed to breach U.S. defenses with the ease of a skilled surgeon. He nodded at Morningstar. "Very well. Keep me posted."

As Morningstar's image faded from the screen, Clayton studied the man whom he was counting on to build a bullet-proof defense to protect the United States against vicious acts of cyber terrorism. Zachary Ishmel had the education, the experience, all the credentials for the job, but America was being laid bare, at the terrorist's whim. The country, and the president, couldn't take much more. Something had to change.

Ishmel stood erect behind a conference chair that reached to the middle of his chest, short fingers gripping the dark leather. "You wanted to see me, sir?"

"I thought we strengthened power and communications defenses around the country after last night's attacks."

Ishmel cleared his throat. "In spite of what Miss Morningstar thinks," he said, motioning to the dark screen, "we believe differences exist in the San Francisco and Houston attacks. I can protect against what we know, but defending against what we don't know is extremely difficult."

Clayton made no attempt to mask his growing frustration. "Preventing unknown methods of attack. Isn't that what Orion 5 is all about?"

"Orion 5 is effective to a large degree, Mr. Secretary, but Orion 6 will put a stop to all of this."

"You tell me we need Orion 6, yet you're still having trouble with Orion 5. Am I confused?"

Ishmel squared his shoulders. "I have a plan."

"Really? "I give you Kirsten Lockhart's staff to help complete Orion 5 and now you have another plan?"

"We're dissipating resources and losing time on Orion 5, which even when completed won't stop many of the terrorist's attacks. I propose we skip a generation of software development and focus all efforts on completing Orion 6."

Clayton felt his face growing warm. "How many times have you told me that we can't skip a generation?"

"Mr. Secretary?" Captain Whistler was at the door. "Excuse me, sir. I can't hold back the networks much longer. They want interviews to discuss the latest attacks."

Clayton shook his head, thinking. The media had to be dealt with, but on his terms. "Fine. But just one interview. Who can be here first?"

"Sheila Carson of WorldNews and her mobile van are already at the garage security entrance."

"Okay, but tell her ten minutes max."

Clayton returned his attention to Ishmel.

"I realize we're skipping generations, but I've thought it through." Ishmel pulled his pipe from his pocket and turned it over in his hand. "We'll have problems. Then we go back and fix things. Iterative development, it's called."

"Fix things? And what if we can't just go back and 'fix things'?"

"If you don't trust my abilities, Mr. Secretary, I—"

"I *have* trusted you, Zachary. And I will remind you that the president of the United States is fighting to keep this country together while we figure out how the hell to complete a job you should have already finished."

Ishmel cleared his throat but waited silently, his eyes unwavering.

"How much time do you need to complete Orion 6?" Clayton finally asked, feeling his support ebbing for this never-ending cause.

"I'll have Orion 6 operational and deployed within forty-eight hours."

Clayton studied Ishmel, wondering which version of what plan would eventually deliver results.

Finally, the increasing threat of further attacks and the president's 72 hour deadline pushed him to a decision. "We'll go with Orion 6. But this is your last chance, Zachary."

Captain Whistler was at the door as Ishmel departed, holding a worldphone in his left hand. "Secretary Karlin on the priority line for you, Mr. Secretary."

Clayton took the phone, surprised to hear from Joan Karlin so soon after the morning meeting at the White House. *What was up?* "Clayton."

"Dusty, it's Joan Karlin."

"This is a pleasure."

"Perhaps not. I wanted you to know that the president has authorized preparatory positioning of Special Forces and CIA agents for Operation Hydra."

Clayton swore under his breath. Operation Hydra could not be allowed to proceed under any circumstances. "Someone got to the president. Who?"

"Don't know, but the latest terrorist attack may have pushed him over the edge. Air Force One turned around three hundred miles outside of Houston. The president is returning to Washington."

Clayton studied Karlin. "This won't look good in the media."

"The media is feasting on this crisis, at the president's expense. Have you seen the piece on Safeguard?"

Clayton shook his head. "No."

"One of those network news internet polls conducted this morning indicated that 61% of all Americans and a growing majority of members of Congress are in favor of scrapping the missile defense system."

Clayton knew the terrorist's demand that President Anston cancel the controversial Safeguard missile defense system would ignite an explosive debate across the country. Anston had used much of his political capital to push approval of Safeguard through Congress. If he agreed to the terrorist's demands now, he would risk political suicide at home and abroad. If he rejected the demand, the mushrooming sentiment against Safeguard would further lower confidence in his handling of the terrorist crisis and seriously split his Congressional support.

"The president doesn't face many good choices," Clayton said finally.

Karlin was silent for a moment. "Any progress on your end?"

Clayton considered the news on the continued delays of Orion 5 and the lack of concrete intelligence on the identity of the terrorists, but decided to spare Karlin the details. She had more than enough on her plate. "No, but I'll keep you posted."

"God be with you, Dusty." The signal went dead.

Clayton set the smartphone on the polished surface of the conference table. Anston's decision to begin preparations for Operation Hydra would be based on more than the Houston strike. The only scenario that made sense was that of an exhausted president, under attack from all fronts, who had been pushed over the line of sensibility. The president was in the crushing grip of a rapidly closing vice. Yes, somehow, Rutledge, or perhaps Ibbs, had succeeded in getting to the president.

Yet he, head of the Orion Project, must accept responsibility for America's vulnerability against the cyber terrorist attacks. Somehow, circumstances had to be brought under control.

But how?

Clayton became aware of the eerie silence surrounding him. The muffled hum of computers and crackling of video displays mixed into some form of cyber recipe, yielding a surrealistic feeling, as if the computers would go on even if their human masters were no longer there. He paced between the conference table and windows overlooking the cyber center, considering his next steps.

No answers came.

"Excuse me, Mr. Secretary," Captain Whistler said from the doorway. "Air Force One on the videophone for you, sir."

The wall display illuminated with the face of Ron Comber. The president's chief of staff appeared drawn and pale.

"Yes, Ron?" Clayton liked Comber. The former two-term congressman viewed his responsibilities as ensuring an open flow of information between Anston and his key advisors. And in Clayton's estimation, he delivered.

"The president would like to speak with you, Mr. Secretary."

Several moments later Anston's image filled the screen. His face was lined with worry. "I'm sure you've heard of my change in plans."

"Yes, sir."

"These terrorist fellows seem to be able to pick their targets and their timing with unerring accuracy. Any comment on that, Dusty?"

"Only that we're still tracing the source of the Houston attack, sir."

"I'm running out of things to say to frantic American citizens being thrown into darkness by unknown assailants that we can't find or defend against. I hope you have some piece of positive news for my telecast tonight."

"I wish that were the case, Mr. President." Clayton considered the situation, searching for a thread of good, but found none. The president had to know the truth. "We're no further along than we were twelve hours ago."

"I don't have to tell you your seventy-two hour window is rapidly shrinking."

Nothing Clayton could say would make either him or the president feel better. "I'm doing everything I can, sir."

Anston pulled a sheet of paper from his desk. "You should know that our colleague Hackworth has introduced a bill, Congressional Directive

614, forcing my hand to initiate Operation Hydra."

Clayton winced at the mention of Dan Hackworth. The powerful Arizona congressman who headed the House Committee on Technology and Terrorism was a highly decorated former Marine pilot and Vietnam POW whose bias toward use of military force mirrored that of Admiral Rutledge. In synch, the two men presented a potent voice. Such a resolution could mean big trouble for the president

"Think the resolution has a chance, sir?"

"Too early to tell. We no longer control Congress, but I still have some powerful allies on the floor."

Clayton detected a tinge of anger in Anston's voice. They both knew Hackworth would use every ounce of his power to embarrass the president. Anston was heading toward a trap. Was there a way out? Only the president would know.

"Another arrow in his quiver for a second shot at your office, Mr. President?" Clayton asked.

"Without question," Anston answered, shaking his head. "The terrorists have handed Hackworth the opportunity to run on a silver platter, and mark my words, he's going to play the opening for all it's worth."

Clayton bristled at the thought of Hackworth using a national security crisis to attempt to unseat a sitting president of the same party.

"I understand Hackworth may summon you to testify, Dusty. Watch out for him."

The two men stared at each other across the miles in silence.

He worried about Anston as he studied the president's weary face. "How are you holding up, sir?"

"You mean other than dealing with the swelling tide calling for my resignation? Hackworth must love that, particularly if he can get me in a defensive position over Safeguard."

"Is there a question about proceeding with the missile defense?"

"Safeguard has always been a hotly debated issue, but as long as I'm in this office, Safeguard is here to stay."

"Don't the terrorists know that, Mr. President?"

"Absolutely." Anston examined Clayton through narrowed eyes. "You and I are thinking alike."

"The defense shield isn't what the terrorists are after, is it, Mr. President?"

"That's right. They have grander plans. The question, Dusty, is exactly what are those plans?"

CHAPTER 13

Logan hesitated in front of the office marked "DIRECTOR KIRSTEN LOCKHART."
Except for the telephone and a vacant inbox, the administrator's desk in front of the office was clean, devoid of any visible sign of occupancy. For an instant, concern gripped him that Kirsten had already moved on.

Then he heard a sound behind the closed door. He took in a deep breath and exhaled. Since meeting with Deputy Director Sherwin and his conversation with Kansas Morningstar, he had run a myriad of scenarios through his head on how to approach Kirsten on his mission. In the end, he decided that the shortage of time allowed but one approach, to be direct. The nature of his mission meant that any hope he and Kirsten might have a fresh beginning was minimal or nonexistent.

Just as he raised his hand, preparing to knock, Kirsten rushed through the opening, knocking her body into his and sending her dark leather attaché to the carpet.

Her face quickly flushed, with a look of anger and surprise. "Brett!"

Brett stared at Kirsten as he reached for the case. Her hair was more copper than he remembered, cut short to her shoulders to frame the beautiful line of her jaw, with clear ivory skin stretched over magnificent cheekbones. Thoughts of his mission momentarily washed away by memories of dinners under the stars at their favorite restaurant in Palo Alto, quiet walks through the pounding surf in Carmel, visits to the Valley of the Moon, where he hoped to purchase a winery some day. Without taking his eyes from hers, he slowly picked up her attaché. "Hello, Kirsten," he said, fighting to keep his emotions steady. "I thought we might talk."

She looked right through him, her green eyes shining with anger. "I think not. Now if you don't mind—" she wrenched the attaché from his grasp.

Brett's hand brushed over Kirsten's soft fingers and for a moment his words froze in his throat. "You look great," he said, finding his voice.

"What are you doing here?" she asked, spitting out her words.

"Special assignment, CIA liaison to the Orion Project."

"Congratulations." Kirsten's green eyes blazed, darkening. "Now if you'll excuse me, I've had a difficult day and was just leaving." She pushed past him toward the elevators, attaché swinging at her side like a weapon.

He took long strides to catch up. "You made a hasty disappearance from California. I was hoping we could have lunch?"

"No thank you. Been there, done that." She increased her pace.

"Look," he said, increasing his stride, "I know you were upset about the way things ended on the encryption project. But I can clear everything up in one brief conversation."

"Send me a tweet. That'll be more explanation than I got ten months ago." She pushed through a group waiting at the elevator and jabbed the button.

He shouldered his way next to her and lowered his voice. Personal discussion would have to wait. "We need to talk. Business."

"About what?" she asked, her back to him.

"Sidney Hirschfield."

Kirsten whirled to face him. Although she was six inches shorter, she pushed her face close to his. "Sidney? Is that why you're *really* here? Why don't you double-dealing government types play your spook games somewhere else?"

"This is about Sidney's safety."

"Right. And your cockamamie 'CIA liaison' story is a giant bunch of crap, isn't it? Well let me tell you something, Mr. Spook. Sidney Hirschfield has done nothing wrong. So leave him – and me - alone."

"Sorry, but I have my orders."

"And as I remember, you never fail to obey orders, do you? Now if you'll excuse me." The doors opened and she pushed into the elevator.

"I'll call you," Brett said as the elevator doors began their closing slide. "One way or another, we're going to talk about Sidney."

"Greetings, Mr. Secretary." Television journalist Sheila Carson pushed a lock of wavy golden blond hair away from her mature, attractive face and flashed Clayton her near-perfect smile. Behind her, a thin, bearded cameraman in a baggy Grateful Dead sweatshirt fiddled with a minicam while a bespectacled young black man began adjusting a rack of lights.

The room set up for press interviews held two leather swivel chairs across a small table set with a pitcher of water and glasses, backed by a wall of computer displays. Clayton slid into his chair and appraised Carson. She looked every bit the ambitious reporter, wearing a double-breasted dark blue jacket tailored to accentuate her figure and matching skirt, accented by a bright multicolored scarf encircling her neck.

Sheila Carson had been the curse of many Congressmen and government officials who had mistaken her engaging smile and sparkling blue eyes as a sign of understanding, or perhaps even personal interest, perhaps causing them to let their guard down. Only when they saw themselves skewered by the sound bites from her barbed questions on the news did they learn their lesson. He would not make the same mistake.

"Thank you for fitting me into your schedule, Mr. Secretary," Carson said in her smooth tone. "We'll be talking about today's terrorist attacks. I've a few gaps you may help fill in. I realize you're short on time, so I'll patch in the introduction afterwards. We can go directly to the questioning. As usual, the red light indicates we're recording. Ready?"

Clayton finished adjusting the small microphone to his suit lapel and nodded.

She beamed that broad smile again. "You look great."

The red light winked on. "Secretary Clayton," she began, "is it true the power and communications systems struck today in Houston had been strengthened this morning utilizing the latest protective measures from the Orion Project?"

"That's correct."

"Then how can you explain the startling success of today's strikes, and particularly their timing, given the president's planned visit?"

Clayton took his time, forming his words carefully. "We put up our strongest defenses, but protection against cyber terrorist attack is like a game of leapfrog, Sheila. This time around, it seems the other side made the greatest leap."

"Your strongest defenses? Is it true the Orion Project's most advanced effort to counter cyber attacks, led by Kirsten Lockhart, was cancelled this morning?"

Clayton knew he had to be careful with his answer. The last thing the American on the street needed to hear was double talk. "The advanced effort you are referencing was placed on temporary hold to allow us to focus on the immediate terrorist threat. The decision was a matter of priorities and timing, nothing more."

"I understand," Carson said, smiling. "For our viewers' benefit, this advanced system learns from prior attacks and builds stronger defenses on its own?"

"Yes, much like the body's immune system."

"Is it possible that this advanced system, had it not been cancelled—"

"Placed on hold."

"Of course. Is it possible this advanced immune system could have prevented the Houston attacks?"

"We have no idea."

"Of course not. Because a system placed on hold can't be deployed to determine if it works, can it, Mr. Secretary?"

Clayton worked to keep his face passive. Carson was getting close to being out of bounds. "I believe I've explained the reasons behind our actions."

Carson shot a glance at her notes. "The White House has remained silent on who might be responsible for these attacks. Who do you think is behind the strikes, Mr. Secretary?"

Clayton knew better than to break the president's silence on the subject. "A number of potential sources are being investigated. I'll leave it at that."

"North Korea, Iran, and al Qaeda have been mentioned. In your personal opinion, would you include them as suspects, sir?"

Clayton felt the heat rising in his body from Carson's pushing, but kept his face calm. "As I said, this isn't an appropriate time to speculate, Sheila."

"Very well." Carson cleared her throat. "Getting back to the Orion Project. Is it possible, Mr. Secretary, that the upgraded defenses from the Orion Project put into place this morning failed during today's attacks?"

Clayton was puzzled. He had nothing to indicate the Orion Project had software problems during the attacks. *Where was she going with this?* "Unless you know something I'm not aware of, we have no evidence of such failures. But I assure you that we would aggressively investigate any such possibility."

"But you're not denying the possibility of such failures, sir?"

Carson's questioning was taking Clayton into territory precisely where he did not want to be in an interview that would be aired worldwide. "The

Orion Project has one of the most rigorous quality assurance programs possible, but such failures
do occur, although highly infrequent."

"'Highly infrequent?'" Carson let the words
hang in the air. "Isn't it true, Secretary Clayton,
that software failures are a way of life in the Orion
Project? Such as today's failures in the final testing of the Orion 5 defense?"

Clayton kept his face calm. *Where had she
gained that information?* "Software development is
an extraordinarily complex process. The rigorous testing undertaken to ensure that all system
components function together means there will
be failures along the path to success. So to charac-
terize the Orion Project as operating with failures
as a 'way of life', as I believe you put it, seriously
misleads the American public."

Carson retrieved a sheet of paper from a
folder in front of her. "And are you aware of
Deputy Defense Secretary Ham Janhre's testi-
mony this morning about potential security problems inside the Orion Project?"

"No."

"This morning, the secretary briefed the
House Armed Services Committee, and I quote:
'It would not be unusual for quality problems in
the U.S. cyber terrorist program to stem from the
cooperation of insiders with outside forces.'

"*Do* you have an internal problem, Mr.
Secretary?" she asked, raising a groomed eyebrow.

Clayton kept his eyes, unblinking, on Carson.
"I'm in no position to respond to comments I

haven't seen from Secretary Janhre," he replied in a measured tone.

Carson shot a glance at the camera before cocking her head questioningly toward Clayton. "Is that a 'no comment' on possible internal problems, sir?"

Clayton fought to keep his expression impassive. "As I said, I have no such information."

Carson clasped her hands and smiled. "Thank you, Secretary Clayton, for joining us." She turned to face the camera. "This is Sheila Carson reporting from the Orion Project." The red light blinked off.

Clayton ripped the microphone from his lapel. "We're off the record, Sheila."

A smile formed on her lips. "*Is* there a problem, Mr. Secretary?"

"Where did you get the Orion 5 information?"

"I can assure you, from reliable, highly placed sources."

Clayton considered the implications of such information being leaked, but his mind locked in on the question that was a good deal scarier. What else in the project was being compromised and by whom?

She pushed back the mane of blond hair covering her forehead. "Is there reason to conceal software failures, sir?"

"You're on the wrong track, Sheila. I suggest you back off."

"My job is to inform the public, sir, nothing less, nothing more."

"Twisting sensitive and confidential inside information?" he shot back. "Looks to me like you have another agenda, perhaps a position with a *major* network?"

She checked her watch. "Well, Mr. Secretary, if that's all you have, I'll put my story together."

"You don't know what you're dealing with here, Sheila." Clayton felt the disapproval permeating his words but didn't change his pitch. "Put out misleading information such as this, and you and your network will bear the responsibility for destabilizing the country even further."

Carson smiled. "Exactly my point, sir. I don't want to add to their panic. So, do you want me to bring the American people *your* truth? Or do you want to see someone else's version of the truth on our program?" She stared unflinchingly at Clayton.

"That, sir, is up to you."

CHAPTER 14

Kirsten rang the bell and waited on the broad porch of the sprawling Spanish-style estate as a melodic tone inside announced her presence. The front doors were massive hand-hewn pieces of wood, probably ten feet high, decorated with Spanish-style lanterns on each side. Ceramic pots decorating the large porch overflowed with color from local flora. She watched the dust from the departing SUV whirl into the dry Tucson morning air. The Tucson sun was high and hot, the air breathless, without the slightest breeze. Beyond the shrubbery in the front yard the landscape was dotted with scrub trees and stretched into the horizon, shining like hammered metal. Mountains in the distance tore a jagged edge out of the intense blue sky.

She felt a growing uneasiness, a tightness spreading through her chest. Should she even be here? Or was this trip mere folly, a wishful but hopeless journey?

The door suddenly flew open and a warm familiar voice greeted her: "I see Palo found you at the airport. Welcome to the Bar-S ranch!"

Kirsten turned toward the voice. She had been looking into the sun and it took her a moment to adjust to the relative semi-darkness inside the house.

She smiled on recognizing the tan, toned figure. Terry Sailor wore a black T-shirt and matching black jeans with his gray-streaked hair swept back into a ponytail and a toothpick that he moved from side to side in his mouth. Many mistook him to be a biker, particularly when he donned one of his large leather jackets, but Kirsten knew he had never been near a Harley. Terry's taste ran to fast sports cars; she would never forget the 120 mile-per-hour ride racing along the Pacific Coast Highway in his 2002 limited edition Porsche Carerra several years earlier.

"Terry, you look great," she said, extending her hand.

"It's the sunshine and working with the horses," he said, placing his arms around her in an embrace. He stood aside for her to step into the foyer, his eyes sparkling atop a wide smile. "You look damn good yourself. As always."

"Thanks for seeing me on such short notice."

"I was delighted to receive your call. You know you're welcome at any time." He offered his arm. "Come, I'll show you around. Then we'll have lunch and catch up."

Kirsten took his arm. "It's been a while."

"Sixteen months, just before your public offering, I believe. Last I heard you were headed to the Orion Project in Washington."

Kirsten shot him a questioning glance. "You've stayed well informed."

"Here and there."

"What about you?" she asked. "I never figured you for early retirement."

"Oh, I keep my hand in the business, now and then."

She admired the fine art on the walls and the ferns and cactus that lined the hallway as they walked. "Beautiful place, Terry."

"Thanks. I like it. The ranch goes back three generations."

Their steps echoed on the smooth Mexican tiles. "I was expecting to hear from you," he said after a few moments.

Kirsten hesitated a step. "Why so?"

"You're in need of help." He stopped to straighten a vase of Bougainvilleas. "Beautiful, aren't they?"

"Yes." Kirsten followed as Terry continued on. "Sounds as though you're staying current on our government's problems."

"I see the news, hear things from old contacts."

Since Terry seemed fully engaged in his ranch, Kirsten wondered if he was still active in technology. "Are you managing to stay current with the wacky things happening on the web?"

He laughed and pulled Kirsten to a stop at a doorway. "Is Bill Gates a multi-billionaire? Here. Take a peek."

Kirsten scanned the room, adjusting her eyes to the dim light. A grouping of computer monitors sat on a wide, curving table facing a large digital wall display. One side of the room contained an array of satellite communications equipment, printers and scanners. The other wall contained a large bookcase and a credenza displaying pictures, awards, and computer memorabilia.

"Nice, Terry." Kirsten wondered what Terry was doing that would necessitate such a powerful array of equipment.

They exited through double doors that opened onto a broad covered veranda overlooking a terraced garden. Kirsten's senses filled with the sweet, pungent fragrances emanating from huge overflowing pots of gardenias and hyacinth.

Terry stood at the railing, head up into the hot wisps of breeze from the desert, staring into the distance. "The mountains and the desert change color from hour to hour, and sometimes, in the morning and the evening, from minute to minute. Everything you see from here to the mountains is the Bar-S Ranch. Over a thousand acres of horses and cattle, raised and cared for in nature's own preserve."

"It's a world apart from where I just came from," Kirsten said. "The terrorist actions have turned the country inside out."

Terry's attention stayed in the distance for several moments, as if he were considering his words. "You're always welcome to stay here if the going gets tough."

"Thanks, Terry," she said, squeezing his arm. "You're a great friend. I need to talk with you, that's all."

His eyes lingered on hers for several moments. "Fair enough. Hungry?"

"If you had spent three and a half hours on Southwest with only two empty pretzel bags and a crushed paper coffee cup tucked into the pocket in front of you, what would you say?"

"Then let's talk over lunch." He motioned to several high fan-back rattan chairs around a circular wooden table where a small Spanish woman was setting a pitcher, several glasses and platters of tortillas, guacamole and salsa.

"May I?" he asked, holding up the pitcher. "Carlita makes the finest margaritas this side of Mexico."

"A man after my own heart." Kirsten took a long sip, and their eyes met over the rims of the glasses. She welcomed the chilled wetness in her dry throat, and nodded approval. She settled into the deep hand embroidered cushions and felt the tangy mixture of the tequila and lime juice begin to sooth her nerves. Kirsten took in the aroma from the glass and nodded. "Patron tequila. You have developed discriminating tastes, Terry. A long way from downing Dos Equis in those rowdy western bars."

"Only the best for you," Terry said, smiling.

She took another sip, feeling herself relax. Perhaps her discussion with Terry would go well after all.

Terry motioned to a platter of chicken, rice and beans. "Please, help yourself. They say Mexican food is good for the soul."

They ate in silence for several minutes. Kirsten took in the beauty of the rolling hills in the distance as she gathered her thoughts. On the airplane that morning she had been over what she would say to Terry many times. She tried to gauge his mood as he refreshed her drink, but couldn't read past the calm, pleasant exterior.

Kirsten settled into her chair, appraising Terry over the rim of her glass. "Terry, in spite of massive funding and resources, the Orion Project is losing the battle with the terrorists."

"I gathered. I saw the news special last evening," Terry commented between bites. "Secretary Clayton didn't appear to be doing so well."

"No, he's not." She pushed aside her glass and placed her elbows on the table, chin on her fists. "May I share some information with you in confidence?"

"Of course."

Kirsten recounted the sudden organizational changes, the confrontations with Ishmel and his staff, the disappointing encounter with Clayton, and the disquieting information on the status of the Orion Project she had gleaned from Karl Breskin, leaving out Karl's name.

"Zachary Ishmel," Terry said, letting the name hang in the air.

"You know him?"

"Hard to be in this business as long as I have and not know him."

"You have an opinion?" Kirsten pressed.

"Honestly? Well, other than his self-righteous arrogance, contempt for other's opinions, and disregard for expert advice, I'd say he's the perfect person for the job."

"Professionally?"

Terry shrugged. "He dreams big, and is rumored to have eyes on that technology czar position over at the White House."

"So he can't afford to fail."

"You mean *seem* to fail."

Kirsten considered Terry's comments. They fit the situation. She would have to be doubly careful in dealing with Ishmel.

Terry poured fresh drinks. "Sounds like you got caught in the Washington political squeeze." He cocked an eyebrow. "Out of your element, Kirsten?"

She toyed with her glass, considering her approach. "It's more than that. Much more. That's why I'm here."

"I know. You've come looking for a savior with a silver bullet."

"I'll get to the point, Terry. I'm here on an unauthorized mission to ask you, beg you if necessary, to assist the Orion Project. You're one of the few people in this country who has a chance of crafting a defense against the terrorists."

Terry chewed on his toothpick in silence for a few moments. "I fought this battle – for a new way of thinking about defense against cyber warfare – a year ago. We have created in this country a tragically fragile technological infrastructure that can tumble down around us as swiftly as a crack of lightning strikes the earth. "All that is needed is a trigger. And now we have one."

"So surely you're willing to help?" Kirsten said, feeling a glimmer of hope.

He shook his head. "As I said, I gave my advice, for which I was rebuked, disgraced in my profession, and forcefully removed from the responsibilities I had worked my entire career to obtain."

His eyes were as cold as dark stones. "No, I'm not going to take that road again, under any circumstances. I'm sorry."

They sat in silence, the only sound coming from the warm breeze rustling the potted flowers.

Kirsten's mind raced. "I understand you've been wronged. Will you at least help identify the terrorists?"

"I'm sorry, Kirsten. I'm staying out of this one."

Kirsten felt the head-lightening effects of the Tequila and ran a finger over the drops of moisture sliding down the glass as she worked to compose her thoughts. She had underestimated Terry's anger with the government. Her trip had been for naught.

"I hope I didn't offend you with my comments," he said, breaking into her thoughts.

She managed a small smile. "I understand, Terry."

He sipped his drink in silence for a few moments, then asked, "So how's the rest of your life? Has Mr. Right come along?"

"Somehow I don't think I'm made out for relationships, Terry."

"You're wrong on that, for certain."

"No, not at all."

Terry slid a hand on hers. "Sure you won't consider my offer to leave the madness you're embroiled in and come enjoy the many wonders of the Bar-S-Ranch?"

Kirsten left her hand for a moment, then squeezed his and slid hers away. "I hope I haven't misled you. I'm here on business."

"I understand." Terry placed his hands flat on the table and stared at them, as if considering what to say. After several moments, he looked at her, the tenseness in his face softening. "I'm not unsympathetic to your situation. I will make a suggestion."

A warm surge of hope washed through her. "Yes?"

"Have you considered Sidney Hirschfield?"

She had thought of Sidney, of course, from the friendship they had forged when he was working on his doctorate at Stanford. With Terry's refusal to help, Sidney was now fresh again in her mind.

"Why do you bring up Sidney?" she asked.

"Well, Sidney *is* one of the world's recognized experts in network computing."

"He's also wanted by the government."

Terry ran his finger around the rim of his glass. "As I said, one of the world's best."

"How well do you know Sidney?"

"We've cooperated from time to time regarding various, well, shall we call them, computing challenges? He's the best and the brightest anywhere. Much better than I ever was."

"He's gone into hiding."

"Yes, but finding him shouldn't be a problem for someone he trusts. You just need to know where to look."

"What do you mean?"

Terry removed a card from his pocket and slid it across the table. "When you called I suspected you might want this."

Kirsten picked up the card. On the back was a handwritten Internet address. "Sidney?"

Terry nodded. "That's all the help I can give, Kirsten. If there's a way out of this horrific mess our country has managed to get itself into, I'm certain you will find it. You have the energy, you have resources, and now you have means at your disposal. In your heart, you know what steps to take. My counsel to you is to take them.

"Come." He pushed back his chair. "You have a return flight to Washington to catch and I have horses to tend to. Palo will drive you to the airport." He kissed her hand, his eyes on hers. "Your visit has brought joy to my day." His hand lingered on hers before dropping to his side.

He turned to go, and then stopped. "There's danger in this terrorist situation, Kirsten. Be careful."

Kirsten watched Dr. Terry Sailor disappear through the twin doors at the end of the veranda. She felt suddenly alone in a vast battle raging all around her. One thing, however, was clear – she had to find Sidney Hirschfield.

Slowly, she became aware of Carlita standing at the doorway of the house, holding her jacket and attaché. Behind her, the SUV waited in the driveway, the bright sun reflecting off the dark tint of the windshield like a beacon aimed her way.

CHAPTER 15

Kirsten locked the door to her office, dropped her empty attaché on the desk, and started opening drawers. From the moment she had left Terry Sailor at the Bar-S Ranch the afternoon before she knew what she was going to do. But she had to move quickly.

The message indicator on her desk phone showed that eleven messages awaited retrieval. Probably the same messages had been received in her smartphone the day before: Clayton's aide, Ishmel, Karl Breskin, Kansas Morningstar, Brett, and several calls from some woman in human resources. Each of the callers had asked her to call immediately. She had considered leaving a message for Clayton, but had decided against it.

No reason to tip him off on her plans. She would call him in a day or two.

She clicked on the TV remote and listened to CNN Headline News as she sorted through her desk. "In his address to the nation last evening," the news anchor said, "President Anston gave no indication that progress was being made on identifying the New Tomorrow terrorists, except to state that a wide range of leads were being followed up on. The president attempted to calm the nation, stating that the terrorists would be caught and brought to justice. In response to questions, the president emphasized that the elevation of the nation's threat level was meant to protect citizens, and was cause for caution and awareness, not alarm. Meanwhile, in San Francisco, which has been three nights without heat or light, a march on City Hall by angry citizens spread last evening into a city-wide spree of bottle-throwing, looting, and outbreaks of arson, causing Mayor Paladin to order a curfew beginning at sundown this evening."

Kirsten placed her passport in the top inside pocket of the attaché, tossed in several final personal items and switched off the news. She glanced at the bookcase. The plaques, pictures and mementos would have to stay.

She had slept little the night before, battling surges of self-doubt. What if she couldn't contact Sidney? Of if he, like Terry Sailor, refused to help? How could Sidney, a fugitive from justice, help under any circumstances? She paused at the picture with the resolute faces of the startup team. Nothing stopped her then. In that moment, she knew that in spite of the odds against her, nothing would stop her now.

The phone on her desk chimed, and Kirsten suddenly felt as though the walls were closing in on her. Time was working against her. She had to go. She closed her desk drawers, snapped the attaché shut, and hurried toward the door.

As she took one final look around while the door slid open, she caught the movement of a figure out of the corner of her eye.

Brett stood in the hall outside the door, hands shoved comfortably in his pockets. "Welcome back. Got a moment?"

Kirsten swore under her breath. Brett was the one person she had wanted to avoid at all costs. "If you don't mind, I have an engagement."

"Missed you yesterday," he said in a casual tone, seeming to ignore her response. "Business in Tucson? Or personal?"

Damn. Kirsten felt the base of her throat grow warm. Brett had wasted no time in putting a noose around her every move. Her smartphone, e-mail, office phone, her apartment, her every action, would be under surveillance. She was suddenly angrier at Brett than she thought possible.

"Sounds like you already know," she said, striving to keep her voice even.

"A cattle ranch seems a bit removed from all of this. Or does Dr. Terry Sailor somehow fit into the Orion Project?"

"Why don't you ask him?"

Brett removed his hands from his pockets and crossed his arms. "We have."

"So you already have your answer. Now if you'll excuse me."

"I was sorry to hear about the organizational change."

"I'm touched by your concern."

Brett's face softened. "Kirsten, I didn't double cross you in California, and I can explain that to you, if you will ever listen."

"I think we'll both be better off if you let the past be the past."

His face softened. "I'm finding that difficult."

Kirsten studied Brett. For a moment she was transported back in time, to the weekends in Monterey Bay, where they splashed through the surf hand in hand, and to the candlelight dinners in Palo Alto. Brett had brought out the best in her and made her sparkle, her friends had said. Her heart had agreed, and somewhere inside, a hint of a wish remained that things could have gone differently between the two of them. But that was not to be.

"I have just a moment," she said, blinking her eyes to clear her vision. "What do you want?"

"I've done some checking. There's no hard evidence Sidney's involved in this terrorist thing."

Kirsten looked squarely into his eyes. "Then leave him alone."

"I have a message for you to give to him."

Kirsten glanced away to conceal her reaction. *How would Brett know about her plan to contact Sidney? Terry would not have talked.* "You seem to know more than I do," she said finally. "Give it to him yourself."

Brett continued as though he had not heard her retort. "If he were to turn himself in, cooperate, and use his skills to help locate the terrorists, perhaps a leniency plea can be worked out."

"Another promise, just like in California?"

"This is about Sidney."

"Fine. You said he wasn't guilty of anything."

"I said no direct evidence of his link to the terrorists was found, but other charges are outstanding against him. I'm sure you know the consequences for evading an arrest warrant; in his circumstances, severe. If he cooperates, now, things will go a lot easier for him."

"If he turns up in my computer lab, I'll be sure to pass your generous offer along. Now, as I said, I'm on my way out."

Brett held his ground. "He *will* get caught, Kirsten. Think about it, for his good."

"Sidney is capable of looking out for himself and I doubt he needs your help. Now if you'll excuse me." She pushed by Brett and into the corridor.

Brett followed, matching her step for step. "What are your plans?"

Kirsten glanced at her watch. She had things to do, and he was going to ruin everything. Unless she hit him where he was most vulnerable and sent him in another direction. She stopped, placed her hand on his arm and smiled. When she spoke, softness filled her voice: "I think you're right, Brett. The pressures of everything in the Orion Project are getting to me. We really should hash out our personal issues."

Brett seemed surprised. "What do you have in mind?"

Kirsten knew from the tone in his voice she had hit home. She squeezed his arm. "How about that lunch you've been asking for, say, tomorrow?"

"Today perhaps?"

"Really, with all the changes, I've got my hands full today." Kirsten gave him a warm smile as she pulled notepad and pen from her purse. "Here." She wrote an address on the notepad, then pressed the sheet into Brett's hand, lingering a moment. "Quiet place. Shall we say twelve-thirty?"

"We'll talk about Sidney?"

She winked. "Let's discuss us first."

"Until tomorrow, then," he said, and turned away.

"Until tomorrow." Kirsten sighed in relief as she watched him turn the corner. Her ruse had bought some time, perhaps, but she knew the real problems with Brett Logan were only beginning.

CHAPTER 16

The door to H 139, one of the House committee offices on the southwest corner of the Capitol's ground floor, had scarcely closed when Zachary Ishmel turned his head toward Dustin Clayton. His voice trembled with anger. "I fail to understand how a group of Congressional representatives, with no technical background and no concept of what we're up against, can ask a series of unenlightened, inconsequential questions and then attempt to make the case that we're headed nowhere. Don't they understand the magnitude, the complexity of the Orion Project?"

"Keep your voice down, Zachary. These walls have ears." Clayton glanced behind them to ensure they hadn't been overheard and increased his pace.

Ishmel's heated response to the hearing did not surprise Clayton. CTOC, the Congressional Terrorism Oversight Committee, had been outspoken critical in their dissatisfaction with the Orion Project's progress in producing a cyber terrorist defense. Congressman Hackworth, the chairman of the committee, had voiced with all the force he could muster, his lack of confidence in the management of the project. He had pronounced with a full-throated combative tone that set staffers on either side nodding in vigorous agreement that "the Orion Project is a crisis second only to that presented by the terrorists."

"Every member of that committee is under intense pressure from their districts, Zachary," Clayton said out of the side of his mouth. "They're doing their jobs, and at the moment we don't seem to be doing ours. I suggest you keep your focus."

Clayton had his own, larger, concerns from the hearing. Clearly, Hackworth saw the terrorist attacks as a golden opportunity to build public support by positioning himself as the public servant who was proactively taking action against the attacks. In his appeal, Hackworth would position himself against the president.

Clayton sidestepped a group of congressional staffers engaged in animated debate and lengthened his stride through the massive Rotunda entrance to the Capitol.

"Their expectations are unrealistic," Ishmel continued, moving his short legs faster. "These uninformed, self-appointed guardians of the people expect everything we do to work perfectly, without a hitch? When was the last time Congress performed like that?"

Clayton grasped Ishmel's arm, pulling him toward the wall, out of the flow of the crowd. "Put your self-protecting rationalizations aside. You have a major Orion 6 system test coming up this afternoon. I suggest you find a way to make things work, and quickly, before we're both facing a different kind of inquiry."

A strong female voice rose over the noise of the crowd: "Mr. Secretary!"

Television reporter Sheila Carson pushed through a knot of naval officers, with a lanky WorldNews cameraman trotting on her tail like a trusted bloodhound.

Clayton swore under his breath. He was not going to allow a hotheaded comment from Ishmel to produce statements that led to tomorrow's headlines. He gave Ishmel's shoulder enough pressure to start the shorter man moving. "Go on ahead and locate my car. I'll catch up with you."

Carson brushed back her blond hair as she reached Clayton and flashed her best smile. "Good morning, Mr. Secretary. I understand you briefed the oversight committee on the Orion Project," she purred in her tell-me-all voice. "What can you share with us?" She tilted the hand microphone toward Clayton. Behind her the Minicam recording light burned bright red.

"You know better than that, Sheila." Dustin measured his words, remembering the earlier interview. "Those meetings are closed, and they shall remain that way." He posted a courteous smile and began to move toward the door.

"Certainly there's some positive aspect of the Orion Project's progress you can share with the American people, Secretary Clayton." She straightened the brightly blue scarf adorning her neck as she walked with him. "Or is it all bad news?"

The Hackworth hearing had left Dustin on edge, making it difficult to fight back a surge of anger. "Why don't you ask the congressman directly? I'm sure he'll be holding a press conference within the hour." He turned and waved farewell.

Carson called out: "Is there any truth, Mr. Secretary, to the rumor that Congressman Hackworth is drafting a measure turning the Orion Project over to private industry?"

Clayton hesitated for a half step, feeling as though the air had been kicked from his lungs. In the hearing, Hackworth had railed about Internet service providers who didn't implement adequate security safeguards to protect American citizens, and attacked the Orion Project as inefficient, bureaucratic and massively expensive, but the proposal Carson spoke of was new to him. Dustin swore to himself, angered that the Orion Project was being used as a pawn to advance Hackworth's self-serving ambitions, and pushed on in silence toward the doors.

Clayton caught sight of Ishmel at the top of the steps to the Capitol. "Any sign of my car?"

"Not yet, sir." Ishmel tilted his head toward a crowd forming at the base of the Capitol. "This group may have slowed traffic."

Clayton scanned the scene. The crowd, many with placards proclaiming "Make the Terrorists Pay!" jammed together, listening to a towering figure dressed in a flowing white robe who stood facing them on the steps of the Capitol. Behind them, news crews with cameras jockeyed for position. A firm line of Capitol police studied the crowd with sealed-in frowns, hands on their clubs. Others barked commands for order, their voices crackling through hand held speakers.

Clayton squinted into the sunlight. The tall figure, wavy silver hair swept back into a full ponytail, looked strangely familiar. *What was it?*

The figure raised his arms, one hand holding a large Bible. "My brethren, in a few short days the timetable set for the leaders of our nation will be exhausted, and the forces of evil that strike our homes will again show their fury. Our government leaders are weak in spirit. Unless we demand that our leaders act decisively to counter the terrorists who threaten our communities, a destructive tsunami will overwhelm all of us. Are we to let the fears and timid actions of a chosen few set our course to destruction?"

No!" the crowd shouted, swinging and waving their placards. "No!"

Clayton placed the identity of the speaker. "Oh, boy," he murmured.

The tall figure raised his hands for silence. "In the name of our Lord, I say we make the leaders of this land take action. Tell them we must strike NOW!"

The crowd surged forward, toward the police line. "NOW!" they shouted. The media cameras swung back and forth over the speaker and the animated crowd.

A black van arrived and disgorged police in riot gear.

"Don't exactly fit the mold of a pacifist preacher, do you, Billy Boy?" Dustin said under his breath.

Ishmel edged closer. "Who is he?"

"In what life? He's had more than a few. In the seventies, he was a Vietnam War demonstrator; in the eighties, well, don't ask. He was rumored to be overseas in the nineties, and recently resurfaced as Brother William, a born-again Christian and political activist for hire."

Clayton spotted his limousine edging toward the corner. "I have a luncheon, Zachary. See you back at the center in time for this afternoon's tests."

Two riot police struggled to pull the man in white toward the van. Boos and jeers rose from the crowd.

"I don't get it," Ishmel said. "This isn't religion. What's his game?"

"Check under Billy Boy's robe," Clayton said as he started down the steps. "Bet you a twenty you find a "Hackworth for President" button."

CHAPTER 17

Kirsten hesitated, scanning the crowd behind her once again. She had taken a taxi to downtown Washington, away from the Orion Project, and then spent an hour walking, doubling back, making certain she hadn't been followed. Satisfied, she started across the street, searching for a path through the throng of young men and women, most clad in jeans and heavy jackets, who jammed the entrance to the cyber café. Some waved signs lettered "Keep the Net Free!" A young red-headed man in a black T-shirt emerged through the door and motioned for them to move on, drawing shouts of protest from the crowd. The wail of police sirens drew closer. Some in the group glanced up the street, broke ranks, and backed away.

Kirsten edged past the crowd and slipped inside the café.

Booths containing computer terminals occupied most of the large room. The room was crowded, mainly young people focused on their computer screens. The smell of coffee filled the air. A café, occupied by a crowd drinking coffee and eating, ran the length of the back wall. Kirsten stepped to the Internet rental counter and glanced around for a clerk. For what she was about to do she would not risk using her computer at work or at home.

The redheaded teen, in her opinion a year out of high school and living his life as a computer nerd, hastened around the counter and stopped in front of her, his eyes still on the front windows of the store.

"What's that about?" Kirsten asked, tilting her head toward the front windows.

"Excitement over some rumors. What d'ya need?"

"I need a terminal. Rumors about what?"

"The feds cramping 'Net access. Like outlawing guns so only those criminals have 'em." His hands flicked across the keyboard. "PC or Mac?"

"PC." Kirsten turned to watch the last of the demonstrators scatter as the police cruiser pulled up. "Perhaps the government should focus more on the terrorists."

"Got that right, miss, and that'll be twenty bucks for the hour." Kirsten passed across a twenty and he handed her an access card and pointed to the far corner of the room. "Booth seven. One hour."

Kirsten tensed. She didn't have time to start over. And she wasn't going to shortchange her chance at contacting Sidney. "I might need more time."

The clerk shook his head and shot a scowling look that had *Take a hike* written all over it. "Ya want - try our other location—"

Kirsten held up her hand and turned away. There was no sense arguing with immaturity. She glanced over the booth numbers and started toward number seven.

She took her place at the terminal, inserted her café access card, and reached in her attaché for the Internet address Terry Sailor had given her. She had one chance to contact Sidney, so she carefully entered the address, followed by a message:

NEED TO MEET, 24 HRS, URGENT. ABSOLUTE SECRECY GUARANTEED. Kirsten

She reviewed the message, and then added: WHAT'S A PUZZLE?

Use of an authentication question was security practice she and Sidney had used on sensitive Internet messages. He was a stickler for knowing for certain with whom he was communicating. Kirsten held her breath for a moment, and then clicked the Send Mail icon.

The message was on its way.

She let out a long breath, leaned into her chair, and scanned the room. A tall, trim figure in a dark blue suit speaking with the red-headed teen at the counter caught her eye. She glanced away and then back to the figure. *Had she been followed after all?* Perhaps Brett had only appeared to go along with her ruse earlier that morning about lunch tomorrow. A moment later, the man walked to a booth two rows over, removed his jacket, and sat at his terminal, never looking in her direction.

Kirsten felt an ache in her stomach, and wrote it off to tension. Then it hit her. The last real meal she had had was at Terry Sailor's. At the counter, she ordered an egg salad sandwich and potato leek soup, and brought a large black coffee back to her booth.

She sipped her coffee and checked her messages. Nothing.

"Ma'am?" An overweight teen waitress with a blotchy complexion stood over her table with a tray. "You order soup n' sandwich?"

"Yes—thanks." Kirsten pushed her things aside to make room.

The spicy aroma of the soup intensified Kirsten's hunger. She finished half the bowl, and then dug into the sandwich. Between bites, she glanced at the man in blue. He was still working at his terminal, but she could see the reflection of his face in the screen. Did that mean he could see hers?

Five minutes stretched to fifteen, fifteen to thirty. Kirsten motioned to the waitress. "Bring me a café latte. No, make that a double." She checked the inbox. Nothing.

Kirsten clicked on CNN.com to pass the time and scanned the news briefs. One article quoted a poll indicating that the president's approval ratings on his handling of the terrorist crisis had plunged to 22%. The article alluded to rumors whipping through Washington of Anston stepping down.

She clicked on an article titled "Ten Most Wanted", a list of individuals wanted for questioning regarding the terrorist attacks. When the pictures flashed on the screen, Sidney was number three. She stared at the image, remembering their first encounter. She had been a guest lecturer for a course in entrepreneurship at the Stanford graduate school of business. Sidney was completing his doctorate in computer science and had audited her course to learn what made the business side of technology tick. He had become enamored with her tales of how to take a product and build a worldwide market leader. They quickly became friends, enjoyed coffee and swapping stories many evenings at Café Barrone, a popular eatery in nearby Menlo Park where students and budding entrepreneurs hung out and networked.

She had become fascinated with Sidney's ability to quickly absorb any subject and see the limitations and possibilities of potential product ideas. Shortly after, she had accepted the position at the Orion Project and moved to Washington. On hearing of his difficulties with the government, she had attempted to reach him. His cell phone had been discontinued, and her e-mails were returned marked undeliverable. Sidney was unpredictable and impulsive. But a criminal? *A terrorist?*

The red-headed teen rushed by, then paused at her booth. "Wrap 'er up," he said.

Kirsten ignored him and the teen moved on to the next booth. She checked her original message. Everything was in order. She reviewed her options if Sidney didn't answer. She could swallow her pride and return to the Orion Project, but Ishmel would thwart her every step of the way. She had previously considered and ruled out trying to get help from her contacts in Silicon Valley. Not enough time remained to work through the approval process to get their help. That left the possibility of making a second run at Terry Sailor, but she understood him well enough to know he was steadfast in his refusal to help.

The teen headed back in her direction, pulling his finger across his throat with a slashing motion. He reached across the table to the access card in the side of the terminal. "Pullin' your plug."

"Like hell!" Kirsten shot from her chair. Grasping his wrist, she bent his hand backward until it cracked, spilling her coffee in the process.

The teen twisted away in pain, staggered back a step, a look of agony covering his face. "You broke my wrist!" he wailed, and surged toward her again.

Kirsten took a step forward, staring at him with steeled eyes. "You want another cracked wrist, keep coming." She knew from her self defense martial arts training that she had only twisted the ligament.

"I'm staying. Beat it," she said. He hesitated a moment, stepped back, then spun and fled toward the counter.

She grabbed her napkins and began mopping up the coffee. Out of the corner of her eye she saw a stocky thirty-something woman with a butch haircut – most certainly the manager – emerge from curtains behind the counter, listening to the teen squeal his story while he motioned frantically toward Kirsten.

Kirsten disposed of the napkins and empty coffee container. As she stared at the manager, a muted chime indicated the arrival of a message. She glanced at the sending address, knowing Sidney would have laundered the connection, a complicated maneuver to disguise the identity and location of the sender, and then read the text, aware that the stocky manager was starting around the counter in her direction:

A PUZZLE IS REALITY FROM A DIFFERENT PERSPECTIVE.

BEST RESTAURANT IN EUROPE, TOMORROW, 1300.

COME ALONE.

Her heart raced as she reread the words. Sidney answered her authentication question and provided a coded response indicating the time and place where they would meet. Sidney's favorite restaurant was in Zurich.

The manager was now strutting toward her, shoulders back, as if gearing for confrontation. Kirsten inserted a flash drive in the PC with the Orion Project's destructor algorithms and typed a few commands, destroying any trail of her message and Sidney's reply.

"I'm calling the police," the woman said with a voice of uncertainty as she approached, certainly aware of what Kirsten had done to the teen's wrist.

Kirsten removed the access card from the terminal and set it on the table, topped it with another twenty dollar bill to cover the additional time, and turned away without speaking. The woman could call whomever she pleased. Her work there was done.

She noted on the way out that the man in blue was nowhere to be seen and smiled to herself as she stepped outside.

She was on her way to see Sidney.

CHAPTER 18

A dim gray light that mirrored Dustin Clayton's spirits filtered through the darkened windows of the limousine as it sped across the Anacostia River and west across the Woodrow Wilson Memorial Bridge.

He had replayed the morning's congressional hearing again and again in his mind. Aside from the scorching criticism of the committee members, one fact kept returning: Hackworth had been well informed about the recent problems of the Orion Project. Too well informed for someone on the outside. How could detailed information on Orion 5 software failures from early that morning have reached the congressman so quickly?

Slowly, he churned through possibilities as the vehicle crossed into the historic old eighteenth-century tobacco port of Alexandria. He had a leak. But who?

He felt simmering anger from the mention of Hackworth's plans to promote privatization of the Orion Project. Discussion of privatization would only serve to further Hackworth's political interests; the turnover, startup and staffing requirements would be complex and disruptive, setting the Orion Project back significantly. Clayton knew his only weapon in this political battle was to produce a defense against the terrorists.

The car slowed as the driver turned onto the waterfront. Clayton stared through the dark windows, considering what lay ahead. He thought he knew the reason why Admiral Rutledge had requested an offsite luncheon. He would soon know for certain.

Clayton stepped from the limousine in front of the small Italian restaurant and drew in several deep breaths of the crisp winter air. He took the creaking wooden stairs to the upstairs dining room two at a time and entered an unmarked private room through the first door on the right. Admiral Rutledge and National Intelligence Director Stuart Ibbs were in discussion over cups of coffee. They paused and looked up as he entered.

Rutledge, attired in razor-pressed dress blues, motioned Clayton to a chair.

"I'm short on time," Clayton said as he sat down.

Rutledge smiled. "Won't take long, Dusty. We've already ordered."

Moments later a waiter entered and set a steaming plate of crab cakes and a bowl of salad in the center of the table, added a fresh pot of coffee, then departed without a word, closing the door behind him.

"The crab cakes here are the best," Rutledge said.

"I'll take your word for it," Clayton replied.

Rutledge smiled and raised his coffee in a toast. "Here's to health."

"And to peace," Clayton added, raising his cup.

Rutledge's smile stayed in place but his eyes darkened a shade. "Peace. Of course. Isn't that why we're here?"

As the crab cake was passed around, Ibbs glanced at Clayton. "How did the congressional briefing go, Dusty?" he asked in his high, raspy voice.

Clayton had an inclination Ibbs already knew the answer to the question. "Why don't you tell me?"

Ibbs stopped chewing and frowned. "Pardon?"

"The congressman seemed unusually well informed about the latest developments in the Orion Project." Clayton eyed Ibbs over the rim of his cup as he took another sip of his coffee. "You wouldn't know anything about that, would you?"

"You know better than that." Ibbs replied.

Rutledge cleared his throat, interrupting the fixed stare between the two men. "I believe Director Ibbs has an update on the terrorists."

The CIA director withdrew a folded sheet of paper from his inside jacket pocket and pushed it across the table toward Clayton.

As Clayton read the computer-printed message a dark sense of foreboding enveloped him:

Mr. President,

In the past twenty-four hours, scores of our colleagues around the world have been harshly interrogated, many wrongfully placed in detention and their equipment confiscated. These unjustified actions must cease, immediately, and those incarcerated freed by noon today. If you do not abide by this reasonable request, we will be required to take action several grades more forcefully than you have seen before.

–New Tomorrow

Clayton handed the sheet back to Ibbs. "And our response?"

"The response is the United States doesn't kowtow to terrorist demands," Rutledge replied between mouthfuls of food.

"The president and I spoke this morning," Ibbs added. "As far as continuing to root out the terrorists, we're staying the course."

"Any closer to identification?" Clayton asked the intelligence chief.

Ibbs shook his head. "We believe New Tomorrow is a combined effort of several terrorist groups. Which ones we don't know." Ibbs shot a glance at Rutledge. "Which brings us to what we wanted to discuss."

Clayton's eyes narrowed as he waited for one of the two men to continue.

Rutledge pushed away his plate and studied Clayton over tented fingers. "Since things don't seem to be going well at the Orion Project, Dusty, we thought you might want to reconsider your position with the president."

So that's it, Clayton thought. Take away Anston's hope for the Orion Project and what was left? Operation Hydra. "The president gave me a time frame. And I intend to use it."

Rutledge tapped the terrorist message with a wiry finger. "Every minute we delay in responding to these terrorists further alarms our citizens, confuses our allies and emboldens our enemies. Sit still and we're setting the stage for further attacks of all kinds. Christ, Dusty, you of all people know a strong offense is the best defense."

Ibbs placed his elbows on the table and leaned toward Clayton. "Dusty, Americans have not been safe traveling or working abroad for years. Now our wives and children aren't even safe at home." He motioned to include the three of them. "We, and the president, have a one-time opportunity to seize the moment, to strike such a deadly blow at terrorism that the world will be safe for Americans for generations to come." Ibbs' eyes grew larger. "This time may never come again."

"Perhaps I missed something," Clayton said, not trying to mask his growing anger. "I thought I was working on a response so we *didn't* let this opportunity pass."

"We appreciate what you're trying to do with the Orion Project, Dusty," Rutledge said in an even tone. "Your effort is well intentioned, but the dog won't hunt. You know that. We know that. You just don't have a solution this time around, but you will have the opportunity in the future, when you're ready. The president deserves to be told the bare, bold, truth."

"Of course." Clayton's suspicions were confirmed. He was boiling inside. "Since our esteemed intelligence agencies can't seem to locate these terrorists, you want me to take the fall and remove any obstacle to Anston proceeding with Operation Hydra?" He shook his head. "You've got the wrong man."

Rutledge raised his eyebrows. "You might want to consider the big picture, Dusty."

Clayton grimaced with distaste. "The big picture? You loose Operation Hydra, executing hundreds, perhaps thousands, and the entire world, even our allies, will be lined up against us. Who knows what ill-bent, half-crazed head of a rogue state will come after us if he thinks he's next on our list. God's sake, Admiral, where's your head on this?"

"I didn't start this terrorist crisis, Dusty," Rutledge said. "Nor, I will remind you, was I charged with preventing it." He let his message hang over the table. "I will not stand by and watch our country be ravaged, while some computer wizards in the Orion Project tweak their latest line of malfunctioning computer code. Nor, I might suggest, should you."

"If I may take a moment," Ibbs said, "let me place our country's situation in perspective. Since the invasion of Afghanistan, nearly 4,000 al Qaeda operatives around the world have been, as some would politely put it, incapacitated."

Ibbs hesitated, his attention focused on Clayton, as if measuring his words. "Operation Hydra is merely a highly-focused campaign in our country's existing war on terrorism, nothing more. You know as well as we that victory over a diffused enemy such as this cannot be accomplished piece-meal. It requires focused, decisive action."

"I believe I've been briefed on all of this," Clayton said. "What's your point?"

"Just this," Ibbs said. "I know you have an aver-sion to Operation Hydra—"

"The very concept is abhorrent," Clayton interjected.

"As you wish," Ibbs continued, "but please hear me out. I have concerns myself. Nonetheless, I want to point out its long-term benefits. Not only will we decimate, even destroy, the major-ity of the world's terrorist organizations, we will cripple their recruiting capability for an entire generation."

As he spoke, Ibbs' eyes brightened, as if some inner rheostat were being turned up. "And with the prospect of a Hydra 2 always looming over the jihadist's head, we estimate the cumulative effects to be one-to-two hundred terrorists off the rolls for every one killed in Hydra 1."

The waiter stuck his head in the door and Rutledge waved him away.

"*This*—" Ibbs' eyes widened, his voice rising, "— this promise of safety for Americans is the legacy Hydra will leave to our children and their children."

Clayton had heard enough. He placed his hands on the table, preparing to push back. "Is there anything else, gentlemen?"

"Just one thing before you head off and do, or don't do, something you might later regret." Rutledge exchanged glances with Ibbs. "Really, Dusty, I hate to put it this way, but there's only one lead dog pulling the sled, and you're not it. Congressman Hackworth's bill is quite specific in directing the president to take immediate and decisive action against the terrorists—"

"Do I have to remind the admiral we don't even know *who* we're dealing with here?" Clayton said.

"Amend that to read terrorists wherever they are. We can do this the best way for the country, allowing the president to demonstrate leadership, to take charge and make the decision, or we can do it the hard way. The option is yours."

Clayton studied the two men. Rutledge and Ibbs had covered every base, playing the president off against Hackworth and the terrorist threat off against the public, catering to Hackworth's intense presidential ambitions but likely willing to cut him aside if the situation warranted. The president was merely a player on their board, a board marked global war.

He fought down the bile rising in his throat. "If you will excuse me. I've had quite enough of this." He stood, pushing his chair noisily across the wooden floor. "I thought I knew you, both of you. But I really don't – don't even recognize who — or what – what you've become."

"A final point before you so hastily depart, Mr. Secretary." Ibbs sighed, then toyed with his cup, his attention locked on Clayton. "One way or the other, the vital actions we've discussed today *are* going to happen. And the president – he's not going to survive this crisis. The only question is where you want to be when the music stops."

Rutledge eased back his chair and pulled himself to his full height, laid his napkin slowly on the table and straightened his uniform. He stood eye to eye with Clayton, their faces inches apart.

"Looks as though you have a decision to make, Dusty."

CHAPTER 19

Kirsten turned and stared out the rear window of the Lincoln Town Car for a third time, watching for any sign of a trailing vehicle. When she looked forward, the driver's eyes glinted at her in the rear view mirror.

"Expectin' company, miss?" he asked, ragged eyebrows moving as he spoke.

She shook her head and tried to return a confident smile. "No. Everything's fine. Thank you." The time since she had made contact with Sidney had passed in a blur. She had rushed to the bank, to the travel agency for tickets, and to her favorite boutique for clothes and a travel case. She didn't detect that she had been followed, but the fear remained. She wouldn't relax until the door on

the aircraft closed and she was on her way to
Zurich.

"Can't be too careful, that's what I say," the
driver said, alternating between watching her and
the road. Wiry wisps of gray hair shot out from
under his faded baseball cap and he spoke with a
gravelly hoarseness that suggested years of serious
smoking.

"I moved down here from New York to get
away from all that bad stuff," he continued.
"Once Rudy G. was out of office, the city went to
pot. When my wife died, that was it. I packed up,
loaded the town car and came here. I don't work
the streets, only trips by appointment, like this,
takin' you to Dulles, but I'm still prepared." He
tilted his head toward the glove compartment.
"Still pack my New York insurance policy, loaded
and ready, jus' in case some punk gets wise."

Keep it in the glove box, Fella Kirsten murmured
under her breath. She stared out the window at
the cloudy, moonless evening punctuated only by
diffused circles of illumination from the street-
lights and occasional light beaming from the windows of office buildings.

She glanced to the rear again. Finally realizing
the futility of her attempts to identify a vehicle
behind them with Brett at the wheel, she eased
her head against the seat, closed her eyes and
focused on easing her tension.

The vehicle decelerated, wheels squealing,
sending her forward. The seat belt dug into her
chest. "What is it?" Kirsten asked, bracing herself.

"Jesus," the driver muttered. "What are these idiots doing?" He removed his cap and scratched his head.

Kirsten took in the picture illuminated by the headlights and frowned. A crowd flooded the street, some carrying torches that sent flames and dark smoke into the evening air. A large poster read in large block letters, "Give them the Missiles!"

"Must be comin' from one a' them demonstrations this evening," the driver said.

Kirsten stayed erect in her seat, shoulders taut. The news had talked about groups who were demanding the president give up the missile defense system and send the terrorists on their way. Hopefully the demonstrators were just crossing the street and the taxi would soon be on its way.

The driver rolled his window down and stuck his head as far out as his short body would allow. "Get outta the road, assholes. I'm goin' to the airport!" he shouted, waving his cap. He glanced at Kirsten in the rear view mirror. "They don' screw with Tony Alisandro this way. I know how to handle this. We'll have you on your way in a few moments, miss."

"Maybe you should take it easy and let them pass," Kirsten said, feeling a sense of unease swell over her.

"Only one thing they'll listen to, and that's authority," the driver said. He laid on his horn and flashed his high beams. "Move it, you scabs," he yelled out the window. "Ya hear me? Move it!"

A group of the protestors stopped and stared at the taxi, then broke from the crowd and started toward the car. Fully alert, Kirsten ran through their possible options in her head. "Can we take another route?"

A thump reverberated at the back of the car. "We ain't goin' nowhere, miss." The driver rolled up his window and clicked the door locks. "Look behind you."

Kirsten twisted in her seat. Every muscle in her body tensed. Demonstrators had cut off traffic behind them. They were surrounded.

"Get away from my car, bastards!" the driver shouted, and laid on his horn again.

The car rocked. Kirsten cringed. *They're trying to get in.* "I don't think that's a good idea," she said.

The sound of fists on metal echoed from the top of the vehicle. A chorus of voices, startlingly close, shouted, "Open up! Open up!"

A sea of agitated faces pressed against the glass. Kirsten worked to keep her breathing calm. She knew she could defend herself quite well, but not against a mob.

"They ain't gettin' my car." The driver waved his arms at the crowd.

The heavy sedan began to rock from side to side. More protestors, some carrying torches, broke from the main group and moved toward the car.

The driver leaned across the seat toward his glove compartment. When he sat up he held a pistol in his hand. He steadied himself and began to wave the gun at the front passenger window.

The vehicle bucked. "Open up!" the voices said, louder.

"Get back!" Heavy perspiration dripped from the old man's brow.

The old man's losing it. Kirsten threw off her seat belt and thrust herself forward, gripping the back of the front seat with her hands. "What are you doing?"

The driver's face was twisted with anger, beyond reason. "I'll show these scumbags a thing or two."

"No!" Kirsten lurched over the seat, grasping for his arm.

"Stay out of this," he shrieked. His elbow caught her in the throat, knocking the breath from her and sending her backward into the seat. His hands were shaking as he pulled the gun to the glass. "This scum isn't going to mess with me."

Kirsten braced herself for the explosion. Only a miracle would save them now. She ripped off her coat and pulled her valise closer as a possible weapon, preparing to fight.

A shrill sound filled the air, first from a distance, then closer. Then she heard it again – whistles, with their urgent shriek of authority, indistinguishable shouts mixed with the clomping sound of running boots, and then a metallic voice through a bullhorn: "Get back! You've been warned. Get back! You are blocking traffic!"

Torches dropped to the ground. The vehicle swayed as though it was about to be overturned. Suddenly, the crowd began to back away. Figures disappeared from the windows, pulled away by the black-gloved hands of the riot police.

CHAPTER 20

Dustin Clayton studied the frenzied activity in the cyber center through the glass in his office, his mind only partly focused on the upcoming Orion 6 test. The calls he had made upon returning from the luncheon with Rutledge and Ibbs had confirmed his suspicions and increased the deep unease he was feeling. Rutledge and Ibbs had not been bluffing; they would be prepared to launch Operation Hydra within the next forty-eight hours. The information from Secretary of State Joan Karlin, reaffirming that preparatory action was under way for the attacks, concerned him the most. Her final words still hung in his ears. "We've got to find a way to stop Hydra, Dusty." His only hope was to deliver a working version of Orion 6, but he needed some luck and a little bit of time. Some help delaying Congressman Hackworth's bill would go a long way.

He touched his intercom. "Maureen, get me Ron Comber and Senator Ralston, and then track down the newswoman Sheila Carson."

Clayton glanced at the three television monitors mounted in the wall to his left. The news shows showed different pictures but carried the same theme: the country was churning in chaos.

A speaker on the desk shot a crisp voice into the office: "We have a testing hold on Orion 6."

His face darkened. Ishmel had expressed optimism about the Orion 6 system test, but was facing his third delay in the past hour. Clayton's thoughts flashed back to the conversation with Kirsten at the Pentagon three days earlier. She had warned him against placing all his bets on one horse. In spite of all the respect he held for Kirsten, in this case he prayed she was dead wrong. *And where was Kirsten?*

His phone blinked red. "Yes, Dusty?" Ron Comber's voice was tired and distant.

"What do you hear about the Hackworth bill?" Clayton asked the president's chief of staff.

"It's being rushed through committee, and could hit the president's desk the day after tomorrow."

Clayton shook his head. This was the day of Anston's State of the Union address. "Any chance the president can pull in some chips at the last minute to head off, or at least delay, passage?"

The line was silent for a moment. When Comber spoke, his voice was laced with a tone of resignation. "The support just isn't there for defeat, and with the looks of the polls from this afternoon, things are getting worse for the president. You're rapidly becoming the only chance the president has left to avoid this Hydra monster."

"I understand. Thanks, Ron." Clayton replaced the handset and studied his reflection in the polished top of the conference table. Comber's final comment summed up the entire situation facing the president: The Orion 6 test had to work.

"Resuming countdown," the voice on the speaker said. "Four minutes."

The second line on his telephone console blinked red, the display indicating Sheila Carson was on the line. "Hello, Sheila."

"This is a surprise, Mr. Secretary," she replied in a smooth, almost cooing voice.

Clayton didn't always agree with Carson's tactics, but he knew she had extensive contacts throughout Congress, and could be trusted. "Off the record, Sheila?"

"Of course."

"Who's driving the Hackworth bill?"

Her voice became formal, businesslike. "What are you after, sir?"

"Just answer the question."

After a short silence, she said, "You're looking for the pressure point? There isn't one. The bill has broad support and is progressing more on the fear factor than anything else, fueled by the growing sentiment on both sides of the aisle that the president isn't dealing effectively with the terrorist situation."

Clayton took a deep breath and plunged ahead to his primary question. "In your opinion, is there any way to stop the bill?"

"Not this time, unless someone can double the pacifist element in Congress in the next twenty-four hours. They're the only ones resisting."

He considered how much more he could learn from Carson, and decided to stop here. "Thanks, Sheila, and keep this to yourself."

"You have my word." She paused, then said, "Anything new for me, sir?"

"You seem to know things before I do, Sheila," he said, and hung up.

Clayton stared at the telephone, trying to visualize what the world would be like after Operation Hydra. Thousands of terrorist and suspected-terrorists would be annihilated in a massive worldwide display of lethal force, but the image that kept returning was the violent response and uprisings against the United States in response to Hydra's killings. And would New Tomorrow be alarmed enough to back away?

The president was caught in the tightening jaws of a trap. If he authorized Operation Hydra, his effectiveness as a world leader would be damaged irreparably; if he withheld military action and waited for the Orion Project to produce a result, the only event which might save him from being run out of office would be if the terrorists behind the attacks were located and stopped.

Or if Orion 6 succeeded, thus stopping the next wave of cyber terrorist attacks.

"Two minutes," the voice on the speaker intoned.

Maureen was at the door. "Senator Ralston is still in special session, sir. Can I get you anyone else?"

Clayton drummed his fingers on the desk, eyes on the talking heads filling the television screens, thinking. Was it his imagination, or was reaching his contacts in congress becoming more difficult?

"Any progress in finding Kirsten?" he asked finally.

"No sir. She wasn't seen yesterday, came by her office briefly this morning, but didn't return after lunch. She's not at her apartment."

"Ishmel seen or heard from her?"

"Not for several days."

"Very well. Let me know the minute you hear anything."

Clayton scanned the office, taking in the personal items that his personal secretary had placed around to make things seem as comfortable as his main office in Homeland Security. The wall and bookcase contained mementos, plaques, awards, and pictures of himself with every president since Nixon.

He pushed himself from his chair, picked up a wooden-framed picture from the middle shelf, and examined the two fresh, eager faces, ready to meet the world. His daughter's arm was slung over Kirsten's shoulders, and the grand vista of Lake Tahoe lay behind them, snow-capped peaks in the distance stretching toward a crisp blue sky. Stephanie glowed with the excitement she had felt over receiving her first major CNN assignment.

He blinked to hold back the moisture forming in his eyes and traced the picture of her face with his finger, remembering her as she had been that weekend, enthused and filled with anticipation, on the eve of her departure.

He had tried long ago to block the image of the lifeless, inert form that had returned via C5A military transport six months later, casualty of a surprise attack during coverage of operations in Iraq from his consciousness, but had failed.

The speaker on the wall came to life: "Orion 6 abort! Repeat. We have a system abort!"

CHAPTER 21

Brett Logan felt his heartbeat surge as he tried to concentrate on anything other than the irritated tone in Nate Sherwin's voice bellowing from the smartphone: "Goddammit, Logan. We hand you the Lockhart woman on a platter and now you say she's missing? What the hell are you doing over there?"

Brett could almost feel Sherwin's hot breath against his face through the phone, and fought the revulsion that was sweeping over him. "Why don't you focus on your job and I'll focus on mine?" he said finally, fighting to keep his words civil.

"So exactly how do you plan to find the damn Lockhart woman and get us Hirschfield?" Sherwin continued.

Brett's angered grip on the phone was so severe that the device slipped from his hand and dropped to the floor, clattering against the linoleum.

"What was that?" he could hear Sherwin shout. "Jesus, Logan. Logan, are you there?"

Brett could hear Sherwin cursing as he reached for the handset and cut the connection, then switched the device off. Worthless distractions he did not need. What he did need was a break.

He paced the cramped area behind the table in the small conference room that he had commandeered as his base of operations and turned his thoughts to Kirsten. She hadn't been seen at the Orion Project and wasn't answering her phones. He had thought her offer for lunch a bit too easy, but he quickly grasped for it at the time, for the wrong reasons. Sucker play on her part, a diversion. She was up to something. Kirsten always, always had a plan. *But what?*

"You okay, Brett?" Nate Sherwin's CIA man Peter Olson stood at the door, a puzzled look covering his face.

"I look that bad?"

"Yep. Someone get to you?"

Brett decided to keep his problems with Sherwin to himself. "Nothing important."

"You sure?"

Brett considered Olson. He hadn't really gotten to know the young CIA contract worker since they met, but he acknowledged to himself that he really didn't care. "I'm sure. Any leads on Kirsten?"

Olson shook his head. "I've checked all the possibilities. The security system confirms she hasn't returned, and the communications guys say she hasn't used her smartphone or wireless notebook all afternoon. She's gone below ground."

"Home? Friends?"

"We checked her apartment. No sign of her. Doesn't seem to have a lot of friends locally."

"Damn." Brett searched his memory, trying to remember if Kirsten had mentioned anyone she was close to, but came up empty.

Olson shot Brett a questioning look. "What's she up to?"

"What do you mean?"

"Well, first a mysterious trip to Tucson to visit a recluse computer genius, then her interest in tracking down the fugitive Hirschfield, and now – disappearing."

Brett shook his head.

"All of this must be tied together," Olson continued. Is she planning something to help the Orion Project?"

Brett studied Olson, who returned his stare with an innocent look. Brett knew he would be wise to assume that anything he said would find its way to Sherwin, so he remained noncommittal. "Not that I know of."

Olson smiled. "Of course. Now what else can I tell you?"

"What about Twitter, e-mail?"

"Standard e-mail messages, except one. See if this makes sense to you."

Olson read the e-mail message out loud: "Travel eastward from A to Z, young maiden, for the margarita gods are with you."

"The margarita gods?" Brett said. "What kind of comment is that?"

Olson shrugged. "Beats me, but I found the travel comment interesting."

"How so?"

"Travel eastward from A to Z. Eastward. As in Europe?"

"Could be." Brett imagined Kirsten contacting Sidney Hirschfield, making travel plans, and then what? "Who's the sender?"

"The return e-mail address was missing."

"Traceable?"

"No."

"Check all flights to Europe in the next twenty-four hours."

"I'll take care of it," Olson said.

"Anything else?"

"I did some checking on Hirschfield. Seems he's been deep into some sensitive CIA and National Security Agency sites."

"Damage?" Brett asked.

"Nothing I could find. He's clever; rarely leaves a trace. But troubles such as system crashes, time bombs, delayed payloads, trap doors could turn up two, even six months from now. Fact is, no one really knows for certain what he's up to. I'm still checking."

Brett appraised Olson. "You seem to be on top of the technical side of things. Why are you helping the CIA chase hackers and thieves when you could be making the big bucks in the private sector?"

"Oh, I prefer Washington. This is where the real action is."

Brett considered Olson's answer. After all, who was he to question someone's interest in public service? "I'm going home to get some rest. Let me know if you come up with something on the flights."

"For sure."

"If I head out, you want to tag along?"

"No. I'll be your point man here, just keep me posted, okay?"

Brett smiled to himself, relieved he would not have to deal with Olson on a trip out of the county. "Will do."

Olson paused at the door. "You going to be okay with this?"

"How do you mean?"

"Well, it's none of my business, but it seems pretty clear you have a thing for the Lockhart woman. If she really does find Hirschfield, she could face charges of aiding and abetting a fugitive unless she turns him in, which appears unlikely. Heavy stuff." His eyes narrowed. "You up for that?"

"It's all part of the job, Peter," Brett said with less conviction than he felt. "Some parts are easier than others."

CHAPTER 22

The first thing Brett Logan noticed about his apartment was the stuffy feeling that closed in on him the moment the door swung shut behind him. He opened a window to let in some fresh air, tossed his coat over the couch, and dropped the day's collection of junk mail on the coffee table. The dirty dishes in the kitchen were not conducive to a big appetite, but he felt the need for something in his stomach. He pulled a bottle of Red Stripe beer from the refrigerator and slid the only food he could find, a frozen thick crust combination pizza, onto the middle rack of the oven and set the temperature to 400 degrees.

He settled into the recliner, took a long drink from the bottle and thought over the possibilities.

He kept coming back to the same answer: Kirsten knew where Sidney was and was on her way there. *But on her way to where?*

Brett took another long swallow and felt the soothing effect of the cold liquid. Peter Olson was right. Pursuing Kirsten to Hirschfield was heavy stuff. Quite heavy. He let his thoughts drift back to better times with Kirsten. He had always admired her versatility and intellect. She could talk XML and Java scripts with the programmers from Google, discuss the future of the Internet with the best of them, or bandy about internal rates of return with investment bankers, all with equal confidence and ease. And he had always been enchanted by her intense emerald eyes, soothed by the soft touch of her hand in his.

Twelve months earlier, the plan for the rest of his life had been clear: after finishing his service in the CIA he would purchase a small winery in the Valley of the Moon north of San Francisco with the proceeds from his grandmother's estate. When Kirsten entered his life, his dream had blossomed to include her and a life together in one of the most enchanting spots on earth. She had stolen his heart.

He drained the beer, staring at the wall but seeing nothing but images of Kirsten. Because he had mishandled communication with her over a business matter that had to remain secret, she had walked out on his life. His dream had vanished like San Francisco mist in the morning sun.

Brett got a second beer and returned to the recliner. Several swallows later, he put his head back. Would there be a second chance for him with Kirsten? He had experienced a surge of hope when he watched her striding purposefully across the floor of the Orion Project. But now? If he followed his orders and brought her and Hirschfield in, his dream would vanish as before.

What if he protected Kirsten and didn't follow his orders? He laid his head back and closed his eyes, returning to Operation Blackbird, the last time he had considered not following his orders. The objective of his team's secret mission had been to hook up with a turncoat Iranian nuclear physicist, code named Blackbird, and ferry him safely out of the country.

Two weeks into the mission, he had made contact with Blackbird and set up arrangements for them to meet and begin his escape. Then, something in the situation hadn't seemed right. He wondered if he should abort the meeting, but his orders came through: "Major Logan, stay with the mission." Too late, he realized he had fallen into a trap, and in sixty tortured seconds in which he could still smell the acrid odor of machine gun fire and hear the anguished, piercing screams of men ripped apart by the thunderous fusillade of bullets. His entire squad, five young Marines, lay dead. He knew every inch of their brave faces, images that would haunt him the remainder of his life.

Brett stared at the ceiling and struggled with the sharp pains that still struck his stomach. *If he had gone with his instinct and ignored his orders, would those men be alive today?* From the first moment of that attack, Brett knew he was through with armed conflict forever.

The switch to the CIA provided the safety of a series of innocuous assignments, mainly industrial espionage, committee work, and special investigations. But the nightmares remained; the repeated, senseless retracing of actions, trying to find that single step, that pivotal error he could correct to turn everything back. The retreat into the private world of interpreting satellite photos in search of troop buildups, secretive biological weapons factories, and new intercontinental missile sites had provided a chance for him to be alone, to have time to try to square himself with his memories, and to lose consciousness of the past in the endless stream of photographs.

The smell of burning bread and cheese shook him from his half-awake state. Brett was pushing from the chair when his smartphone chimed.

"It's Peter," the husky voice said.

The serious tone in Olson's voice jerked Brett's mind alert. "What's up?"

"Hope you're packed. Your Miss Lockhart's not as smart as she thinks."

CHAPTER 23

The low winter sun was a fading pale disk behind a gray curtain of clouds that shrouded Lake Zurich, providing no warmth to the wind swirling off the Limmat River. Beyond the lake, half-hidden in tumbling clouds, Kirsten could make out the peaks of the Alps, white with snow. She cinched the wool scarf tightly around her neck and increased her pace, silently cursing the hotel concierge who had told her that the restaurant was within comfortable walking distance. It seemed that every step across the Quailbrucke, the bridge that spanned the East and West banks of Zurich, brought more powerful blasts of the frigid air.

Her tumultuous departure from Washington the evening before, followed by an anxiety-ridden night of sleeplessness on the flight across the Atlantic, had left her on edge. By the time she had checked in to the Baur au Lac hotel an hour earlier, even the long hot shower had not been able to calm her. Doubts about Sidney and about the entire plan raged on in her mind. She couldn't shake the ever-present fears that somehow, in spite of all of her precautions, she had been followed.

The transfer to the Zurich-bound Swiss flight at Charles de Gaulle had raised no suspicions for her. The aircraft had been full and the passengers seemed preoccupied with talk or reading. Her fear of leading the CIA to Sidney had been with her from the start and had not waned. Meeting Sidney in a public place wouldn't have been her first, or even second, choice, but it had been his. They would spend only a brief time at the restaurant, and then they had to move to someplace quiet, private, and safe. A place to talk away from prying eyes and ears.

A black Mercedes sedan with dark windows slowed as it passed her and pulled to a stop at the curb in the first block after the bridge. Kirsten eased her pace. The vehicle remained at the curb, engine running. She was on the verge of turning back when the sedan pulled away and in a moment was gone around the corner.

She ducked her head into the wind and continued on. The Kronenhalle restaurant, occupying the ground floor of a five-story gray building with gold crowns above the windows, came into view. She increased her pace.

"Reservations for Lockhart," she said to the maitre d'. Kirsten shed her coat and scarf for the attendant, eager for the comfortable warmth of the room to seep into her body. She had asked the concierge at the hotel to request a table at the rear of the restaurant. Now she silently forgave him for suggesting the chilly walk as she was led past the paintings by Matisse, Bonnard, and Picasso. The room was formal, almost stiff. Crystal lamps adorned with butter-colored silk shades and vases of white gladioli were strategically placed throughout. She was shown a small booth in the corner, grateful to have a view of the goings-on.

She ordered a café latte, sank into the cushioned seat, and scanned the room. Businessmen, their dark suits contrasting against the white tablecloths, and older couples chatted in low tones. None had afforded her as much as a glance as she entered. Satisfied for the moment, she settled into the soft cushions and thought of Sidney. If anyone could help with the terrorists, it was Sidney. His intellect was so widely respected at Stanford that students had flocked to watch him work while professors vied for a role in his thesis research, hoping a piece of the brass ring Sidney would bring home would also be theirs. Facebook and many other firms had reportedly offered him a king's ransom of stock options and free reign on his research. Sidney was a true force of nature, a legend in his own time. Kirsten ran her finger around the rim of her cup, savoring the images of her time with Sidney. Where had he gone wrong? *Or had he?*

She scanned the room again and then pulled a copy of the *International Herald Tribune* from her attaché. The headline in the newspaper leapt out at her: "NATO Issues Strong Warning to U.S." She read and then carefully re-read the opening paragraph:

> Representatives of the NATO alliance, meeting in emergency session, voted yesterday strongly advising the United States against taking military action in response to the latest attacks that have shaken America. The sharply worded two-page statement from the NATO ministers read: "The nations of Europe will in no way support preemptory or provocative military actions, of any type, in any theater, by the United States in response to recent acts of terrorism," and called on President Anston to cease any such preparations immediately. The statement expressed its deep concern for the U.S. and stated that all NATO nations stand by to provide 'thorough and unfailing support' in finding those responsible for the attacks and bringing them to justice.

An adjoining article dismissed the "dismal progress" of U.S. cyberterrorism efforts that had left the country open to attack, specifically the Orion Project. A discussion of Orion 6 readiness was detailed in an eye-popping account of the prior day's software failures. Details were provided, the article said, by "an informed but anonymous source." Kirsten felt her stomach tighten. Who would be so low to leak such damaging information on the Orion Project?

She folded the paper, set it aside and sipped her coffee. The initial adrenaline rush from believing that Sidney might be able to deter the terrorists had worn off, leaving a family of doubts behind. Was this a fool's errand? Could she convince Sidney to help the country that had cruelly separated him from his family and now hunted him? Who was to say he could succeed where legions of programmers on the Orion Project had failed? Was she placing him at risk by coming to see him?

Slow down. One step at a time. Kirsten scanned the restaurant and let out a long breath as she rotated her shoulders to ease the tightness in her back. Step one was to connect with Sidney. She frowned as she checked her watch: twelve minutes past one. Sidney had always been punctual. She ordered a second coffee and waited.

One-thirty. Where was he? She felt a rising dread that something had gone wrong. Her unease increased as she contemplated the possibilities. What if Sidney's message to her had been somehow traced? What about the black Mercedes? Could he have been apprehended on the way into the restaurant?

Perhaps he was out front, waiting for her. Kirsten slid from the booth, motioned to the waiter that she would return, and walked slowly to the front of the restaurant, trying not to appear anxious. The reception area was empty. She pulled open the door and stepped outside. Sidney was nowhere to be seen. The black Mercedes was gone.

Kirsten returned to her booth, contemplating a range of options that led to one conclusion. Without Sidney's presence, she had no place to turn, except to return home. She reached for her cup and noticed a folded slip of paper under the saucer that hadn't been there earlier. Thinking it to be the bill, she opened the fold. She sucked in a quick breath as she read the five handwritten words: "Meet me in the toilet." No signature, no initials.

Her mind whirled through the possibilities. *Meet who in the toilet?*

"Is everything okay, madam?" the voice said with a polished Swiss accent.

She must have stared at her waiter blankly for several moments, for he examined her with raised eyebrows.

Kirsten gripped the note tightly. Did she hold in her hand the only chance to reach Sidney, or was this a trap? What was her role in this puzzling game? It mattered not. She had come this far and she wasn't turning back now. "Yes, but I'll be going." She pushed twenty Swiss francs across the table, slid from the table, and hastened past the waiter.

She threw a quick glance behind her as she reached the toilet, and then pushed through the door.

Except for the cleaning woman shining the mirror above the basins, the room appeared vacant. Kirsten walked to the back wall, turned and faced the door, frowning. The stalls were empty.

She checked her watch once, then again, aware of the sound of her heart hammering in her ears. *What was going on?* She glanced at the mirror and caught the attendant watching her. Kirsten returned the stare. *Was this a trap?* Uncomfortable, she started toward the door, but stopped as the attendant stepped in front of her.

"You're being followed." The attendant spoke in clear English with a strong Germanic accent.

Followed by whom? Before Kirsten could say anything, the attendant reached inside a stall and retrieved a large shopping bag. She pulled clothes and a pair of large sunglasses from the bag and thrust them toward Kirsten.

"Put this coat on and tuck your hair under the hat," the young woman said, speaking rapidly. "Go to the Bahnhofstrasse shopping district and mix with the crowds. Retrace your tracks. Watch for anyone who might be following you. At 4 o'clock go to the Hauptbahnhof station."

The sudden rush of events had sent Kirsten's mind reeling. Had the young woman been sent by Sidney? "Who are you?"

"We haven't time for that now. At the station, look for a blue two-door van at the curb. Enter on the passenger side, tuck your head down, and lock the door. Let no one in. Got that?"

Kirsten hesitated, then donned the coat and pulled the hat over her hair. The young woman spoke with an intensity that left her feeling little thought for arguing.

The woman pushed Kirsten toward the door. "Go! Now!"

"What about my coat in the restaurant?"

"Leave it. Go!"

CHAPTER 24

The rush of frigid air outside the restaurant greeted her with the force of a whip, shooting pain into her lungs. She hailed a cab, waited anxiously on the lower step as a curious pair of two men, one tall and well dressed in a tailored overcoat, the other two full heads shorter with tight curly hair whose jeans showed beneath his worn rain jacket exited, and slid into the back seat. She gave the driver directions and he navigated a U-turn to follow Ramistrasse back across the Limmat to the shopping district.

She twisted in her seat, scanning for the black Mercedes, anyone who might be following, but saw nothing and gave up. The Bahnhofstrasse, where the elite retail showplaces of Globus, Jelmoli, Cartier and others sat beside worldwide financial institutions such as Swiss Credit and A. Sarasin & Cie, was alive with shoppers and the business crowd. Mercedes were jammed hood to trunk. Limos were double-parked, waiting.

A light icy rain began. Umbrellas splashed moving islands of color on the sea of tan and black overcoats. Kirsten cracked open the window, relishing the bracing feel of the crisp biting air on her flushed face. Then she closed her eyes and prayed for the first time in years.

Kirsten paid the taxi halfway down the boulevard and hurried into the crowds. She paused at a window and checked her reflection. The maroon wool hat pulled low over her face, together with the large oval sunglasses, presented an image even she did not recognize.

The questions that had sprouted in her mind at the restaurant, and more, were still with her. What was going to happen when she entered the van? Who had followed her to the restaurant? What did the young woman have to do with Sidney? Or did she?

Too many questions without answers. Kirsten turned back the way she had come and walked with the shoppers, thinking. She stopped. She had no other way to contact Sidney, nor could Sidney contact her. Her only option was to plunge ahead.

She entered the Hauptbahnhof Station shortly before four o'clock. Clusters of students with backpacks moved about the station, sharing cigarettes and chatting. She stopped at the schedule kiosk and pretended to read the schedules, watching the large doors where she had entered. All she saw were people rushing to their trains, people waiting, reading newspapers, sipping coffee.

She moved with the crowd, stopped to look behind her, then turned toward the exit. Outside the terminal, Kirsten stopped and glanced in both directions. *Which way?* In spite of the winter chill, she felt herself begin to sweat.

She walked around the building, acting as though she knew where she was going, scanning the vehicles. A blue van was parked several cars ahead, in front of a Mercedes SUV. She dodged around a group of older men, their heads bowed in close conversation, and stopped beside the vehicle. The Ford Econoline had no markings.

She hesitated, looking both ways, and tried the passenger door. The door clicked open, and in a swift motion, she sucked in a deep breath and leapt into the seat, pulling the door closed behind her. She snapped the lock closed, then scanned the inside of the van. With the exception of a small black handset with a short antenna protruding from the driver door pocket, the vehicle was empty. No papers, no used coffee containers, nothing.

She pulled on the glove compartment handle. Locked. Several feet behind the seats a curtain separated the passenger area from the rest of the vehicle. She started to reach over the seat to look behind the curtain when she saw two Zurich police officers approaching. Her pulse quickened as she remembered she was a foreigner occupying another person's vehicle. She slumped down and pulled the hat further over her eyes. The men paused, eyeing the vehicle. She cringed as one of the officers removed his sunglasses and squinted through the side window. The other officer pointed to a sticker on the front windshield displaying a shield above a series of numbers and made a motion to move on.

Kirsten let out a long breath. She checked the side view mirror and watched the moving crowd for signs of the young woman, Sidney, the CIA, anyone she might know.

The driver's door burst open. The young woman from the restaurant, now wearing a black leather jacket and jeans, her head topped with a dark cap, leapt into the driver's seat. In a single motion, she pulled her hat from her head and tossed it behind her, sending a mass of dark, auburn hair tumbling to her shoulders.

She started the engine, backed away from the curb, and swung into the afternoon traffic.

Kirsten started to speak but was stopped by the sound of voices conversion in German. A second or two passed before she realized she was hearing a police band broadcast coming from the communications handset.

She studied the driver. The young woman looked to be in her mid-twenties. Her auburn hair flowed naturally over her shoulders, framing strong jaw lines characteristic of many Europeans. Her hands were gloved in fine Moroccan leather.

She wore a fitted cashmere jacket over dark wool slacks, with lightly polished boots, most certainly Italian. Not a working girl, Kirsten thought.

"Who are you?" Kirsten asked, searching for some clue on the woman's plans.

The young woman ignored her.

"Where are we going?" Kirsten pressed, her voice displaying false confidence.

The young woman drove in silence. Kirsten started to speak again but the woman shot her a stern, dark glance. They cleared downtown and headed into the suburbs. Kirsten laid her head against the seat, fighting to collect her thoughts. Was this one of Brett's misguided antics? She quickly discarded the notion. He and the CIA would not be so indirect as to use a young unidentified woman. She thought back to the article in the paper she had read in the restaurant and felt her discomfort increase.

Kirsten pulled her smartphone from her purse, but in a swift motion the young woman snatched it from her hand and placed it in the door pocket next to her. Kirsten had had enough. She wanted out of the vehicle. "Look, I—"

A flicker, a movement of the curtain behind the seats caught her peripheral vision. Kirsten tensed. She saw the young woman glance into the rearview mirror and nod. Kirsten shoved herself against the passenger door, head pressed hard against the cold glass.

In the reflection of the windshield, Kirsten saw a slim figure emerge from the darkness behind the curtain. She felt the wetness of her hands slide against cool metal as she gripped the door handle, waiting.

"Hello, Kirsten," said a soft voice, anxious but firm. "Who are your friends?"

Kirsten twisted in her seat toward the figure. It was Sidney.

CHAPTER 25

"**Y**ou lost her?"

Brett Logan studied agent Rick Fliorina as he struggled to come to grips with the news.

The stocky, broad-shouldered Italian CIA operative shifted uncomfortably in the doorway. "May I come in?"

Brett stood aside and motioned to an upholstered chair that provided the hotel room's only seating.

"We had a mix up of communications between the Paris agents and my team," Fliorina said, perching uneasily on the edge of the chair.

"What kind of mix up?"

"Turnover problem on her arrival. Don't worry, we'll find her." He spoke with a tone of

confidence that did not match the look of discomfort that filled his face.

"What about your text message that your men
had located her at the Baur au Lac?"

"They followed her, then lost her again in the
crowds at Hauptbahnhof Station."

Brett moved past Fliorina to the window and
gazed over Lake Zurich. Mid-afternoon's icy rain
had turned to snow before the clouds moved on
in the evening, leaving behind a black-cloaked
sky punctuated with brilliant stars. Somewhere
out there, in the lights that reflected on the water
from the city, Kirsten was on the run with Sidney.
Where are you, Kirsten?

"We'd better come up with something, or I
came halfway across the world for nothing," Brett
said, fighting a combination of exhaustion and
frustration. If Peter Olson hadn't traced Kirsten's
travel plans and made arrangements for Brett
to go on a Defense Department courier flight to
Zurich, Brett would still be at the Orion Project
while Kirsten pursued her mission, whatever that
mission was, thousands of miles away. He wasn't
going to lose her now.

Logan leaned back in his chair, watching
Fliorina. "What's your plan for finding her?"

"The agents who picked up her trail at a flight
change at Charles de Gaulle are interviewing staff
at the IBM Research Lab," Fliorina continued,
"just in case she contacted someone there, but so
far, the most recent anyone at the Lab has heard
from her was two weeks ago."

"Not surprising." Brett knew that IBM's Zurich technology center, with its research arm in cyberterrorism, would be a logical contact for Kirsten, but not if she came surreptitiously, and especially since she was most likely here to see Hirschfield.

Brett studied Fliorina in the reflection of the glass. "Let's talk about finding Sidney Hirschfield. What's your background for this assignment?"

"Master and PhD in computer science, University of Paris. Five years in Interpol cyber security. Four years with the Agency, six months of which has been here in Zurich."

"So you're our top European cyber nerd?" Logan asked, smiling.

Fliorina tipped his head in acknowledgement. "The current term is geek, but thank you for the compliment."

"Tell me – what progress have you made on Hirschfield?"

Fliorina pulled a CIA-issue HP Netbook computer from his briefcase and set it on his lap. "Since he fled the U.S. he has become invisible." Fliorina patted the closed Netbook as he spoke. "I've pulled in all the chits from my contacts at Interpol and we've checked every possible place he might be on the web, but he has no presence whatsoever. He has no Twitter chatter, has a discontinued Facebook account, and certainly does not expose himself on YouTube. No websites, no blogs, no e-mail addresses, nothing. It's like he doesn't exist."

"How then, does he conduct his affairs?" Logan asked.

"Through others – or via false addresses and sites. Would be a cake walk for him to set up. And he can mask traces of his location and site ID's by routing his communications through robot sites that are changed continually, sometimes hourly."

"He must communicate with somebody? Who?"

"We're hitting the chat rooms, the Computer Societie Internationale, the cyber cafes, you name it. The kid casts a long shadow in the world of cyber computing and is clearly a legend in his own time but lives a stealth existence. The comments we received on him border on reverence, but if he's in town, it's a surprise to the European tech crowd."

Logan frowned at the news. "If he is in Zurich, he must live somewhere."

Fliorina patted a hand on the Netbook. "We've run every possible trace on public records. The city has no registrations, licenses, or permits in his name, no phone service, financial accounts, or records of any type. If he's in Zurich, he officially doesn't exist."

"Any tricks up your sleeve with that fancy computer?" Logan asked.

The question brought a smile from Fliorina. He held up the small computer. "This baby has more cryptographic-decoding, password-busting, website stealth entry capabilities than existed in the Agency's Cray supercomputers just two years ago. Together, she and I can go almost anywhere in the world."

"Love the sci-fi techno-babble description; I'm quaking in my boots. But any progress?" Logan asked.

Fliorina looked away. "Not yet."

"So much for high tech."

"I'm not done yet."

"How about this – he's a foreigner, has to register with the government if he's staying here for any length of time."

Fliorina shook his head. "Like I said, there are no government records of him." He shrugged his shoulders. "Besides, the locals may not be much help anyway."

Logan raised his eyebrows. "Beg your pardon?"

"It's just that the Swiss seem to have a soft spot for American fugitives. You saw how they handled the Polanski affair."

Logan turned toward the window and mouthed an obscenity. A lost trail on Kirsten, no signs of Hirschfield, and the clock ticking away on a ridiculous assignment with a hard deadline. He was due a break, but at the moment had no idea where it might come from.

"What does the Lockhart woman want with Hirschfield anyway?" Fliorina asked, breaking the silence.

"She knows he's suspected of being implicated with the terrorists, and may be trying to warn him."

A puzzled look filled Fliorina's face. "And then do what?"

"We'll ask her that when we find her. Who do you have on this?"

"Right now it's us, my technical guy and the two Paris agents."

Brett's phone chimed and the display indicated Sherwin was calling. Deciding he wasn't up to dealing with Sherwin about the latest news on Kirsten, he ignored the call and set the device on a side table. He massaged the back of his neck, trying to ease away the tiredness and tension as he traded glances with Fliorina.

"You have kids?" Brett asked, breaking the silence.

"Boy six, and one on the way in two weeks." Fliorina smiled the way only an expectant father can. "Sonogram says our prayers have been answered and we're about to have a daughter join the family."

"Congratulations." Brett added his smile to Fliorina's. He had wondered how married agents in the post-9/11 world had been able to balance the ever-present dangers and intense demands of their job with the needs of a family. He felt a warm admiration for Rick Fliorina, for the dedication and courage that he had to maintain every day to keep his life going.

"How about you?" Fliorina asked.

"Never married."

"Still looking?"

Brett smiled. "Always."

Fliorina's phone chimed. He answered, listened a moment, and held the device out for Brett. "Sherwin," he mouthed quietly.

Logan swore under his breath as he took the phone. "Yes?"

"You damn well had better wrap things up quickly, Logan." Sherwin's voice was a pitch higher than normal. "You have company. Bad company."

Now what? Brett felt a shiver of apprehension flash up his neck. "What's that?"

"Less than an hour ago we intercepted an encrypted message to a German hit team headed to Zurich. Somehow, they know we're looking for Hirschfield, and they have orders to find him first."

As Brett listened to the details from Sherwin, his mind whirled with possibilities. "A hit team looking for Sidney? Why?"

"How the hell would I know?"

"How would anyone even know we're here?"

"Let us worry about that. Now listen to me. The team could be following the Lockhart woman to Hirschfield. I assume you have her under surveillance?"

Brett felt a sharp pang of fear for Kirsten. This news changed everything. He glanced at Fliorina and sucked in a long breath. "We lost her."

"Jesus!" Sherwin boomed in Brett's ear. "How in *hell* does a team of experienced agents lose an untrained civilian in broad daylight?"

Brett had nothing to say and remained silent. At the other end of the line he could hear

Sherwin swearing and relating the story to someone near him.

"You're a lost cause, Logan," Sherwin continued as he came back on the line, "but for the sake of two civilians you'd better get your ass in gear. I'm diverting a plane your way. I expect you to find Lockhart and the Hirschfield kid and have them ready to board by six tomorrow morning." The connection went dead.

Brett handed the phone to Fliorina and stared out the window in silence. Trying to block vivid images of a hit squad taking out Kirsten on a Zurich street, he reconciled an action that he had vowed in the aftermath of Blackbird never to take again.

"That didn't sound good," Fliorina said.

"Do you have an extra weapon?"

Fliorina's eyebrows shot up. "You're not armed?"

"I made myself a promise several years ago. But things have changed."

Fliorina paused, as if waiting for more, then nodded. "I have one in the car. What's up?"

"The stakes have just gone up. We need to break this chase open."

Fliorina motioned at his laptop. "I need a little more time."

"No—now, before someone gets killed."

"Before who gets—"

"Kirsten and the Hirschfield kid, for openers."

"How will this—"

Logan jumped to his feet. "Just give me a god-damn lead!"

"Okay – let me think – what would be Hirschfield's most important need in Zurich…?"

Logan needed more information. He pressed his phone's speed dial for Peter Olson.

"Transportation…housing…computer equipment…"

An inner voice spoke. Logan cancelled his call midway through and snapped his fingers. "Internet access."

"Yes!" Fliorina smiled as his hands flew over the laptop's keyboard. "*Secure* access, to be specific."

"Meaning…?"

Fliorina stared at his Netbook screen. "Meaning, if Hirschfield is indeed in town he may have ordered installation of satellite high-speed telecommunications links."

"Or perhaps he has upgraded someone else's facilities, in their name." Brett felt a small sense of hope for the first time since his arrival.

"I'm on it." Fliorina tapped a series of commands into his Netbook and scanned the screen. "There's quite a list of network upgrades from the telecom company here over the past eight months."

"Under Hirschfield?"

Fliorina looked at Logan, eyebrows raised. "If you were Sidney Hirschfield would you hang out a 'Doing Business' sign?"

"Better kick your machine in high gear," Brett said, pulling on his jacket, "because as of this moment U.S. citizens Kirsten Lockhart and Sidney Hirschfield have life expectancies measured in hours."

CHAPTER 26

Kirsten paced in silence, her impatience building, as she listened to Sidney and the young woman discussing the building's security system. Every minute she didn't get Sidney talking about the U.S. attacks was a lost minute in the terrorist deadline.

The van ride from the city had been circuitous, with Sidney quiet, on the alert for followers. He had watched the rear for signs of a tail as they circled through neighborhoods, doubled back, stopped, and doubled back again. Just when she thought they were going to execute a third double-back, they had made an abrupt turn up a curving, heavily wooded driveway and crunched to a stop between a large two-story home and a small cottage in the rear. Sidney had led her into a small rustic building with high windows and pitched shingle roof. Inside, covering the space of a four-car garage, was a modern computer lab.

The lab was pure Sidney. A slate-gray semicircular table in the center of the room held twin flat panel computer displays and a set of ergonomic keyboards. Except for a framed photograph, the desk was devoid of books, supplies or paper. Kirsten looked at the photograph closer. The picture was of Sidney and a young woman, arms around each other, standing on the great expanse of lawn which stretched toward the Eiffel Tower. She had never known Sidney to have pictures of women around him, not because he didn't like them, but because he had other priorities.

Kirsten continued her examination of the lab. The communications equipment and mass storage devices occupying ceiling-high metal frame racks against the far wall were as sophisticated and powerful as she had seen in the Orion Project. Two wall-mounted high-def television monitors adjacent to the communications equipment flashed newscasts, one a CNN American broadcast, the other a German station, both in muted silence. A small kitchenette and a door that Kirsten presumed led to a lavatory were at the far end of the room.

The young woman who Sidney had introduced on the van ride as Katrina Mendollfson was busy at a small table against a far wall in front of a keyboard and a trio of small video monitors.

Sidney alternatively moved between her and his computer desk, fingers skipping across the keyboard, pausing to study the screens.

Kirsten checked her watch for the third time in as many minutes. Time was getting away from her. "Sid, we *must* talk."

"Not now," he replied without looking up. A moment later he sprang from his desk chair and joined Katrina in front of the trio of video monitors. Kirsten noted that even during this stressful time, Sidney still exhibited an authority, a sense of purpose that gave him an air of inevitability, as though everything he attempted would unfold the exact way he expected. If she could get his assistance – she *would* get his assistance – he would need every ounce of that confidence he could muster.

Sidney leaned over Katrina's shoulder. "The afternoon surveillance scans are clear," she said. "No signs of activity."

"You checked the rear?" he asked.

"Twice."

"The main house?"

"Clear."

"Okay. Reset and activate the motion sensors, and make sure all surveillance cameras are operating."

Kirsten's first thought had been that the intense concern over security precautions had not been triggered by her visit, but she sensed more was going on than she knew.

She put the thought aside as Sidney broke away from the security monitors and crossed the small room, motioning her to a seat. He pulled up a computer chair from the semicircular desk to face her. He leaned forward, arms resting on his knees, eyes full of question.

Kirsten took her first opportunity to really look at Sidney and saw how much the strained months had changed him. His fun, playful gaze had been replaced by an unwavering stare from coal-black eyes. Dark wavy hair that once fell over his forehead was slicked back above his Buddy Holly-style glasses. The fun-loving student she had once known had become in a short time a serious, perhaps hardened, man. Only his dress was the same, black jeans topped by a black turtleneck, and Adidas sneakers. He still wore the TAG watch his parents had given him when he received his PhD.

Sidney ran his hand through his hair. "You don't know who was following you?"

"As I told you in the van, I took every precaution. I don't believe anyone was following me."

"You didn't notice a black Mercedes?" he pressed.

The memory of the black car on the bridge came back to Kirsten. Perhaps Brett had somehow followed her, but if not, she could neither understand nor explain the day's puzzling events. "I remember a Mercedes, on the bridge, but it moved on and I never saw it again."

Katrina joined them, placing her hands on Sidney's shoulders. "Sid, this is getting us nowhere." She spoke in a brusque tone that betrayed resentment. "I told you this before, and I'll tell you now, we're being set up."

Kirsten returned Katrina's hard stare, wondering what really troubled her. "I would never set Sidney up."

"I agree," Sidney said to Kirsten, "but it is probable you were followed by the Feds."

Kirsten was tiring of the inquisition. "If by some chance I *was* followed, we seem to have lost them."

"Perhaps, perhaps not," Sidney said, leaning closer to Kirsten, "but you need to understand the position we're in because of you. If it weren't for Katrina, chances are we'd all be cornered in some windowless interrogation room at this moment, staring into spotlights and fielding unfriendly questions from large men in dark suits."

Katrina nodded, her eyes dark and cold. "Sid, I can feel it. We've been compromised. We need to get out of here."

Kirsten had expected any number of circumstances when she located Sidney, but an angry, interfering girlfriend hadn't been one of them. She checked her watch. The president's State of the Union speech, and the terrorist's deadline, was two days away. Sidney couldn't be allowed to go anywhere. "Sid, I need to speak with you. Alone."

The room was silent except for the hum of the equipment as the three of them exchanged glances. Finally, Sidney said to Katrina, "I agree we all have to leave. Pack some things while I talk with Kirsten."

Katrina hesitated, still staring at Kirsten. "Don't be long. And tell your friend she can skip the B.S. Remember who writes her paycheck." She turned toward the security monitors. "I'm switching off the alarm sensors," she said in a sharp tone, and then left the way they had come in, closing the door with a bang behind her.

Sidney reset the alarms and returned to his seat across from Kirsten.

"Have you heard from your parents?" Kirsten asked, knowing that Sidney's parents lived in San Mateo, thirty minutes south of San Francisco.

"Yes. They're shaken up but okay."

"Good." Kirsten glanced toward the door. "Katrina going to be okay?"

"Katrina and I have existed here safely, in anonymity, and you come into town and everything changes. She fought against your visit and now, in her view, this lab, her house, everything's at risk."

"You know I wouldn't have contacted you if it weren't urgent."

"You're here because of the attacks in the U.S." Sidney said matter-of-factly.

"Yes." Kirsten took a moment to order her thoughts. She had had hours on the plane to consider how best to approach Sidney for help, but the complications on her arrival and Katrina's anger toward her had affected Sidney's attitude. Still, she was out of time, and the best approach would be the direct one. "The Orion Project is in trouble. We need your help against the terrorists."

"The government drives me from my home, sending me into exile, harasses my family, and so I should forget and forgive and play savior for a country which persecutes me?"

"Sid, I'm only here because we've run out of options."

"I'm not one of your options. You can take me off your list."

"I know you're angry, Sid, but it's a mess back home. There's turmoil, anxiety, fear, everywhere you go. The terrorists have the upper hand. No one even knows who they are."

"Your esteemed government can't say they didn't see it coming," Sidney said. "There have been warnings, many of them, all ignored. The Internet is one of the most deadly delivery mechanisms of creative destruction ever developed. There's no warning, no political posturing, no troop mobilizations to see on spy satellites, no missile launches to detect, no signs whatsoever, just a silent strike out of the ether."

"That's exactly why the Orion Project needs your help."

"The Orion Project defenses are too little, too late." Sidney paused. "Except possibly for Orion 6."

"Sid, that's why I'm here. Orion 6 is in trouble."

"Can't help you." Sidney rose from his chair and walked to the security monitors in silence.

Kirsten followed, deciding to take a different approach. "Sid, what kind of trouble are you in back home?"

"Nothing serious, except to the back-climbing hotshots in the government looking for fall guys," he shot back.

Kirsten placed her hand on his arm. "You can't go on living like this, Sid, and you know it. You'll get caught by the government, on their terms. Is that what you want?"

"I have to be smarter than the other guy, that's all." His tone was confident, almost cocky.

"This isn't about being smart, it's about resources. You're outgunned a thousand to one. It's purely a matter of time before the CIA finds you, and yours is running out." Kirsten paused, and then plunged ahead, using a thought that Brett had given her. "Sid, if you help me, you may have a chance for leniency, a new start at home, and for your parents."

"A fresh start? I don't believe that, and neither should you."

Kirsten realized she was getting nowhere. She glanced around the lab. "Is there any water?"

Sidney motioned to the kitchenette. "The refrigerator's got bottled water and soft drinks. Grab me a couple of Pepsis."

Deep in thought as she made her way to the cooler, Kirsten stumbled on a protrusion in the floor, nearly losing her balance.

"Watch your step," he said.

Kirsten studied a latched wooden door set in the floor. "Secret hiding place?" she asked.

"Basement or tunnel, I think. Katrina says it's a holdover from World War II."

Kirsten returned, careful to avoid the protruding latch. Sidney popped open one of the cans and drained the contents.

She took a gulp of her water, then a second, letting the cool liquid coat her throat while she considered her options. "You're running and hiding. Is this any life for Katrina?"

"Don't involve her in this."

"Seems to me she's already involved."

"I owe Katrina everything. I was at my lowest point, running from one dismal boarding house to the next, changing disguises, afraid to show my face, and waking up each morning thinking that that day might be the last time I would see the outside of a federal prison. I had no one to turn to.

"Katrina braved the odds and brought me here, upgraded the computers and communications, put in a new security system, and added emergency backup power. She did whatever I needed to stay in touch with my world." Sidney surveyed the room. "Katrina's parents died in a ski accident in Italy. Her father had used this room for trading international currencies."

Sidney opened the second Pepsi and took a long pull. "She's unlike any friend I've ever had. I don't have to prove myself to her like the others, who gathered around like groupies to witness my latest daredevil hacking feat, then disappeared into the night with their real friends. For the first time in my life, I have someone who is really special."

"Sounds to me like a relationship worth protecting."

Sidney kept his attention on the security monitors and remained silent.

Kirsten glanced at her watch. "Sid. Listen to me. The terrorist crisis is a golden opportunity, perhaps your only opportunity, to get your freedom, your life back."

He raised his eyes to hers.

"Don't you see that?" she persisted.

"I wish things were that easy. The situation is more complicated than that."

"More complicated than what?"

"Those responsible for the San Francisco attacks are worlds apart from the ego-driven hackers and thrill seekers who capture the evening news. They're dead serious about their beliefs, and have attack scripts that have yet to be seen."

A seed of suspicion reached full size in Kirsten's mind. "Jesus, Sid. You know who these terrorists are, don't you?"

Sidney glanced away, quiet.

"Don't you?" she pressed.

"All I can say is these are vicious people you want to avoid at all costs."

Suddenly, the pieces came together, sending a shiver up Kirsten's back. Sidney's preoccupation with security, Katrina's anger over Kirsten's presence, and now the news that Sidney feared the terrorists all added up to one conclusion. "Sid, are you in danger from the terrorists?"

Sidney blew out a long breath. "If I help or appear to help the U.S., I will be in more danger than you can imagine." His eyes flickered with concern. "I'm sorry I agreed to let you come here, Kirsten. You're in the wrong place, at the wrong time."

CHAPTER 27

Brett had collapsed in the chair, consumed with frustration, when Rick Fliorina spoke. "I may have something."

Brett jerked his head around. "Talk to me."

Fliorina's hands were skipping over his keyboard. "I've secured a list of high-speed Internet connection upgrades for the past four months. That's the good news."

"The bad news?"

"It's a long list."

"So narrow it."

Fliorina looked up. "Any suggestions?"

"You're the hotshot. Do what you have to do."

"I'll need time to—"

"We don't have time."

"You don't have to be such a prick about it." Fliorina returned to his keyboard, working in silence.

Logan rolled the options through his mind. He could have Fliorina concentrate on somehow contacting Kirsten, to warn her, but that would take Fliorina away from the only real possible lead they have to pursue, the Internet upgrade. And that could be a fool's errand. He started to call Fliorina's men at the train station for a third time, to press them for news – any news – on sightings of a young American woman that afternoon, but put his phone down. The agents needed to focus, not talk to him. He could call Sherwin to ask if there was an update on—"

"May have it!" Fliorina said, almost shouting.

Brett shot across the room, his face pressed close to the computer screen. "Have what?"

"I researched Sidney's Facebook account—"

"You said the account was closed."

"I have my ways – anyway, I did a reverse 'six degrees' search of contacts, and—"

"Speak English, for God's sake."

"Degrees of separation between friends on Facebook is a hobby of mine; I've developed some search algorithms, and you won't believe some of the—"

"Get to the point," Brett said, anxious.

"Here's the drill. They say we are all six degrees of separation from everyone else in the world. So I was interested in anyone here in Zurich who knows Sidney or knows someone who knows Sidney, or who—"

"I get the point. Go on."

"So I found a good-sized group of people here in Zurich who "Liked" Sidney or were "Liked" by him on Facebook. But none were on my telecoms upgrade list. So I went to the next degree of separation, got a smaller number."

Brett motioned him to move on.

"The point is, Sidney knew three people who knew a young woman in Zurich, a Katrina Mendollfson."

"And…?" Brett searched Fliorina's face for a clue.

"Her name matches one on my list of Internet upgrades."

"Got an address?" Brett said, feeling his pulse surge for the first time since arriving in Zurich.

"Working on it … hold on … got it, sent it to my phone to let the GPS do its work."

They bolted for the door and were halfway down the hall to the elevator by the time the door to Brett's room closed behind them.

"You going to tell me what the hell's going on?" Fliorina asked, his shorter legs moving rapidly to keep up with Brett.

"What do you hear of the German National Democratic Party?"

"NDP, the right-wing extremist group? Nothing good. Why?"

"They're after Hirschfield." He glanced at Fliorina as they reached the elevator. "What can you tell me about them?"

Fliorina blew out a long breath. "These guys are one of the largest pro-Nazi, anti-American orders in Germany, with a reach all over Europe, even into the U.S. They're relentless, and considered highly dangerous. Why their interest in Hirschfield?"

"Find Sidney and we'll both know." Brett jabbed the elevator call button a second time, then ran toward the EXIT door at the end of the hall. "Let's take the stairs."

They were at the second level when Fliorina's phone sounded. "My team. Meet you in the lobby," he mouthed, and waved Brett on ahead.

Brett called for the car, then found a quiet area of the main lobby near a frieze by Bernini and shoved his hands in his overcoat, pacing as he considered the latest twist of events. Sherwin chasing Kirsten, Kirsten chasing Sidney, and now fascist militants coming out of nowhere. *What the hell was going on?*

He checked his watch. Where was Fliorina? He had started toward the stairs when the door burst open and Fliorina rushed past a family being ushered to the elevator by the bellman, tripping momentarily over a luggage cart before recovering. "My team has no leads at the station – told them to wait on standby, ready to move."

They sprinted through the lobby toward the car.

CHAPTER 28

Kirsten watched as Sidney began shutting down his computer systems. She estimated she had ten minutes max before they would be in the van heading for another location and any possibilities of securing Sidney's help would be over. "You're in trouble. Tell me what's going on, Sid."

"You don't want to know."

"Try me."

Sidney studied Kirsten for several moments and then blew out a long breath. "A little over a year ago I formed a group with four of the brightest guys anywhere on the Internet to do some totally new, outside-the-box creative work on ways to defend computer systems against cyber attacks. We called ourselves the Cyber Riders. We came up with a number of breakthroughs, sophisticated methods for tracing incoming signals back to their source that far exceeded the existing state of knowledge. Unfortunately, in our initial live tests things went awry. We lost control of the systems and penetrated a number of super secret National Security Agency sites."

"Is that how you got in trouble with the government?" Kirsten asked.

He nodded. "That's when the hounding from the Feds began and I had to leave the U.S."

"So what did you do then?"

"We knew we were onto something big, so once I got set up here we continued our development, being more careful in our testing. One day I received a message from a group who said they were also researching means to deter cyber attacks. They asked if we would like to pool our efforts with theirs. The Riders and I wanted to continue our work on our own so we sent them a response saying we weren't interested. Less than an hour later, we received a return message, threatening us if we continued our work alone. This time we didn't answer."

"Did you and your friends keep working?"

"Yes."

Sidney's face became drawn and pale. Kirsten could see he was troubled. "Are you all right?"

Sidney's voice cracked. "A week later one of the Riders was found dead in his car at the bottom of a ravine off the Santa Cruz highway, along with his girlfriend."

"My God," Kirsten said, taking in a sharp breath. "An accident?"

"The police report indicated my friend had been forced off the road at a turn toward the summit. After seeing the report, I told the other Riders to stop work and lay low." He shook his head. "One didn't."

"What happened?"

"His body was found several days later in his San Jose apartment, hacked to pieces and thrown in the bathtub. My name was written on the wall in blood."

Kirsten grimaced at the grisly image. "Did you consider contacting the authorities?"

"Sure, and get busted in the process, or worse yet, have the publicity lead the killers to me?"

Kirsten now understood the reasons for Sidney's extreme security measures and Katrina's anger at their being located. She wasn't certain she wanted to hear the answer to her next question but she asked anyway. "The fourth Rider?"

"He's safe, laying low."

Kirsten tried to put together the pieces. Someone didn't want Sidney's work to succeed, to the point of committing multiple murders. *But why? And who?* "Who was the group who contacted you?" she asked.

Sidney stopped what he was doing and locked his eyes on hers. "New Tomorrow."

Kirsten tried to stifle her feeling of horror. "Jesus, Sid."

"I know."

The pieces suddenly began to make sense. Kirsten ran Sidney's story around in her mind, imagining the terrorists discovering that Sidney's group potentially held a means to deter their planned attacks on the U.S. They had taken swift action, but hadn't reached Sidney. Yet. Leaving the country had most certainly saved his life.

An idea hit her, something Terry Sailor had said to her. "Sid, does this have anything to do with Backflash?"

All expression vanished from Sidney's face. Only his eyes, dark and unblinking behind his glasses, betrayed the questions within. "Where did you hear about Backflash?"

"From a friend, but trust me, it's gone no further."

"For your own good I suggest you keep it that way."

Sidney's response told Kirsten that she was on to something. "Tell me about it."

"The concept is an offensive rather a defensive response to cyber attack."

Kirsten felt a stir of hope as she considered the potential lurking in Backflash. "You said offensive. Does Backflash return an attack of its own?"

"It attacks when operational, which it's not. There's no telling what it might destroy if it got loose in its current state. We're dealing with extremely sophisticated stuff here."

"Okay, let's say Backflash were operational. Then what?"

"I'm not getting involved in your battles, but it couldn't be used, because Backflash only works in response to an attack. I haven't watched much of today's news, but I don't believe the terrorists have announced the location of their next strike."

Kirsten reflected on his answer. If Backflash had to be implanted in every major U.S. computer site to be an effective deterrent, then it provided no deterrence. "Sid, there has to be a way."

"Doesn't matter," Sidney said, pushing from his chair, "because we're leaving for another hideaway until things blow over."

Kirsten felt a rising dread that events far outside of her control were conspiring to doom her mission. "Sid, I came to get your help, and I still need it."

"Can't help you. We'll figure out how to get you on your way in a few days."

"A few days will be too late."

"Sorry. Can you hit those lights in the back?" Sidney asked, motioning toward the kitchenette. "I'll deactivate the sensors until we get to the main house."

As Sidney turned to the alarm keyboard and rapidly began entering commands, Kirsten felt any remaining hopes for stopping the terrorists fade and then vanish.

CHAPTER 29

Brett sprinted up the curving driveway, conscious of the crunching of his shoes in the frozen snow. A light wind was rising, scattering a mist of snowflakes from the trees. At first sight of the two-story house, he slowed, mist escaping from his mouth in measured puffs, and shot a glance behind. The car was barely visible in the darkness, with Fliorina inside as backup.

He examined the residence. Thick trees surrounding the house swayed in the evening breeze, filtering dim illumination from the winter moon in a changing pattern of light and shadow. He knelt and let his eyes wander over the house. The wood and stone structure was dark except for two windows downstairs projecting a yellow glow. He checked his watch. Ten thirty. Perhaps Miss

Mendollfson was out, or in bed. The question was whether she had company.

Recent car tracks in the fresh layer of snow snaked around the house and disappeared in the darkness. He ran through his options: front door announcing his presence via the doorbell, or approach around the back. Stealth triumphed over frontal assault. He rose from his crouch, careful to stay in the shadows, and edged along the tree line to the back of the house. He rounded the corner and froze. Thin, high windows in a smaller stone structure beamed diffused ribbons of light over the driveway, illuminating a van tucked in the shadows next to the main house. He knelt, consciously slowing his breathing to listen to the quiet of the night for sounds from the cottage. Above, branches rustled in the wind.

Something caught the corner of his eye, a glint, a movement. He waited. The glint flashed, for an instant, again. Under the eves of the sloping roof a small, moving tube reflected a twinkle of the light from the window. At the far end of the structure, he saw a second, synchronously moving surveillance camera. He squinted in the darkness, searching for indications of infrared sensors or motion detectors. If they were there, he saw no signs. Brett let out a silent breath of thanks for whatever had caused him to stop when he had. A yard or two more and he would have been in the range of the cameras.

He wondered if Sidney would be inside and if Kirsten would be with him. He blew out a long,

silent breath. Too many ifs and too many con-
flicts. He wanted Sidney but much more than
that, he wanted Kirsten out of this picture.

He pulled his phone to his lips and spoke in
a whisper. "Rick, I'm approaching a cottage in
back. Come in and take the main house from the
front."

He crept back into the shadows of the larger
house, then stood quietly, listening. A hint of
muffled voices, a man's and then a woman's,
drifted from the cottage. He heard no sounds of
alarm, but couldn't chance that the German team
wasn't inside. He timed the sweep of the cameras: four seconds. Nowhere near enough time
to approach the building without giving warning.
How would he get close? He scanned the large
house, the yard, and stopped on the van, which
was closer to the small structure.

Slowly at first Brett backed away, using the
shrubs for cover, then turned and sprinted
around the front of the house and toward the
cottage from the other side. At the back of the
main house, he stopped, measuring his breathing. The van stood between him and the cottage.
He studied the slow swinging arc of the cameras.
When they swung in the other direction, he
sprinted to the van. The cameras retraced their
arc. He crouched and sprinted the twenty feet to
the cottage, feeling a tingling of his extremities.
His senses were bringing him into a heightened
awareness of his surroundings, as if he were viewing the scene from several angles at once.

He hugged the wall, sliding along the cool stone toward the door, light from the high windows beaming over his head. He took several deep breaths and counted to twenty-five to slow his breathing. The voices from within were clearer. He considered his next move. The door was made of heavy, timbered wood, crosshatched with riveted bands of darkened metal from top to bottom. Crashing in would not be an option.

Brett's thoughts were interrupted by an abrupt silence from within. Had he not missed the eye of the cameras after all? Had they heard something? The darkness was quiet. All he could hear was the faint swishing of the camera's ceaseless sweep above his head. Across the drive, the main house remained quiet, lights still burning upstairs.

Then, as quickly as they had stopped, the voices resumed. Lights from the windows at the far end of the small building went out. *Were they coming out?*

The door cracked open, beaming a sliver of light into the darkness. The crack became a thin gap and held for a moment. Brett tensed. It was as though someone were looking outside, checking. The lights inside went dark.

He edged a step closer and braced, preparing to lunge. *Might as well get this over with. Put the kid on the plane, then turn in the badge and forget the whole sorry mess—Sidney, Kirsten, the CIA, everything.* He cursed himself for getting involved in a mission tangled with personal interests, then took a deep breath and leapt forward. Weapon in hand, Brett hit the heavy wooden door hard with his shoulder, swinging it open into the room. He collided with a tall, thin figure who fell backward into the darkness.

"Jesus!" a male voice screamed.

A female voice shouted, "What the hell? Who's there?"

Brett recognized Kirsten's voice but stayed in his crouch, weapon ready, as he scanned the room. He had the advantage, his eyes already accustomed to the dark. Sidney was on his knees, hands searching the floor for his glasses, Kirsten crouched next to him. They were alone. Brett eased up and felt along the wall behind him for the lights, then swung the door closed. The relief of finding Kirsten safe became overshadowed by the emptiness that engulfed him over what lay ahead.

"Son of a bitch," Kirsten exclaimed. "Brett."

Sidney pounded the floor with his fist, his face twisted with anger. "Shit—shit—shit! I told you."

Brett had not looked forward to this moment. He tried to swallow, but his throat was dry. "Your journey is over, Kirsten," he said, conscious of the crack in his voice. Sidney was hours from facing intense interrogation in Washington. As for Kirsten, he saw only trouble, but he would have to save the speculation for later. They needed to leave, to find somewhere safe.

"Who's in the main house?" Brett asked.

Kirsten exchanged quick glances with Sidney. "No one," she said.

Her tone left Brett all the more convinced the Mendollfson woman would have to be dealt with as well, and silently hoped that Fliorina had things under control. "We'll see about that." He motioned toward the door. "We're leaving. Get your things together."

Kirsten placed her hands on her hips. "You have no right to be here."

"Please don't make this any harder than it is, Kirsten," Brett said. "We're going on a trip."

Sidney bolted to his feet and dashed to the security computer on the far wall, hands tapping at the keyboard. Bolts snapped closed on the door to the lab with a series of loud clicks.

Brett burst across the room, covering the distance in three long strides, and pulled Sidney from his chair. "What are you doing? Open the door."

Sidney shrugged and returned Brett's stare. "Too late. The security system is engaged."

Brett turned and studied the door. Heavy wood reinforced with steel bands. Strong hinges. It would take an explosive device to open. He scanned the security setup where Sidney sat. The three monitors presented crisp, high-resolution images with a night-vision green tint of the quality one would see in military and espionage work. The system had a German name Brett didn't recognize, and he quickly concluded that he would stand little chance of reversing Sidney's action.

"Cut the crap, Sidney" he said. "You don't know what you're dealing with here."

Sidney's voice held a taunting confidence: "Is that so? This is private property. Where's your search warrant?"

"Different rules. We have to get out of here, now. Open the door."

Kirsten shot Brett a mocking look. "Looks as though you're not making the rules."

Brett felt drained from the long trip and the emptiness of his mission. "Stay out of this, Kirsten."

Kirsten met his stare, unblinking. "I'm already in, all the way."

Brett shook his head. He knew reasoning with Kirsten was like negotiating with a hungry bobcat. "That's something you'll have to live with."

"And what are *you* living with?"

"I have my orders."

"Orders? Orders?" Kirsten slapped her hand against her forehead. "Of course. Is that what's at stake here, your fading, tenuous career? Want some perspective, Mr. CIA? Has it ever occurred to you that while you're chasing an innocent civilian halfway around the world our country is on the brink of chaos? In the mindless pursuit of your orders have you thought for even a minute why I might be here?"

"My job is to bring Sidney in, not to speculate on the state of the nation."

"Our country is in a state of siege, poised on the brink of war, and you're focused on some politically motivated, trumped up orders to capture a young computer graduate who might offer a way out? Isn't this about getting your priorities straight?"

"Give it up, Kirsten," Sidney said. "He's a robot with a programmed mission. Nothing short of a short circuit or total rewire is going to change his direction."

"Okay – here's the grownup news, folks," Brett said, blowing out a long breath. "There's something bigger going on here, bigger than my orders, bigger than Sidney's arrest warrant. There's a German hit squad targeting Sidney, and perhaps you, Kirsten, that may be here at any moment. You want to play games and wait, Sidney, I suggest you start praying."

CHAPTER 30

The sight from the War Room overlooking the Orion Project cyber center deepened Dustin Clayton's growing sense of concern that his effort to combat a cyber terrorist attack would produce a defense too late. Or none at all. The Orion 6 implementation display lay dark, a silent reminder of the day's testing failures. The technical staff sat quietly at their computer terminals, exchanging glances or attention seemingly fixed in time on their computer screens.

As he contemplated his next steps, Clayton listened to the growing alarm in the tone of the news reports from CNN, Fox, and WorldNews on the wall-mounted monitors behind him:

"A growing number of 911 services around the country report their systems are either down or crippled, leaving police and fire response services in cities such as Detroit and the Watts section of Los Angeles unable to cope with a soaring tide of emergency calls...."

Dozens of web-reliant retailers are reporting their systems are down or crippled from attacks. A spokesperson from Amazon.com referred to its entire business operation as inoperable . . . .

Reports are coming in of communications and power outages sweeping the country, raising fears for those in hospitals requiring medical care . . . ."

The videoconference screen above the television monitors filled with Kansas Morningstar's image, breaking Clayton's concentration. Behind her, the large intrusion display was a wall of animated light, alive with flashing, multicolored dots signaling cyber attacks on U.S. facilities. "I'm ready with the updated threat analysis you requested, Mr. Secretary."

Dustin had steeled himself for an unpleasant assessment from Kansas, but hoped somewhere in her analysis there would be a thread of hope for battling the New Tomorrow terrorists. He muted the television broadcasts. "I assume you have some leads?"

Kansas hesitated a beat, and then said, "Actually, just the opposite, sir."

Clayton felt his stomach tighten. "Meaning?"

"The New Tomorrow terrorists seem to be staying out of the attacks. Perhaps we're seeing some copycats."

Clayton glanced at the pictures on the silenced television monitors and tried to reconcile the images with what Kansas was telling him.

Kansas continued as though she were reading his mind. "Sir, what hasn't been reported is that the FBI and several key defense sites are also down."

Jesus, Clayton said to himself. Ibbs had been right. Other cyber zealots around the globe had become bold and were jumping into the fray. In a matter of days, the nation would plunge further into panic. *And at what point would panic become chaos?* "Your recommendation?"

"Sir, unless the U.S. can show some means to protect its infrastructure, we expect the attacks to continue to increase. Bottom line is, if we don't get Orion 6 operational, we're going to have a wildfire on our hands like this country has never seen."

"If I may interrupt, Mr. Secretary?" Maureen Connelly, Clayton's personal assistant, stood in the doorway, her polished, erect manner and impeccable hair and clothing taking at least ten years away from her sixty. "There's a piece on WorldNews you will want to catch, sir."

Clayton nodded but kept his attention on Kansas. "Anything else?"

"Not at this time, sir," she replied.

"Keep me posted." Clayton swiveled toward the wall of television screens. He was greeted by Sheila Carson's image, but his eyes locked on the man she was interviewing, Congressman Dan Hackworth.

Clayton motioned to Maureen to turn up the volume. Hackworth was speaking in his politician's baritone. "Our nation is under attack. If Secretary Clayton and his management team cannot deliver a working cyberterrorism defense that will ensure the safety of American citizens, we must bring in those who can."

"Are you referring to privatization, Congressman?" Carson asked.

"Absolutely. Vigorous, swift action is required. I believe a crack counter-cyberterrorism team drawing from private industry should be assembled and dispatched to the Orion Project within the next twenty-four hours."

"And their mission?"

Hackworth's expression hardened. "Immediate assumption of command. The United States government has proven time and again that it is not in the business of software development. Our country's technology infrastructure was developed by private industry. I have long argued that the protection of that infrastructure should be in the same hands. The president's lack of action to halt the stumbling of the Orion Project is, in my opinion, indefensible. The time to take action is long past."

"Get me Ishmel," Clayton said to Maureen. Fighting the terrorists and struggling with internal issues wasn't enough. Now he could be facing a squadron of watchdogs and meddlers, meaning progress on the Orion Project would slam to a halt. *Hackworth wouldn't mind that at all, would he?* he thought, recalling the luncheon conversation with Rutledge and Ibbs.

Zachary Ishmel's dour image filled the videoconference screen. A group of technical staff clumped around a bank of computer terminals, heads down, behind him.

"Your Orion 6 deadline has passed," Clayton said, doing nothing to conceal his frustration. "Where are we?"

"We've experienced some unexpected delays. I told you we would have results, and we will."

"You're aware of the escalation of attacks around the country?"

"As I'm sure you've been told, nuisance strikes, nothing more."

Clayton studied the image of his technology director. Ishmel's excuses were becoming increasingly thin, and now he began to question whether the two of them were even fighting the same war. "When will you have progress?"

"This is the world of software, Mr. Secretary." Ishmel's jaw clamped tightly around his pipe. "We knew there would be risks when we jumped directly to Orion 6. Take no chances, you get no progress."

No progress is exactly where we are, Clayton thought.

"Excuse me, sir." Maureen was in the doorway again. "There's an emergency airborne alert underway. Your chopper will be on the roof in two minutes."

Clayton drew in a quick breath and gave Ishmel a final glance. "I'll be in touch once I'm aloft. You have six hours, Zachary, or we'll be having a different kind of conversation."

Clayton pulled the collar of his overcoat tightly around his neck against the wind that whipped across the roof of the Orion Cyber Center, his eyes straining for signs of the helicopter. He wondered about the alert. President Anston had ordered readiness tests of the National Emergency Airborne Command Post, Kneecap in shorthand, as preparations for possible military engagement loomed over the nation's capital.

The flying Command Post, a custom built nuclear-hardened Boeing 747, was designed to be America's flying communications and command center during war. With aerial refueling, the aircraft could stay aloft for three days at a time. An earlier version had been dubbed the Doomsday Plane by the media, giving the operation a Dr. Strangelove aura. In Kneecap exercises, the selected participants did not know whether the alert was real or a trial run. They would not know until they were on board and airborne.

The unmistakable, distant sound of the rotors beating the air reached Clayton just as he saw the dot on the horizon moving rapidly toward him. Twenty seconds later, the noise from the chopper's engine and rotor blades grew deafening as the beetle-shaped assembly of steel with its extended landing pods dropped onto the marked circular landing area thirty feet away. He rushed under the spinning rotors, blasted by their downwash of freezing winter air, and was pulled on board by two waiting crewmen.

The powerful engines had the Sikorski 1B helicopter in the air, nose down and climbing rapidly, before Clayton was strapped in his seat. He watched the building shrink and then disappear in the clouds. He guessed the helicopter had been on the roof less than five seconds. He leaned his head against the vibrating headrest, catching his breath and adjusting to the dim light in the compartment.

"Hello, Dusty," a mature, twangy woman's voice said.

Clayton peered across the darkened interior. Joan Karlin stared at him across the compartment, next to two burr-cut Marine guards in crisp flight gear. "Madam Secretary," he said. "This is a surprise."

Her eyes twinkled. "You know better."

Clayton waited. He knew the secretary of state rarely left anything to chance, and their being together in the helicopter would be no exception.

Karlin tilted her head toward the flight deck. "Will you excuse us?" she said to the Marines.

She waited for the young men to move out of the compartment and then steadied her gaze on Clayton. "I wanted to talk with you, face to face."

Clayton respected the secretary. Her folksy Texas manner and silver-haired matronly look masked a keen mind and sharp wit. A cattleman's daughter who had fought her way up through the rough and tumble world of Texas politics, she had demonstrated in her three years in national office that she would press vigorously for what she believed, even if it meant crossing every other member of the Cabinet and the military establishment on the way.

"I've been on the phone most of the day with my counterparts in France, Germany and the United Kingdom," Karlin said. "We're scaring the bejesus out of them that we're going to launch a damn global conflagration in response to this terrorist crisis."

Clayton nodded in agreement.

"I can handle them," Karlin said, leaning forward. "What concerns me is all the talk about lack of progress in the Orion Project from that numbnut Hackworth and the headline-seeking talking heads on television. I want to hear the truth from you. Where are we?"

Clayton knew better than to try to finesse Karlin. She was way too sharp for that. "We're doing everything possible, but at the moment, I'm afraid the terrorists have the upper hand."

Karlin studied Clayton for a long moment. "You know as well as I the retaliation we're going to experience if the unspeakable horror of Operation Hydra is unleashed."

"Some believe Hydra will kill many of our terrorist enemies and intimidate the rest," Clayton said, offering the contra view.

"B.S. We'll kill a few thousand terrorists, and ignite tens of thousands more to action against the United States. The streets of America will never be safe again.

"In addition," Karlin continued, "every major alliance, every friend the United States has in the world, perhaps including Britain, will be in jeopardy. It will set our world leadership position back a generation."

Clayton glanced away. He agreed with Karlin, but his feelings had been overridden in the hysteria enveloping the president's military advisors.

"Have you checked your watch?" she asked.

Clayton glanced at the time. "I know."

"That's right," she said. "Twenty-four hours remain until Anston's State of the Union speech." She shifted in her seat, edging closer. "What have you heard about the resignation rumors?"

Clayton had heard whispers, but tried to keep his attention on his job. "I'm out of that loop, Joan."

"No you're not. Our allies are deserting us. Russia, China, North Korea and God knows who else are on military alert status, and the president is being outmaneuvered at home. William Anston is one of the only voices of moderation in the country. Lose him, and this nation will spin out of control like tumbleweed in a prairie storm."

She paused, as if feeling the need to let her words sink in. "You're our only hope."

Clayton studied his hands, unsure of what to say. He agreed with Karlin's assessment of the political climate, but he didn't have an answer to the terrorist threat.

Karlin leaned toward him. "Tell me you can pull an ace or two out of your hold cards at the last minute."

"I don't know how many cards I have left, Joan. I honestly don't know."

The two sat listening to the vibration and steady roar of the helicopter for several long moments.

"Well, I'd rob the deck, Dusty, because no action, however ridiculous it sounds, is more ruinous than Operation Hydra, so trust your instincts and play your hand out."

The helicopter banked sharply into a tight turn. Karlin grasped her seat. "Jesus!" she gasped. "Damn flying grasshoppers. Don't trust 'em." The sound of the rotor blades deepened. A moment later, the vibration level in the cabin increased and the helicopter began to lose altitude.

"Madam Secretary, Secretary Clayton," the pilot announced, "sixty seconds to touchdown."

As the helicopter descended, the two Marines had Karlin ready at the door. "We're all counting on you, Dusty," she said in parting.

An instant after the wheels hit the runway, she was down the steps, Clayton behind her. Flanked by the Marines, they rushed across the tarmac to the plane towering above them, three stories tall, white except for a blue strip and the legend "United States of America" along the length of its fuselage. The gleaming 747 sat poised at the end of the runway, engines running and ready for immediate takeoff.

The sky filled with the thunder of approaching choppers. Clayton squinted into the darkness. A procession of machine-gun-toting helicopters roared toward them and circled the aircraft. Moments later the president's helicopter burst through the clouds. Marine One banked and made a rapid descent, engines roaring, and settled in a swirl of wind onto the runway next to the 747.

Clayton exchanged glances with Karlin as they ascended the stairs of the aircraft. The president did not normally take part in Kneecap exercises.

What was up?

CHAPTER 31

Brett Logan found it difficult to diffuse his frustration. Sidney refused to open the door to the cottage unless he was free to leave on his own, with Katrina.

He felt his unease escalate as he tried for the second time to reach Rick Fliorina on his phone. Nothing. He was still puzzled and concerned about the German's knowledge of Kirsten's plans. He must get her and Sidney away from the cottage and in safe hands, as quickly as possible. He checked his watch. *Where was Rick?*

Brett took a few moments to check the bathroom and survey the cottage for another exit. There was none. No door other than the entrance, and the windows were too small to allow passage of an adult to the outside.

His shoe caught on a slight depression in the floor. Looking closer, he saw a tarnished metal handle imbedded in the wood flooring together with the outline of a trapdoor. He looked at Sidney. "What is this?"

Sidney turned away, ignoring the question. Brett faced Kirsten and repeated the question.

Kirsten stared at him for a moment, then answered, "According to Sidney, that is a trapdoor to a tunnel leading to the back of the property – a holdover from the war."

"Is the tunnel open?" Brett asked.

Kirsten glanced at Sidney, who shrugged disinterestedly.

Brett made a mental note to keep Sidney away from the trapdoor lest the computer genius get a creative idea about escape.

He glanced at Kirsten, and found her watching him. He sensed that she was taking stock of the situation, considering her next move. Sidney sat next to her, arms crossed and his face expressionless.

"Running out of ideas?" she asked Brett.

Brett ignored her and tried again to reach Fliorina. Still no connection. He checked the smartphone and tried once more. Nothing.

"Having trouble?" Sidney eyed Brett with a peculiar mixture of anger and triumph. "The lab's security system cancels out all outgoing and incoming cellular signals. Protection against invasion of privacy. You know all about that sort of thing."

Brett blew out a long breath. "You have no idea what you're dealing with."

"Really?" Sidney cocked an eyebrow. "You seem to be the one who's locked in, out of contact with your colleagues, unable to carry out your orders. Perhaps you're the one who doesn't know what he's dealing with."

"I suggest you cut your antics," Brett said, suddenly aware of the edge in his tone. "I'm telling you, we have little time to get to safety."

"As I said," Sidney shot back, "Give me – and Katrina – a five minute start and then you can go wherever you wish."

Brett turned to Kirsten. "Get Sidney to open the door."

Kirsten started to respond, but was interrupted by a woman's scream coming from the security monitors.

"Sid!" the woman screamed. "Sid! Are you there?" The security monitor to the main house filled with the image of Katrina struggling with someone off camera.

Sidney bolted from his chair, shooting it across the floor. "Katrina!"

"Get him away from me," she shrieked. "He's got a gun."

Brett crowded next to Sidney in front of the computer screen, grave possibilities tumbling through his mind.

Katrina was pulled from the screen. "Stop, you beast!" she screamed.

A moment later, Rick Fliorina's image appeared on the screen. "Brett?"

"Let her go, you animal!" Sidney shouted.

Brett pushed closer to the screen, relieved to see the other agent's face. "I've been trying to reach you."

"Ditto," Fliorina answered.

"Goddamn it, Sid," Katrina shouted from off camera. "I told you it would come to this."

Fliorina struggled to hold Katrina away with one arm. "What next, Brett?"

Brett ran through the possibilities. They needed help. "Call in the Paris agents. And tell them to bring an explosive to blow the door."

Fliorina look puzzled. "Explosive?"

"Unless hot-shot here changes his mind, we're trapped in here," Brett said.

"Okay. I'll be back to you."

"Rick, my phone won't work in here. Call me over the conference system when you have an arrival time for the agents."

The screen went blank. "Let her go," Sidney said to Brett. "She has nothing to do with this."

"She does now," Brett said. "Harboring a wanted fugitive is a crime."

"She's a Swiss citizen. You can't touch her."

Brett motioned Sidney into a chair at the computer desk. "Stay put, got it?"

Sidney flashed Brett a sharp look and turned to his keyboard.

Brett checked the time. Once the Paris agents arrived, they would caravan in two cars directly to the airport, keeping Sidney and Katrina separate. They should be safe there as they waited for the arrival of Sherwin's plane. *Then back to the states, a final debrief with Sherwin, and he and the CIA would be history. He would manage somehow without his pension.*

Sidney motioned Kirsten to his computer. "Look at what the CNNAmerica.news is saying," he said. Brett joined them, watching over Sidney's shoulder.

"Within the past hour," the report said, "the terrorist group calling itself New Tomorrow distributed a message over the Internet, reminding United States citizens of President Anston's looming deadline for cessation of all work on Safeguard. An excerpt from their message reads as follows:

> To the people of America. If your president fails to meet the condition outlined in our previous messages to cease all work on your missile defense system, we will have no course except to expand our attacks on your country. Any loss of life, for any cause, is regrettable, but you may lay the responsibility for losses that you, your families, and friends may sustain directly in the hands of your president if he does not meet our peace-seeking request. The report continued, "We have no comment yet from the White House, but we do have an update from our capitol correspondent on the rising call for the president's resignation over his handling of the terrorist crisis that grips the nation."

Sidney shook his head. "What a goddamn, sorry mess."

"We'll get them," Brett said.

"No you won't." Sidney laid the words down like a bet.

"Pardon?" Brett asked, frowning.

"I said you'll never find them."

Brett studied the young face across from him. *How much did Sidney know and wasn't telling?* "You have something to say?"

Rick Fliorina's image appeared on the conferencing screen. "Brett, we're looking at fifteen, maybe twenty minutes for the backup team."

"Damn." Brett checked his watch. "That the best they can do?"

"Even that's being optimistic."

"Keep me posted, and, Rick, watch the front of the house."

"What did you mean," Brett said, returning to Sidney, "that we won't find the terrorists?"

Sidney leaned into his chair and clasped his hands behind his head, his eyes narrowing. "You're thinking in the wrong paradigm."

"Care to translate?"

"The New Tomorrow terrorists are dispersed in small, well-disguised locations around the world, organized into loosely knit self-sufficient cells. Even if you get lucky and take out a few cells, others immediately take over as though nothing had happened. Any manhunt, even one of worldwide proportions, will fail to stop them."

Thoughts of hundreds of Special Ops forces taking out thousands of suspected terrorists coursed through Brett's mind. "But you know where they are," Brett said, fishing.

"As I said, in this war, the world of the physical is a thing of the past."

Brett was tiring of Sidney's mind games. "I'm sure we'll figure it out."

"Not without some help."

Brett felt a tinge of suspicion. "You offering?"

"Selling, actually."

"Meaning what?"

"I give you the information on the terrorists, you let me, Katrina, and Kirsten go free, now and forever. No caveats, no exceptions, no screwy CIA funny business at the last minute. Deal?"

Brett knew he was in a hard place. He had no authority to authorize a deal, but he had complete responsibility for Kirsten, Sidney, and Katrina's safety. He could lie to Sidney, get the information and then renege. But that was not his style. He decided to go with things the way they were.

"Here's what I can do. You tell me what you have on the terrorists, we all leave here together, and I commit to you I will plead your case when we return to the U.S."

"Not good enough," Sidney said, shaking his head.

Brett glanced at Kirsten for support, but she looked the other way. So the cards had been laid. They would wait for the backup agents to arrive.

"What a shame for you to misjudge this opportunity," Sidney said. "I was under the assumption you were after the terrorists, but now I see Kirsten was right. Your misguided—"

The cottage suddenly shook from the sound of an explosion.

Brett pushed Kirsten to the floor. "Stay down!"

"What was that?" she asked.

A louder, closer explosion rattled the racks of communications and computer equipment. Ceiling tiles dropped from above, skittering as they hit the floor. The lab's small windows lit up with waves of flashing light.

"Fire!" Kirsten screamed.

Sidney bounded out of his chair and rushed to the security screen. "Katrina. Katrina!" He stabbed at the communication connection again and again. "Katrina, it's Sid." The screen was blank, the speakers quiet. He slammed his hand on the desk until his face twisted in pain. "Katrina, do you read me?"

Sidney flipped the security monitors to views of the grounds.

Brett pushed his face close to the screens, scanning for signs of Fliorina and Katrina. Flames burst from the windows of the main house, reaching for the roof. Columns of dark smoke streamed from bright orange flames into the sky. Any minute the flames would reach the van, hurling hot, twisted shards of metal in every direction. They had to get out, now.

Sidney pointed to one of the screens. "Look." A figure in black, then another, silhouetted by the light of the fire, sprinted around the corner of the main house, toward the computer lab.

Amidst the noise of the fire Brett heard two shots from a hand gun, followed by a series of short bursts from an automatic weapon. Thoughts of Rick Fliorina and Katrina flashed through his mind but he knew he had to stay focused. He figured they had less than a minute until the cottage was also engulfed in flames. He mentally calculated the odds of their getting out by rushing through the front door but quickly discarded the idea. They would be picked apart.

Brett was part way through a plan to move Kirsten and Sidney to the back of the cottage, taking on the attackers himself when a bright explosion ripped the door off its hinges, shaking the cottage with the jolting force of an earthquake. Flying wooden chunks from the door and splinters of glass flew into the small room, accompanied by a searing fireball of heat.

Suddenly, Brett felt as though he had been thrown into a world of slow motion. He felt no pain, heard no sounds as he was thrown backwards, crashing into the wall. He shook his head and gasped for air. For a moment he thought he caught a glimpse of Kirsten across the room through the swirling dust and smoke. He called her name as he clawed his way through the debris toward where he had seen her, but his voice was lost amidst the roar of the fire.

He rubbed his eyes and scooted forward, pushing aside tangles of loose wiring, remnants of computer screens and smashed CPU's. It was a small room. He would find Kirsten somehow. His heart jumped as he felt the touch of cool flesh. Kirsten's hand twitched once, twice, and then grasped his with the force of an animal's claw. He scissor-kicked his body around and moved closer until he could see her face. Her skin was black from smoke, her hair a twisted mass of straw. She stared at the ceiling blankly, her chest heaving from gasping breaths. "Kirsten! Kirsten, speak to me" he said, then repeated as he shook her shoulder.

Her eyes flicked toward him, showing a look of recognition. He exhaled a sigh of relief and squeezed her hand. "Easy goes it," he said. Slowly, he pulled her to a sitting position.

She sputtered and coughed, then asked in a raspy voice, "Where's Sid?"

Brett placed his fingers to his lips and listened. Brett thought he heard a voice. He squinted into the smoke but could not see farther than his outstretched hand. Then he heard the sound again. It was Sidney, sounding as though he were across the room, crying out for help.

Kirsten struggled to get up. "We've got to get Sid —"

"I'll get him. I want you to move toward the kitchen, to the trap door. We'll meet you there." Brett squeezed her shoulder and nudged her forward.

The fire roared closer, gaining in intensity and sound as its flames feasted on the wooden floor and timbers of the ceiling. In a swift motion, Kirsten broke from Brett's grasp and plunged into the black smoke. "*Sidne-e-e-y!*"

"Jesus!" Brett dodged a wall of flame as timbers collapsed from the roof, sending bright hot burning coals shooting across the room. The heat burned, like the sting from a thousand bees, against his face and arms. He hooked his forearms over his eyes, took a deep breath, and plunged into the hot, swirling cloud in the direction Kirsten had gone.

CHAPTER 32

Dustin Clayton studied the faces of the dozen military officers and civilian officials occupying the compartment on the 747 Command Post, searching for signs indicating whether the exercise was a drill or for real. The aircraft had made a steep climb from Andrews Air Force base and made a sharp turn toward a westerly course. If the nation were girding for war, the aircraft might be taking the president and specifically designated officials to the nuclear-hardened command center buried deep in Cheyenne Mountain in Colorado.

Clayton hadn't seen Secretary Karlin since boarding. She would most likely be in the Briefing Room, where the latest intelligence on war exercises and preparations was passed to the senior administration official on board, in this case President Anston. If this exercise were for real, most of the other senior members of government would be in secret hideaways, ready to function if the country were physically attacked.

Clayton laid his head back against the seat and stared at the ceiling of the aircraft. Why, in the midst of the sense of urgency surrounding the Orion Project, had he been invited aboard?

"Mr. Secretary?"

Clayton snapped out of his thoughts. Ron Comber, his normally cheerful face lined with exhaustion and strain, approached and said, "The president would like to see you."

Clayton snapped away his seat belt and stood. "Right behind you."

As he followed Comber, Clayton reviewed what he would tell the president. He hoped that he would uncover a positive note to offer on the Orion Project, but came up empty.

The corridor was congested with serious-faced staffers rushing to and from discussions, notebooks and smartphones in hand. Clayton paused as they passed the Battle Staff compartment, trying to sense the tone of activity. Battle Staff was the largest operational component of the aircraft. In this room data was assimilated on potential threats and war options and passed on to the Briefing Room. The operation's fifteen-member staff of communications and intelligence experts were head down, intent on their computers and telephones, communicating between one another in the frenzied but efficient shorthand of gestures and clipped acronyms that reminded Clayton of his experiences in flight operations during military maneuvers. *Was Battle Staff preparing for conflict or running through exercises?* As he turned away with his question unanswered, his stomach twisted with unease.

Comber opened the door for Clayton as they reached the president's compartment. "The president is waiting for you."

Clayton's first glimpse of President Anston was a shock: in the previous twenty-four hours the Chief Executive had aged five years. Anston's face had a shallow, sunken look and he appeared to have lost weight. Only the firm set of the president's jaw and the intensity of his eyes gave away the focused energy that had driven his ascendancy to the White House.

Anston was in a discussion with Joan Karlin and Gene Richards, his National Security Advisor. The president motioned Clayton toward a sofa on the bulkhead. "We're just finishing up."

Clayton scanned the president's compartment. The room was as he had remembered it from prior visits, the gold pile rug and the blue upholstered sofa with gold trim where he took a seat. A working desk bolted to the floor separated the president from two cushioned armchairs where his visitors sat. The constant vibration and hum of the engines was a reminder that they were airborne.

"We're going to face extraordinary damage control, worldwide," Richards was saying. "The media will be all over you. I don't have to tell you what that will do to your reelection chances."

Clayton studied the presidential seal monogrammed in the carpet and listened.

"Assuming I make it to the election," the president said. "What's your take, Joan?"

The secretary of state leaned toward the president. "Sir, we flaunted our 'shock and awe' tactics in Iraq. This hydra massacre, if we unleash it, will be all shock and zero awe. The United States will be left standing alone in the world, isolated from our allies, and we will further enflame terrorist actions against us. I firmly believe our children's children will still be paying the price for Operation Hydra two decades from now."

"Looks like I'm damned if I do and damned if I don't," Anston said.

Karlin and Richards were silent.

The president drummed his fingers on the blotter covering his desk and then flashed his visitors a brief smile. "Thank you," he said in a tone of dismissal.

After the door closed, Anston took a long drink from the iced tea that was always by his side. "Tell me, Dusty," he asked after a satisfied sigh, "why is it the simplest things in life seem to bring the greatest pleasure?"

Clayton wasn't fooled a bit by Anston's folksy Oklahoma manner. The president continually fine-tuned his skills to disarm those he met with, even if it were with a lifelong friend from early days. He knew the president was switching gears, clearing his mind for discussion.

"Perhaps because in a world filled with uncertainty," Clayton answered, "the simplest things are always the same, Mr. President."

Anston leveled a clear-eyed stare at Clayton. "Can you stop the terrorists?"

Before Clayton could answer, Ron Comber was at the door, pointing toward one of the telephones that were anchored to Anston's desk. "Admiral Rutledge for you, Mr. President."

Anston squinted as he checked his Rolex. "He's early. Tell him fifteen minutes."

"The admiral says there have been some changes."

"Damn it. Tell him I said no changes. Fifteen minutes." Anston fixed a stare at his Homeland Security Secretary. "Well?"

Clayton swallowed hard. In the most difficult hour this president had faced, he was going to let him down. "Mr. President, I can only give you minimal assurance that we'll be ready by the terrorist deadline."

The lines shooting up Anston's forehead deepened. "It's a good thing I'm not a paranoid man," he said, staying in his Oklahoma accent. "Otherwise, I'd listen to my gut tell me that something is dreadfully amiss." Anston leaned into his chair, studying Clayton over the top of his reading glasses. "You know why I say that?"

"No, sir."

"Because everything, absolutely everything, is going wrong. Our esteemed National Intelligence Director can't find a cyber terrorist wearing a bulls-eye on a street corner and the head of our armed forces thinks mass murder is going to win a totally new type of war." Anston swallowed more of his iced tea. "To add to that, our allies are joining forces against us, and a congress controlled by my own party is after my head."

"Excuse me, Mr. President?" Ron Comber was at the door, his hand grasping a blue folder emblazoned with the Presidential Seal. "Prime Minister Thompson is on the line, and when you're ready I have an updated Presidential Daily Brief for you."

Anston nodded. "I'll take the call first." He motioned Clayton to stay put and reached for the secure phone on his desk.

"Yes, Martin." Anston was silent. As he listened his eyes narrowed. "No, Martin, in spite of what the media may say, no final decisions have been made. You have my personal guarantee that there will be no military action without discussion with you beforehand. What's that? Yes, you know I'm deeply appreciative of your concern, as well as that of our other close allies, on that issue, Martin, but I stand firm behind the missile defense system." Anston paused and listened for a moment. "No, we're not becoming isolated. Yes, of course. I realize you're speaking for the others as well." Anston glanced toward Clayton and shook his head as he listened. "Yes, Martin. You have my word. I'll keep you posted."

Anston replaced the receiver and stared at Clayton. "Easy for them to say for us to hold the horses. They aren't being attacked."

Clayton waited. He knew the president well enough to know that talking things through out loud was his way of dealing with frustration.

"You know what?" Anston continued. "Sometimes I think the whole world is going topsy-turvy on us. If you listen to our allies some- times they sound just like the damn terrorists. Or some of our congressmen. They all have demands. France and Germany have always felt Safeguard placed them in jeopardy, wanted it cancelled, and now they've used this damn cri- sis to drag the Brits over to their side. It makes you wonder who in the hell we're really fighting. Everyone seems to want to blame our basic desire to protect ourselves on some grand scheme for world domination.

"As for Operation Hydra—" Anston scowled as he banged his fist on the desk. "That damn 9/11 commission spelled trouble from the start, but little did we know that congress would slip the commission's Hydra recommendation into the legislation. Christ, you know my feelings, Dusty, but in a few hours the decision will no longer be in my hands."

Clayton nodded. He knew congress was in emergency session, hours away from its final vote on Hackworth's bill requiring the presi- dent to take action that would include initiating Operation Hydra.

"Mr. President." Comber stood at the doorway again. "We're behind schedule in a major way. I had to tell the Russian Ambassador that you could not be interrupted."

"I tell you what, Ron," Anston said in a brisk tone. "You just keep telling people that. I'll be through here when I'm through."

After the door closed the president folded his hands on the desk and stared at Clayton. "I need you to come up with a way to stop these terror-ists. I don't know what untried solutions haven't been tested or what crazy ideas some of your tech-heads may have conjured up in their sleep. It doesn't matter what it is, Dusty. I need you to pull out the stops and find a defense – even the *pretense* of a defense. I'm counting on you."

Clayton returned the president's look for several lingering moments before responding. "I can't make any promises, Mr. President."

"Find a way. We're under wartime rules now. Anything – anything – you need is yours."

"Anything?" Clayton repeated.

"Just ask, Dusty."

Clayton brushed past uniformed men and women in the crowded corridor, past coatless mid-level cabinet staffers, his mind lingering on the meeting with the president. Stuck between an attack-driven military, a revenge-driven congress, and a fear-stricken nation, the president of the United States increasingly stood isolated and alone.

He didn't notice the immobile figure of the National Intelligence Director until the men almost collided.

Ibbs' harsh tone brought Clayton out of his thoughts with the power of fingernails on a chalkboard. "What the hell do you think you're up to, Dusty?"

The corridor suddenly became quiet. "I'm sorry?" Clayton replied.

Ibbs' face was flushed with anger. "Do you have any idea what's happened? Any idea?"

"What are you saying?"

"I've lost two agents, all because of some harebrained scheme of one of your people, interfering with an official government operation. You owe me an explanation."

"Hold it a goddamn minute, Stuart. What the hell's going on?"

A passing Marine hesitated and Clayton waved him on.

"Your Miss Lockhart turned our mission to find a wanted fugitive inside out and Americans are dead."

"What mission? What are you talking about?"

"A private residence outside of Zurich, where a suspect in the terrorist attacks was holed up, was firebombed. Your Miss Lockhart was in the middle of it. Two of our agents, several civilians, perhaps more, are dead."

Kirsten? A bolt of fear seared through Clayton's chest. He searched Ibbs' face. "Who?"

"No known survivors. They're bringing what's left of the bodies out for identification."

Clayton backed away, the memory of his daughter's lifeless body tearing through his mind. The fear in his stomach was now a raging pain. "Oh my God. Not again."

CHAPTER 33

Distant sounds of Brett's voice echoed through Kirsten's head. She coughed, trying to clear the smoke from her lungs, and sucked in a breath of air. A gut-wrenching stench reeking of mold and animal excrement doubled her over in spasms of nausea. *Where was she?* Her mind swirled, then memories slowly formed from her mental haze of Brett dragging her, choking from the smoke, through the intense heat to the opening in the floor of the computer lab and half-carrying her down the rickety stairs into the darkness as the cottage collapsed in a cascade of flames above them. She slowly cracked open her eyes.

Brett's face was inches from hers, his skin black from the smoke. Kirsten could see the fatigue etched in his eyes. She tried to push up on an elbow.

He grasped her arm, steadying her. "Take it easy."

She felt her body stiffen. "Sid! Where's Sid?"

"Behind you and doing fine," Brett answered, glancing behind her, "but you're the one I'm worried about. You took a nasty fall down the steps, then lost consciousness. Sidney and I carried you through the tunnel."

She tried to take a deeper breath but the pain in her lungs stopped her. "Anyone follow us?"

Brett shook his head. "The cottage collapsed as we escaped, sending a firefall of burning embers through the opening to the tunnel. No one could have survived in there."

"Where are we?" she asked.

"At the end of the tunnel. We're trying to figure out how to get out."

Kirsten twisted her head and blinked, trying to see in the darkness. Half a dozen steps away, Sidney stood on the highest of three stone steps, ripping at a mass of roots entangled in what she thought to be a metal grate. His iPhone was propped close to him, sending a beam of light, probably from a torchlight app or something similar. Sidney glanced her way with a thin smile, then wiped his forehead on his shirt and continued to rip at the roots.

Kirsten felt a blanket of relief wash over her. Sidney was safe, for now.

"What's Sid doing?" she asked Brett.

"Trying to get us out. The tunnel provided a hiding place during World War II and possibly an escape route. We're trying to see if that grate leads to the outside."

She looked into the darkness of the tunnel. "Can we go back, wait until the fire cools?"

"No, the tunnel entrance caved in under the weight of the collapsing cottage. That end is sealed."

A flood of thoughts about dying in an airless tunnel swept through Kirsten, but she tried to brush them aside. She refocused, turning her attention to Brett. She winced at the sight of the burns on his arms. "You can't use your arms."

"Not as bad as they look," he said.

Another reason to get out soon, she thought. As if they needed one. Kirsten's senses were returning and her vision adjusting to the dim light. She felt the damp, cool earth beneath her. She glanced over Brett's shoulder. The tunnel through which Brett must have carried her was damp with icy pools of water. She shivered, suddenly aware of the cold. If they didn't get out of the icy water soon the tunnel that had saved their lives would quickly become their frigid tomb.

"Damn," Sidney said, breaking her concentration. He lowered his arms from the roots. "They're not budging. Is there something to cut with? A knife, nail file, anything?"

Brett motioned Sidney aside. "No, but let me try." He took Sidney's place on the top step and began pulling at the twisted roots.

Kirsten caught a motion out of the corner of her eye. She turned and froze at the sight. Small eyes glowed at her from the darkness. Rats. She scanned the tunnel. *Where would this adventure end?* Not here, she vowed. Not in some stench-filled, rotting hole in Switzerland.

"Let me help," Kirsten said to Sidney. She started to rise and then slipped to the earth, her head spinning.

"Take it easy." Sidney extended a hand and pulled her to her feet.

Kirsten glanced behind and shuddered. The glowing eyes were back, a dozen or more, edging closer.

"I think I'm getting somewhere," Brett called out. "Hold my legs to keep my feet from slipping."

Sidney put his arms around Brett's legs, digging his feet against the side of the wall for support.

The tunnel suddenly went black. "Damn!" Sidney said. "What a time to run out of juice." Kirsten automatically looked for her phone, then realized it, along with her purse, wallet and passport had been consumed by the fire.

Sidney cursed softly as he fiddled with his phone until a dim light glowed on his screen. "We've got maybe two minutes of juice – got to hurry."

"Give me some light," Brett shouted. "I've got an opening." Scraps of vegetation and clumps of dirt splashed into the wet muck from above.

Sidney focused the beam where Brett was working. Portions of a rusted metal grate showed through openings in the roots.

"If we're lucky," Sidney said, "that's the opening that will take us to the forest behind the house."

"I felt the grate move a bit," Brett said. "Steady me." He ripped away another handful of roots and pushed on the metal. He paused, breathing heavily, and then pushed again.

Kirsten grasped Brett's legs to give support. She felt his muscles tighten, release, then tighten again as he strained against the grate.

"Come on, come—" one of Brett's feet slipped on the rocks and he fell, missing Sidney's grasp, into the mud. His nostrils flared with the rhythm of his rapid breathing. "So damn close." He pushed himself from the floor and climbed back on the stone stairs and kept pulling at the roots.

Kirsten held her breath as long moments passed. All she could do was watch and wait. A sliver of light slowly appeared where Brett was working.

"I'm through!" Brett said, his breath coming in gasps. Cold air rushed into the tunnel along with a dim shaft of moonlight.

He grasped bunches of roots with each hand and pulled his body through the narrow opening, using his feet for leverage.

"Anyone out there?" Kirsten asked, wondering if a welcoming party would be waiting for them.

"Seems safe at the moment." He reached through the opening and extended his arm to Kirsten. "Come, quickly."

Kirsten stepped to the top rock and steadied herself on Sidney's shoulder, stepping on the tips of her toes as she reached for Brett's outstretched hand. Slowly at first, Brett pulled her through the opening. Outside, she collapsed on the ground, gasping, as the shock of the first gasps of frigid winter air tore at her lungs. The freezing air was sweet after the stale stench of the tunnel.

Brett pulled Sidney through the opening. Brett and Kirsten collapsed on the earth, breathing heavily. Sidney stood motionless, staring at the flames and billowing smoke across the tops of the trees, his lips pressed into a thin, straight gash across his face.

Kirsten pulled herself to her feet and scanned the area. They had emerged in a small clearing encircled by thick shrubs and underbrush, with tall trees beyond. The moon had dropped beyond its zenith, backlighting the top of the forest with a pale, frosty glow. The shrill sounds of sirens surrounded them.

Kirsten shivered at the shock of the cold. The skin on her face was icy. She put her arm around Sidney's shoulders.

"Katrina!" Sidney suddenly pushed her arm away and rushed toward the flames, stumbling over rocks in the darkness.

Brett caught Sidney before he reached the bushes, pinning the younger man's arms back.

He pulled Sidney back to where Kirsten was sitting.

"Stay put, both of you," Brett ordered in a hushed voice. "We still don't know who we're dealing with, or where they might be."

"Leave me alone." Sidney struggled to escape from Brett's grasp. "I'm going to find Katrina."

"Not just yet, Sid," Brett said in a firm tone.

"Sid. Sit down." Slowly, Sidney dropped to the ground. Kirsten placed her arms over his shoulders and hugged with all the comfort she could muster for both of them.

Brett glanced to the rear. "I'm going to take a look." He slid through the thicket of shrubbery, toward the forest. The moon had dropped and the long shadows from the trees seemed to reach out and swallow him up, leaving only empty darkness and the distant sounds of the fire.

As they shivered together, Kirsten could feel Sidney's sorrow. *What had she wrought?* The turbulent events of the past twenty-four hours made her feel as though she had been dropped through a trapdoor into an alternative universe. Her quest had brought the CIA down on Sidney, perhaps destroyed his life, and had nearly killed them all. And what about Katrina? She put her thoughts aside, not wanting to consider the worst that might have happened.

"Sid?" she asked finally.

Sidney sat in silence, his face turned toward the flames in the sky.

"It's going to be okay, Sid," she said, praying she was right.

Five minutes passed, then ten more. Kirsten fought the cold. They couldn't last much longer. *Where was Brett?* They needed a fallback plan in case something had happened to him. But what?

Sidney pulled away, his face twisted in pain, and started to stand. "I'm not waiting any longer. I'm going to the house."

"Shhhh…" Kirsten clamped a hand over Sidney's mouth. She listened to the quiet of the forest, thinking she heard movement.

Moments later, Brett pushed through the bushes, carrying a flashlight, thermos, and an armload of blankets. He dropped the blankets on Kirsten's lap. "The fire captain is sending paramedics. Just hold on a bit longer."

"The main house…?" Sidney asked.

Brett glanced between Kirsten and Sidney. "The house and the computer lab are gone, leveled." His voice was hollow; his words hung in the darkness.

Sidney sucked in a quick, ragged breath. "Katrina?" he whispered.

Brett stared at Sidney, and then averted his eyes. "No signs of anyone, Sid. I'm sorry."

Kirsten watched Sidney's face turn ashen with certain understanding. She could imagine Katrina trapped in the burning house, unbearable heat tearing at her skin, choking from the thick, dark smoke. She felt her own tears well up inside of her.

Sidney howled – a raging, tortured voice that bellowed from his chest and filled the woods. He slumped to the snow and pounded his head into his hands, his body lurching with anguish. "I don't understand, I don't understand . . . ."

Kirsten wrapped blankets around Sidney's shoulders, feeling the convulsions wracking his body as if they were her own. She snuck a hand under the blanket to Sidney's arm. "Sid, this is my doing. I'm sorry."

He pushed her away, then wrenched a rock from the snow and flung it into the bushes. "She was by best friend – and I haven't had many of those. She was only trying to help me. She didn't deserve this." His voice trailed off, leaving only the sounds of the fire in the distance.

Kirsten looked up as Brett tucked blankets around her and placed a cup of hot coffee in her hand. "The other agent?" she asked quietly, searching his eyes for any sign of good news.

He blew out a ragged breath. "No."

A searing pain tore at her chest. Where did it stop? "Whoever followed me did this."

"Don't do that to yourself," Brett answered. "There's much more going on here than we know about."

"I'm not doing anything to myself." Kirsten's throat tightened. If it hadn't been for her, Sidney would not have been traced to Zurich. There would have been no firebombing. She had had a dream, but now her plan was over, with senseless

death and destruction seared in her memory forever. "I'm responsible."

Sidney raised his head in a slow jerking
motion. His eyes were swollen and red like
embers. "No you're not."

Kirsten could see an anger in Sidney's face she
hadn't seen before.

"They're going to pay," he said, speaking
through clenched teeth.

Kirsten was suddenly alert. "Who's going to
pay, Sid?"

His eyes hardened. "The ones who did this to
Katrina. The same ones who got my friends."

"Sid, let's let the authorities take care of—"

He swirled and faced her, is anger now filling
his eyes. "No—I'm going to take care of this."

"We don't have a way to—"

"I have an idea."

Kirsten waited.

Sidney's eyes glinted behind his glasses.
"Backflash."

Kirsten glanced toward the computer lab.
"Your computers. They're gone."

"My work is saved in a safe place and can be
retrieved." Sidney pulled the blankets tighter
around his neck. "But there's a catch."

"What's that?" Kirsten asked.

"You have to get me inside the Orion
Project."

"Won't fly." Brett checked his watch then
pulled his phone from his jacket pocket.

"What are you doing?" Kirsten asked.

"Calling the Paris agents for pickup. We have a plane to catch."

"Can you give me a moment?" she asked.

"For what? To consider how to give Sidney carte blanche to our country's cyber defense systems?"

Her eyes met his. "Brett. One minute."

He lowered the phone.

"Thank you," she said, then turned to Sidney. "Backflash only works as a response to an incoming attack. What makes you think they're going to attack the Orion Project?"

"We're going to set it up so that New Tomorrow will be salivating to strike the Orion Project. But they won't know what's in store for them."

"I'm not following you."

"Simple," Sidney said. "The key is Orion 6."

"Time's up," Brett said, raising his phone.

"Damn it, Brett, will you wait?" Kirsten said.

It took Kirsten a moment to understand what Sidney was saying. *Of course.* He had said the terrorists were fearful of Orion 6. "Sid, do you mean to use their fear of Orion 6 against them?"

"Bingo," he said.

Kirsten hesitated. "But how?"

"That little detail of striking that chord of fear is up to you."

Brett raised his phone. "I'm making that call—"

"Shut the hell up!" she said. "I'm thinking." She thought through some scenarios, discarding them all. Then, in a flash, a powerful but simple idea, a ruse, hit her. *But would it work?*

She motioned to Brett's phone. "I need to make a call."

"You know that's out of the question," he answered.

"Give me the phone, Brett," she said, not trying to hide the edge in her voice.

"Forget this nonsense. I'm taking Sidney – and you - in."

"Brett, has it occurred to you that someone out there is afraid Sidney may be able to provide a way out of this terrorist mess and was trying to stop him?"

He shook his head. "You're operating on suppositions and –"

"Let me give your CIA pea-brain the big picture here" she said, her face now inches from his. "Orion 6 is dead, a joke. The U.S. has no defenses against more terrorist attacks. If someone does not stop those attacks, our country is going to become embroiled in a world-wide conflict that could last for years. Any – *any* plan that offers the possibility of stopping those attacks must be executed. Sidney is offering the only play in town, and we have to take it."

"Let me get this straight," Brett said. "You want to propose opening up the U.S. for a terrorist attack so you two can spring some kind of counterattack?"

"Yes — and I'll have the backing of Homeland Security Secretary Dustin Clayton behind it,"

Kirsten said, aware she was way over her head in her bluff.

Brett shook his head. "You're insane."

Kirsten stuck out her hand once again. "Give me the goddamn phone and we'll find out."

Bright lights swung through the trees. Sounds of an engine and tires crunching through the snow grew closer, then stopped. Two doors opened, and then slammed closed.

Kirsten glanced over her shoulder toward the sound, then back to Brett. "Katrina is dead. Your friend is dead. Many more will die unless somebody makes the tough decisions and stops this. Let me make the call. If I'm turned down, you're out nothing."

"And if you're not turned down?"

The sounds of running boots cracking the undergrowth came closer.

Kirsten leaned closer to Brett. "Sidney did some research. I know all about the loss of your team in Operation Blackbird. I can imagine the pain you must feel every day of your life."

Brett stared at her in silence.

She took a deep breath. "Brett, unless somebody does something, we're going to be at war around the globe in two days. We don't get many chances like this life to make things right."

Kirsten held her breath and studied him. "What do you say? Want to set the Blackbird record back to even?"

CHAPTER 34

"**M**r. Secretary!"

Clayton disregarded the anxious voice and brushed past blurred faces in the busy corridor of the 747, ignoring greetings and attempted conversation.

Ron Comber stood in the middle of the passageway, blocking Clayton's path. "Sir, you have a flash traffic priority call coming in through FEMA."

Clayton started to push past the chief of staff. Leave it to FEMA, the Federal Emergency Management Agency that could find any high-ranking government official at any time, to track him down at this moment. "Not now."

Comber thrust the phone in Clayton's path. "I think you'd better take this one."

The line clicked several times, followed by a distant, urgent voice: "Sir, it's —" the line hissed and crackled.

He steadied himself from the sound of a voice he had never expected to hear again. The name caught in his throat for a moment. "Kirsten?"

"Yes, sir."

Clayton fought his confusion, searching for words. "This can't be you."

"I'm a bit shaken up, but it's me." The voice was hollow and distant, as though it were coming from a deep well.

"I heard—"

"I can imagine—"

"—that you—"

"*Please* listen, sir."

"Tell me what happ—"

"We haven't much time. I have a plan that may thwart the terrorists."

Clayton pulled in a long breath and exhaled slowly. It had been a long day.

"Ready, sir?"

"I'm listening."

"There's some things we need to do, all of which necessitate that you trust me. Some of these may be difficult. . . ."

CHAPTER 35

Clayton absently ran his forefinger over the cut on his cheek that was the result of a hasty shave and shower following the unplanned early landing of the Doomsday plane. "I hope to God you know what you're doing on this one," President Anston had said after agreeing to return the plane to Washington.

Clayton laid his head against the soft cool leather of his office chair, eyes lodged, unblinking, on the uniform rows of tiles marching across the ceiling. "That goes for both of us, Mr. President," he said to himself.

"Mr. Secretary?" Maureen Connolly stood in the doorway to the office, dressed in a fresh set of winter Air Force blues. "Newswoman Miss Carson to see you."

Sheila Carson stepped into the office, smartly dressed in a matching skirt and jacket with a turtle neck sweater underneath, and strode toward Clayton wearing her normal look of confidence.

"Thank you for coming so quickly, Sheila," Clayton said, extending his hand. He gestured toward a chair at the polished conference table set with a tray of croissants, coffee and tea. "Coffee?"

She glanced at her watch as she sat across from him. "At this early hour I'm afraid I'm going to need several of those, sir - black, please." her voice still heavy.

"Four a.m. *is* a bit early, I know, even for you high achievers," he said, passing her a cup of coffee. "We'll see if I can make it worth your while."

Sheila blew on the mist rising from the coffee, her eyes signaling sudden interest. "Just so I get my interview recorder and iPhone back on the way out, Mr. Secretary."

"In due time. For now, Orion Project communications are locked down. Phones, messaging, satellite transmissions, everything. And as for this meeting, until I say so, it never happened."

The cup stopped halfway to her lips, her expression feigning fear. "Trapped, am I?"

"If you and I see eye to eye," Clayton said, studying her closely, "you'll be the last person to leave this facility in the next twenty-four hours."

"And on the oft chance you and I don't see eye to eye?"

"We have sleeping facilities and a 24/7 commissary. You'll be quite comfortable."

"You're serious," she said, her manner suddenly stiff and formal.

"As I said, we're locked down."

She pursed her lips as if preparing for an attack. "Is this some kind of spiteful gag on the press for last night's Hackworth piece?"

"Nothing as insignificant as that." His tone was polite but serious.

"Really?" she said, raising a groomed eyebrow. "My, this all sounds so mysterious and controversial."

"When," he asked, "have you avoided controversy?"

"You have a point there." Sheila's eyes studied him.

Clayton folded his hands on the table, gauging the newswoman sitting across from him. *Was she up for the journey he was about to propose?* He leaned toward her.

"How would you like the story of a lifetime?"

She tilted her head, eyebrows cocked, while she silently mouthed his statement, as if questioning its sincerity. "In return for . . . what, exactly?"

Clayton hesitated. He had been over Kirsten's plan again and again in his mind. Many actions had to fall perfectly into place like interlocking pieces of a complex puzzle. Even then, any chance of success depended on the terrorists taking the bait.

The person he had selected to bait the hook was sitting in front of him. He studied Carson for a moment and then plunged ahead. "To answer your question, in return for leaking a story on how we plan to defeat the next wave of terrorist attacks with a cyber defense that doesn't exist."

"'A cyber defense that doesn't exist.' My, my," Sheila said, a look of mock puzzlement forming on her face. "Are you suggesting I engage in some form of disinformation?"

"You might call it that."

"Are you asking me to compromise my professionalism, Mr. Secretary?"

"Actually, I thought I was playing to your strengths."

She throated a quiet chuckle. "You *are* in a charming mood, if I may say so, sir." Sheila placed her hands on the table and tapped her manicured fingernails on the surface with the beat of a slow marching drum. "What else?"

"That's it."

And what is my 'story of a lifetime?'"

"The inside tale – with appropriate editing of top secret material, of course - of how we took the terrorists down. Once this is all over."

"And if you fail to take them down?"

"Then you will have other stories to cover, none of them as pleasant, I'm afraid."

Sheila's face became an unreadable mask for several long moments as if she were undecided or weighing the odds. Finally, she said, "Fair enough." She glanced around the room. "Where is my confidentiality agreement? Security disclosures? Communication guidelines? You have things for me to sign?"

Clayton shook his head. "This is a private agreement that begins and ends with me and you. Verbally."

"And how do we communicate verbally – and in this case - covertly?"

"I'll be covering that with you. Are you in?"

Carson beamed a full smile. "Mr. Secretary, I wouldn't miss this opportunity for all the scotch in Ireland."

Clayton knew he was taking a chance that Carson's extraordinary passion to advance her career offered a risk, albeit one that he had already carefully considered. That same desire would also curtail her actions if he played his cards right. "You understand that you play by my script and my script only, not one you conjure up to advance your personal cause or dream up over a couple of drinks."

"Understood, Mr. Secretary."

"One rogue action from you and I will make absolutely certain no media outlet will touch you again."

"Glad to have that out of the way," she said, her eyes flashing. "So, since we have an accommodation and are now, figuratively speaking of course, in bed together, may I perhaps address you by the more familiar 'Dusty'?"

"In the privacy of this room, Sheila, you may call me whatever you like, as long as you follow the rules."

Carson flashed a broad smile, leaned into her chair and crossed her legs, then threw an arm over the back of the seat, pressing her breasts tightly against her knit sweater.

"Okay, Dusty. Do what you have to do. I'm all yours."

CHAPTER 36

The pulsating hum brought Kirsten out of a troubled slumber. Her eyes blinked open and, heavy with fatigue, closed again. She willed her hands to move. Her fingers slid over a curved, cool, smooth surface. The hum became more distinct, more like a vibration. She still had the scent of smoke from the fire in her nostrils but she noticed something else, the smell of leather.

Where am I?

Slowly, the memories seeped into her consciousness: The terrifying sound and heat of the fire. Black smoke choking the air from her lungs. The wretched stench and darkness of the wet, bone-chilling tunnel. The call to Clayton, then the rush to the airport to board the government jet. A hurried takeoff in the predawn darkness.

Her eyes opened again. *She was on her way to the United States.*

She pushed erect in the seat and pushed up the blind covering the window. Sharp rays of morning sun punctuated a gray curtain of clouds, sending light into the aircraft. She ran her hands over the sweat suit the female pilot had loaned her. She touched her fingers to her face. The medics had helped wash off the mud from the tunnel, but her skin was dry and chapped from the cold, her hands cracked and swollen.

A familiar voice brought her out of her thoughts. "You okay?"

Kirsten turned toward the sound. Brett was leaning across the aisle, studying her with concerned eyes.

"I'm fine." She winced at the sight of his bandaged arm and the reddened skin from the heat burns on his face. "What about you?"

"I'll live."

Kirsten studied the pained look on Brett's face for a moment and turned away. Katrina Mendollfson and agent Rick Fliorina were no longer among the living. She, Brett and Sidney were the lucky ones. *Where was Sidney?* She twisted in her seat and scanned the cabin. Sidney was heads down over a laptop computer, pencil tucked behind his ear. His face was tight, lips stretched taut until they were almost white. The two agents who had arrived with the aircraft occupied a pair of seats beyond him. One shot a curious glance in her direction. She wondered for a moment if, in Sidney's grief over the loss of Katrina, he had overreached on how he might be able to help against the terrorists. She pushed the thoughts aside. Sidney was their only hope. At the moment she needed some answers from Brett or her plan might be destroyed.

She turned her attention to Brett. "What happened back there, in Zurich?

"Someone was on to Sidney, or you. We found out two hours before I arrived at the house that a hit squad was on his tail."

"Why a hit on Sidney?"

"I was hoping you might be able to tell me."

"Level with me."

"I've told you everything I know."

Kirsten tried to put aside her frustration with Brett and focus on her plan. "I need your help."

"What kind of help?"

"There's a leak inside the Orion Project, someone who will blow the whistle on our plan the minute he gets wind of it."

"How do you know?"

"Just look at the news reports. They know every glitch, every hiccup, in Orion 6. I need you to find him, or her, and stop the leak."

Brett shook his head. "I'm in a tough position already."

"I know. But if this person isn't stopped, he could sabotage everything to the point where nothing Sidney or I do matters."

"You don't have to deal with the deputy chief of staff of the CIA."

"Look, Clayton has placed everything on the line. He overruled the CIA director to re-route this plane and arranged twenty-four hours of amnesty so Sidney can work at the Orion Project."

"That's admirable. But he's a cabinet secretary and I'm an on-the-outs CIA agent." Brett pressed his face close to Kirsten. "Tell me something. Regardless of what Secretary Clayton has done, do you really think Orion technology director Zachary Ishmel is going to stand aside as you swoop into the cyber center, disrupt his operation, and give a wanted cyber criminal carte blanche access to the systems of the Orion Project?"

Kirsten studied the back of the seat in front of her. She knew her plans would send Ishmel into a fury, in spite of Clayton's directions. "I'll take care of Ishmel. You take care of finding the saboteur."

Brett turned toward the window in silence. A few moments later he faced Kirsten and blew out a long breath. "You're bad for my health, but count me in."

"Thanks." For the first time in many months Kirsten smiled at her former lover and meant it. He still conveyed the appeal he always had. But that was then and this was now. Time for business.

She hooked a thumb toward the back of the plane. "Let's see what Sidney is up to."

CHAPTER 37

Kirsten and Brett slid into the two seats across from where Sidney was working. Kirsten waited, not wanting to interrupt.

Sidney glanced up but kept his attention on the computer screen.

She noted that the laptop Sidney was working on was labeled FOR CIA USE ONLY. She glanced at the two agents facing them from across the row and smiled. Both returned blank, sullen stares. "Nice fellows you work with," she said to Brett, keeping her tone low.

Brett shook his head. "Tell me you wouldn't be upset if the guy you were assigned to arrest was snatched away from you, given a mysterious reprieve, carte blanche on his actions, and a private jet trip to Washington."

"You have a point."

"Let's talk," Kirsten said to Sidney. She rose and tilted her head toward the empty area in the front of the aircraft where she and Brett had been sitting. She didn't need to satisfy the agents' thirst for information.

"What do you have?" Kirsten asked Sidney once the three of them had taken seats around a small circular table at the front of the plane.

"The San Francisco blackout is pretty much what I thought," Sidney said. "Bombs purchased through eTerror triggered through trap doors."

"Beg your pardon?" Brett asked.

Kirsten glanced at Brett and then at Sidney. "Sid, you may need to translate for our non-tech associate."

Sidney's expression flickered with irritation for a moment. "The real danger in outsourcing information technology tasks is not loss of jobs. It's loss of security. Why? You don't know *who* is actually doing the outsourced work. Hundreds of millions of lines of computer source code have been outsourced and sub-sub-contracted. Much of the work is performed in Malaysia, India, Russia, and former eastern bloc countries."

"So we lose control of what is actually being done with that computer code?" Kirsten said.

"Correct," said Sidney. "Plus, these are countries with significant sections of their population holding strong hatred of the U.S., thus increasing the risk of subterfuge."

Brett nodded. "So what happens?"

Sidney blew out a long breath. "Software in the U.S. has been found to contain hidden 'trap doors' inserted by those with questionable motives that allow access by anyone holding the key. In addition, some systems have hidden code to cause system malfunction, known as 'logic bombs' that can be triggered through the trap door, resulting in system failure. The power and communications blackouts in San Francisco were caused by someone entering mainframe systems through the Internet, accessing a trap door, and setting off a bomb, causing system failure." Sidney snapped his fingers. "Bingo, the lights go out and the dial tones go silent."

"And who has the keys?" Brett asked.

"Most keys historically remained with their creator – until a market developed for their distribution."

"Let me explain," Kirsten said. "This is where eTerror comes in. ETerror.com is an online auction bazaar in cyberspace for cyberterrorism. Their offerings include trap doors, time bombs, attack scripts, whatever the terrorist needs to create cyber mayhem. All sold to the highest bidder."

"And the problem is not limited to power and communications systems," Sidney added. "Groups like New Tomorrow – given enough funding – can invade and disrupt air traffic control systems, military defense systems, conceivably just about anything they want. Does take some strong technical savvy, however, which few people have."

"And distribution of these weapons…?" Brett asked.

"Pretty simple," Sidney said. "A combination of skilled tech freelancers, probe farms, bot networks for power and privacy."

"Bot networks? Probe farms? Slow down, you two." Brett pulled a pad of paper from a cabinet by the table and pushed it in front of Sidney. "Draw me a picture."

Kirsten read the look of frustration on Sidney's face.

"I said I'd help you," Brett said to Kirsten. "I need to know what I'm dealing with."

Sidney squared the pad in front of him. He drew three boxes on the sheet, the first labeled "Payloads," the second "Access," and the third "Delivery," and connected the first to the second and the second to the third with arrows. "The terrorists' destruction machine consists of three pieces." He tapped the column labeled "Payloads." "This is what we've been talking about so far."

Sidney tapped a finger on the column labeled "Access". "Kirsten is talking about the access to computer networks that allows attacks to take place. Today's networks are protected by arrays of firewalls, intrusion detection systems, and a host of other defensive means—"

"As in Orion 6?" Brett interjected.

"Yep. With today's defensive tools that actually work, getting to the access point, the trap door, is increasingly difficult. My hunch is that

New Tomorrow buys access to large groupings of computers, or farms, which do nothing but probe personal, government and business computer networks, evaluating defenses and searching for openings. Sites with detected vulnerabilities that meet the terrorists' profile targets are ranked according to desirability and provided for a price. This is similar to methods used to steal credit card information from banks, identity theft, that sort of thing." Sidney looked up at Brett. "With me so far?"

"This smacks of a big business," Brett said.

Kirsten shook her head. "Billions and growing faster than online pornography."

"How does New Tomorrow pay for all of this?" Brett asked.

"Support from Iran, North Korea, other rogue states, terrorist groups, and who knows," Sidney said.

The pitch of the engines changed and the plane started its descent. The darkness had started to fade, with rays of sunshine coming over the horizon behind them. Sidney tapped "Delivery." "Once the payloads and the sites to be attacked are identified, the question becomes one of carrying off the attack without being identified. New Tomorrow may use its own resources if time is critical, or line up robot, or bot, networks, which are arrays of interconnected personal computers that have been compromised for this purpose, almost all without the owner's knowledge. Current estimates place the number of robot networks worldwide at 50,000 or more. The size of these captured, or zombie, networks varies widely. I've seen evidence of bot farms containing more than 400,000 machines. There is a huge and rapidly growing black market for use of such networks."

"So that's the New Tomorrow strategy?" Brett asked. "Won't the Orion Project or other defenses turn the tide at some point?"

"We believe their attacks are most likely prelude rather than end game," Kirsten said.

Brett shifted in his seat. "Prelude to what?"

"Once the U.S. has been softened up by New Tomorrow's strikes," Kirsten answered, "many of our communications, power, transportation, and some key military systems will be compromised, some seriously. With the country in disarray, attacks with chemical, biological, perhaps even nuclear weapons will become much easier for terrorist groups."

"So the question," Brett said, "is 'who is New Tomorrow?'"

Sidney shook his head. "Don't know, and for now, don't need to know. Backflash, if it works, will render their assault farms, wherever they are, and every system in their internal networks inoperable."

"*Will* Backflash work?" Brett asked.

"We'll find out. It's highly experimental."

"And what if it runs amuck?"

"There will be collateral damage in areas of the web. It's a chance that has to be taken."

Kirsten asked Sidney, "Once we reach the Orion Project, how much time will you need to have Backflash ready for use?"

Sidney laughed, almost a child's chuckle, only deeper. "How good do you want your chances that it will work?" I can have Backflash ready in six - eight hours, but place the odds of success at less than 20%; I presume you want to aim for the 50%-plus success probability."

Kirsten nodded. "Higher than that. Much higher."

"Ten hours uninterrupted may give you 60-70%," Sidney said. "No way can I offer you more than that. And even then, it may go haywire. Then we're dealing with unintended consequences. New ball game."

"Can't have that," Kirsten said, shaking her head.

Sidney stared at his hands for several moments, as if sorting through the Backflash code in his mind, then said, "Twelve hours, full access, uninterrupted. Even then, there are risks. Huge risks."

Kirsten had mentally gone through the schedule from their moment of arrival until the time they needed to start their ruse prior to the president's speech. They didn't have twelve hours, eight tops. She would just do whatever she had to do to get Sidney the resources he needed. They would launch when they had to and pray Backflash was ready enough.

Brett glanced at Kirsten and shook his head. "You're hoping to destroy an unknown, unseen enemy with an unfinished, untested system that may wreak havoc with other computer systems across the country? And on top of that you expect the terrorists to come to you?"

"In a nutshell," she said. "Problem with that?"

"Jesus," Brett said, shaking his head.

The pilot announced their final approach into Langley and turned on the seat belt signs. "Stow your gear and tighten up, everyone. It's going to be bumpy."

Sidney passed a handwritten sheet to Kirsten. "This details the computing resources I'll need to support our plan. Now if you'll excuse me, I need to put some serious effort into our surprise for the terrorists." Sidney tucked the laptop under his arm and retreated to his seat in the back.

The aircraft angled into a sharp curve as a storm of hailstones banged against the windows. Kirsten studied the sheet Sidney had given her, considering what lay ahead when they reach the Orion Project. Skirmishes and power plays with Ishmel's staff over Sidney, some of them ugly, were in the cards. She knew she had to mentally gird for war.

A severe bump shot the plane's left wing up sharply, sending the aircraft downward to the right. Brett's hand grasped Kirsten's arm, releasing her from her thoughts. As she looked at the burns on his face, it occurred her that the chance they were about to have to best the terrorists, to do something for their country, was due to the person sitting next to her. "Brett?"

"Yes?"

"No matter what happens, I want you to know you did the right thing."

"What right thing?"

"Letting me make that call to Clayton."

He turned his head toward the window as the plane's nose pitched down in final descent. "I guess we'll see, won't we?"

CHAPTER 38

Kirsten felt a hush roll through the Orion Project cyber center as she, Sidney and Brett Logan cleared security and rushed down the center aisle toward the control center where she had had her encounter with Zachary Ishmel just days earlier.

Row by row, like toppling dominoes, work ceased; conversations between computer technicians, communications specialists, and managers stopped in mid-sentence. Heads turned in their direction. Some stood at their desks to get a better look. Kirsten saw brows furrowed with concern and eyes filled with questions.

She glanced at Sidney. His eyes glinted as he scanned the rows of computer workstations and the massive wall displays. He had the look reserved for a man with newly acquired wealth assessing the array of gleaming chasses displayed in a Ferrari showroom. "This should do quite nicely," he said under his breath.

Kirsten spoke to Brett in a low tone out of the side of her mouth. "I want you to stay close to me, scan the audience periodically, say nothing unless I speak to you, and above all, look official. Hang your CIA identification on your jacket breast pocket, and –" she scooped a mini-headset with microphone from an empty desk as they passed and handed to Brett "—wear this. Understood?"

Brett donned the headset and nodded. "Understood."

Zachary Ishmel had not been in his office to meet them as promised on arrival, but Kirsten had not been surprised. She scanned the large room and caught sight of him at the base of the main aisle with his back to her. Testing director Mario, project director Karl Breskin and several others flanked Ishmel on either side.

The men were bunched around a bank of computer screens, heads down, in animated discussion. Looming above them, indicators on an intelligence display flashed an array of multicolored lights indicating cyber attack activity across a map of the U.S. In contrast, the Orion 6 implementation screens lay quiet and dark.

Kirsten girded herself for the confrontation with Ishmel. Her telephone conversations with Clayton over the Atlantic had prepared her for an unwelcome reception. According to Clayton,

Ishmel had characterized her plan as "a dangerous, ill-conceived stab in the dark, a technological train wreck that will jeopardize the Orion Project and irreparably harm Orion 6 progress." Kirsten understood. Clayton's endorsement of her plan was a clear signal that called Ishmel's sagging Orion 6 project into further question. The professional reputation Ishmel had spent a lifetime creating was being threatened, and he would fight her with everything he had. Even with Clayton's support, at this moment she was on her own, one-on-one with Ishmel. She would have to play her cards perfectly.

Kirsten stopped behind the men, motioning Sidney and Brett to stand next to her. "Hello, Zachary," she said in a firm voice.

The group's heads swung toward her in unison. Ishmel's expression showed no intent to hide a look of irritation. Mario wore a twisted scowl while Karl Breskin flashed a tentative smile. The others stared.

"This is Sidney Hirschfield," Kirsten said, motioning to Sidney, "and my security director, CIA senior agent Brett Logan."

Ishmel ignored them both. He removed his empty pipe from his mouth, his eyes dark, and motioned to a small desk and computer terminal several rows over. "Your computing facilities are available, as requested by Secretary Clayton. Now if you'll excuse me, we have important things to tend to." He spoke in a loud, clear tone so all around him could hear.

Kirsten glanced at the computer setup and saw it to be woefully inadequate to meet the resources she needed for Sidney. Ishmel stared at her for a moment more, then turned away. "This equipment won't do, Zachary, and you know it," she said.

Conversations, sounds of movement, the clicking noise of computer keyboards, fell silent in the vast center behind her. Technicians pushed back their chairs and rose to watch the encounter.

Ishmel turned to face her. "I will remind you that this center is my responsibility — the staff of 300 behind you, the computers, the satellite links, the security, everything. We are here for one purpose, to protect the United States of America against attacks by cyber terrorists. Until relieved of that responsibility I will allocate computing resources as I deem necessary." He threw out his chest and lifted his head in a look of superiority. "Now as I said, please step away. We have important work to tend to."

Kirsten knew Ishmel was playing to his audience, publicly demonstrating that she and Sidney were unwelcome intruders in their midst who must be banished. He wanted to humiliate her in front of the Orion Project staff, to rob her of respectability and any chance of the support she would need for her plan to succeed.

She stepped closer to Ishmel, her face inches from his, and kept her voice low and calm. He had raised the stakes to winner take all and she had to up the ante or fold. "We can do this the easy way or the hard way, Zachary. Your choice. One hour ago Secretary Clayton signed Homeland Security Emergency Preparedness Directive 314 giving me 'any and all resources necessary' from the Orion Project for Sidney to do his work. If you persist, I will have agent Logan –" she motioned toward Brett "—go to Secretary Clayton's office to get a copy of that directive and return with his security detail. You and your management team will be officially detained and escorted out of the facility in front of your staff, at which time your authority here – and perhaps your government career – will effectively be over."

The mocking expression on Ishmel's face turned to anger mixed with frustration, and then softened. "It's been a busy time – I may have been a bit hasty in my response. I am certain we can work this out to your satisfaction," he said.

"Good start, Zachary," she said quietly. "Now I want you to smile like you mean it, shake Sidney's hand, and clap him on the back in a public show of welcome."

Ishmel shrugged. "Well, let's not get carried away—"

Without taking her eyes from Ishmel, Kristen motioned to Brett. "Agent Logan, you may proceed as I directed."

Ishmel's shoulders promptly lost their swagger, making him look smaller. "Wait!" he said. "I…uh…uh… I of course welcome all of you!" The members of Ishmel's management team standing behind him shifted uneasily from foot to foot as they watched, some looking away, unable to hide the growing distress spreading over their faces.

"Good start," Kirsten said. "After you welcome Sidney I want you to introduce him to your management team and then make a public announcement to the cyber center."

"An announcement to…?"

"An announcement welcoming the celebrated cyber specialist Sidney Hirschfield, who is to be afforded every courtesy and full access to the resources of the Orion Project during his stay."

Kirsten pointed to a headset sitting on an adjacent desk. "Make it, Zachary," she said.

"I'm going to get you for this," Ishmel said to Kirsten under his breath as he reached for the headset. Better watch your back."

"Keep smiling, Zachary," she said cheerily, then patted him on the back like they had been good friends since college.

Ishmel set his shoulders back, flashed a broad smile and began his announcement: "Attention, your attention, please. We are pleased today – no, we are honored – to have celebrated Internet technologist Sidney Hirschfield working with us. I want each of you to provide Mr. Hirschfield every courtesy as well as full access to the resources of the Orion Project to . . ."

Kirsten let out a long sigh of relief as Ishmel spoke. But an ominous feeling still lurked within; she had not seen the final clash with Zachary Ishmel.

A nudge knocked her out of her thoughts. Brett held up his smartphone. "I've been summoned upstairs to an emergency meeting with the Deputy Director of the CIA," he said in a hushed voice.

She nodded, keeping her eyes on Ishmel. "You're done here—go."

"I may be in need of an emergency directive myself," he said as he turned to leave. "By the way, you didn't tell me about the 'Homeland Security Emergency Preparedness Directive.' What exactly *is* that?"

Kirsten returned an innocent look, like the child denying having dipped into the cookie jar. "I have no idea. Now get to your meeting."

CHAPTER 39

Brett Logan stood silently, waiting, as the door to the conference room slid closed. Because of what happened in Zurich, he knew this was to be a difficult meeting. There was no predicting what Sherman might do.

Nate Sherwin wore a frown as he turned from the windows overlooking the Orion cyber center. He motioned to a leather chair at the conference table. "Please, have a seat."

"I'd rather stand, thank you."

"Suit yourself." Sherwin slid into a chair and crossed his legs, appraising Brett. "You should know the director holds you personally responsible for the avoidable loss of lives in Zurich."

Brett had thought about agent Rick Fliorina many times since the fire, and what he could have done differently. He had retraced his actions over and over in his mind, trying to find that single step, that key decision he could correct and turn everything back, but he always came up empty.

"What do you have to say for yourself?" Sherwin asked.

How about go fuck yourself?

"Whose clever idea was it," Sherwin continued, ignoring Brett's silence, "to screw up his orders and let a prisoner make a personal phone call halfway around the globe to thwart the arrest of a suspected terrorist?"

Brett maintained his silence.

"You've created a hell of a mess for yourself – for everyone," Sherman said. "Ever consider that?"

"Yes." *And much more*, Brett thought. He fought back the distaste he felt for Sherwin that threatened to cloud his objectivity, only to realize he had lost any hope of objectivity in a shrub-encircled clearing outside Zurich, ten hours earlier and thousands of miles away. He had committed.

Sherwin stood and walked toward Brett, closing the distance between the two men until he they were a foot apart. "You have some temporary protection provided by Clayton but essentially have less than twenty-four hours as a free man. After that, it's going to be a long while before you see sunshine."

Brett felt a growing urge to take out Sherwin's windpipe with one chop and hope for the best with a plea of self-defense, but rational thought got the best of him.

"Tell you what. You don't deserve it," Sherwin said, "but I'm going to make you a deal."

Nerve ends prickled on the back of Brett's neck. Sherwin had the power to do as he pleased. A deal meant something was up. Something that couldn't be good. Brett felt his phone page again. "What kind of deal?"

"The Lockhart woman's foolhardy scheme cannot be allowed to succeed."

"Her scheme is not my affair."

"You made it your affair in Zurich when you participated in the death of agent Fliorina. Your assignment then was to bring in Sidney, and you failed. Your assignment now is to stop her. Pull that off and I'll see how I can make things easier for you."

Brett felt a tug of suspicion. Kirsten's plan held the only hope in sight to deter the terrorists. "Why would you want to stop—"

"Let's just say some powerful people have plans they don't want derailed."

Brett couldn't believe what he was hearing, but he was beginning to get the bigger picture: the terrorist attacks weren't the major focus. The response from the U.S. was what mattered. He made no effort to repress his anger. "Yours is the kind of help I don't need, Sherwin."

The security officer was at the door. "Sir, your time is up."

"Listen, Brett," Sherwin said, his voice suddenly conciliatory. "This Lockhart woman's got you between the legs, I understand that. Been there myself. But I'm telling you, you're up to your neck in dog shit on this. I'm trying to help you dig out of it. For your own survival, put an end to her crazy goose chase, her hopeless charade, and save yourself twenty years of hell."

Sherwin patted Brett on the shoulder and was gone.

CHAPTER 40

Dustin Clayton stood quietly as the door to the Oval Office closed behind him, waiting. President Anston was at his desk, signing documents.

President Anston looked up with a smile. "Good to see you, Dusty." He pointed to a chair. "Make yourself comfortable. This meeting could get bumpy."

Clayton nodded and took seat.

"The Sheila Carson piece this morning on the power of your Orion 6 defense was impressive," Anston said with a knowing smile. "Even had me believing it, and I know better."

"There's none better at creating illusions than Sheila."

Anston managed a bit of a smile. "I must say I admire the beauty of the false illusion created by the plan, and the trap it so neatly sets."

"We still have to get the terrorists to take the bait. Plus, we do have one major vulnerability."

Anston raised an eyebrow. "That being?"

"There can't be a leak on this. We are doing everything possible to keep the details of Kirsten Lockhart's plan secret. Exposure would derail the entire counterattack plan.

Anston looked at his watch. "Rutledge and Ibbs will be here momentarily to get their marching orders. Anything you need from me before they arrive?"

"No, sir."

Anston patted a document on the center of his desk. "I pulled in every chit I had with the pacifist element to stop this damn Hackworth resolution, but when the votes were counted, it wasn't enough."

"I'm certain you did, sir."

Anston poured hot tea from the pot and studied the steam rising from the cup. "You know, Dusty, our cherished political party has changed since that wave of kids was swept into office in the mid-term elections. The freshman crop Hackworth has on his side has no idea of the carnage they are triggering with Hydra. They've been sold a bill of goods. Christ, they probably think this whole Hackworth resolution is some sort of global *Call of Duty* video game."

Clayton studied the president. Anston was a courageous man by nature, a born politician who had maneuvered with the wind at his back all his life. Now the fair winds had turned to an ugly storm. "Any chance for a veto?"

Anston gave a half-laugh. "Wouldn't last a New York minute before being overturned. Besides, how would *that* look in the press? No, I only managed one break, a compromise hammered into the resolution. I still give the final order. And that, my friend, is my only ace in the hole, if I have one."

Clayton hesitated, formulating his thoughts. "Hackworth, Rutledge and Ibbs are all in this together, aren't they?"

"Like blood brothers."

"Delay is their enemy at this point. I can only encourage you to forestall the start of Hydra as long as you can, sir."

"Agreed." Anston tapped the Hackworth resolution with his forefinger. "Once Rutledge has the go-ahead, how much time before Hydra starts?"

Clayton thought back to his days as head of the military. "Depends on how closely our teams are positioned to their targets."

"What's your best estimate?"

"Probably by this evening. And most of the attacks will be over twenty-four hours after that."

"And there you will have it. William Anston, peace-loving leader of the free world, will deliver a State of the Union address this evening in the hallowed halls of our Congress explaining how mass execution of the leaders of every major terrorist organization on earth is going to solve a cyber terrorist problem at home that we can't fix ourselves." He stared at Clayton. "How will that look in the history books?"

The door to the Oval Office opened. Ron Comber stepped aside, allowing Admiral Rutledge and Stuart Ibbs to enter. Neither spoke as they took chairs opposite the president.

Clayton watched but did not acknowledge the two men. As a result of their luncheon, his relationship with them had changed. He would never see them through the same eyes again.

Comber remained in the doorway. "Mr. President, the NATO delegation has landed at Andrews and will be here shortly."

Anston nodded. "Let me know as soon as they arrive."

The president scanned the three faces before him. "Before I sign this resolution, I want every last avenue of hope for alternative action discussed one final time." He flashed a riveting stare at the director of national security. "Stuart?"

"I see no other course. It's clear we must proceed immediately with Operation Hydra, Mr. President."

Admiral Rutledge looked at Clayton for the first time since entering. "I'd like to know what's behind this media attention on Orion 6."

"Just reporting progress," Clayton said with a shrug, returning a blank stare.

"This wouldn't be a scheme to attempt to derail Hydra at the last minute, would it?"

Anston shot Rutledge a sharp look. "Let's stay on track, Admiral. What else?"

The Chairman of the Joint chiefs straightened in his chair. "Our teams are moving toward final position. We are prepared to commence Operation Hydra an hour before your State of the Union address."

"And what about retaliation?" Anston said.

"One of the benefits of Operation Hydra's fast-strike strategy, Mr. President," Ibbs said, "is to destroy the enemy's capability to fight."

"Do you two really believe that B.S.?" Anston asked, glancing between Ibbs and Rutledge.

Rutledge stirred. "Certainly there will be attempts to disrupt our command and control capabilities. I'll be onboard Kneecap to ensure continuous worldwide communications across the military. Our forces will be on full worldwide alert, ready to take immediate retaliatory action against anyone who chooses to exhibit provocative action. This business will all be over in less than forty-eight hours, Mr. President."

Clayton studied Rutledge when he heard the word Kneecap. It would of course make sense for the head of America's military to be in the flying command post during Operation Hydra, but the need to do so left him cold.

"I suppose you and your cohort Hackworth are aware that we will have exactly zero support from our allies on this Hydra exercise, a point our friends from NATO are going to drive home to me as soon as they arrive here?"

"Some things worth doing do not always appear so, Mr. President," Ibbs said.

"Cute, director. You should use that to explain Hydra's consequences to the American people and see how you do."

Ibbs shifted in his chair and made a pretense of muffling a short cough.

Anston eyed Rutledge as he slid the Hackworth resolution in front of him. "Okay, run how this works by me one more time."

Rutledge shot a glance at his watch before answering. "As you know, Mr. President, Operation Hydra is based on the principle that 'The head goes and the body follows.' Phase one consists of rapid, forceful removal of leaders, suspected leaders, and key supporters of terrorism, worldwide, carried out by our worldwide fleet of drones, supported in a coordinated effort by the CIA and our Special Ops teams, together with full use of our forces already positioned overseas. We have run exercises on similar actions for several years. In phase two, the disorientation, fear, and retrenchment from phase one allows the infusion of operatives into terrorist groups to gather intelligence, intimidate, and eliminate further as needed. Phase three is the public relations misinformation campaign to place the operation in the best light."

"God help us," Anston said through a long breath.

Ibbs leaned forward in his chair, his eyes brightening. "And then there is always Hydra 2—"

Anston pointed a long finger in Ibbs' direction. "Don't push me, Stuart."

Ibbs glanced at Rutledge and eased back into his seat.

"I don't have to remind you we didn't start this, Mr. President," Rutledge said.

Anston ignored the comment and focused on Clayton. "Anything to add, Dusty?" he asked, reaching for a pen.

Clayton shook his head. Unless the Orion 6 deception prevailed, war would soon be the order of the day. "My dissent has been registered, Mr. President."

Anston slid the Hackworth resolution in front of him, affixed his signature, then stared at the document in silence.

After a period of silence, Rutledge cleared his throat. "Do I have immediate authorization to proceed, sir?"

The president kept his eyes on the document for a few lingering moments, then looked up. He leveled his presidential pen at Rutledge. "You start any action, and I mean *any,* before I give the word, I'll have every last stripe and star stripped from your sleeves before sun up. Got that?"

Rutledge returned the president's admonishment with a steely stare. "Yes, sir."

"That's all, then, gentlemen," Anston said.

America's military chief rose from his chair and straightened his uniform. "Mr. President," he said with a sharp nod, then strode toward the door.

Anston waved a motion of dismissal toward Ibbs without looking at the director's face.

Clayton rose and followed. As he reached the door, he noticed Anston had swung his chair around and was staring out the window. The nation was now closer to overt acts of aggression the outcome of which no one, including the President, could predict. All that was clear was that Anston would carry the burden for what happened over the next forty-eight hours, whatever the outcome would be, for years to come.

CHAPTER 41

Still reeling from the confrontation with Sherwin, Brett Logan pulled up a chair next to Kirsten and Sidney, who were huddled around Sidney's workstations. "I came as soon as I got your message. What do you have?"

"It's more what we don't have," Kirsten said in a quiet voice. "We're missing some of Sidney's working files."

"Serious?" Brett said.

"Major setback," said Sidney.

Kirsten swung her chair to face Brett. "Remember our discussion on the plane about the leak, the potential for sabotage? This is why I need you."

Brett glanced away and tried to get a grasp on his thoughts. If he helped Kirsten, Sherwin would have him put away. His decision had been made before the door to the conference room slid shut behind Sherwin. He had taken an oath of office to defend the United States and that was what he intended to do.

"Any leads?" Brett asked.

"Sidney initiated some traces, but couldn't get further than here." Kirsten tapped a finger on a message on the screen that blinked RESTRICTED ACCESS.

"Where do I start?" Brett asked.

"By getting some help."

Brett thought for a minute. He knew few people on the Orion Project. Kansas Morningstar was one, but her expertise was intelligence. Plus, he was certain she could not be pulled from her work. The other was Peter Olson. "I can ask Peter Olson – he's the resident CIA tech genius."

"Your choice," Kirsten said. "I just need this handled, or we're dead in the water."

Brett pointed Olson toward the computer on the far wall of the small conference room and pulled up a chair to be next to him. "Sidney explained his problem," Brett said. "Any ideas on who we're dealing with?"

Olson carefully laid his suit jacket over one of the chairs and smoothed the material before replying. "It always comes down to motives. You know that. This center is packed with people who've put their lives into the Orion Project and who would die to see Sidney fail."

"Can you narrow that down?"

"Let's review the circumstances. We know Sidney was working in a tightly restricted area of the network, so whoever destroyed his files had top-level access. And Sidney's tracing led to an area of the internal network with even greater restricted access."

Olson rolled up the sleeves to his white shirt and addressed the computer terminal. "Let's see where Sidney's trail leads us."

Brett watched as Olson maneuvered through a series of screens, several of which had flashed RESTRICTED ACCESS. "You can get inside?"

"I can get into just about anything." Olson said without looking up. "That's why the agency hired me. Give me a minute here . . . ."

Brett gave up trying to gain any understanding of Olson's actions. He paced the small room, checking his watch every thirty seconds. Olson was right. Any number of Ishmel's staff would possess the capability and knowledge to get to Sidney's work. But how could the culprit, or culprits, be identified?

"You think Sidney's scheme has a chance?" Olson asked.

"You're asking the wrong guy."

"Let me take a shot at an answer, then. How does it work?"

"How does what work?"

"You know, Backflash, Sidney's defense."

"I told you, I'm the wrong guy to ask."

"Okay. Just trying to be helpful."

Brett paced in silence.

"Sidney must be on to something, though," Olson said, "or Secretary Clayton wouldn't have castrated Ishmel and given your gal friend the chance to turn the Orion Project topsy-turvy."

Brett let the Kirsten comment drop. He was annoyed by Olson's cockiness, and realized that he had never warmed up to the young agent since the time they met, but didn't really know why. He kept pacing. You played the cards you were dealt, and he was dead in the water without Olson.

"What's your relationship with Sherwin?" Brett asked, changing the subject.

"About the same as everyone's, I guess. I keep my head down, do my job." Olson kept his attention on the screen as he talked.

"Which really is what?"

"Sherwin wants to know what the Orion Project is up to. I give him information and get to stay employed."

"Information about me?"

The reflection of Olson's smile was visible on the computer screen. "Only what's relevant," he said.

"You know about my meeting with him this morning?"

"Enough to know you're digging a big hole for yourself by doing what you're doing."

"So you're adding another shovel to help me?"

"Nothing personal, but you don't need my help to self-destruct with Sherwin."

Brett resumed pacing and tried to shake Olson's comment by concentrating on one aspect of his discussion with Kirsten that had been troubling him, on the way to Washington. She had said that there had been a series of failures in the Orion Project going back several weeks. Were these failures premeditated attacks or merely troubles along the difficult path of software development? Two attackers would indicate a broader set of motives than someone attacking only Sidney, and a more dangerous problem.

Brett checked his watch. They had been in there nearly an hour. "Any progress?"

"Not yet. I keep hitting the same 'Restricted Access' firewall Sidney ran into that requires special privileges for access. I'm going to try a maneuver, a trick that may get us past the access block, but there's a possibility we'll get discovered by the system security people, and then we're locked out for good. You up for that?"

"Do we have a choice?"

"Not really, just keeping you in the loop." Olson's fingers danced over the keyboard. "I'm going to try a cryptographic code-breaking sequence I developed. It conducts intelligent interrogations of pass code possibilities in sort of a stealth mode, hopefully without letting system security monitors know what I'm doing." Olson finished tapping in commands, tilted his head while he read the entries, and tapped the mouse. "That should do it."

After a few moments, Olson leaned closer to the screen and said, "Well, well. Peter's crypto-magic strikes again."

Brett hurried around the conference table and looked over Olson's shoulder. "You have something?"

"Possibly." The words "EXECUTIVE USE ONLY – CONFIDENTIAL" filled the screen.

"We're looking at Zachary Ishmel's private domain," Olson said with a note of triumph in his voice. "I've heard whispers about this. Let's see what we've got." He hummed to himself as a series of screens flashed by on the monitor.

"This seems to be a strange place to look for sabotage," Brett murmured. "Are you thinking Ishmel's involved in some way?"

Olson shot him a glance. "The world's full of strange things, and strange people. Like we said, it all comes down to motives." He scanned the screens, pausing occasionally. "The first thing I like to search for is what people have been trying to delete, particularly where there have been multiple attempts." He turned to Brett. "You know, where people are acting anxious?"

"How do you find something that has been deleted?" Brett asked.

"You can thank Bill Gates and Microsoft for that. It's the nature of computing. Data and file deletions stay on the system until permanently removed or archived by the systems staff. System staffers have been known to fall behind on their data management duties depending on their workload or, you know, their motivation level."

Olson continued his humming as he scanned the screens. "Well, here's something that has had three deletions over the past forty-eight hours." The screen was titled "Orion Project Testing Data." A chart displayed a line that alternated red and green as it crossed a broader, blue line, spread over the previous thirty days.

Brett squinted, trying to read the information. "That's a big deal?"

"Testing results usually aren't, but *secret* testing results where someone has seemingly become obsessed with deletion? That leaps off the screen and crackles with suspicion to me."

Brett pointed to the line that alternated red and green. "What's with the change of colors?"

"Standard procedure. Operating results within acceptable limits, the blue line, are shown in green. Above acceptable limits, the results are shown in red."

"Lots of red," Brett observed.

"You got that." Olson clicked on the red line. An expanded chart showing only the red portions of the graph filled the screen. "This analysis shows that approximately a sixth of the systems coming out of production experienced failures during testing. Not good performance by a long shot, but not catastrophic." He toyed with the keys, humming. "So why the rabid interest in deleting the data…?"

Brett checked his watch. "Where does this revelation leave us?"

Olson leaned toward the screen. "Wait, this is normalized data. Let's see what the raw figures say." He tapped the mouse again and the screen filled with a fresh set of charts. "Well, well."

"What's that?" Brett said, leaning closer.

"No wonder Orion 5 and Orion 6 have been delayed. Remove the softening bias of normalization and we have a new picture. At this level of software failure rates, the project has been imploding for several weeks."

"I hate to sound confused" Brett asked, frowning, "but what's this got to do with Sidney's problem?"

Olson stared at the screen, humming. "Could all be connected somehow. Let's start with what we have. Why would Ishmel hide data on testing results?"

Brett felt his patience slipping.

"These figures may indicate why Ishmel made the grab for your Miss Lockhart's staff," Olson said. He swiveled his chair toward Brett. "Try this out for size. Orion 5 is falling rapidly behind due to software quality problems. Ishmel is motivated to keep the word from getting out so it won't ruin his career, so he makes a desperate move by grabbing your girlfriend's resources to catch up."

"Stow the personal talk, Olson."

Olson smiled. "So things move along okay until boy genius Hirschfield hits the scene, and now they're worried he might discover their situation or, worse yet, trump all their work and steal their glory. Make sense?"

"So someone plots to stop Sidney," Brett said.

"Bingo. A few well-targeted strikes stop or at least delay Sidney's work. I can tell you from what I've heard that Ishmel's staff would do anything to keep Backflash from upstaging Orion 6."

"I don't understand why someone at Ishmel's level would be involved in this sort of thing."

"Perhaps someone on his staff," Olson said. "But I'd be surprised if Ishmel wasn't in on the scheme. The stakes are enormous for him."

Brett considered Olson's argument. The trail from poor software to sabotaging Sidney's work was speculative, but possible. "Seems like a long shot."

"You have something else for us to run down? I can continue searching, but it could take hours."

Brett knew he was short of time and options. Better to pursue Olson's lead and see where it led than continue to churn through data. "Fine. You know Ishmel's staff. Where do we start?"

"I suggest his testing director, Mario. As Ishmel's enforcer, he is in on everything that goes on in the cyber center. I've seen him butt heads, even shove a reluctant engineer over a desk, to make sure things happen the way Ishmel wants."

Brett pulled on his jacket. "You pull Mario's background information and I'll bring him here."

"I was going to ask you earlier" Olson said, watching Brett. "Lose your weapon?"

"Gave it up a few years back," Brett said.

Olson swiveled in his chair. "Really. Why?"

"Another time, perhaps."

When Brett returned fifteen minutes later, Olson sat at the conference table where he was leafing through a stack of printed sheets. "Mario is on the way, against his will," Brett said. "He was furious." He glanced at the stack of paper as he removed his coat. "Find anything?"

Olson looked up. "I printed out a copy of the test reports as well has Mario's personnel file. He has a straightforward technical career. Cut his teeth in private industry and moved to the Orion Project with Ishmel."

"So the two of them go back a ways?"

"Twenty years."

"What about his background checks?"

Olson pulled a group of sheets from the stack and slid them across the table.

Brett leafed through the pages, not knowing what he was looking for. He stopped as he read the fourth page and turned it around for Olson to see. "Make anything of this?" he asked, tapping a finger on a paragraph in the center of the page.

Olson's eyebrows shot up. "Perhaps nothing, out of context. In context, perhaps everything. I suggest you push it when the time's right."

Brett scanned the remainder of the background checks and found nothing of interest.

The conference room door slid open. Mario, his face amber with rage, stormed to the conference table. "What's this all about?"

"Have a seat." Brett motioned toward Olson. "I believe you know Peter Olson of the CIA?"

Mario stayed standing. "I haven't time for this nonsense. We're in the middle of major software testing."

"Software testing. Exactly what we'd like to ask you about," Brett said. "Perhaps you can explain. Why have the software failure rates on the Orion Project been skyrocketing?"

"Skyrocketing? By whose count?"

"By yours." Olson tossed several sheets of test results across the table toward Mario. "Look familiar?"

A deep crease shot across Mario's brow as he glanced down at the charts. "Where'd you get these?"

"You've been hiding something, haven't you?" Olson asked.

Brett didn't know where he was headed, only that they had to push Mario to see where things led. "Looks like someone has been destroying data to mask problems in software development. Know anything about that?"

Mario's eyes smoldered. "That's crap and you know it. You can't intimidate me, hotshot."

Brett stared back, unflinching. They had evidence of a potential cover up, but needed more. Time to push. "Your background information is being checked by the CIA at this moment," he lied.

"This is bullshit." Mario turned to leave.

Olson stood and moved between Mario and the door. "I believe you were asked a question about destroying data."

"I don't have to answer your asinine questions," Mario said.

"I probably don't have to remind you," Brett said, "but willful hiding or misrepresentation of official government information with intent to deceive is a federal crime."

Mario's eyes danced between Brett and Olson.

"Think about it," Brett said. "Jail time."

"You can't prove a thing," Mario said.

"What's behind the slippage of Orion 6?" Olson asked.

Mario's face darkened.

"Does Ishmel know about the destruction of data?" Brett pressed.

"Why don't you ask him yourself?" Mario shot back.

"Of course, if you want to take the fall for this alone," Brett said, "that's your choice."

The room was silent.

Brett shot a quick glance at Olson. He was beginning to doubt that Mario was going to talk. They had to push further. He took in a deep breath. "Based on your falsification of records to hide problems, I'm wondering if you want the Orion Project to succeed at all."

Mario took a step toward Brett, his hands clenched into fists. "You have no right to accuse me. This is a fabrication of lies."

"Let's talk facts, then." Brett flipped several pages of Mario's security folder. "Is it true your real name is Hans Marconi Samplinski, of Russian and Italian parents who emigrated from East Germany to the United States in 1986?" He walked around the table and fixed a steady gaze on Mario. "Want to talk loyalties for a minute?"

"You son of a bitch!" Mario lunged so quickly Brett didn't have a chance to defend himself before the muscular man had him pinned to the floor. He winced in pain from his injured arm as he struggled to break the strong man's grip but felt himself losing ground. Suddenly, Mario's hands went limp and he slumped to the floor.

Olson stood over him, massaging the side of his hand. "Haven't had to use that chop to the neck since training."

"Thanks," Brett said, rubbing his arm.

"Looks like you have your man." Olson paced around Mario's body, jabbing him with his shoe. "Get up, hotshot. You and your boss's little game is over."

CHAPTER 42

K irsten pushed against the wall, trying to find shelter from the winds gusting across the roof of the Orion Project building that sent dark, brooding clouds rushing toward the capitol.

She shivered both from the plunging temperatures and the huge uncertainties facing her. Mario's detention had sent a seismic wave through the technology center, disrupting work and raising the anxiety of the exhausted staff. Silently, she prayed the report she had transmitted to Clayton about the incident with Mario, emphasizing the necessity for Clayton to reestablish order in the technology center had hit its mark. Less than six hours remained for Backflash to work.

She scanned the clouds, listening. Minutes earlier, Maureen Connolly had called, saying Clayton's helicopter was en route from the White House. On landing, Clayton was to proceed immediately to a video conference with the Pentagon. Kirsten pulled her coat tighter against the cold and waited. She would only have one chance to see him.

The door to the roof swung open, framing a familiar figure in the light.

She held her hand over her eyes to shield them from the stinging wind. "Zachary?"

Ishmel's reply, "Shit!" slashed through the sound of the storm with a fury all its own. Leaning into the wind, he crunched across the icy snow toward her. "What the hell are you doing here?"

"I came by your office, several times," she said as he flattened himself against the wall, breathing heavily.

Ishmel jammed his gloved hands into the pockets of his overcoat and cast a momentary look at the sky. When he turned back, his beard was frosted with ice crystals. His face was twisted with anger.

"You're history, Kirsten, and that juvenile delinquent fugitive friend of yours is going where he belongs." A stream of white mist followed the words out of his mouth, then was whipped away by the wind.

"You and I need to talk," she said.

"We have nothing to discuss."

"I didn't want you to be blindsided. I want you to know that Clayton is aware of—"

"Blindsided, you say? You have nerve. Why don't you ask Mario about being blindsided? You've disgraced him and humiliated me to my people. Have you no shame in this spiteful quest for revenge?"

"What you did is inexcusable, Zachary," Kirsten said, raising her voice to be heard over the howl of the wind.

"As soon as Clayton arrives, I'm having you removed from this building," he shot back.

Kirsten looked away. Ishmel's rage blinded him from the truth, making it impossible to get through to him. She watched the stream of her breath, reviewing again the rapid events of the past hour. Under questioning, although absolving Ishmel from involvement, Mario had confessed to a cover up designed to mask the failures of the Orion Project, but no more. The Orion Project's rapid collapse over the past several weeks was now fact, not presumption. She had explained it all in her report to Clayton. She had acted quickly, properly, and out of necessity.

The first *thump-thump-thump* reverberations of the approaching helicopter reached her. Kirsten turned her face to the sky. Her heart pounded in time with the approaching rotor blades and then raced ahead.

The helicopter broke through the clouds and slowed its descent, rotating to line up for landing. Engines whining, the chopper bounced once in the wind, then settled on the roof. Kirsten tucked her head further into her coat to protect herself from the waves of frigid air hurled over the rooftop by the whirling rotors.

The ladder had scarcely touched the roof when Clayton emerged.

Ishmel pushed past Kirsten, stepping between her and Clayton.

Clayton pulled the collar of his overcoat higher against the wind. His face was lined with concern, his eyes hard. "Yes, Zachary?"

"I must speak with you," Ishmel shouted. The helicopter's engines increased in pitch. A moment later, the noise became a shrill scream. The chopper leapt into the air, its rotors fighting for a grip on the sky, and tilted away from the building, disappearing into the clouds.

"This woman," Ishmel thrust a gloved hand toward Kirsten, barely missing her face, "is destroying the Orion Project with her outrageous disregard for protocol and for security."

"You're referring to Mario's detention?" Clayton asked.

"Yes, that," Ishmel's voice cracked with anger, "and her storming into my technical center with a hunted fugitive in tow, taking over our systems. God knows what's going to happen."

Clayton waved Ishmel to silence. "Miss Lockhart's got the green light, Zachary. We're staying the course with Backflash."

Ishmel reached inside his overcoat. "In that case, sir, you leave me no choice." He thrust an envelope carrying the seal of the Orion Project toward Clayton. "I cannot and I will not continue with my responsibilities under these circumstances."

Clayton blew out a long breath of frost crystals. "I'm afraid you're too late for that, Zachary."

The door to the building burst open. Two security guards, heads up into the wind, rushed toward Ishmel. The anger dropped from Ishmel's face, replaced by shock and disbelief.

As Ishmel was escorted into the building, Clayton faced Kirsten, his eyes squinting in the blowing snow. "We've stopped all work on Orion 6."

Kirsten started to reply but stopped as Clayton motioned her to stop.

"This ballgame is all yours," he said. "For all of our sakes – and the country - I hope to hell you can deliver."

CHAPTER 43

Kirsten stared at the image in the mirror of the women's lavatory, oblivious to the sound of the running faucet. Her communications headset lay on the counter, silent.

What had she wrought?

Since embarking on her journey to save the Orion Project three days earlier, she had left a trail of disarray and death. The detention of Ishmel and Mario had brought all work on Orion 6 to an end. Key staff had been reassigned to work on supporting the Backflash deployment, and others were told to stand by but not to leave the cyber center. Sidney was rushing, passionate to finalize his work, but someone had struck again. Any more strikes, she knew, and any hope of Backflash being ready would vanish. The firebombing in Zurich that caused the deaths of Sidney's girlfriend Katrina and the CIA agent haunted her the most. *Who would be next?*

The voice of a news reporter on the television in the sitting area behind her grabbed her attention: "We now bring you the latest on the food shortages sweeping the country."

She stared at the television image in the mirror. The newscast showed a supermarket with citizens rushing grocery carts through near-empty aisles. Lines wound from the checkout counters to the back of the store.

"Markets across the country are quickly emptying of food and water," the reporter continued, "as many citizens prepare for what many believe may be a major wave of terrorist attacks tonight following President Anston's State of the Union speech."

Kirsten closed her eyes. Who was the enemy? Was it the faceless terrorists who had ignited the spark or the growing media-fueled firestorm that panicked citizens more? Was she, as Ishmel had shouted over his shoulder while being led away on the roof, "a dangerous force whose misguided actions are playing into the terrorist's hands?" In her frenzied zeal, had she become part of the problem?

She opened her eyes. The screen showed a line snaking around the corner of a Wal-Mart store and into the parking lot. The camera closed in on the tortured face of a young woman, frozen ice caked on her hair, clutching two small children to her chest, begging with security guards to be let in the store.

The image switched to a wind-blown reporter in front of the store:

> "As you can see, unrest continues to rise around the country even though our colleague Sheila Carson reiterated last hour that her latest information confirms the Orion Project still plans to distribute its Orion 6 terrorist defense software prior to the president's speech this evening. In related news, White House sources have denied rumors sweeping the capital that the president will resign at the conclusion of his speech."

"Ops to control."

Kirsten shook her head to come back to the present at the sound of Karl Breskin's voice. She grasped the communications set from the counter and pulled it to her head.

"Yes, Karl?"

"We're ready."

Brett put a finger to his lips, smiled at the executive assistant like he was a regular visitor and tapped twice on Walt Washington's door. The door swung open and Washington stood in the entrance. Seeing Logan, his expression changed from curiosity to anger.

"May I see you, Director?" Logan asked, glancing at the concerned face of the assistant. "Privately?"

After a moment, Washington stood aside as Logan entered, then said, "First you shackle Dr. Zachary Ishmel, an innocent man, then come barging in here. You have some nerve. What do you want?"

Brett decided to sidestep the question. "The Orion Project has a serious security problem. I'm here to see who else may be involved."

"Dr. Ishmel is a good and proud man who has served his country for many years," Washington replied. "I consider his arrest a deliberate disregard of his personal rights."

"As I said, I'm looking for accomplices."

"Then look under your nose."

"Beg your pardon?"

"That renegade hacker Hirschfield who has been given the run of the house, for starters."

Brett ignored the bait for an argument. "He's being watched. I'm searching for information on someone who may have worked with Dr. Ishmel or his associate Mario, someone who is sabotaging work on the Orion Project."

"And exactly how am I supposed to help?"

"I'm interested in reviewing your communications records for Ishmel's staff."

Washington let out a mocking laugh. "Agent Logan, you are out of your mind."

"We've got a serious problem here, sir, and you can help solve it."

After a strained silence, Washington said, "My operation has more than eighty-three terabytes of encrypted and compressed digital and optical storage packed with phone logs, Internet messages, memos, and the like. That includes every email, every message anyone on the premises created, and never sent: clandestine love notes, raging flamer memos, and perhaps even fantasy acts of espionage composed during a fit of anger.

"Toss in Facebook posts, Tweets, security videos, building access records, original and updated background checks, special investigations, and you are facing a lifetime effort with your little research project. I suggest you take your treasure hunt elsewhere. You are wasting your time here."

"Aren't we getting off to rather a bad start?" Brett asked, easing his tone. No need to further inflame Washington's feelings.

Washington examined Brett with narrowed eyes. "Your words, sir, not mine."

The two men stared at each other in silence.

"I'm here on government business regarding the safety of our country," Brett said. "If you have a problem with that, I suggest you make a call to Secretary Clayton's office." Brett studied Washington's face and waited, hoping the bluff would hold.

After several moments, Washington pulled a pen from his jacket pocket and poised it over a small note tablet he removed from his desk. "Exactly where in the eighty-three terabytes of data do you care to start?"

"I'm interested in memos, telephone conversations, and Internet messages, over the past two to three weeks."

Washington snorted a small laugh. "Exactly how much time do you have, Agent Logan?"

"We'll start with internal e-mail and Internet messages." Brett glanced at his watch. "I have little time. Anything you can do to help will be appreciated."

Washington pushed away from his desk. "You can use the computer on that desk against the far wall. I'll handle the passwords to get you logged in."

Brett's phone chimed. He turned from Washington to answer.

"Brett, it's Peter. Find anything?"

"Just getting started. What have you got?"

"I've run those checks you asked for on the web address you got from Hirschfield."

Brett straightened. They were overdue for some progress. "What about the address extension?"

"'de' is the country designation for Germany. I've double and triple checked this. The site belongs to an auto dealership in Hamburg. Respectable business."

Brett mouthed a profanity. He had held slim hope for some connection between the web address and what had happened in Zurich, but now that trail, too, was dead.

"Brett?" Olson asked.

"Yes?"

"You sure we're not being led down the primrose path here?"

"Meaning?"

"First this squirrelly web address. Then every time I try to get close to Hirschfield, to keep an eye on him like I'm supposed to, he gets secretive. He gives me an uneasy feeling, like he's up to something."

Brett fought the impulse to believe Sidney was playing on the other side of the terrorist battle. He would let Sidney proceed with Kirsten's plan, at least for now. "Sidney's not attacking his own work. Let's stay focused on the saboteur."

Brett stared at his phone after disconnecting the call. None of the pieces were fitting together. How had the Germans been tipped about Kirsten's going after Sidney? Was the leak the same as the saboteur? He shook his head. Ishmel and Mario didn't seem likely candidates to undertake murder. No, someone else inside knew everything. But who?

"Agent, you with me?" Washington studied Brett with an expression of annoyance.

"I'm with you."

"You're set up. The highest level access we have." Washington tugged his crisp shirtsleeves toward his wrist and extended his palms toward the computer. "Search your heart out, and call me in the spring when you're done."

"Wait." Brett examined the database search screen. He had no time for false starts. "Can you give me some guidance here?"

"I agreed to provide you with access to full access to our records, and that does not include serving as your data retrieval tutor."

Brett scrambled for words. "Are you using standard Defense Department search tools?"

"Pretty much."

"How pretty much?"

"Listen, agent, I've done my job." Washington straightened his suit coat and swiveled on his heel for the door. "From this point, you are on your own."

"Chief Washington," Brett called out, using the Seal's Navy rank. "From what I know about you, we were on the same side in Iraq, and, believe me, we're on the same side here."

Washington hesitated but didn't look back. "Zachary Ishmel did not and would not falsify government records. He is an honorable man. You are mistaken on this one, sir. I suggest you look elsewhere."

The closing of the door left Brett alone with his questions, a ticking clock in his head, and a room silent except for the quiet rush of the computer fans.

CHAPTER 44

Kirsten studied the faces of the Backflash deployment team around her, considering their chances for success. Step one had gone well: Clayton's address over the cyber center's video system, giving his full support for Kirsten's project and the vital importance of its success, had had its intended effect. The technicians in the cyber center had settled down and were focused on supporting the intended Backflash deployment – assuming the terrorist attacks were to come. The staff needed for deployment was in place. Step two was to ensure her team was prepared to carry out the complex task of preparing for Backflash deployment.

Step three was up to the terrorists.

Her team appeared ready. Her friend Karl Breskin, jacket removed, his white shirtsleeves rolled up his forearms; a young Chinese woman in a black turtleneck with short cropped black hair Kirsten didn't recognize; and Kansas Morningstar, intent in the study of the deployment plan Sidney had prepared, formed a semi-circle around her. Sidney sat one row over, focused on his workstations.

Kirsten extended her hand to the young Chinese technician. "And you are…?"

The young woman stepped forward. "Susan. Susan Chan."

"My apologies, Kirsten." Breskin placed a hand on Chan's shoulder. "In the rush I didn't have the chance to introduce you. Susan is taking over for Mario."

Kirsten studied the young woman, hoping she was up to the task ahead. "Here is our game plan. Everyone listen up. Our detailed deployment plans have been sent to each of your smartphones, but let's recap where we're going. We will be taking the cyber center out of Lockdown status, thus opening up for incoming traffic, at approximately 1800 hours tonight, leaving the center vulnerable to attack. This is necessary if we are going to go through the motions of distributing Orion 6 to communications, power and transportation networks across the country. As we all know, Orion 6 is not operational. Efforts have been made in the media to lead the terrorists to believe that Orion 6 *is* operational. We anticipate the terrorists will use this opening in our defenses to attack and attempt to disable the Orion 6 distribution. Make sense so far?"

The faces on the team nodded.

"Good," Kirsten said. "When they do attack, Sidney will launch Backflash to turn their own incoming strikes against them."

Kirsten paused, taking stock of where they were. Each of her leaders managed a team of dozens of technicians, and thus had to understand the full picture of the plan. Time to go through the details. "All right, everyone, let's take it from the top."

"Ops is ready," Breskin said. "I'll be handling the countdown sequence, which is scheduled to run fifty minutes. We'll report status on the readiness display."

Kirsten glanced at the front wall of the technology center. The words "Backflash Deployment" glowed in bright red letters on a large black-background screen.

Breskin pointed to his headset. "Remember, we'll be broadcasting on channel 1. If you have something private to say, switch to channel 2 and key in or speak the individual's communication code."

Kirsten nodded to the young Chinese woman. "Communications?"

Susan Chan cleared her throat. "Communications ready. We will use minimum channels for the simulated outbound Orion 6 transmission, leaving clear channels for incoming terrorist access."

Kirsten waited a moment, then added, "And clear channels outbound for Backflash?"

"Oh, yes - that is correct," Susan Chan said.

Kirsten studied the young Chinese, hoping Breskin hadn't made a mistake with her. Communications was critical to the success of the effort.

"Recovery?" Kirsten said, looking at Breskin.

"Backup systems and emergency power are operational and standing by," Breskin answered. "There will be no disruptions due to the attacks or external factors."

"Good," Kirsten said, then turned to Kansas Morningstar. "Intelligence?"

Morningstar raised her dark eyes to Kirsten's and held them in silence.

"You ready?" Kirsten asked.

"Yes. Are you sure about this?"

"You have a concern?" Kirsten asked.

"Only about what could happen to the country's technology infrastructure if Backflash attacks the wrong target and gets out of control."

Sidney looked up from his computer and shot Morningstar a sharp stare. "You focus on identifying the proper targets, and I'll do the rest."

Kirsten motioned to Morningstar. "Go ahead with your briefing on detection of incoming threats."

Morningstar edged past a desk packed with computer screens to face the group. "My group's mission is to identify and confirm potential terrorist attacks against the Orion Project." She motioned toward the blue-background intelligence display next to the readiness screen Breskin had referred to earlier. "Sector A on the intelligence display monitors the Orion Project Internet site as well as our Intranet, which runs our internal communications. As you know, these sites, just like their counterparts at the CIA, FBI and other government agencies, routinely receive attacks, but such hits are typically of a low danger level, from hackers, crackers and espionage outfits looking for information."

Sidney glanced up from his workstations. "Sector A won't be the terrorist's point of entry."

"True," Morningstar agreed, "but we're monitoring just in case.

Kirsten agreed with Morningstar's low-threat assessment of potential Sector A attacks from outside, but worried about the threat from within. She glanced at her smartphone. No word from Brett on his progress.

"Sector B," Kansas said, "covers our Extranet, where we share information with our technology partners, vendors, and government agencies. The terrorists may attempt to sneak in via this path. But accessing Orion 6 systems through the Extranet, while possible, would be difficult, and in our opinion take more time than they can spare."

"Still a point of exposure," Sidney added. "Every government agency, every partner, every supplier who interacts with the Orion Project creates new points of vulnerability. Be alert to Sector B, everyone."

Morningstar continued: "The sweet spot in the terrorist's minds is Sector C. Sector C is where we monitor the dedicated fiber-optic and satellite communications circuits that support Orion Project systems collaboration and dispersion with the outside world. We expect the attack, if there is one, to come in here."

"Please cover the attack warnings," Kirsten said.

Morningstar nodded. "Every attack on the Orion Project will show as a flashing star in the Sector where it occurs. Once we have confirmed intrusion, an attack that has entered our systems, you will hear an audible *'ping, ping, ping'* throughout the center as long as the intruding signal is active. A digital display will count the seconds from entry."

Morningstar paused for a moment, scanning the faces of the group. "As usual, we'll also be operating the U.S. intrusion display showing major attacks anywhere else in the country." Behind her, the U.S. intelligence display map glowed on a background of green.

"That's it," Morningstar said. "Questions?"

"Seems to me Sector C would present a difficult attack point for the terrorists," Breskin said. "Isn't this where we have our strongest firewalls and most advanced protection measures?"

"That's correct," Kirsten said. "The toughest, and we just made them tougher."

Susan Chan raised her hand. "I don't understand. If we want the terrorists to attack, why are we strengthening our defenses?"

JAMES D. MCFARLIN

"Simple." Sidney studied Chan for a moment, as if considering the purpose of the question. "If we don't, they'll only get suspicious, and stay away."

"But what if we keep them out?" Chan asked.

Sidney waved his hand in dismissal. "They'll zap through the security measures like lightening through a golf umbrella. Our problem is going to be reacting quickly enough."

Peter Olson had been listening from a distance and wandered in close to the discussion. "Is there a place where I fit in this?"

"Thanks, Peter," Kirsten said in a voice that was quiet yet firm. "We have everything handled." She wished he would focus on helping Brett find the mole.

"I can be of help in your Sector C surveillance," Peter said.

"I said we're set. Thank you."

"As you wish. Olson waved a hand in dismissal and turned toward the workstation he used on the floor of the cyber center.

Kirsten motioned to Sidney. "Your turn, Sid."

Sidney swiveled his chair to face the group, ticking off points on his hand as he spoke. "We have twelve seconds, max, to identify, confirm, intercept, lock on, and counterattack the terrorist transmission, or the game's over."

The deployment team exchanged glances.

"Kansas, once you identify a potential terrorist intrusion," Sidney continued, "you have six seconds to confirm the attack and route the signal to my computer cluster."

"Which is eight seconds less than normal," Morningstar said.

"Timing will make or break us," Sidney said. "The terrorist's objective will be to get in, do their damage to Orion 6, and get out quickly. Then they'll vanish, our opportunity for counterattack lost. We'll have nothing to trace to the source. So, once I have a confirmed signal from Kansas, I'll do a final authentication, then move immediately into the Backflash launch sequence."

"What happens then?" Chan asked.

Sidney studied the group. "We wait."

"And everyone stays in position," Breskin added.

Sidney turned to Susan Chan. "I need pure electronic quiet inside this center. Other than the critical internal communications in support of our mission, the Orion Project must be electronically silent. No exceptions. Clear?"

"Clear," Chan replied.

"And even when Lockdown is disengaged," Kirsten said, studying the faces before her, "we can't take a chance on any messages leaving this center. If the terrorists get any indication, any hint, of our plan, they'll stay away, and we're dead in the water. Understand?"

Chan nodded.

"You're sure?" Sidney asked, raising his eyebrows.

"Yes," Chan replied.

Kirsten studied Sidney. He would leave absolutely nothing to chance. She knew he would continue checking every aspect of the deployment process until the countdown began. She rued the day for anyone he was depending on who missed a cue.

"Finally," Sidney said, "for Backflash to work, we need all defenses down."

"Removing the defenses in the cyber center is the next to last step of the countdown," Breskin said. "I'll see to it personally. After that it's your show."

"Any other questions?" Kirsten said.

The group exchanged silent glances.

"Okay," Kirsten said, "once the defenses are down, we'll wait until the terrorists make their move."

"At that point," Sidney added, "we've turned the Orion Project into one big, luscious honey pot."

Kirsten made eye contact with each member of the team. "Ready, everyone?"

"Oh," Susan Chan asked. "What happens after the counterattack?"

Sidney's expression hardened. "If Backflash finds its targets, the terrorists will be gaining a renewed respect for the term 'killer app.' Most of their computers, attack systems, and communications networks will be severely crippled, if not disabled."

"Get to your positions, everyone," Kirsten said. "We've got the A-Team here. Let's act like it - and make this a night the terrorists won't forget."

CHAPTER 45

Kirsten felt pinpricks in the tips of her fingers. The countdown was nearly complete. Three days of madness had all come down to this.

Karl Breskin's voice echoed in her headset: "Ops to control."

"Yes, ops," Kirsten replied.

"Prelim checks complete. Proceed with deployment?"

Here we go. "Roger."

Lights in the center dimmed. Sound levels subsided to a hush. Kirsten riveted her eyes on the readiness display while she monitored Karl's countdown over her headset.

"Backup?" Karl said.

"Systems backup ready, ops."

"Recovery?"

"Ready and standing by."

"Communications?"

The line was silent.

"Communications?"

"Hold up, ops," the high-pitched Chinese voice said.

Kirsten swung her head toward the communications area in time to see Karl rush in that direction. *What was up?* She tried to swallow and realized her mouth was dry. She twisted the cap from her bottled water and took a long swallow. Then another. She started in the direction of the communications group.

"Control?" Karl's voice said.

"Yes?" Kirsten answered.

"Communications go. Continuing countdown."

She let out a long breath. "Roger."

Karl continued the countdown: "Intelligence?"

"Intel ready," Morningstar's melodic voice said.

"Satellites?"

"Satcom connections established, ops."

"Firewalls?" Kirsten asked.

"Down," Karl answered.

Kirsten glanced at Sidney. He drummed his fingers on his computer desk, face intent on the screens in front of him, one leg in constant motion. She shifted her attention to the Backflash deployment display on the large screen.

All steps in the countdown except the release of "Lockdown" had switched from red letters saying "STANDBY" to green letters stating "READY." The monitor showed Backflash in red letters saying "STANDBY".

"Ops to control. Preparing to release Lockdown," Karl said.

Kirsten checked the time: 15:05. She glanced over the tech center. The staff was motionless, silent. Waiting. She moistened her lips. "Roger, ops. Proceed."

She struggled to keep her attention on Karl's voice as fragments of shifting memories flashed through her mind.

Sidney's shrill voice shot through her headset: "What the hell? Hold it!"

"What?" Kirsten bolted for Sidney's desk, pulling the microphone away as she ran. "Sid! Talk to me."

Sidney glanced between his terminals. "Everything was perfect. I was making my final checks, and now it's not executing." He slammed his fist on the desk. "Jesus!"

Kirsten's headset beeped. "Control?"

She pulled the microphone to her lips to respond, then hesitated. No need to broadcast the problem. "Channel 2, ops." She switched to the private channel and waited for Karl's call.

"What's the problem?" he asked a second later.

Kirsten glanced at Sidney, looking for any expression of hope, but he was intent on his

computer screens, his face a mixture of frustration and anger. "We've got a temporary hold,
ops," she said.

"Anything I can do?" Kirsten asked Sidney.

"Negative."

Karl lowered his voice. "Kirsten, you
know we can't hold on a standby status. With
Lockdown disengaged we're a sitting duck. The
terrorists can make their attack and we'll have
nothing."

"What are you suggesting?"

"If you need time, we'll be forced to back off
and restart when you're ready."

"Give me a minute, Karl." Kirsten placed a hand
on Sidney's shoulder. "Tell me what you think."

"I don't make mistakes like this," Sidney said.
There's only one possibility. Someone's been into
Backflash again."

"How much time do you need?"

"I can't tell you. Someone has full system
access to my work, but I do know that the son of a
bitch isn't smarter than I am."

Kirsten pressed her fist into her forehead.
Had she been set up? Was the Orion Project
team, loyal to Ishmel, laughing behind their
computer terminals? Was Sidney, exhausted from
the calamitous events of the previous twenty-
four hours, over-wrought from Katrina's loss,
no longer able to function clearly? Or had they
missed something, someone?

"Kirsten?" Karl asked over her headset.

Kirsten bit her lip. They were already short on time. Backing off was not an option. Not yet. "Maintain hold status until I get back to you."

"I can't leave the cyber center vulnerable without Backflash," he said.

"Karl," Kirsten said, hearing the tension in her voice. "Listen to me. We'll work through this. I need some time."

He was quiet for a moment. "I'll give you five minutes."

Kirsten bit her lip as she listened to Karl's announcement echo through the cyber center: "Temporary hold. Stay on station. Repeat, stay on station."

Kirsten turned her attention to the sabotage problem. Had someone else been out there all along who was waiting to strike again? She scanned the center. Karl and the rest of his team were speaking in hushed tones in the control area. Peter Olson was busy at his computer terminal. Kansas Morningstar waited in the intelligence area, hands on her hips. A sea of blank faces manned row upon row of computer terminals. Some turned to others in hushed conversation. *Where are you?* She touched Brett's number on her smartphone.

He answered immediately. "Yes, Kirsten?"

"Any luck on finding other conspirators?"

"I'm doing everything I—"

"Sidney's been hit again."

Brett was silent.

"I need you to stop what you're doing," she glanced around to see that she couldn't be overheard, "and run a special check on a Susan Chan in communications."

"We've been through everyone's background."

"Brett," Kirsten tried to slow her rapid breathing, "we're goddamn dead in the water down here. I need your help on this."

"Fine." He hesitated. "Kirsten, are you certain about Sidney - that he's not just opening the Orion Project to the terrorists?"

"We've been through that."

"Think about it again, Kirsten. While there's still time."

"Let me know about Susan Chan," Kirsten said, and clicked off.

She tucked away her thought doubts and slid into a chair next to Sidney. "Anything?"

"No," he mouthed, and kept working.

Kirsten mentally flipped through the options. Continuing to hold for Sidney only kept the center open to attack. Starting over took precious time, but she had no sense of how much time Sidney would need, and even if he were to restore Backflash to operational status, what was to prevent the saboteur from striking again?

She heard Karl's voice over her headset: "Any progress?"

She swallowed hard. "No."

"I've got to terminate deployment." Karl was silent for a moment, and then said, "I'm sorry about this, Kirsten."

The lights in the tech center went up. Kirsten felt the breath go out of her as, one by one, the status designations on the Backflash readiness display switched from bright green READY to a blinking red TERMINATED. In sixty seconds, the entire display was a shimmering carpet of red.

Technicians pushed away from their computer consoles and stretched. Some exchanged questioning looks; others clustered in small groups, talking quietly. The time read 15:20. Kirsten slumped into a gray plastic chair and rubbed her tired eyes until she forced herself to stop. She thought about Clayton, the one person who had believed in her. How would she break the news, and where did the circumstances leave him?

She dropped her head into her hands to think, aware only of the rapid clicking of Sidney's computer keyboard. What else could she do? Was she too close to the problem to see it?

An official young voice worked its way into Kirsten's consciousness. "Miss Lockhart? Excuse me, Miss Lockhart?"

"Yes?" Kirsten raised her head. The light blue eyes of a young Marine Corporal stared into hers.

"You have a civilian visitor at street level security, Miss Lockhart. We informed him no visitors were allowed in, but he was quite persistent. Says it's critical he see you."

"Tell whoever it is I'll get back to him."

"Yes, ma'am." The corporal turned away, then stopped and examined a slip of paper she carried in her hand. "The gentleman did have a message for you, Miss Lockhart. He said he brings fair winds from Arizona."

Her head snapped up. *Terry Sailor - from Tucson?*

Ten minutes later Terry Sailor, in western boots, jeans and leather jacket, cleared security and in his easy, swinging gait followed the Marine toward Kirsten.

Terry's hug shot warmth through Kirsten's body. "What in God's name are you doing here?" she asked.

"I knew you were close to a big deadline," he said, smiling. "Thought I might be able to help."

Kirsten ran a hand through her hair. "We've got what looks like sabotage. There's nothing you can do. Besides, only Sidney's familiar with what he's doing."

"Actually, I *am* familiar with what he's doing," Terry said, stroking his ponytail.

Kirsten frowned. "What do you mean?"

"I've collaborated on Backflash all along."

"You?" You're the one he was working with?" Kirsten glanced over her shoulder toward Sidney, whose head was buried in his computer screens. "I guess he didn't see you come in."

Terry smiled. "Perhaps he did. We've never met."

"That we can change." Kirsten grasped Terry's hand and drew him to Sidney's work area. "Sid, there's someone here who'd like to meet you."

Sidney kept working, eyes fixed on his computer screens. "Yes?"

"Does the name Terry Sailor sound familiar?"

Sidney's hands froze above the keys. He turned his head and stared into Terry's eyes. "You're kidding me." He leapt from his chair, his face lit with a sweeping smile, and grabbed Terry with a bear hug.

Terry placed both hands on Sidney's shoulders. "Kirsten mentioned this saboteur problem. You must be a bit worn, guy. Need an assist?"

"Actually," Sidney said, eyes flickering to his workstations, "I've just about recovered. The real problem is what we do when this happens again."

Kirsten's headset beeped on channel two. "Kirsten, we've rechecked everyone, just as you asked," Brett said. "Nothing."

"Even your own people?"

"Yes, and ditto on Susan Chan."

Kirsten squeezed the bridge of her nose to try to relieve the pressure on her pounding head. "Keep at it, Brett. We're missing someone."

"Give me some time."

"We're out of time, Brett. Just do it." Kirsten mashed the button to click off the communication. *Was Brett really on board?*

Terry slipped a toothpick in the left side of his mouth. "More trouble?"

Kirsten struggled to hide her disappointment. *When do the good guys get a break?* "We have a little saboteur problem."

"Mind if I take a shot at it?"

Kirsten placed her hand on his arm. "If I thought it would do any good, Terry, I'd say go ahead."

"You might be surprised," Terry said, scanning the area. "Got an extra workstation close by?"

Kirsten edged closer to Terry, making certain her headset was off. "What are you thinking?"

"Let this saboteur come to us."

"How?"

"Get Sidney's system back on line. While he's doing that, I've a few clever traps and traces I can set up. Then go into your normal countdown. I'll monitor every step of the process. When your saboteur strikes again, I can give you a better than fifty-fifty odds, depending on how clever this guy is, that I can nail him."

"What do you need?"

"Full access to Sidney's systems and to the Orion Project's internal network."

Kirsten studied Terry's earnest face. She needed to stay focused on the Backflash deployment. On the other hand, there would be no deployment if Sidney couldn't keep Backflash operative.

"Okay, you're on." Kirsten glanced at the time display. "How much time do you need?"

"Depends how the access routines and protocols are set up here," he said, slipping out of his leather jacket. "Perhaps sixty minutes."

"You've got twenty."

CHAPTER 46

Brett's eyes ached from scanning the small characters and symbols flashing by on the screen. Since the latest sabotage attack, he had widened his search. More complex keyword and topic-based inquiries had produced results containing thousands of internal memos, external communications, and e-mail messages. He leaned away from the screen and stretched his good arm. He was searching an electronic haystack of immense proportions and getting nowhere.

He carefully composed alternative versions of the search criteria. Small, even subtle, changes could produce markedly different data. The screen instantly painted the search results in order of their fit on the screen. He speed-read topics, scanned text, paged down, scanned again.

And again. *Too much data. Somewhere there must be a clue.*

The door behind him slid open, then closed. Brett leaned closer to the screen, squinting at a new group of search results. *Come on, come on.* Brett felt as much as heard the slow, deliberate steps on the carpet, closer now. He turned, ready to spring from his chair just as a strong hand clamped his shoulder.

"What the hell?" he exclaimed.

"Sorry to interrupt." Walt Washington released his grasp. "Thought I'd see how you're doing."

Brett returned to the screen. "In the future you might consider announcing your presence."

Washington extended his large hand. "Did some checking. Seems we're on the same side after all. Guess I owe you a big apology, Major."

"Thanks, Chief, but save it for later. I've got a new problem."

"I heard about the latest sabotage downstairs," Washington said. "Looks like your problem has a new dimension. What do you do now?"

"Keep searching."

"Want me to take a look?"

"Look for what? You said it yourself. There's too much data." Brett studied the screen that for more than two hours had echoed his requests, disgorged responses, then waited for the next round, its cursor blinking its cadence, as if daring him to take another shot at its massive storehouse of intelligence. He tapped his fingers on the desk. The answer was right in front of him, if he only asked the right questions. *But what were the right questions?* Something Kansas Morningstar had said on his first day in the Orion Project tugged at the back of his mind.

Brett spun his head toward Washington. "Walt, do you have Daisy on this system?" Brett used the newer name for what had once been called Carnivore, the FBI's controversial data searching software tool that many thought infringed on personal privacy rights.

"Yes, but using Daisy is going to require specific authorization from the top."

"Clayton's not available. Will my orders from him do?"

Washington stared at the computer for several long moments before returning his attention to Brett. "Let's find this saboteur."

"Ops to control."

"Yes, Karl?" Kirsten replied.

"We have a communications hold"

"What's the problem?"

"I'll handle it. Stay where you are. Estimate countdown to start approximately sixteen-ten hours."

Kirsten stared at the readiness display, listening to Karl's announcement over the broadcast system and thinking. Barely enough time. Was everything ready? She gave up trying to outguess the possibilities. Her mind was operating on overload, numb from fatigue and from the grinding pressure of not knowing what to expect next.

She noticed Terry Sailor watching her from his computer station a row over. Several seconds later, she fell into a chair next to his and flipped her microphone away. "All set, Terry?"

"In waiting mode now."

"What are the odds you'll detect something?"

He shrugged. "Depends on how clever our saboteur is. On balance, I'd say thirty percent."

Kirsten blew out a sigh. "Not good odds."

"Best we've got."

"Guess you're right on that—" Karl's voice in her headset jarred Kirsten out of her thoughts: "We're starting," Breskin's voice said in her headset.

Kirsten squeezed Sailor's arm and stood. "Gotta go. Find us our guy."

She pulled the microphone to her mouth. "On the way, Karl."

CHAPTER 47

The moment the soundproof door to the underground White House Situation Room closed behind him, Dustin Clayton felt he had stepped into another world. A phalanx of flag rank officers, shirt-sleeved aides and intelligence specialists worked banks of phones and moved rapidly between small groups and computer terminals. Secretary of State Joan Karlin balanced two telephones as she huddled with advisors at the far end of the large polished conference table. Faces were strained with fatigue. The cumulative effect of three dozen animated voices gave the room a loud, almost unruly, bazaar atmosphere.

The Situation Room, informally known as the Woodshed, is located in the basement of the

West Wing. The room is largely filled by a long polished-wood table in the center, surrounded by high-backed black leather chairs. The windowless room contains six flat-screen video monitors, the largest filling the south wall at the end of the table from the president's chair.

On a videoconference screen, National Intelligence Director Stuart Ibbs was speaking with Admiral Rutledge, who was aboard the flying command post. President Anston stood with a phone to his head in front of a screen displaying a digitized map containing red dots representing planned locations of attacks.

Clayton hesitated, reviewing the map. Militant *jihadi* groups operated in more than seventy countries, providing hundreds of targets for Operation Hydra. Red dots marking suspected terrorist cells in Indonesia, Algeria, Yemen, Jordan, Italy, Turkey, Morocco, Spain, the Philippines, most of Southeast Asia, and many others were targeted. More than four thousand CIA agents and Special Ops forces were on their way to deployment, supplemented by more than two thousand killer drones, many of which had been previously programmed for some of the targets, awaiting orders. The U.S. was sweeping past cooperative efforts with local governments and taking matters into its own hands. Clayton shook his head in worry as he considered the consequences.

He listened to the Operation Hydra countdown preparations as he worked his way around the conference table through knots of aides toward the president: "All nonessential commercial air traffic suspended . . . National Guard called out on nationwide alert . . . train stations under military guard . . . vacations cancelled for fire and police personnel . . . U.S. forces on full alert across the globe." He passed Ron Comber, who held a phone tightly to his ear. "Yes, Governor. The president supports using Army reservists to augment the National Guard in the Los Angeles uprisings. No, I wouldn't expect you would hear from him this evening."

The deputy director of the FBI glanced up from a conversation on a speakerphone and nodded to Clayton. "I'll repeat, senator. The presence of agents will not protect the FAA's flight control centers. That's one reason why the president has ordered all commercial flights grounded beginning at 5 P.M. Yes, he's aware of the economic implications."

A bank of television screens tuned to the major news channels filled the far wall. One channel flashed images of frenzied citizens looting a grocery store in downtown Los Angeles; another covered the growing demonstrations in Washington, with thousands of citizens waving placards saying "Impeach Anston." At what point, Clayton wondered, does a president lose the ability to govern?

On a third screen a windblown reporter stood at the nearly deserted entrance to Manhattan's 59th Street Bridge, making a report:

"With this evening's terrorist deadline rapidly approaching, the workers in Manhattan are voting a big 'no confidence' in President Anston's ability to deal with the crisis. In addition to the thousands of those who took the day off, many of the city's workers left early today, darkening stores, restaurants and office buildings, leaving streets, including this famously busy bridge, nearly empty of vehicles. Even the familiar fleets of yellow taxis are missing."

"Dusty." Anston waved Clayton over to where he was speaking with Rutledge on the videoconference screen. Clayton took a place between the president and Stuart Ibbs and listened.

"We have reports of intelligence leaks on Operation Hydra, Mr. President," Rutledge was saying. "I recommend we commence operations immediately before our targets go deep underground."

Rutledge's face was taut with tension, his eyes sparkling with energy. Behind him, the frenzied activity in the flying command post mirrored that of the White House Situation Room.

"Hold a moment, Admiral." Anston leaned close to Clayton, his voice lower. "Be straight with me. What's your confidence level in this entrapment plan of yours?"

As much as Clayton wanted to give the president encouraging news, he knew it would be a grave disservice if he were to overstate his position. Unlike the precision military exercises

that had been his way of life, the unpredictable, ever-changing scenario playing out in the
Orion Project defied rational assessment. He
could not calculate the odds, only hope at this
point.

"Sir, it will be at least an hour before we have
anything to report," Clayton said quietly, turning
his head away from the video screen camera.

"Damn!" Anston said.

"Mr. President?" An Army two-star stood
halfway across the room, his hand covering the
mouthpiece of a telephone. "Sir, the Russian
president is on the line again."

"Joan," the president said with a tone of
urgency to Secretary of State Karlin, who quickly
placed the person she was speaking with on hold.
"Take that call from President Vladir. I'm sure
he's calling, as most the leaders of Europe have,
to remind me that our taking any overt military
action will have serious repercussions."

"Your response, Mr. President?" Secretary
Karlin asked.

"Tell him that I believe we have every right to
defend ourselves and that I'll call him before my
speech this evening."

Anston let out a long breath and examined
the Operation Hydra attack displays for several
long moments, then glanced back to Clayton. "All
right," he said softly, seemingly to himself.

The president turned to the videoconference
screen where Rutledge's image waited stiffly, as
though frozen in time. "Hold up, Admiral."

"But, Mr. President," Rutledge said in his gravelly voice, "we're proceeding per the Hackworth resolution."

Anston's voice turned chill. "I said hold, damn it! Now you hold and hold fast until I get back to you."

Rutledge mouthed an obscenity as his image faded from the screen.

Stuart Ibbs, who had watched the exchange, said, "Mr. President, there's a timing issue. Preparations for the pre-emptive cruise missile launches must be coordinated with our ground teams."

"Missile launches? What missile launches?" Anston looked as though he was going to explode.

"We have to strike far and wide, quickly, Mr. President," Ibbs said without hesitation. "Terrorists are going to come at us for the rest of this century until we're plucked clean if we don't take them out now."

Anston slammed his fist on the table, turning heads. "Jesus Christ!"

CHAPTER 48

Kirsten felt an increased uneasiness she couldn't shake. The clock was moving steadily toward the time of the president's speech. Sidney's progress was difficult to measure. The more she asked him the less communicative he became. Then there was the potential of another attack on Sidney's work, a possibility that hung over her like a heavy cloud. With each passing minute they lost a bit more flexibility to deal with—

"Control?" Karl Breskin's deep voice in the headset interrupted her thoughts.

"Yes, ops?" she answered.

"Ready to step through deployment status."

Kirsten shook her head to clear her thoughts. "Take me through it. Backup systems?"

"Backup ready," Karl answered.

"Recovery?"

"Ready."

"Communications?"

"Ready."

"Communications satellite links?"

"Comsat ready."

"Firewall?"

"Firewall engaged."

She focused on the large Backflash readiness display and ran the high-risk areas through her mind once again. Backup and recovery had to be bullet-proof; the tolerance for software or data transmission error was zero. Communications had to provide an uninterrupted outgoing channel, or Backflash, if they got to that point, would never make it to the terrorists.

Kirsten checked the time: 16:24. "Ops," she said.

"Yes, control?"

"You're certain communications is solid?"

"Roger. I'm on station here personally."

"Okay, ops. Hold for my word."

"Ready when you are. I'll disengage Lockdown on your order."

She turned toward Sidney's work area. His hands darted between keyboards, paused momentarily as he studied one of the screens, then resumed their frenetic movements. His left leg was in constant motion, in tempo with his hands. Kirsten studied the commands flashing across the screens, waiting in silence. Terry Sailor, at a desk next to Sidney, glanced in her direction for a brief moment before returning to his computer screen.

"Waiting for me?" Sidney asked without looking up.

Kirsten was conflicted. Backflash would only have one opportunity to do its work. But timing made or broke the entire operation. "Yes," she said finally.

Sidney spun in his chair to face her. "Two words: not ready."

"We are out of time, Sid."

He spun back around in his chair, his attention on his computer monitors. "Need one hour."

Kirsten blew out a long breath. "I can give you twenty minutes. That's it."

Sidney paid no attention to her and kept working.

She switched on her communications set. "Ops?"

"Ops here, control," Karl Breskin answered.

"We have a twenty minute hold."

Walt Washington pulled his chair closer after Brett discarded screen after screen of search possibilities. "You're not smiling, Major."

"For good reason." Brett swore under his breath. Daisy, formerly known as 'Carnivore' in the CIA because of its power in getting to the meat of multitudes of data, was complex software, tricky to operate. He discarded one approach and took Daisy in yet another direction. Keywords, phrases, names, combinations. The possibilities were endless. He went over his methods again. With so much data, the odds overwhelmingly favored disregarding key facts. Another search. Nothing.

Brett leaned into his chair, staring at Washington. "Is nothing going to work?"

"Maybe we're getting ahead of ourselves."

"Meaning?"

"Let's go back to basics. Think like the saboteur for a moment."

"Go on."

Washington pushed away his chair and leaned against his desk, arms crossed over his chest. "If *you* were the inside guy – or gal - and knew about the Orion 6 trap and this secret counterattack weapon the Hirschfield kid is readying, wouldn't you want, at any cost, to get a message out?"

"Got that, but I'd know we've been operating with communications silence under Lockdown."

"Don't forget, Major, for fifteen minutes a while back Lockdown was disengaged."

"But all outgoing messages were blocked."

"Did everyone know that?" Washington asked.

"I'm not following you."

"Remember what I said about our trapping messages attempted but not sent?"

Brett's pulse raced as he considered the possibilities from what Washington was saying. He motioned for Washington to take his place in front of the computer. "Here. You know what you're looking for."

Washington squared himself at the keyboard. "I'm not a whiz on this system, either. Give me a minute."

Brett paced the area behind Washington in silence. Two floors below, Kirsten was preparing for the launch of Backflash. Somewhere, the saboteur was waiting, preparing for the right moment to strike. He grabbed his phone, then put it aside. She had her hands full, and did not need the distraction. He would call her if he had news.

Kirsten approached Sidney's desk. "Need to wrap it up, Sid."

He continued working, ignoring her.

She waited a few moments. "Sid—"

"Fine! We'll go with what I have."

"We don't have the time to—"

He swiveled his chair and stared at Kirsten. "Don't think I don't understand that. I have four dead friends I want to avenge. You've got the best I can do."

"I understand," she said, and patted him on the shoulder. "So you're okay to proceed with deployment?"

"I thought I just told you—"

"Got it, Sid."

Kirsten switched to channel two and spoke Kansas Morningstar's communications code.

"Yes, Kirsten?" Morningstar answered.

"Final check. Identifying the terrorists has center stage. You ready?"

"Yes."

"Remember, you only have six seconds to identify and lock on the terrorist signal."

"I know."

"Two minutes, on my count." Kirsten paused. "Good luck to us all." Kirsten switched to the open channel. "Ops."

"Yes," Breskin answered.

"Disengage Lockdown."

The lights dimmed. One minute passed. Then two. An eerie silence fell over the center as the staff of 300 went into launch readiness. The final two elements necessary for Backflash readiness changed from bright red to green as Lockdown read DISENGAGED and Backflash read READY.

The time was 16:32

The intelligence intrusion display sprung to life. Two, then a half dozen, an array of flashes appeared in Sector A, the Orion Project Internet site. Sectors B and C were empty of intrusion attempts.

Kirsten considered the odds. *Had Sheila Carson's broadcasts been enough to lure the terrorists?* If the terrorists had moved the deadline in direct response to the threat to them posed by Orion 6, they would see something soon. If not, the remaining time until 18:00 would be quiet and uneventful, and after that would be a barrage of attacks. She hoped. The time read 16:40.

Silence. Another series of flashes in Sector A; a swarm of flashes in Sector B. No audibles.

Kirsten kept her attention on the readiness display as the minutes passed. Each sixty seconds seemed like an hour. The clock had advanced just four minutes, to 16:44.

Channel 2 beeped and she switched signals. Terry Sailor's voice rang in her headset with an urgency she hadn't heard from him before. "Come look at this."

Kirsten hurried across the twenty feet to Sailor's work area. "What's up?"

"I've got a possible trace."

"Where?"

"See?" Sailor stabbed his finger at a line of computer code. "If I'm right, this is an attack algorithm that is set to deactivate Backflash in less than thirty seconds."

"Can you delete the code?"

"Yes, but are you sure?"

Kirsten hesitated. What if he were wrong? Deleting the instructions might impact the Backflash deployment. Should she check with Sidney? Ten seconds remained. No time.

"Delete the code."

She leaned closer to the screen, her face next to his as he depressed the DELETE key. "Do you know who did this?"

"Trying to find . . ." Sailor keyed instructions to the computer and then tapped the screen where the trace ID displayed the picture of the originator. "Know him?"

Kirsten caught her breath as she recognized the face. She placed a hand on the desk to steady herself. *How deep did the conspiracy in the Orion Project go?*

"Look at this," Washington said, shaking his head.

Brett stopped pacing. "What?"

"Seems we had a pent-up desire to communicate." Washington jabbed a long finger at a list of entries scrolling down the screen. "We're looking at a queue of over a hundred messages that were composed to some level but didn't make it out."

Brett glanced at his watch. "So read them."

Washington pushed his head closer to the screen and scrolled down the page. "There's messages to loved ones, internal stuff, flamer hate mail to Clayton over the Ishmel mess, and messages to a number of foreign countries. Where do you want to start?"

A distant alarm sounded inside Brett's head. "Wait. Is there a message carrying an address with a '.de' extension?"

"Hold on." Washington's fingers ran over the keys.

Brett checked his watch.

Washington stopped scrolling. "There's just one."

"One's all we need." Brett pushed his face closer to the screen.

Washington touched a dark finger to an entry. "Know this sender?"

Brett froze when he saw the picture. Memories of the firebombing roared into his mind, turning initial disbelief into terror. Like a row of matching bars on the winning turn of a slot machine, the improbable pieces fell into place. He was staring at Peter Olson.

He pulled his phone and called Kirsten, but was sent to voicemail. He texted her a message. No response.

"Come with me!" he said to Washington, then whirled toward the door and bolted from the room.

CHAPTER 49

Kirsten twisted her head to the row behind her. Peter Olson's face met hers. Their eyes locked, his glinting with anticipation above a sneering grin, hers still registering surprise. He eased out of his chair, pushing it away and unbuttoning his suit jacket as he stood.

Kirsten ran through the possibilities, none of them positive. She pulled her eyes away from Peter Olson's stare for a moment, searching for security. The nearest guards were at the entrance. She inched her hand toward the headset control unit clipped at her waist. If she could open the channel her words would be heard to her team.

Olson must have seen her ploy. In a swift move, he vaulted over a row of computer

411

terminals and ripped the communications con-
troller from her waist. "Lose the headset."

Kirsten backed away. The surveillance cameras, someone, had to see that something was
amiss.

"I said, lose it." Olson stepped closer, his eyes
dark and menacing.

Slowly, Kirsten removed the headset, with the
control unit dangling, and placed it on the desk.
She was aware of Terry Sailor close by, facing
Olson, arms loosely at this side. Sidney slid from
his chair. Kirsten motioned him back, toward Karl
Breskin.

In her peripheral vision, Kirsten saw that
all work in the center had ceased. Staff members stood at their computers, speaking to one
another in hushed tones, straining to hear. She
saw motion at the entrance, figures rushing
through security, and hoped it was Brett.

"Why?" she asked, stalling for time.

Olson smirked. "Why this? Or why Zurich?"

"The fire?" Kirsten couldn't believe what she
was hearing.

"Casualties of war, I'm afraid," Olson said.

"You goddamn murdering son of a bitch,"
Sidney screamed. He bolted past Kirsten, lunging
toward Olson.

Terry Sailor caught Sidney's arm and jerked
him to a stop.

Olson slid his weapon from its holster so
quickly Kirsten wasn't aware what was happening.
He grabbed her arm, and in a deft single motion,

twisted her around and put a chokehold across her neck, jabbing the gun under her chin. "You and I have one more job to do," he said with a hiss. His stale breath blew hot across her ear.

Kirsten heard commotion and rushing footsteps. Brett ran to a stop ten feet away, breathing heavily, with Walt Washington right behind. "It's over, Peter." He inched toward the German, hands open and away from his body. "You've served your purpose. Nothing more can be accomplished. Put down your gun and we'll talk."

"It's not that simple," Olson said. He edged away from the group, toward a security elevator behind him, pulling Kirsten with him so that she served as his shield.

Kirsten's vision began to get fuzzy. She struggled to break Olson's hold, trying to get air. She opened her mouth and started to speak, but his grip tightened, lodging the sound in her throat.

Walt Washington stepped forward. "You'll never make it out of here, Olson. Let her go and we'll talk."

Olson pushed his gun tighter against Kirsten's neck. "Tell your men to drop their weapons."

Washington's eyes flickered between Olson and Kirsten, as if calculating his odds.

"Drop them!" Olson demanded.

Without taking his eyes from Olson's, Washington released his gun and motioned to the guards. They slowly dropped their weapons to the floor.

"That's good," Olson said. "Now kick them away, raise your hands and keep them there."

The clatter of metal weapons being kicked across the tiled floor filled the silent room.

Olson backed slowly away, his arm tight around Kirsten's neck. He caught his heel on the foot of a desk, and for an instant glanced toward the floor.

Terry Sailor bolted from the group and lunged toward Olson, arms outstretched.

Olson swore in German as he swung his gun from Kirsten's neck and squeezed the trigger once, and then again. The roar of the weapon filled the center with screams and sent technicians diving.

For a moment, Terry Sailor's mouth and eyes opened in shock, then disappeared in a sea of blood. The first bullet struck the center of his face. The second entered his mouth and smashed through the back of his head, spewing a stream of crimson blood. His body jerked, then spun backward from the impact, tumbling over a desk before slumping to the floor.

"Terry!" Kirsten kicked wildly at Olson's legs, trying to break free.

Olson struggled to steady himself as he took aim at Sidney. "You're done, geek."

"No!" Brett lunged in front of Sidney an instant before the weapon roared twice. Brett's white shirt erupted with a bright crimson stain. He lurched, then spun backward, taking Sidney to the floor with him.

The scream caught in Kirsten's throat. She twisted and jerked, trying to reach Olson's face, to claw at his eyes, but the force of his grip was too great.

Walt Washington started to reach for his weapon on the floor.

Olson swung the gun, still smoking from the earlier shots, and leveled it at Washington's face. "Want to make it four, black man?"

Shuffling backward, Olson pulled Kirsten through the elevator doors, then jabbed the CLOSE button. Silently, the small cab began its descent. Olson loosened his grip but Kirsten felt the heat of his rapid breath against the side of her face.

"So you're the one with the cowardly friends who kill innocent civilians," she said, spitting her words.

Olson tightened his grip. "Best be quiet."

"What weird insanity occupies the mind of a traitor?" she said.

He smiled. "I'm not a traitor. I'm—"

The elevator jerked to a stop and a voice came over the speaker: "It's over, Olson. We're bringing you back up. Put down your weapon."

Olson jabbed his gun further into Kirsten's neck and stared at the camera. "Play games with me and you can say goodbye to your hotshot scientist here."

A moment later, the elevator continued its descent, and then stopped. Kirsten took note that they were on Sublevel 4. She instantly knew where Olson was taking her.

The doors slid open to the brightly lit corridor. Olson edged his head out of the car, glanced in both directions, and then pulled her behind him, pausing to lock the elevator in place. The hallway, bright with overhead lights reflecting on the shiny floors, was empty. He grasped her arm tightly and pulled her roughly down the hall and around the corner, stopping at the door labeled POWER SYSTEMS.

"Open it."

Kirsten remembered from her visit with Karl Breskin three days earlier that the room could be secured and sealed off from the rest of the building. Not far away, she could hear the clatter of boots on the exit stairs. Time to stall. "I'm not cleared."

"Oh, you're funny." The back of his hand hit her full force, knocking her head into the wall.

He shoved the gun against her neck. "Open it!"

Kirsten's face felt like it had been slammed into a bed of sharp needles. She put a hand to her cheek. A warm stream of blood ran down her face onto her wrist and dripped to the floor. The sounds of the boots were closer. She hesitated.

"Now!" Olson pushed the gun harder, sending waves of nausea over her.

Kirsten passed her wrist over the biometric implant reader and entered her pass code.

The sound of running boots grew louder.

"Hurry, damn you!" Olson hissed.

The door clicked twice and swung open. Olson shoved her through and slammed the door behind them.

Kirsten stood with her back to the door. "There's no way out of here," Kirsten said, summoning all the energy she could muster to keep her voice from cracking. She hoped Olson did not know of the emergency escape elevator, but that hope was dashed a moment later.

"I think we both know better than that," he said, and with a rough shove pushed her ahead of him, nearly sending her face-first to the floor.

"What do you want from me?" she asked.

"This way." Olson pushed her roughly ahead of him, past still generators and humming electrical devices toward the computer workstations where Kirsten had seen Karl monitor activity in the Orion Project. Olson motioned her closer and clamped the back of her neck with a strong grasp of his hand. "You," he said, placing his face close to hers, "are going to buy me time. Then we're going on a trip to the surface. Behave yourself and you'll be okay."

Kirsten returned his stare. She wanted to keep him talking while she figured out a way to stop his escape. "Time for what?"

"I'm going to send a little message."

Kirsten suddenly understood. He was going to use the outside communications link to get a message to the terrorists. Somehow, she had to stall, but how? She scanned the room, carefully, without turning her head.

Olson slid into the chair at the workstation, his gun leveled at her chest. "Stand where I can see you. Back a bit. Hold it."

"Why are you doing this?" Kirsten asked, hoping to distract him from his work.

Olson throated a small laugh. "Always looking for simple answers, you Americans. How about this: money – plus the once in a lifetime chance to tip the scales of destiny just a little bit."

She had to buy some time. "That makes no—"

"Shut up!" he said, his voice echoing through the room.

With one hand he pecked at the keyboard, while his other held the gun leveled at her. "Cute, your Orion 6 deception, with the newswoman Sheila Carson and all that," he said. "But in sixty seconds your secret will be busted wide open."

Kirsten slowly raised her hand and wiped the blood away from her eyes, trying to focus. Walt Washington's SWAT team would be gathered outside, figuring their moves.

Olson must have read her mind. "The fools outside will use their time discussing tactical plans for entry to save your life and by then I'll be done."

Kirsten bit her lip, thinking. He was right. If security tried to enter, she would be riddled with Olson's bullets before the SWAT team had cleared the door. She had to find a way to disarm Olson, even temporarily, before the team entered.

She tipped her head toward the entrance. "When they come in, you're a dead man," she said.

"Ladies first," Olson said, showing a thin smile. He kept typing on the terminal.

Kirsten edged her foot to her left. She had to move, a bit at a time, so he didn't notice.

A voice over the security speakers jarred the silence. "Olson, this is security director Walt Washington. Can you hear me?"

Olson glanced at Kirsten, but ignored the voice and kept pecking at the keyboard with his free hand.

Kirsten slid her foot further to the left. Olson was slowed by only using one hand, which would give her a bit more time. A small slide forward, then another.

"We can triple, quadruple what they're paying you," she said.

Olson smiled and shook his head. "You still don't get it, do you? Money is not the object."

"Even if you make it to that elevator," Kirsten said, sliding closer, "you will be a hunted man for the rest of your life. Is that any way to—"

"Shut the fuck up!" he shouted.

"Let Miss Lockhart go free," Washington said over the intercom. "She has nothing to do with this."

Olson ignored the comment and continued pecking at the keyboard.

"We can work this through," Washington continued. "I want to send someone in, one person, unarmed, to talk with you."

Kirsten gauged the distance between her and the computer console where Olson worked. She could make the leap, perhaps five feet, but only if Olson became distracted.

"We are almost there…" Olson said softly to himself as he reviewed the screen.

Kirsten stiffened. There would be no time for Washington's men to stop Olson now. It came down to her. She slid a small step closer. Olson was not allowing himself to be distracted by Washington's ploy. Within a few seconds, the message to the terrorists would be on its way.

She studied Olson's positioning, the angle of his gun arm. How long would it take him to focus on her, aim and fire? She would duck and hit him head-high, toppling him from the chair, hoping Washington's men would enter the room before Olson overpowered her. Either way, she had to stop his message. She measured her breath to slow the racing of her heart.

"Olson." Washington was back on the speaker. "You have thirty seconds. Then we're coming in. Don't make us do this the hard way."

Olson motioned to Kirsten. "Time to get the elevator, sweet pea."

She hesitated.

"Do it!" he screamed, his face a scowling mask.

Kirsten hoped her movement would give her the opportunity to make her move toward him. She started toward the elevator, watching Olson out of the corner of her eye, gauging the distance between them.

Olson tapped at the keyboard with his empty hand. "Okay ... here you go...." he whispered in a soft tone.

Olson lowered his head toward the screen, his fingers poised to send the message. For a fraction of a second, his attention was distracted. His gun hand was lowered a notch, pointing at Kirsten's feet.

Kirsten knew she had one chance, and this was it. Using momentum from her steps toward the elevator, she took a deep breath, pivoted and sprung toward Olson. She knew the minute she turned that she had misjudged. She was too far away, too late. It was as if she were watching in slow motion . . . his initial look of surprise, replaced by the beginnings of a satisfied grin . . . his hand coming up with the pistol . . . the blinding flash from the muzzle and ear-splitting crack of the weapon as it discharged.

And then darkness.

CHAPTER 50

Conversations in the White House Situation Room had fallen to a hush.

"Delay is compromising our mission, Mr. President." The large wall screen exaggerated Rutledge's hawkish features, giving him a larger-than-life image that dominated the room. Behind wire-rim glasses, the admiral's eyes narrowed to slivers. "What are my orders, sir?"

Clayton could see the turmoil raging through Anston's mind reflected on the president's face. To withhold the attacks would be in direct defiance of congressional directive and could lead to the end of his presidency. But the fallout from Operation Hydra would, in Clayton's view, result in even more precipitous consequences.

"Proceed to your first station," Anston said, shooting Clayton a sidelong look. "But you god-damn hold for my order, Admiral." Anston hesitated a moment. "Admiral!"

"Yes, *sir*!" Rutledge said finally.

Rutledge's image faded and all eyes turned to the wide screen view of the Flying Command Post, bathed in bright lights, perched at the end of the long runway with takeoff lights blinking. Military sentries conducted a final check of the area, then pulled away from the aircraft. Moments later, the four massive Pratt & Whitney engines, each larger than a Prius, increased their shrill whine to a high, screaming pitch. Constrained by massive interlocking brakes, the aircraft rocked in place, like an overanxious runner at the starting line awaiting the signal from the starter's gun.

Slowly, almost imperceptibly at first, the world's heaviest 747 began to move, building speed. Fifty seconds later, the Doomsday Plane leapt from the runway with a massive roar, banking sharply into the sky before disappearing into the tumbling gray clouds that framed the growing darkness.

Somewhere in the room, a quiet voice said, "God help us all."

Anston diverted his attention from the screen, focusing on Clayton. "Remember, Dusty - I'm stalling, giving you until 6 p.m. But that's all the time you have."

Clayton watched the president stride away, wondering about the source of the confidence that seemed to remain in Anston's step. He made a note of the president's instructions, wondering what the strict time frame would mean to Kirsten. He motioned to Maureen Connelly. "Get this reminder to Kirsten."

He didn't feel the hand on his forearm until after he heard Joan Karlin's raspy voice and Texas twang.

"Dusty - can we talk?" Karlin asked.

Clayton gave a final glance at the display screen. The image of the empty sky had been replaced by the heading OPERATION HYDRA, and was being filled with a grid containing data on targets, estimated kills for each, deployment time, responsible agency, and a series of codes he knew to indicate priority and alternative plans.

Clayton circled the conference table, following the secretary of state to a space away from the crowds. They sat at a corner at right angles to each other. Her face was filled with resolve, her eyes red and swollen.

"Yes?" Clayton asked.

Karlin tossed her reading glasses on the table and studied Clayton. "What's the progress on your end?"

"We're in the final attempt." Clayton hesitated. Karlin could take the brute truth as well or better than anyone in the room. "But we have problems. I'm not holding out much hope."

Karlin's voice became confiding. "This damned crisis has given birth to life of its own. We need an interdiction strategy."

"Meaning?"

"Once those teams start taking out their targets, many of the terrorist's host nations — Christ, all of them — are going to consider our actions as a violation of every treaty the U.S. has ever signed, perhaps an invasion. You and I know their reactions will provoke further response from us. At home, we're quickly reaching the point where the president is going to lose his ability to govern. We need to defuse things before we turn this little green planet of ours into a goddamn Sunday barbeque."

Clayton stirred. "What are you suggesting?"

"Excuse me, sir." Clayton's executive assistant Maureen Connelly rushed toward Clayton, holding a secure phone and his overcoat.

Clayton glanced at Connelly. "One moment."

Karlin placed her hand on Clayton's forearm and squeezed. "You know exactly what I'm suggesting, Dusty. Anston needs to act while he still has the power to stop this bloodbath. He must replace the warmonger Rutledge – now, and put an end to Operation Hydra."

"What about the congressional directive?"

"Christ, Dusty, I don't know. The president will have to call in some chits, finesse it somehow."

"Sir!" Connelly said to Clayton, anxiety filling her voice. "There's been a siege, and shooting, at the Orion Project."

He spun his head toward her. "Casualties?"

"Yes, sir."

"Kirsten?"

Connelly hesitated a beat. "Miss Lockhart has been taken hostage."

Clayton dropped his head into his hand, suddenly feeling as though his throat were in a vice. "Get my chopper."

"Pilots are on board and it's warming up, sir."

Clayton cleared his thoughts and studied Karlin as he stood to leave. She was right of course. America's finger was on a global trigger, and the last chance to stop a conflagration was less than an hour away. He glanced in the president's direction. "I'll see what I can do."

"Excuse me - Madam Secretary?" A military aide with an anxious face stood across the table from Karlin. "The call with the NATO ministers is ready."

Karlin knocked her knuckles on the polished surface and pushed away from the table, her eyes never leaving Clayton's. "I know you have other issues facing you, Dusty. But the president listens to you. Talk to him, man-to-man. Before the world comes crashing down around us."

CHAPTER 51

Kirsten was certain of it.

The nightmarish menagerie of memories tumbling through her consciousness had all been a dream. Everything was fine. *But if those events hadn't happened, why was her head splitting with pain and her ears filled with the pitched shrill of sirens?* She blinked, then blinked again. Her eyes were filled with blurred images of a tall black apparition and moving figures with white armbands emblazoned with red crosses. And how did she explain the deep, echoing voices she kept hearing?

"Miss Lockhart…?"

The echoing voice spoke again: "Miss Lockhart, can you hear me?"

She pulled her eyes open wider, then closed them as she was pulled down toward an inky-dark place, like a deep cave in the earth . . . .

She willed her eyes open until her vision came into a hazy focus. She lifted her head and squinted, looking around her. The tall black image coalesced into the face of Walt Washington. Behind him, fuzzy images moved in and out of her vision, one of them squatting over an inert form on the floor. Blood ran down the wall beyond the desk. A security officer paced, issuing instructions into the phone pressed against his head. The computer chair Olson had occupied lay upside down against the wall.

"You're a lucky lady," Washington said. "Bullet grazed your head. The medic's temporary bandage will hold you for now. But we need to get you medical attention."

Kirsten fought the wooziness that engulfed her. "How long have I been out?"

"Just a few minutes. Now you really need to rest."

Kirsten pushed herself up on her elbow, fear filling her heart, as images of the shooting upstairs filled her consciousness. "Sidney? Brett?"

"Agent Logan is being airlifted to Bethesda Medical. Nasty shoulder wound, but he'll be fine. Mr. Hirschfield has a minor arm injury. He's being treated upstairs."

"Thank God." Kirsten said a silent prayer of thanksgiving. *What about Terry?* She fought the ghastly memories of Terry's body being thrown to the floor by Olson's bullets. "Terry Sailor?"

Washington's face tightened. "I'm sorry."

Kirsten's body wracked with a sudden convulsion. She doubled over on the floor, struggling with the heaves of anguish before catching her breath.

"You going to be okay?" Washington asked.

"Yes." She glanced toward Olson's body and fought the urge to crush his skull with anything heavy within reach. "And him?"

"He didn't give us any choice."

In spite of the pain in her head, her mind began to clear. "Message! Did Olson send a message?"

Washington motioned toward the computer terminals. Their screens and keyboards lay in splintered sections over the desktop. Loose wires hung toward the floor. "We don't know. The equipment took a lot of damage." He gently pushed Kirsten's head back on a pillow fashioned from his suit coat. "Now you need to take it easy."

Kirsten let her head collapse into Washington's arms. *Did Olson's message make it out?* There would be no way to tell, but it no longer mattered. She struggled with what was left of her energy and pushed herself up on her elbow, fighting to keep the figures in the room from fading out.

"What time do you have?" she asked.

Washington glanced at his watch. "17:15."

Kirsten closed her eyes. A quarter past five. Time had run out. Her plan had failed. The terrorists would throw the nation into chaos. The U.S. would certainly launch a counteroffensive that couldn't be won by military strength but would cost countless lives at home and across the world. She struggled to get her feet under her, her breath coming in short gasps. "Must reach Clayton."

"The secretary's on his way, Miss Lockhart." Washington eyed her sternly. "His orders were to cease all operations."

"I've got to get upstairs." Kirsten placed her hand on Washington's shoulder to steady her legs. "Help me up."

Washington frowned at Kirsten's wobbly stance. "You've done quite enough, miss. I wouldn't recommend moving any–"

"I said I'm going upstairs."

"Very well." Washington motioned to one of the security men. "I'll send someone with you."

Kirsten waved the man away. "Please, no." She needed time to think. "I'll be fine," she said in a voice weaker than she wanted it to be. "I want to be alone." She studied Olson's lifeless body. Even in death, his face projected rage. Her rage matched his, but she had no place to direct it. Not now.

Kirsten focused on placing each foot in front of the other, one halting step at a time, weaving her way in a slow, winding gait toward the hallway.

The elevator doors slid silently open. Kirsten braced herself and stepped into the brightly-lit

compartment where what seemed a lifetime earlier Peter Olson had slammed her against the
cold metal. The car started upward. She stared in
shock at the unfamiliar reflection in the mirror.
Her face was still red where Olson had hit her.
Dried blood was caked from the cut just below
her left eye. A red-stained head bandage thrust
strands of hair forward and up at odd angles.
Kirsten squeezed her eyes closed and prayed that
when the elevator doors opened, somehow the
dreadful memories would be nothing more than
a bad dream. The Orion cyber center would be in
normal operation, Backflash deployment underway, her friends well and smiling.

"Excuse us, miss."

Kirsten had not heard the doors slide open.
She blinked, wondering for a second where she
was. The Marines standing in front of the elevator
examined her with solemn faces.

In the instant her eyes dropped to the
stretcher between the two young men, the night-
mare of reality shattered her desperate prayer of
hope. Kirsten grasped the door of the elevator
to steady her legs and stood aside as the Marines
wheeled Terry Sailor's motionless form onto the
elevator.

It took her a moment to realize that the voice
echoing in her head came from one of the young
Marines: "Sorry, miss, but we must move on."

When the doors slid together, Kirsten knew a
chapter in her life had closed with them forever.

CHAPTER 52

*W**here was Sidney?*

Kirsten steadied herself with both hands on a table next to the elevator, trying to will the tense pain in her head away as she scanned for signs of Sidney in the cyber center.

An eerie silence hung over the massive room, giving it the feeling of a giant vault. Shattered computer displays and overturned chairs littered the blood-smeared floor where Peter Olson had made his stand. The pungent smell of gun smoke permeated the air. Technicians wearing dazed expressions sat or stood at their workstations while others wandered the aisles alone or talked in hushed tones. The Backflash deployment display cast a ghostly glow, its countdown sequence frozen in time. Backflash had failed without having a chance. The terrorists had won.

She caught sight of Sidney at his desk, rubbing a white bandage that covered most of his right forearm. She released her grip on the table and took tentative steps forward, willing her feet to move in his direction.

Sidney rose as she approached and gave her a long hug. "Thank God you're okay." He helped her into a chair. "You don't look well."

"You don't look so good yourself," she said. Sidney's eyes were swollen and red, his face pale. He appeared as though he had aged ten years since she had seen him an hour earlier.

"We heard about the battle downstairs," he said. "Sure you're okay?"

"I'll be fine." She studied his bandage. "You?"

He nodded. "A flesh wound is all."

After a moment, he placed a hand on hers. "I'm sorry about Terry Sailor."

"I am too, Sid, and about Katrina." She stared past him, not knowing what else to say.

They sat in silence, both taking stock of the cyber center as Sidney toyed with his keyboard. She wondered what would happen that evening when the next wave of terrorist attacks streaked through the complex web of computer networks that encircled the globe, striking deep into their intended targets in the United States.

"If only Backflash had had its chance," she said finally to break the awkward silence. "We ran out of time."

Sidney nodded, and they continued studying the center together. His head stopped first. He stood. Her eyes followed his.

"You see what I see?" he said.

"Yes. The countdown frozen in place?"

"Yep. No need to restart." He swung his chair to his workstations. "We may still be able to—"

"Continue the countdown!" she said, feeling a surge of adrenaline. She checked the clock. 17:40 – twenty minutes until their deadline.

Kirsten stood and checked the readiness displays. The attack readiness state had not changed during her absence. Each deployment indicator announced READY except for two: Lockdown read ENGAGED; Backflash read STANDBY. A flicker of hope stirred somewhere inside of her.

"Backflash?" she said.

"I can be ready – five minutes."

Kirsten retrieved her headset from the desk where Peter Olson had tossed it an hour earlier and checked the indicators on the control unit for readiness. She winced from a jab of pain as she pulled the headset over her bandage. Twenty minutes remained until the deadline. If they circumvented procedures, it might be possible to have Backflash ready by then.

She selected channel 2 for privacy. "Ops?"

Karl Breskin's husky voice came on line immediately. "Kirsten. My God. Are you all right?"

"Yes." Kirsten scanned the center for his large frame. "Where are you?"

"In security, answering questions."

"I need you down here. We're continuing the countdown. I want Lockdown lifted. Now."

Breskin hesitated. "Did you hear the cease operations order from Secretary Clayton?"

She pressed her eyes closed. As long as Lockdown was engaged and the cyber center closed off to the outside, Sidney's effort had no chance. Karl Breskin was the only one who could reinstate communications with the outside world.

"Karl, two innocent people died in Zurich. Another two here. Brett's in the hospital. This is just a down payment of what's to come unless we take action."

Kirsten fought to keep her voice from shaking. "We're going to finish this. Get down here."

"Kirsten," he said, "deployment takes over an hour. There isn't time."

"We'll take shortcuts, do whatever we have to do. I'll take responsibility. Just get the center open."

"There's no guarantees," he said.

"We ran out of guarantees sixty minutes ago."

Breskin was quiet for a moment. "You know I'm with you. But there will be hell to pay with Clayton." He clicked off the line.

Kirsten called Kansas Morningstar. "Kansas, it's Kirsten. Yes, I—I'm fine. Can I count on you for an accelerated Backflash launch?"

"I'm ready and waiting," said Morningstar. "But what—"

"Just get ready. We start in two minutes."

A minute later, Kirsten blew out a long, steadying breath. Mustering all the air of command she could find, she faced the vast cyber center and switched to the broadcast channel. "Attention. This is Kirsten Lockhart." Conversations ceased and faces turned toward her. All motion in the center stopped. "Prepare for immediate resumption of Backflash deployment. I repeat. Prepare for immediate resumption of deployment, two minutes from my mark. Five, four, three, two, one, mark."

The still silence in the center ended with an outbreak of activity. Technicians broke from their groups, rushed toward their workstations, and addressed their computers. The lights in the center dimmed. Darkened display screens flickered to life.

Kirsten fought with every ounce of her energy to ignore the sharp pain in her head, to focus her thinking. The time display showed 17:45. Fifteen minutes remained. Even if Backflash proved to be operational, scant time remained for the terrorists to take the bait, and little assurance that they would.

Kirsten listened to Breskin proceed with the check-ins.

"Intelligence?"

"Reactivating sector monitoring," Morningstar said. On the blue intelligence display, Sectors A, B and C of the Orion Project reappeared.

"Remember, everyone," Morningstar added, "attacks are on visual only until we've locked on a probable terrorist intrusion. Then we go to audible."

Kirsten had never imagined she would pray to be attacked, but at this moment, she found herself anxious for the "ping" indicating a possible terrorist intrusion.

"Once we have a possible incoming, we pass the signal to Sidney," Morningstar continued.

"As a reminder," Sidney interjected, "you've got six seconds to identify."

"I'll handle my end," Morningstar replied.

Kirsten understood what had gone unsaid: the six seconds Sidney was allotted provided precious little time to confirm and lock on the terrorist signal and then launch Backflash.

A minute went by, then two. Kirsten keyed Breskin's code. "What are you waiting for?"

"Working on it. You know Clayton has arrived."

"Thank you. Now get going, Karl."

17:54.

A moment later, Breskin's tense voice boomed over her headset: "Communications?"

"Open channels and ready," Chan replied.

"Backflash?"

Sidney gave Kirsten a nod, then adjusted his headset and poised his hands over the keyboards. "Let them come."

The display readiness screen blazed in all green except for lockdown:

Backup	READY
Recovery	READY
Communications	READY
Intelligence	READY

Satcom	READY
Lockdown	ENGAGED
Backflash	READY

Channel 2 beeped on Kirsten's headset: "Ops to control."

"Yes, Karl?"

"Disengage lockdown?"

Kirsten glanced toward the entrance to the center. Would Clayton arrive in the midst of all of this? "Confirm disengagement, ops."

Breskin's voice boomed throughout the center: "Ten seconds to release of Lockdown. Nine, eight, seven, six, five, four, three, two, one."

The final step to enticing the terrorist attack was confirmed: the Lockdown display switched to DISENGAGED.

The Orion Project cyber center was open and vulnerable to attack.

The time display read 17:57.

"Lockdown disengaged." Breskin's voice echoed through the silence that coated the center.

No one spoke. Every face in the center focused on a computer screen or the intelligence intrusion display.

17:58.

The intrusion display was dark. Nothing.

17:59.

A flash and then several more appeared in Sector A. Kirsten tensed. Two, then three hits in Sector B. Across the room, Morningstar's intelligence group hunched over their computer terminals, fighting against time to confirm a possible terrorist attack. Morningstar paced behind the rows of computer terminals manned by her staff, watching and waiting.

"Easy as she goes," Sidney said. "If they come like I think they will, they'll probe, gently at first, checking soft spots, moving around, then they'll strike."

More hits in Sector A, then flashes in B. Were these normal hacking attacks or terrorist probes? Kirsten felt the pain of her fingernails digging into the palm of her hand. Still no audible.

Someone tapped Kirsten on the shoulder. She turned to see Clayton enter the center, make eye contact, and head toward her.

"Kirsten, you're okay!" he said as he reached her.

"Yes, sir."

He scanned the activity in the cyber center. "What's going on here?"

"Doing what you ordered me to do, sir. Stop tonight's attacks."

"What you've been ordered to do is to cease operations."

"I deserve one last chance to get this done for you. Can you alert the president that we need until 18:30?"

He stared at her for a few moments. "Get this done, then take care of yourself." He turned and was gone.

18:06.

Kirsten watched the intrusion screens. The giant cyber center was silent, the staff motionless, waiting. The seconds dragged by.

18:15.

"See anything, Sid?" she asked.

His eyes darted between the intrusion display and his computer screens. "No."

Kirsten kicked a chair, causing faces to turn in her direction. "Damn you, come on," she said under her breath.

18:20. The center hadn't a sound.

Kirsten looked over at Sidney, a feeling of resignation rising inside of her. The terrorists must have received Olson's message.

Morningstar's anxious voice broke the silence in Kirsten's headset: "Control!"

"Yes?"

"They're taking out CERT."

In the time it took Kirsten to focus, the CERT indicator lights on the green U.S. intrusion display blinked red for incoming attacks, then went to solid.

"Wait! Jesus, they're going after the NIPC" Morningstar said. The lights for the National Infrastructure Protection Center site blinked red before going to solid. An instant later, the Air Force Space Command site in Colorado began blinking red.

"Give me a reading," Kirsten shouted.

"They're preparing for a major national attack," Morningstar replied.

Kirsten shook her head. The terrorists weren't going for her trap.

Technicians glanced up from their screens toward the intrusion display. In the back of the center, workers stood to get a better view. Confused voices came over the broadcast channel, seeking clarification.

Sidney's head shot around toward Kirsten. "Stay focused! This is all a diversion."

Kirsten signaled Breskin. "Karl, keep everyone on station."

Morningstar's voice rang out: "Incoming, Sector C!"

Sector C exploded with a constellation of flashing lights.

"Game on!" Sidney exclaimed, hunching over his terminals.

Kirsten focused on the time display: *six—five—four—three—two—one.*

"Intrusion confirmed." Morningstar's voice was tense, clipped.

The audible confirmation signal filled the room like a gong, *"ping—ping—ping—ping."* An instant later a second audible joined the first, *"ping—ping—ping—ping"*, then another, and another, blending into a chorus of high-pitched signals.

"Goddamn! Multiple hits," Sidney cried out. His hands raced across his keyboards. "Should have known."

Kirsten watched as Sidney's computer screens lit up with incoming signals. He selected one, another, then another, and then discarded all three and selected another. His eyes narrowed. He spoke to himself as he worked: "Which one?"

Sidney was half out of his chair, face inches from his computer screens, his hands dancing across the keys.

Five, four, three, two, one. Kirsten held her breath.

Sidney's fingers raced across his keyboard.

The attacks continued. The electronic displays flashed with the intensity of a fireworks show, and looked as if they were going to explode.

Sidney's face was even closer to his computer screens now, his fingers a blur of motion.

Then, just as they had began, the flashing lights indicating attacks began to disappear. Moments later, any signs of the terrorist attacks were gone. Sector C was dark. The audible signals went silent, leaving only a retreating echo as a reminder of their presence.

A hushed still fell over the center, all attention on the darkened displays. No one moved.

Kirsten glanced to the readiness display. All indicators glowed READY except Backflash, which blazed LAUNCHED in luminous red.

"All sectors clear." Morningstar announced.

"Everyone remain on station," Kirsten said.

Five minutes passed.

"Continue clear," Morningstar announced.

Kirsten checked the time display: 18:36. Eleven minutes had passed since the attacks had begun.

Breskin's voice echoed over Kirsten's headset. "Engage lockdown?"

Kirsten let out a long, measured breath. They had done all they could. Waiting longer, she knew, would accomplish nothing. "Roger, ops," she replied.

Lights in the center rose to normal.

Behind Morningstar, the intrusion display was quiet. "Resetting sensors," she announced.

Throughout the center technicians slowly stood, their faces showing a mixture of relief and wonder. Most glanced toward one another in questioning silence.

Kirsten pulled off her headset. She pressed her face close to Sidney, her voice a hoarse whisper. "Sid, did you get them?"

Sidney's pursed his lips in silence, scanning the screens arrayed before him.

"Sid, talk to me." Kirsten held her breath, frozen in time as she waited.

He pushed his chair back, glanced at the quiet intrusion display, then again at his computer terminals. "I believe," Sidney said, his breath coming in heaves, "that for now, the bastards just met their match."

Kirsten tossed her headset aside and extended her fists toward the ceiling in a sign of victory. In the next moment, she had Sidney in her arms, hugging him with all the energy she could muster. The fact that she had strength to hold him at all was a measure of how she felt. For she was tired, far too tired to speak.

CHAPTER 53

The marine guard closed the door behind
Kirsten, closing out the brightness from the
hallway. She hesitated, adjusting her eyes to
the dim light. The only movement in the quiet
room at Bethesda Hospital came from a muted
wall-mounted television that shot shimmering
colored images onto the far wall. She edged
forward and tilted her head around the thin
white curtain that encircled the bed.

Brett lay motionless, his eyes closed. His bandaged chest rose and fell rhythmically, almost
imperceptibly, under the sheet. A lone IV fed
his left arm. A young doctor, a lieutenant commander, stood next to the bed, head down, making entries into an electronic memo pad. He

glanced up after a moment and flashed a quick smile.

"Evening, Miss Lockhart," he said with a clipped northeastern accent.

"How did you know?"

"It's in your eyes." The doctor tilted his head toward Brett. "Besides, our guest here has been asking about you."

Kirsten's eyes flickered back to Brett. "How is he, doctor?"

"Your friend's a lucky man. The bullet passed through his shoulder without serious damage. Fortunately, the medics got him in time to control the bleeding. He needs to take it easy." The doctor shot Kirsten a knowing smile. "Perhaps you can help him recuperate, somewhere where it's quiet." He wrote a number on the back of a card and handed it to Kirsten. "I'll check in first thing tomorrow. If you need anything, call me at this number any time."

The door closed behind the doctor, leaving the room in silence. Kirsten eased into the chair next to the bed. She ran her eyes over the burn bandages covering his arm and the new wrappings on his chest, each injury producing a flood of memories that for the moment she did not want to relive. After a moment, she slipped her hand into his.

Brett stirred, his breathing interrupted. A moment later, he opened his eyes, thin slits in a pale face. A flicker of recognition produced the beginnings of a smile. His hand tightened around hers.

"Burned, beaten and shot. You're quite a mess," she said softly.

"I've got to start keeping better company." Brett's words were hollow, and seemed to arrive slowly, as if from a great distance. "And you?"

"Survived with only a messed-up hairdo plus the need for a good dose of painkillers and an extra layer of makeup."

"The terrorists. How did we do?" His voice was weak, and Kirsten leaned closer.

"We stopped them," she said, squeezing his hand. "But save your energy. We'll have lots of time to talk."

"I'm a tougher goat than these doctors here give me credit for." Brett's eyes narrowed for a second, then softened. "You know how sorry I am about Terry Sailor."

Kirsten felt her throat constrict. Brett's expression told her he knew what she was feeling.

"Terry always will be special."

"How's Sidney?" Brett said in a hoarse whisper.

Kirsten showed a hint of a knowing smile. "He's doing well." She hesitated. There would be time to explain about Sidney later.

"Olson?" Brett asked.

"Didn't make it."

When Brett continued, his voice was stronger. "Peter Olson was right in front of us all the time. If only I had seen through him earlier."

"Don't do that to yourself," she said, giving a double squeeze of his hand. "We were all fooled."

Brett frowned. "Are we clear with Ishmel and Mario, or should I hire a bodyguard?"

"You're clear. Clayton is hitting them with criminal charges, borderline treason. Both are in custody, their lives as they know them are over."

Kirsten listened to the rhythm of his breathing, recalling memories of Brett's twice saving Sidney, his decision to risk everything on her plan. She moved her face closer to his.

"Brett, I want to thank you for taking a chance on me."

He smiled, letting his eyes linger on hers. "I know good odds when I see them. What's next for you? Heading back to California?"

Kirsten placed her other hand on his and studied him in silence for a few moments, considering all that had happened and all that was to come. She took a deep breath.

"Clayton's asked me to stay on, to head up the Orion Project."

Brett winced as he smiled. "Congratulations."

"He's given me authority to bring Kansas Morningstar over to head up the defensive ops section."

"Good choice."

"And you – headed to the California wine country?" she asked.

"Who knows where I will be when Sherwin gets through with me."

"Nate Sherwin is in custody with Ishmel."

"Well – that simplifies my life," he said.

Kirsten let out a short breath. "I would like – ah – very much like you to consider heading up an expanded counter-terrorist operation in the Orion Project."

Brett's eyes gave away his puzzlement. Then he said in a weak voice, "Aren't you acting out of character?"

The room fell silent except for the hum of the medical equipment and muffled steps passing in the hallway. "We all wear masks," Kirsten said. "Sometimes because we have to. Sometimes because we're protecting ourselves."

She ran her hand loosely through his hair. "Either way, most of the time it makes us forget who we really are. But you made me realize who I really wanted to be."

Brett's eyes softened and then closed.

"Of course," she said, "if you take the position, it means we'll be working closely together."

His eyes opened. "That poses an interesting question."

Suddenly, the room seemed to close in, a cocoon of white, around her. All sense of sound and smell vanished. Only Brett occupied her senses.

"Yes?" she asked.

"So you really think we can stand working together?"

Kirsten felt a warmth come over her. "Actually, working together may not be enough. Not nearly enough." She leaned forward, her chest feeling the warmth of his, and kissed him fully on the lips.

CHAPTER 54

Clayton kept one eye on President Anston's phone call with the British Prime Minister and the other eye on the television. The newscaster stood in front of San Francisco's Ferry Building, mist fanning from his mouth. Behind him, the brilliant lights of the city's skyline sparkled against the early evening sky.

"Tonight's relative calm across the United States is in stark contrast to the conditions of the past week," the reporter said. "How close the United States actually came to military action as a result of the terrorist attacks is not yet known and will be the subject of intense discussions for weeks, perhaps years, to come."

Anston paced behind his desk, looking out onto the darkness, a telephone clamped to his ear. "Martin. Please, Martin. You're the first stop on my European swing. Yes, we have fences to mend. We are no way escalating any position of aggressive pre-emptive actions." Anston frowned, shaking his head. "No, Martin, the missile defense system stays. Catch my speech tonight."

Clayton marveled at the vitality he saw in the president. Anston's face had regained much of its color and the bounce had returned to his voice. The tension around the jaw and the eyes had eased. The commander in chief had shed the ten years added during the events of the last several days.

The image of Sheila Carson on the television snapped Clayton back to the present. He listened to the voice-over of the commentator.

'The one newsperson who steadfastly clung to her belief in the Orion Project, WorldNews commentator Sheila Carson, now finds herself the subject of national attention. Be sure to tune in to Carson's new program *Prime News Live!* debuting tomorrow evening as she takes you behind the scenes inside the daring plan known only to a few that thwarted the terrorists, an effort that involved technological deception on an international scale, a fugitive computer genius, and quite possibly reached as high as the White House."

"See you tomorrow, Martin," the president concluded.

Anston hung up the phone and shot a sideways glance at the television monitor. "Looks as though the Carson woman fared well on all of this, thanks to you," he said, appraising Clayton with an amused look.

"Yes, sir."

"What's next, a documentary on your career?"

Clayton turned his face toward the television monitor in an attempt to hide the beginnings of the smile on his face. Anston was having fun with him, and who was he to stand in the president's way?

"Think we'll hear from our Arizona friend?" Anston asked after a moment, his tone serious again.

"Don't think so, Mr. President. Reports are Hackworth is refusing all requests for interviews."

Anston gave Clayton a wry grin. "The media doesn't seem to like him."

"No sir."

The president was quiet for a moment, eyes distant. "We just experienced a close one, Dusty. Too close. If it hadn't been for that ingenious plan of yours, we would be having a different discussion."

"Except the plan wasn't mine, Mr. President."

"Well, I pray your people haven't emptied their well of ideas." Anston retrieved a sheet of paper from a side drawer and pushed it across his desk. "This came in from the New Tomorrow group minutes before you arrived."

Clayton frowned as he read the message out loud: "We'll be back."

"Think they will?" said the president.

Clayton understood that the cyber terrorism battle would be fought in many forms in the future. "Only that we've just begun this war, sir, not won it."

"Does this mean," Anston said, "that all the cooperation we're getting from Chancellor Eckhart in rounding up these extremists who had a problem with our missile defense system won't buy us a single scalp?"

"Possibly not, Mr. President. Cyberspace is a virtual place, with many places to exist and hide. We've entered a fifth dimension of warfare, after land, sea, air, and space in which we do not hold the winning cards. We've a major job ahead of us."

Anston nodded. "Sounds like the opening of my State of the Union address."

Clayton glanced at the antique clock against the wall. The president's nine o'clock speech was a bit over an hour away. A detailed discussion on the continuing threat of cyberterrorism would have to wait.

"I've been thinking about my second administration," Anston said, leveling a stare at Clayton.

Not knowing where the president was headed, Clayton waited.

"We've got a bit of global fence-building to do," Anston continued. "Joan Karlin is retiring from State. Any suggestions?"

"Not at the moment, sir."

Anston gave Clayton a studied look for a long moment. "Very well." He handed Clayton a pen. "Before we go, leave the details on the kid who K.O.'d the terrorists. What was his name again?"

"Hirschfield. Sidney Hirschfield."

"Yes, Hirschfield. We owe him. I'll have Comber call over to Justice and see what can be done on leniency for his crimes, whatever they are. We should be able to get him a short sentence, two to three years, max, and then he's out."

"I was going to speak to you. It may be too late for that, Mr. President."

Anston's face showed surprise. "In what way?"

"Hirschfield was sent to Bethesda for treatment, and, well—"

"Let me guess." Anston's expression turned to mock amazement. "In a moment of lax security, he slipped into the night."

"Something like that." Clayton tried to conceal a smile. "But somehow I'll bet we haven't heard the last of him."

"Mr. President." Ron Comber stood halfway through the door. "It's time, sir."

"Three minutes." Anston opened the top drawer of his desk and removed a thin stack of papers. "This speech is longer, and a Texas mile more comfortable, than the one I thought I would give. Thank God for that." He placed the documents inside of his jacket pocket and rose. "Well, Congress is waiting."

"I do have one question before you go, sir."

"Yes?"

"I was on my way to the Orion Project when the final decisions were made. How were you able to halt the Operation Hydra attacks?"

"Hydra attacks?" Anston threw his coat over his shoulder and smiled as fully as Clayton had seen in days. "What attacks?"

Their eyes locked in the manner of two friends who knew and understood one another well.

"Understood, Mr. President."

"Tell me something, the truth, now," Anston said, straightening his shoulders. "I have the damnedest time getting people around here to level with me." He ran his hand over his dress shirt. "Is this too pink for television?"

"Looks great, sir," Clayton said, grinning.

Ron Comber was at the door again. "Mr. President."

"A moment, a moment." Anston selected a long Cuban cigar from a humidifier in his desk and took an appreciative sniff of the rich aroma. "Lara won't let me smoke these in the White House, even in victory, so I'll smell up the limousine on the way home.

"You know, Dusty," Anston said, "some things I just don't understand. Now Rutledge I get. His credo that power isn't power unless you use it, that sort of thing. He'll have that to think about in his newly found retirement. But Ibbs is a mystery. Leaking confidential information to the media and making backdoor deals with Hackworth. I just don't understand."

Clayton raised an eyebrow and waited for the president to finish.

"He twisted way off course on this one, Dusty."

Clayton nodded in silence.

Anston paused at the door. "Sure I can't persuade you to take over State? Pay's not much better but you get to see the world."

Turning down the president's direct request was difficult, but Clayton knew what he had to do. "You have others far more capable, Mr. President. As for me, I've dodged too many bullets in the past forty years, and this last one was a squeaker. I'll stay where I am through the election and give special attention to the Orion Project to make sure things are on track. Then it's home to the farm for me. After that, the young people will have their chance."

Clayton shifted his attention to the window, past the flags of the four services, his mind in the distance. "We're facing a vastly different new age of threats, of warfare. It's their world now."

THE END